About

Alan Gorevan is an award-winning writer and intellectual property attorney. He lives in Dublin. Visit his website at www.alangorevan.com

By Alan Gorevan

NOVELS:
Out of Nowhere
Better Confess
The Kindness of Psychopaths

NOVELLAS:
The Forbidden Room
The Hostage
Hit and Run

SHORT STORY COLLECTION:
Dark Tales

ANTHOLOGY:
The Thriller Collection *(contains The Forbidden Room, The Hostage, and Hit and Run)*

The Kindness of Psychopaths

Alan Gorevan

Copyright © 2020 by Alan Gorevan

All rights reserved

No part of this book may be reproduced, stored in a retrieval system or transmitted by any means without the written permission of the author.

This book is a work of fiction. People, places, events and situations are the product of the author's imagination. Any resemblance to actual persons, living or dead, or historical events, is purely coincidental.

ISBN: 9798692557339

THE KINDNESS OF PSYCHOPATHS

PART ONE

JUNE

CHAPTER 1

Valentina López Vázquez stepped into her back garden, startling the sparrows which had been hopping around on the grass. The birds shot into the air, chirping and regrouping on top of the hedge. They peered down at Valentina as if they were curious about the phone she held in one hand and the pregnancy test in the other.

Good news? Bad news?

Maybe it was all bad.

Valentina's phone buzzed. She didn't want to check it, didn't want to read any more of the filthy messages. But curiosity got the better of her.

She felt sick reading the message, but he was the one who was sick, this creep, detailing what he wanted to do to her.

Valentina glanced around, hoping the tranquil space would calm her. Though small, the square garden was lovely. Half of it was grass, the other half paved, filled with ceramic ornaments, hanging pots and flower boxes.

The summer she moved here with Barry, Valentina had planted lavender. The plant was in full bloom now, and it reminded her of a happier time. She watched bees flit from one purple flower to another.

Her phone buzzed.

Another message from the unknown number.

She looked back towards the house. It was one in a row of terraced two-beds. Unlike her neighbours' houses – the one on the left with red brick and the one on the right with yellow – the walls of Valentina's house were plastered smooth and painted white, like a Mediterranean villa. The house glowed in the morning sun, looking bright and modern compared to the other properties.

She was going to miss this place. She'd been so happy here.

Mostly.

It would have been wonderful to raise a family in this lovely Dublin lane, but that was never going to happen.

Soon she'd be gone.

They'd get out of here, put the house on the market the minute the paint was dry. Then begin a new life in Barcelona. Her parents would be glad to have her home. They'd discover Barry was a good man, even if he looked rough.

Valentina tied her long, dark hair in a ponytail. It was ten o'clock. Her shift at the charity shop started at ten thirty, but she was never going to get there in time unless the painter finished soon.

Through her sunglasses, she looked up at her bedroom window where Aidan Donnelly had been working for half an hour.

The stringy young man they had hired to paint the house was sitting on her bedroom windowsill, stroking his chin, and gazing at Valentina. His lips were parted and there was a dreamy expression on his face.

Goosebumps broke out on Valentina's arms. A feeling of dread spread across her chest, snaking up to her throat.

Why was he staring at her?

Aidan wore a sleeveless white vest, which showed off his tattoos. A Mayan pyramid was inked on one arm, a humanoid face with three eyes on the other. His black hair was short at the back and sides and longer on top, waxed into an Elvis-style quiff.

There was something murky and unwholesome in his eyes. Valentina didn't like the way he rubbed his upper lip constantly and how he left droplets of urine on the floor when he used their toilet.

Though Aidan gave Valentina the creeps, she was damned if she was going to be intimidated in her own home.

She kept looking at him as she removed her shades. When he realised she was watching him, he quickly disappeared from sight. Back into her bedroom.

Valentina wondered why he was taking so long there. She imagined him going through her private things. Handling her possessions.

She turned her attention back to the pregnancy test as the result appeared. Two pink strips told her she was pregnant. This was the second test she had taken, as she wanted to be sure before she told Barry.

She looked at her phone. It was tempting to let him know the news now, but later would be better – over a nice dinner. Barbecued chicken and a few glasses of chilled white wine.

She hated that Aidan was in the house, ruining this moment. Bringing up WhatsApp, she tapped out a message to Barry.

I don't like being alone with this guy.

He might not see it for a while as he had clients all morning. In any case, Valentina hated relying on other people. She'd handle this herself.

She stood up and marched into the kitchen, pausing only to set the pregnancy test down on the kitchen table, before she made her way upstairs, walking loudly on the carpeted steps. Aidan should know that she was coming and that she meant business.

As she approached her bedroom door, there was a loud crash.

She hurried forward, pushing open the door to the bedroom. Aidan was standing over her bedside locker, which lay on its side. Valentina's socks and panties lay scattered across the floor.

"I'm really sorry," Aidan said. "It was a complete accident. I'm so clumsy – always knocking things over."

Heat rushed to her cheeks – fury at the thought of Aidan going through her underwear. He must have been looking through her things, then panicked when he heard her coming. He took a step towards her.

"I've got it," Valentina said, holding up her hand to stop him coming closer. She scooped up her clothes.

Three of the walls were peach colour now. Only one remained to be painted. The smell of paint turned her stomach. "I can finish the painting myself," she said.

Aidan frowned. "But I'm nearly done."

"I'll pay you the full amount anyway."

"I won't be long."

"No," Valentina said. "Thank you, but no. I will finish. I have to go out soon."

"Okay," he said. His face was wrinkled with confusion. "I'm sorry. If it was about your clothes—"

"Leave it. I said I will finish."

Aidan set about getting his things together, while Valentina carried her socks and underwear to the spare bedroom. She dropped them on the bed and waited there. She listened as Aidan brought his stepladder downstairs, the steel clanging with every step. The front door creaked open. Aidan lugged the ladder outside.

Valentina could be firm when she wanted to be. The confrontation hadn't been any fun, but at least he was leaving now.

Valentina checked through the drawers of the desk that sat in a corner of the spare room. This was where she kept all her stationery. She found an envelope and put the money she owed Aidan inside.

Suddenly she heard a groan from outside. What was Aidan doing?

Valentina walked onto the landing. She paused to listen but heard nothing more. At the top of the stairs, she looked down.

The front door was ajar.

"Aidan? Are you okay?"

Nothing.

No answer.

She jumped when her phone buzzed with a text message. It was the anonymous number again.

Let's play.

She swallowed, trying to stave off panic as her pulse began to race.

"Aidan?" she called.

She waited but when she heard nothing further, she began to descend the stairs, gripping the banister with one hand and clutching the cross around her neck with the other. The cross was made of smooth mahogany. Her father had given it to her for her tenth birthday and it always reminded her of him. She released it and let it hang next to her other necklace – the one Barry had given her, with a bright yellow sunflower pendant.

"Aidan?" Valentina called when she reached the bottom of the stairs. Her mouth was dry.

Silence pressed in on her, throbbing in her ears as she waited for him to answer.

If she wanted to see outside, she'd have to go closer to the door. She didn't want to do that, but she didn't want to turn her back on the door, either.

She lifted her phone and dialled Barry's number. It went straight to voicemail. She ended the call without leaving a message. Speaking would have meant breaking the silence.

Someone might hear her.

She tapped out a text instead.

Call me ASAP. I'm scared.

Valentina had to force herself to walk over to the door, to pull it open. By then, she could hardly breathe.

Something was very wrong.

She peered outside.

The back doors of Aidan's van were wide open.

What she saw inside it made her mouth fall open in horror.

"My god," she whispered, gripping her cross.

She turned to run, but it was too late.

CHAPTER 2

Detective Sergeant Joe Byrne stepped out of the shop, holding a paper cup in one hand and a grease-stained bag in the other. Rush hour traffic was gone, but Morehampton Road remained busy. Jaguars, BMWs, a couple of Teslas. A lot of buses too. Joe had forgotten how much traffic passed through Donnybrook, heading south to University College Dublin and north to the city centre.

His bag contained two breakfast rolls. Egg, sausage and bacon, on soft round baps. The paper cup was extra-large, full of dark, bitter coffee and only a hint of milk. A chocolate bar was stuffed in his suit pocket.

Joe needed all of it.

He'd been driving through the night, leaving his Kilkenny apartment at 6:45 am, after working the late shift. Too angry to sleep, he had stayed up all night, aimlessly flicking through dozens of TV channels.

He'd driven 130 kilometres, arriving in Dublin after three hours. A crash on the N7 had made the journey a nightmare. A Nissan had careened off the road and veered into a line of trees, grazing every one of them for half a mile before smashing head-on into a brick wall.

Back when he'd been on motorcycle patrol, Joe had worked scenes like that.

Once he had arrived in Donnybrook, Joe had zeroed in on the nearest place he could grab some food, which was the deli counter in this shop.

A few steel tables and chairs were set up outside the door, separated from the footpath by a canvas barrier. No one sat there, no one but Joe. He slumped in the nearest chair and began to demolish his food.

The June air was warm, the sky a brilliant blue.

Donnybrook Cemetery stood on the other side of the road, its metal gates set into a stone archway. The gate was chained up tight, but leafy tree branches reached over the stonework.

Joe's destination was Donnybrook Garda Station, next to the cemetery. Three storeys tall, the station was a boxy grey building that looked about as much fun as a colonoscopy.

Joe finished the first roll and wiped the ketchup and melted butter off his hands with a napkin. Then he started in on the second roll. At thirty-five, he was aware that it would soon start to take a little more work to keep in shape. Especially if he kept eating like this. So often though, he had to grab food whenever a case allowed. And at those moments, he reached for the nearest thing, whatever it was.

Being a detective was like being a reporter. You went where you were told. Four weeks ago, Joe had learned he was being transferred to Donnybrook. He'd declined. His boss in Kilkenny wasn't interested in talking about it. As far as he was concerned, Joe worked in Dublin now.

So here he was. Day one.

Starting on the late shift.

Detectives worked six days on, four days off. Ten-hour shifts. Of the six days on, there were two early starts, two late starts, and two nights. Joe had never got used to the pattern. Today's late start meant reporting at 10:00 am, finishing at 8:00 pm.

But Joe figured he'd be done with Donnybrook by 10:05 am.

He'd rather quit than work in his old neighbourhood.

Not that he minded leaving Kilkenny. There was nothing for him there but an overpriced apartment and a dying aloe vera plant.

He was willing to go anywhere – except Donnybrook. It was weird that he was being transferred here. The first thing the force did when you left training academy was move you far from home so you wouldn't be policing your own community. And then you tended to be transferred to a variety of places, none of them very close to home. But Joe had grown up near here, had gone to college down the road. So why had he been sent here?

After the second roll, he polished off the chocolate bar, and drained the dregs of his coffee. He wiped his hands one more time and got to his feet.

His ten-year old Honda Civic was parked around the corner from the shop. Slipping behind the wheel, Joe started the car and eased up the road, past the front of the station, then turned down the narrow road where the entrance to the car park was buried.

It was a sprawling car park with dozens of spaces. He drove right up to the building, parking next to the big steel door, in the only free space at this end of the lot.

He checked himself in the mirror and realised that he'd forgotten to shave. Nothing he could do about that now, which was a shame, because his dark brown stubble was pretty obvious. He combed his blond-brown fringe back with his fingers and wiped a dab of butter from the corner of his mouth.

As soon as he stepped out of his car, a Ford Escort screeched to a stop behind him. Old and grey, the car wheezed like it smoked sixty cigarettes a day. Ignoring it, Joe turned and walked towards the building.

"Hey!"

A man's voice. Harsh. Indignant. Arrogant, too.

Joe didn't even look around. He hit his key fob to lock the Honda and kept walking. Behind him a car door opened and closed, the engine still running.

"Are you deaf? That's my space."

Joe kept walking as uneven footsteps came up behind him. His muscles tensed.

"I'm talking to you."

A macho attitude was thankfully rare on the force, but Joe had a feeling that the man behind him was one of those uncommon cases. And Joe was in no mood to play nice. He was tired after the drive and annoyed at getting pushed around.

Being ordered to Donnybrook had brought emotions bubbling to the surface. Memories, too, of the worst period of his life.

When someone grabbed his shoulder, Joe spun around, his hand already balled into a fist.

Joe froze once he caught sight of the man. Like him, the guy was in his thirties. But he stood a foot shorter than Joe's six one. He had a round face, thin dark brown hair, and an expression of smug indifference. He wore an ill-fitting suit. But, most noticeably, he was clearly unwell.

He leaned on a crutch and his skin had a disgusting greyish hue. The man's mouth twisted into a sneer as he read Joe's intention.

"You want to take a swing at me? Go ahead."

Joe took a slow breath. Let it out.

"Forget it," he said, turning his back.

"You're still in my spot."

"And I still don't care," Joe said.

As he walked away, he felt a twinge of guilt – the guy really didn't look well. But Joe hated bullies, even sick ones.

He reached the station's back door at the same time as a woman in a dark suit. Shoulder-length brown hair, hastily applied makeup. She paused in the doorway, cradling a bunch of manilla folders under one arm, and squinted at Joe. Her eyes had the probing gaze of a new plainclothes officer. Late twenties and stressed-looking – Joe figured her for a detective garda, which put her one rank below him.

"Can I help you?" she asked.

"Where can I find the Inspector?"

"You must be our new sergeant."

Joe gave her a grudging nod. He didn't bother telling her that he wasn't going to stay.

"Detective Garda Anne-Marie Cunningham. Pleased to meet you, sir."

They shook hands.

"The Inspector?" he prompted.

"If you'll follow me."

Cunningham led Joe into a long corridor that reeked of lemon disinfectant. The walls were covered in pale yellow paint.

He followed Cunningham up a flight of stairs. At the top, she keyed in a code to get through a locked door. She led him down another identical corridor and stopped in front of a door at the building's back corner. She said, "This is Detective Inspector O'Carroll's office."

"Thanks."

"You're welcome, sir."

She turned and set off back down the steps. Joe rapped on the door with his knuckles.

"Come in."

Detective Inspector David O'Carroll sat at his desk drinking a cup of tea. It was a few years since they'd seen each other, but O'Carroll hadn't changed. A few touches of grey appeared in his carrot-coloured hair, but the forty-something-year-old still had the wiry fitness of a man who cycled ten miles a day. He jumped up from his chair and came around the desk.

Joe said, "Sir."

"Don't call me that, for god's sake."

They shook hands. Joe smiled, feeling a little of his tension dissipate. The two men had been stationed together for several years. O'Carroll had always been a good friend to Joe.

It looked like he still suffered from OCD. His room was tidy to the point of being sterile. The desk was bare except for a computer and his beverage.

"Good to see you, David."

"You too, Joe." He took a step back and looked Joe over. "I have to say, I was expecting worse."

"Why?"

He shrugged. "I heard about the hospital. They said you went pure mad and nearly killed yourself."

Joe flushed.

"Who the fuck said that?"

O'Carroll's expression hardened. Informality was one thing, insubordination another. He pointed to a swivel chair, and said, "Sit down, Joe."

CHAPTER 3

Wall to Wall Fitness was located on a corner just off Abbey Street, in Dublin's north inner city. It was a small studio with two rooms, plus a kitchen. The building's ground floor, below it, was occupied by an Indian restaurant, where Barry Wall often grabbed lunch.

Wall was working in the studio's front room, training a young actress named Holly Martini. She was fine-featured and petite, and Wall felt like a giant when near her. He stood six foot two and weighed 230 lbs, all of it muscle.

Right now, they were sitting on the floor, facing each other, their legs stretched out in front of them. Holly was finishing her cool-down, a series of light stretches to end the session.

The room had a persistent smell of curry from the restaurant below, but there wasn't much Wall could do about that. The weather was so hot that he needed to leave the windows open.

Wall's only employee was training Holly's co-star in the other room. The Americans were in town to film a new TV show. Luckily for Wall, their hotel was a short distance away, so they were training with him.

"Good," he said when Holly completed the last stretch. She struggled to her feet.

"That was the toughest workout of my life," Holly said in her L.A. drawl. "I don't think I could do another squat if you'd paid me."

Wall walked her to the door, where she grabbed her light hoodie, and slipped it on over her Lululemon outfit. She moved with her usual grace, even when exhausted. Perhaps that came from being on camera all the time, having every movement scrutinised.

"That's what I'm here for," he said. "See you again on Wednesday."

Holly hesitated.

"I was thinking," she said. "Would you like to get a drink some time? I mean, I'd love to pick your brain about my diet, because I'm having a hard time believing my nutritionist's advice right now."

Wall smiled. She was a very attractive woman. Most men would have jumped at the chance to have a drink with her.

"I'm not wearing it this minute," he said, holding up his hand, "but I have a ring that belongs on this finger."

Holly blushed.

"I'm sorry," she said. "Of course you have a wife. I'm dumb."

"Don't worry about it. Wednesday at eleven, okay?"

"Sure thing. Bye."

Wall shook his head as he watched her walk briskly out of the room. If he was single, he would have said yes in an instant – but Valentina was everything he'd ever wanted. He decided to check his phone before the next client arrived.

He ducked into the kitchen and grabbed his phone. There was a missed a call from Valentina. Some text messages too. He looked at the first one.

I don't like being alone with this guy.

Wall always said his wife was a drama queen. All the same, his eyes narrowed as he read the second message.

Call me ASAP. I'm scared.

Probably nothing, Wall thought.

He phoned her back. The call went straight to voicemail.

It was eleven o'clock. Valentina was meant to be working today. She had given up her job at the bank once they decided to move to Spain. To occupy her time until the move, she volunteered three times a week at Oxfam. Wall phoned the shop and spoke to the woman who ran the place.

"Is Valentina there?"

"No. She didn't turn up today. I wondered what happened. Is everything—"

Wall ended the call.

No, he thought, with a sinking feeling. *Everything is not alright.*

Valentina never turned her phone off, never let the battery run down. Never turned up late for anything. This just wasn't like her.

Wall scrambled downstairs and out onto the street. He sprinted to the car park where he left his Hyundai.

Got behind the wheel. Got moving.

Called Valentina again.

Still no answer.

He drove across the city and out to the suburbs. By the time he reached the lane where he and Valentina lived, his heart was pounding so loud it scared him.

From the lane, all you could see was a stone wall with a row of high wooden gates. Few people realised what nice little houses hid behind them. Unlike most of the neighbours, Wall and Valentina usually left their gate open, as it was now. Aidan Donnelly's van was gone, as Wall would have expected.

He parked, hurried to the door and let himself in. He called out Valentina's name.

Nothing.

No reply.

His voice echoed around the house. As he stood in the hall, he got an uneasy feeling. He wasn't sure why until he noticed that their wedding photo on the wall was upside-down. Wall stared at it. Why would Valentina do such a thing?

Unless it wasn't Valentina who'd done it.

Entering the kitchen, he saw the bowl of fruit on the island in the middle of the kitchen was upside-down. He corrected it, put the apples and bananas back inside.

He walked around the ground floor, wondering what else was wrong. In the sitting room, the clock on the mantelpiece was upside-down.

In the dining room, the decorative Spanish plates on the wall had been hung upside down.

Wall was about to head upstairs when he happened to look out the window to the back garden.

A cluster of little pink-white objects stuck up out of the grass like mushrooms. Wall slid open the patio door and stepped outside. At the edge of the grass, he hunkered down so he could get a closer look.

Fingers.

They can't be real, he thought.

Then he noticed Valentina's wedding ring on one of those fingers.

CHAPTER 4

"Sit down," Detective Inspector O'Carroll repeated.

Joe threw himself on a wobbly swivel chair in front of the desk. It creaked under him. O'Carroll sat down too, wiping an imaginary grain of dust off the desk with the back of his hand.

Sunlight streamed into the office through a window looking out onto the car park.

Joe hadn't meant to raise his voice, but he hated it when people talked about his private life.

O'Carroll said, "People are concerned about you, Joe. Whether you're fit to work."

"No one's concerned. I don't know where you got that from."

"I hear you live in the pubs down in Kilkenny."

Joe winced. He had overdone it before his trip to hospital, but a brutal case of pancreatitis had stopped him drinking.

"Not anymore," Joe said.

"Now that you're here — part of my team — I want to know you're in decent shape."

"I'm fine—"

"Good."

"But I'm not working here."

O'Carroll knew why. Joe had made the mistake of confiding in him years ago, when they'd been posted together. Back then, they'd shared their struggles with each other. O'Carroll had told Joe of his doubts about being a gay officer in such a conservative institution. Joe had told O'Carroll about the woman who had ruined his life. O'Carroll knew all about Lisa O'Malley, knew she lived in Donnybrook.

And he'd *still* summoned Joe here.

Joe couldn't help suspecting that O'Carroll had done it deliberately. Was it some misplaced attempt to help him?

O'Carroll said, "Let's be clear. You're here to do a job."

"Let *me* be clear. You can let me stay in Kilkenny or you can fire me."

"You're stubborn enough to throw away your career?"

"I guess I am," Joe said. "Anyway, I heard you have a detective sergeant here. As far as I know, Donnybrook has only ever needed one."

O'Carroll leaned forward.

"You're right about that, but the thing is, our sergeant, Kevin Boyle, is in poor health."

Joe thought of the loudmouth in the car park. He said, "The guy on crutches? What's wrong with him?"

O'Carroll shook his head. "Kevin has had a litany of health problems this year, from pneumonia to a broken foot. I suspect there's some underlying condition, but it hasn't been diagnosed yet. He's missed a lot of time, and I need someone to pick up the slack. Forget about that quitting stuff. Wait till something happens, and you get sucked into a case. I remember that look on your face."

"What look?"

"When you're trying to solve a crime."

"Do you even have crimes around here?"

Donnybrook was an affluent area. Joe imagined it was one of the easier postings you could get.

"We have enough." O'Carroll got to his feet. "Let me show you the station. I know, I know. You're not going to work here. I'll give you a tour anyway. We can have tea and a biscuit afterwards."

"Okay, but I'm not changing my mind."

O'Carroll kept the tour brief. Joe followed him upstairs and saw the incident room. They returned to O'Carroll's floor where there were a hundred tiny offices, then went downstairs again to the communications room, the public office at the front, the long corridor from the public office to the other side of the building. Everywhere they went, O'Carroll introduced Joe to his colleagues.

Joe saw the interview rooms, and the holding cells. All of them were empty. They were the source of the disinfectant smell Joe had detected when he arrived.

They passed the door that led out to the car park. And in the corner of the building, beside the exit, was the District Detective Unit. If Joe accepted the transfer to Donnybrook, this would become his new base.

It was a tight series of three rooms, connected by open doorways. Every inch of the place was stuffed with files and folders.

As he had elsewhere in the station, O'Carroll made the introductions. But here, there were familiar faces. First, Anne-Marie Cunningham, the detective garda who'd shown Joe the way to O'Carroll's office.

Then there was Detective Sergeant Kevin Boyle, the sick man. He managed to look smug despite his health issues, whatever they were. Joe shook hands with him for O'Carroll's sake.

"Home sweet home," O'Carroll said, looking around the room.

Boyle put on his suit jacket. Cunningham did the same.

O'Carroll said, "Where are you two going?"

Joe had forgotten how curious David O'Carroll was. He was one of those people who wanted to know everything that was going on.

"We're due in court," Cunningham said.

O'Carroll nodded. "Of course. Go ahead."

After the two of them left, O'Carroll took Joe back to his office. They spent a while catching up, having not really spoken since O'Carroll's wedding. Joe hadn't attended, since he didn't think he could stand the sight of two people getting married. That would only make him feel more alone.

Joe was about to push O'Carroll for his decision – fire Joe or let him continue in Kilkenny – when a call came through from the station sergeant. Two uniforms had responded to a call-out to a nearby house. A young woman was missing from her home and there were signs of violence.

O'Carroll turned to Joe. "I have no one else to handle it," he said.

Joe was eager to get back to Kilkenny, but he couldn't ignore a missing person report.

"I'll deal with this," he said. "And then I'm leaving."

O'Carroll made no comment. Joe wrote down the address of the crime scene and headed for the car park.

CHAPTER 5

Barry Wall stood in his sitting room while he waited for the emergency services. A squad car was the first to arrive. Two officers who looked like children presented themselves on the doorstep. One of them was chewing gum. Wall pointed them to the garden. They went and looked. Then the guy stopped chewing gum and got on his radio.

An ambulance arrived soon after, followed by a second squad car. This time, no one was chewing gum.

Wall stood in the middle of his sitting room while half a dozen men and women stomped around his home. More arrived every few minutes, but no one seemed to be looking for Valentina. He rubbed his bare arms. Goosebumps had broken out on his pale skin. The clock on the mantelpiece was still upside down. Wall stared at it and wondered what the hell had happened in his home.

The third officer to arrive, who looked even younger than his colleagues, kept asking the same inane questions. Wall finally interrupted.

"Just find my wife, will you?"

"I understand you're upset, Mr. Wall. We're doing everything we can."

"No, you're wasting time talking to me. I've told you everything I know."

"I understand it might not seem important, but I'd really like to go through a few more questions with you."

Ignoring him, Wall walked over to the front window as a white van pulled up. *Technical Bureau* was written on the side. Forensics.

At once, the Technical Bureau officers started setting up a cordon, blocking off most of the driveway and forcing everyone to walk on the strip of grass next to the driveway to get to the house.

A Honda pulled up on the street outside. The driver parked behind the Technical Bureau van and made his way up the driveway. Blue shirt, red tie. Mid-thirties, same as Wall. Scruffy-looking. Unshaven. Wall didn't like the look of him. He hoped he wouldn't have to rely on this man to find Valentina.

The man exchanged a few words with an officer at the front door, then made his way up to Wall.

"Detective Sergeant Joe Byrne," he said. They shook hands.

"Are you going to ask me the same stupid questions as the last guy?"

"No, I'm going to find your wife." His eyes were pale blue, very clear. "Can you tell me what happened?"

Wall went through it again. Valentina's texts. The missed call. Arriving home to find her missing, except for—

He couldn't say the word, so instead he pointed towards the garden.

"May I?" Byrne said.

Wall nodded and followed the detective through the dining room and out the back door. A photographer was already there, snapping away on a Nikon. Byrne hunkered down, examining Valentina's severed fingers, each of them planted in the grass like a lollipop.

Wall's stomach heaved, and saliva flooded his mouth. He turned away and got sick into a pot of lavender.

"Come on," Byrne said, and led him indoors, as if Wall might not be able to find his own way. The detective got a glass from the cupboard and filled it with water from the tap.

"It's my house," Wall said. "I'm able to get a glass of water."

"I know," Byrne said.

Wall rinsed his mouth out and set the glass down on the counter. He caught Byrne looking around the kitchen, his eyes passing lingering on every surface.

"Are they definitely your wife's fingers?"

"Yes," Wall growled. "Now can you find Aidan Donnelly?"

"The painter. How much do you know about him?"

"Not enough, clearly. I didn't think he was dangerous."

"Where did you find him?"

"My brother works in real estate. He knows a lot of decorators, so I told him I needed someone."

"Any idea why Aiden Donnelly would want to hurt your wife?"

"I don't know. He's a man."

"You're a man. I'm a man."

Wall glared at the detective. "Some men…"

He couldn't finish.

"Anyway," Byrne said, "we're trying to locate his vehicle."

"I should never have left her alone with a stranger."

Just then an officer from the Technical Bureau came down the stairs. She held a clear plastic evidence bag containing blood-spattered garden shears.

"They were in the bedroom," she said.

Wall felt dizzy. Someone had used those shears on Valentina, on the hands that he'd kissed that very morning.

Byrne said, "This strike me as cruel."

"Of course it's cruel," Wall said. "It's insane."

"I mean, it looks personal."

"What are you getting at?"

"Aside from Donnelly," Byrne said, in a cool tone, "do you know anyone who'd want to hurt your wife?"

"No one. Everyone loved Valentina. No one who knew her would do such thing."

Byrne said nothing.

Wall knew he didn't believe him.

CHAPTER 6

Valentina López Vázquez and Barry Wall's house had a narrow strip of grass out front. Joe and Wall stood there, not talking. The personal trainer was a big guy, heavily muscled and there was something forceful about the way he moved his body. But Joe was pretty sure Wall hadn't attacked his wife. He had an alibi, a training session with some Z-list actress. They were outside because Joe didn't want him muddying the crime scene.

Wall's brother, Ken, lived in the Wicklow mountains, an hour's drive south, but he had an office in Dublin city centre. Joe had asked Wall to have his brother come and collect him. Wall grumbled but did it. Now he kept rubbing his short, brown hair as he waited for Ken to arrive.

The house was swarming with uniforms and forensics people. On Joe's current posting, he'd seen a lot of traffic accidents, minor burglaries, things like that. But he hadn't dealt with serious violent crime for a while. He'd forgotten how busy this kind of crime scene was.

He had the sinking feeling that he might be dealing with a murder.

Joe heard the roar of an engine.

"That's him," Wall said.

Joe followed him out the gate. They walked around the cluster of emergency vehicles to a gleaming red Jaguar at the side of the lane. Ken stepped out of the car in a crisp suit and a cloud of cologne. He had a much smaller frame than his brother, but he wasn't a stick figure. It was just that everyone looked small next to Barry Wall. Ken was maybe forty, with a shiny bald head, and heavy brows over his grey eyes.

Ken said, "Tell me it's not true. Is Valentina really missing?"

Wall said, "She's…"

His voice broke.

Joe had uniforms out canvassing the neighbourhood, but it was a Monday morning, and he wasn't optimistic. The back garden was sheltered by trees and bushes so no one would have been able to see the fingers being planted in the grass.

They were looking for a sick individual. Joe wasn't a psychologist, but cutting off a woman's fingers with garden shears struck him as remarkably malevolent. He didn't expect a ransom demand. Instead, he figured that the attacker had taken her somewhere quiet so he could enjoy more time with her.

The thought made Joe mad.

At the same time, he felt a surge of adrenaline. O'Carroll had been right. Joe was on a case again and he wasn't thinking of quitting. He was focused on finding Valentina López Vázquez as soon as possible. And catching the sick bastard responsible.

Barry Wall had no doubt about who that was.

"Any news on Aidan Donnelly?" he kept asking. "Have you found Aidan Donnelly?"

According to him, the painter had been in the house alone with Valentina that morning. Valentina's text messages suggested she was afraid of him.

"Why López Vázquez?" Joe said, pausing next to Ken Wall's Jaguar.

"What?"

"Your wife didn't take your family name when you got married. I'm just wondering why."

Ken scowled.

"You're asking my brother about names? Why don't you focus on what's relevant?"

"We don't know what's relevant yet."

"Pride," Wall said. "She was proud of the family name and didn't want to give it up."

Joe nodded. Some men didn't like proud women. Statistically speaking, they were probably after a man.

Joe took Ken's number and promised to update the brothers when he could. They were reluctant to leave, so Joe left them at the Jaguar and told the uniform at the entrance to the house not to let them back in.

He wasn't a damn babysitter.

Joe walked through the house, pausing only to gaze at a photo of Valentina that hung on the wall. She had long, dark brown hair, matching brown eyes and a friendly, open smile. Hard to imagine someone wanting to hurt her the way they had. He continued to the back garden and watched as forensics pulled the fingers out of the grass and placed each digit in an evidence bag.

Hold on, Valentina.

He walked through the house one more time, soaking it all up, and taking stock of where things stood. The neighbourhood was still being canvassed, Donnelly's van was still being located, CCTV footage was being sought, and the forensics team was still working the house. There was nothing more he could do there.

He decided to head back to the station. O'Carroll would want to hear how his first day was going.

CHAPTER 7

Detective Inspector David O'Carroll was sitting at his desk, eating a packet of crisps when Joe knocked on his door. He ditched the half-eaten packet in his bin while Joe brought him up to speed on the disappearance.

The windows looking out onto the car park were open as wide as they'd go. It was mid-afternoon and the sun blazed down.

"Let's set up an incident room," O'Carroll said.

Joe had expected him to say that. The incident room was the command centre of an investigation, used when a case demanded a team effort. Serious crimes, basically. It was a huge machine. Roles might be assigned to twenty or thirty officers, depending on the investigation.

O'Carroll picked up the phone and spoke briefly to someone on the other end of the line. His boss, Joe figured.

O'Carroll ended the call and said, "I know this is a lot to throw at you on your first day, but I'd like you to be SIO. I've just cleared it with Superintendent Kavanagh. That okay with you?"

The Senior Investigating Officer was the person in charge. Joe had taken the specialist training, but this would be his first time actually acting as SIO.

"Sure," Joe said.

"If you can't hack it, I'll take over."

"I'll hack it."

O'Carroll called a meeting while Joe headed upstairs.

The incident room occupied almost the whole top floor of the station. A long conference table ran down the length of the room, surrounded by about twenty chairs. There was a white board at the top of the room. Joe made his way there. Beside the white board, a window looked out onto the old cemetery next to the station. The left side of the room looked out onto Morehampton Road.

Joe was still gathering his thoughts when the room began to fill up. He waited until everyone available was there, including O'Carroll.

Anne-Marie Cunningham was back from court. Joe assigned her the role of Incident Room Coordinator.

Kevin Boyle was still out, and Joe was glad of that.

O'Carroll stood beside Joe and helped him assign the rest of the roles to people whose names he didn't even know yet. The family liaison officer, the CCTV team, the exhibits officer, interviewers, the inquiries team, the house-to-house team, crime scene examiners. Some of these people were out in the field, doing their job already – such as the crime scene examiners.

Joe opened a book of tasks – which amounted to an elaborate, numbered to-do list – and doled them out.

By the time he had sent everyone away to complete their tasks, afternoon was turning into evening.

He hadn't had lunch yet and desperately needed to refuel while he had a few minutes to spare.

He grabbed his jacket and set off walking down the road towards the nearest Tesco, thinking he'd grab a sandwich. It was a beautiful evening, but Joe found it hard to put Valentina López Vázquez out of his mind, as he walked.

She'd been missing for hours now, and they still had nothing.

The supermarket was busy. Joe found a grab-and-go food section inside the door. He selected a chicken wrap from the fridge, then continued down the aisle, grabbing a banana in the fruit section, and looking for the coffee. He found the aisle and chose the strongest coffee they had.

When he turned to head to the counter, he saw a woman halfway down the aisle. Her back was to him, and she was reaching for biscuits from the top shelf. Nothing eye-catching about her clothes – she wore blue jean and a green T-shirt. But there was something about the way she carried herself that grabbed Joe's attention. Something about the way her hair fell.

He took a step in her direction. Then another. His mouth became dry.

The woman gave up trying to reach the biscuits, and turned around. Joe felt a jolt when their eyes met.

It was her.

Lisa O'Malley.

Joe stared at her. She stared back. He wondered if he'd changed. She had, but not in a bad way. Her sparkling eyes were still the same – the colour halfway between grey and pale blue. Curly, toffee-coloured hair, parted in the middle. Green loops hung from her ears.

Joe had Googled her over the years. Pathetic, but he hadn't been able to help himself. Even when he tried dating other women, he looked Lisa up every few weeks. Sometimes he was rewarded with a new picture on social media or an update on her website.

She took a step towards him.

He took a step towards her.

Two metres separated them.

"Hello, Joe."

The sound of her voice brought the past rushing back.

Joe couldn't speak. Waves of nervous energy pulsed through him. He just stared at Lisa, feeling like he was in a dream. He had fantasised about what he'd say if they ever met again. Now that she was standing in front of him, his mind was blank.

"What are you doing here?" Lisa said.

Joe cleared his throat.

"I was transferred to Donnybrook. This is my first day. You still live here?"

"For my sins," she said. She nodded to the top shelf. "Can you help me reach the biscuits? I'm not tall enough."

He didn't.

A teenage boy appeared at the end of the aisle, his arms festooned with avocados. He came towards them.

"Mum, do you want the ripe ones or the ripen-at-home ones?"

He stopped when he saw them.

Mum.

Joe was aware that she'd had a kid. He stared at the boy with a kind of appalled fascination. He was a big lad with gentle eyes and messy hair just like his mother's.

Did Lisa have a boyfriend, a husband? Joe tried to read her face but it gave nothing away. The boy looked from Lisa to Joe, and back again, confused.

Lisa said, "Joe—"

His phone rang.

He answered it and listened.

The search team had found Aidan Donnelly's van.

CHAPTER 8

Lisa O'Malley walked quickly, only glancing back to make sure that Christopher was still following her. The road was busy, cars streaming past. Exhaust fumes choked her nostrils.

Home was an elegant red-brick that lay a ten-minute walk from the supermarket. Today, she made the journey in seven minutes.

As much as a freelance web developer had normal days, this had been one. In the morning, Lisa had called out to a small law firm. After lunch, she'd consulted with the owner of a dry cleaning shop. Everyone wanted a decent website.

She'd done some work on her laptop between appointments, and over lunch. Everything had been so normal.

Until now... After so many years, Joe was back.

If she'd heard he was working in Donnybrook, she would have been able to steel herself. To get prepared for the inevitable encounter, and it *was* inevitable given how small the suburb was, and how close she lived to the station.

But no. Suddenly he was just there, standing in the supermarket aisle. Still filled with rage, a decade and a half later.

Joe hadn't changed much. He'd grown into his looks. Those piercing blue eyes were now set in a leaner, harder face. She'd felt something stir inside, when she looked at his sandy hair, the strong physique. A memory of their time together. Lisa didn't like the sadness she now saw in his eyes.

Once home, she made a stir fry while Christopher showered. She was glad to be alone with her thoughts for a while. She dreaded having to answer more questions. After Joe rushed out of the shop without his purchases, Christopher had asked who he was.

Lisa had said, "Someone I haven't seen in a long time."

It had been the best she could come up with, when she was still numb with shock. She'd hurried to the counter to pay before he could ask anything else.

Christopher appeared in the doorway. Her teenage son hadn't even been born the last time she saw Joe. It had been so long.

"What's burning, Mum?"

"What? Nothing."

Then Lisa realised that this wasn't quite true. The chicken and peppers in the frying pan were somewhere between burnt and cremated.

She took the pan off the heat at the same time as the smoke alarm began to scream. Christopher opened the door to the garden. Then he went into the hallway and waved his hand under the alarm, trying to make it stop. Finally, it did, and Christopher came back into the kitchen.

"I don't think we can eat that," he said, peering at the frying pan.

He was right. Lisa tipped the food into the bin and ditched the pan in the sink.

"Fine. Let's have a pizza."

"We didn't get any."

"Really?"

"I told you we didn't finish working through the shopping list."

"Are you sure we don't have a pizza?"

She went to the fridge and looked but Christopher was right. He was always right when it came to food.

Christopher said, "We can order something."

"We just went shopping. We must have something."

"Yeah, well." He shrugged.

"Let's have French toast."

"For dinner? Okay. Fine with me."

It was Christopher's favourite breakfast and was easy to make. Usually they didn't have it for dinner though. She got eggs out of the fridge.

Watching her crack them into a bowl, Christopher said, "That guy…"

"What guy?"

"In the shop, Mum."

"What about him?"

"Mum. Is he – was he – I mean, were you and him, like, together in the past?"

Lisa whisked the eggs furiously.

"Why do you ask that?"

"Because you're acting weird."

"I had a long day."

"I've *never* seen you act so weird."

"Joe is just someone I used to know. It's been a long time. That's all. It was a surprise."

She took a clean pan out of the press. Heated up a little oil and waited. Christopher watched silently for a minute.

"Is he…" Christopher swallowed. "Is he my dad?"

Lisa thought desperately. Her son had become more preoccupied with his absent father as the years went by. Especially this year. She put the whisk down. Thought for a second. Said nothing. Thought again.

"I'll take that as a yes," Christopher said.

He walked out of the kitchen, slamming the door behind him.

CHAPTER 9

Joe parked the Honda on a quiet road a mile from Barry Wall and Valentina López Vázquez's house. In front of him, the van they'd found was bookended by two squad cars. Four uniforms stood guard, their faces grim. A football field lay on one side of the road, a wall on the other.

Joe's legs felt light as he stepped out of the car. It was the adrenaline coursing through him.

He tried to keep his focus on Aidan Donnelly, but running into Lisa O'Malley had hit him hard. He took a breath and reminded himself that a woman's life depended on him.

Overhead the sky was still a brilliant blue. The early evening air was still warm. Joe heard music booming from the distance. The smell of barbecued chicken and burgers.

As he walked over to the van, one of the uniforms nodded a greeting.

Joe said, "You open it up yet?"

"No, sir. We waited, like you said."

"Good."

"We're not sure it's the van you want."

He pointed to the empty space where the licence plate should have been. Removed to slow down identification. Joe wondered why the vehicle had been left out in the open. The road was quiet, but it was still a public place. Cars passed by. Donnelly must have known the van would be found sometime.

Joe walked all the way around it. There was no one in driver's seat or the passenger seat. He slipped on a pair of gloves and tried the driver's door. It opened. He stepped up and glanced around but there wasn't much to see. A tabloid newspaper and a half-empty bottle of fizzy orange sat on the passenger seat, together with a tattered paperback called *Extra-terrestrial DNA and Humanity's Destiny: Exposing the New World Order's Plan*.

He stepped down and walked around to the back, steeling himself. It was possible he was about to find a corpse. He pulled out his 9mm Sig Sauer and pointed the gun at the van.

"Okay. Open it up."

One of the uniforms pulled open the door while the other three stood watching.

The painting gear in the van caught Joe's attention first: brushes and tins of paint, rollers, roller trays and turpentine. The van was full of them.

Then he saw a figure lying across the van, at the far end.

He stepped up into the van.

No. Don't be dead, Valentina.

But it was a man. He looked to be in his twenties, thin, stubbly, wearing a white vest, and showing tattoos. The man matched the description of Aidan Donnelly. He seemed to be asleep, with his head resting on a pink jumper.

The van's licence plates lay beside him.

"Mr. Donnelly?" Joe said. He kept the Sig trained on the figure. "Are you Aidan Donnelly?"

Nothing.

Joe leaned forward and kicked the man's arm. He shifted, then sat up quickly.

"What's going on? Where am I?"

"You better tell me where Valentina is."

He squinted as if he didn't understand. "What?"

Joe looked around the van but there was definitely no one else there.

"Where's Valentina?"

"Where am *I*?"

"Get up," Joe snapped.

Donnelly got to his feet. Unsteady, he staggered towards Joe, who grabbed him to stop him falling. Up close, Joe could smell the gin on his breath.

A flash of turquoise lace poked out of the pocket of Donnelly's jeans. Using a pen, Joe slowly pulled the lace out. Donnelly didn't move. It was a pair of ladies' panties.

Joe was shaking with rage.

"I'm going to find her," he said. "And I'm going to make you pay."

CHAPTER 10

Christopher O'Malley paced from one end of his bedroom to the other. The floorboards under the carpet creaked with every step.

Not eating dinner was weird, but anger had ruined his appetite. Mum had lied to him his whole life, and she'd only admitted the truth because of a chance encounter in the coffee aisle. Christopher couldn't believe it.

He had tried to play a computer game, but couldn't concentrate. He hadn't even known that was possible.

He wanted to break something, but he wasn't sure what. His laptop? The window? Footsteps came down the hall. Christopher heard three knocks on the door.

"Go away."

Mum said, "Can I come in?"

"No."

"Please?"

"No."

She opened the door. "We should talk."

"Why did you ask if you were going to come in anyway?"

She stepped inside. Her voice became stern. "Don't talk to me like that. Now calm down."

"Why should I? I thought you told me the truth, for all those years, and now I find out you're the biggest liar in the world."

She sighed and sat down on the edge of Christopher's bed.

"Maybe I could have handled things better. I was trying to do the best thing for you."

"Telling me my dad is some American guy is the best thing for me? When actually it's literally a complete lie?"

"Sit down."

"No."

He wouldn't sit down with her and be nice. Not after what she did, the way she betrayed him.

"*Sit down,* Christopher. Now."

He scowled, then dropped his ass onto the bed.

"I've asked you a million times who my dad is."

"I know," Lisa said. "What I told you had a grain of truth in it."

"He's not American. He's from Dublin."

"Don't use that tone."

"You care about my tone, but you don't care about me."

Mum massaged her temple like she had a headache.

"Of course I care about you. You're the most important thing in the world to me."

"Yeah, right."

She patted his leg.

"Okay, Joe's not from America. He's from around here. We met at university."

"Great." Christopher injected as much sarcasm as he could into his voice.

"Do you want me to tell you or not?"

A long pause.

Christopher said, "I guess. What's his name?"

"Joe Byrne. We dated for a while. When I found out I was pregnant, he was in America."

Christopher looked up for the first time.

"Why?"

"He got a place on a student exchange programme and went to New York for a year."

"Was he training to be a police officer there?"

Mum smiled. "No. He was studying philosophy."

"Why did he go there, if he was your boyfriend?"

"I insisted. I thought it would be a good opportunity for him. I didn't know I was pregnant."

"Oh my god. I have grandparents somewhere?"

"Joe's parents are dead."

"Both of them?"

Lisa nodded. "It was a hit-and-run many years ago."

"Whoa," Christopher said.

Mum took a breath. "Anyway, Joe always said he didn't want kids. Then I found out I was pregnant and he was away in another country. Seemed like the best thing was to… cut him loose. I didn't want to put pressure on him to do something he didn't want to do."

"Wait. You mean he doesn't even *know* I'm his son?"

The idea seemed so incredible that Christopher laughed out loud. But Mum wasn't laughing.

"I stopped talking to him. When he returned to Ireland… well, he was upset. He went and joined the force, like his dad. His father had been a detective too."

A surge of anger returned. Christopher got to his feet. "All this time, you could have told me, but you didn't. And you could have told him."

She stood up too. "I did what I thought was best – because I love you."

"That's a weird way to show it, Mum."

Christopher felt tears streaming down his face. Not knowing what else to do, he sat down again. He felt so angry and betrayed. But he could also see that his Mum was upset, and he hated that. She wrapped her arms around him. She held him in silence until the tears stopped.

"I'm sorry," Christopher whispered.

"It's okay. I'm sorry too."

He pulled away so he could blow his nose.

Mum said, "I know it's a lot to take in. We can talk about it more tomorrow, okay? I think that's enough for one night. We're probably both a bit overwhelmed."

"Yeah, okay."

"You want to look at something on TV? Maybe an action movie? We can pig out on Haagen-Dazs."

"I'd just like to be alone for a while."

"Okay. If you want to talk, you know where I am."

She kissed him on the forehead before leaving the room. Christopher thought for a moment. Then he began to form a plan.

He had a better idea than watching TV.

CHAPTER 11

Christopher waited in his room until Mum phoned Granny. When she was deep in conversation with her mother, Christopher slipped downstairs and let himself out the front door as quietly as he could.

He hurried down Morehampton Road. The sun was low, but still bright and strong. It was a beautiful evening.

And Christopher had a father.

He couldn't contain his excitement. He wanted to learn everything there was to know about Joe.

He passed the old cemetery and turned in at the gate of Donnybrook Garda Station. When he went up to the entrance, he found the door closed. But there were lights in the station's windows. He went up to the door and knocked. When that achieved nothing, he banged on the door. Then he went back out onto the street and knocked on the window there.

There were people inside. He was sure of it. He returned to the door and was about to bang again when it opened suddenly. A big man in a uniform appeared in the doorway.

"What's this?" he shouted. Christopher melted back, unable to speak. The garda's expression softened. "Was that you banging on my window?"

"Sorry."

"Well, what is it?"

"Um, yeah. I need to talk to Joe Byrne."

"Who?"

"Joe Byrne? I thought he works here."

"I don't know any Joe Byrne. Do you mean the new lad?"

"I guess so."

"He's busy." The garda made to close the door. "You might catch him tomorrow."

"Wait, please, it's an emergency."

"What sort of emergency?"

"Um – a family emergency."

The man gave an exaggerated sigh. "Come in, then. I'll see if I can get him for you."

Christopher followed the officer into the reception area. There was a counter on the right with a door leading off into a room behind. That must have been where this man was working when Christopher disturbed him.

There was another door beside the counter, leading in the same direction. The garda ignored both of those doors and turned to a third door. Like the others, it was protected with an electronic code.

"Stay here," he said, and disappeared through the doorway.

CHAPTER 12

Interview Room 1 at Donnybrook Garda Station contained two small, square tables and four hard chairs. A barred window looked out onto the car park at the back of the station, so at least you could keep an eye on your car while you grilled a suspect.

In the corner was a large box containing the recording device. The rest of the world may have moved on from DVDs, but not here. Legislation specified that interviews be recorded on DVDs, so DVDs it was.

Joe sat at the table on the right side of the room. Aidan Donnelly was opposite him. There was a space in the centre of the room between the two tables. Anne-Marie Cunningham sat at the other table, her chair turned to the side so she could face Donnelly.

The fourth chair was empty. Donnelly had waived his right to a solicitor, which was fine with Joe.

But he still hadn't said a useful word, and that wasn't fine.

Donnelly couldn't explain why Valentina's jumper was in his van or why her panties were in the pocket of his jeans. He couldn't explain why he had a scratch on his arm, or why he'd been found where he was.

Joe didn't believe a word of it.

"Where is she?" he asked again.

"I couldn't tell you. I hope she's alright."

"You were the last one to see her. If she's not alright, I suspect you're responsible."

"I didn't touch her."

Donnelly had no criminal record, not even a parking ticket. But that didn't mean he was innocent.

Joe said, "Alright. Tell me again what happened."

"I… finished the painting."

"And then?"

"I woke up in the back of a van to find you lot arresting me."

"You missed a few hours. What happened between you leaving her house and us finding you?"

"I don't know. Nothing."

"Clearly something happened. Valentina went missing from her home. Someone cut her fingers off and left them in her garden."

Aidan Donnelly shuddered. "That's horrible."

"What do you think happened to her?"

"I have no idea."

"Humour me. If you had to guess, what would you say?"

He hesitated. For the first time, a thoughtful look passed over his face.

"You wouldn't believe me."

Joe leaned forward. "Try me."

"Nah," he said.

"Go on. I'll hear you out."

He stared at Joe for a moment, then leaned forward, resting his elbows on the table.

"Alright, but it'll sound mental."

"Go on."

"They must have wanted her. The ones up there."

Joe glanced at Cunningham, but she seemed equally confused.

"What do you mean?" Joe asked.

"They're trying to find out how she works, or putting something inside her. Maybe cutting off her fingers wasn't to hurt her. Maybe it was a test. That might be how they do it. Or putting a tracking device in there?"

"What the hell are you talking about?"

Donnelly flicked his eyes towards the ceiling. "You know."

Cunningham said, "Her neighbours?"

Donnelly scowled. "No. Above."

"Her boss?"

Donnelly shook his head. Cunningham glanced at Joe.

"God?" Joe said.

"They'd be like gods to us. The ones up there, because they're so far ahead of us."

Joe groaned and dropped the pen he'd been fidgeting with. He'd remembered the choice of reading material found in Donnelly's van.

"Are you talking about aliens?"

Donnelly shook his head. "I told you it would sound mental."

"How else do you explain what happened to me? I finished painting. I went outside. There was a flash of white light and I woke up hours later. Missing time. You know what I mean?"

He'd become animated while he spoke, waving his hands. Cunningham rolled her eyes.

Joe said, "Was there a bar on the spaceship?"

"I don't know about that."

Donnelly had refused to be breathalysed, but Joe knew gin when he smelled it, and Donnelly had stank of it when Joe took him into custody. However, he wasn't acting drunk. He was acting insane.

"Maybe the gin was part of the testing."

"Get real," Joe shouted. "A woman is missing. She's probably lost a lot of blood by now. Tell us where she is so that we can help her."

"I didn't do anything. Maybe the ones above are still working on her. With the technology they have, maybe they can put her fingers back on."

Joe felt like reaching across the table and smacking Donnelly. As he was considering doing just that, four hard knocks rang out on the door. Joe turned to find a uniform standing in the doorway.

"Sorry to interrupt. You're needed, Detective Sergeant Byrne."

"Let's take a break," Joe said.

He followed the garda out into the corridor, thinking O'Carroll must want him for something.

"What is it?"

"There's an emergency," the garda said.

"Another one?"

"Not a crime. A family emergency."

"Whose family? I don't have one."

"Well, there's a lad who wants to speak to you and he seems to think different."

CHAPTER 13

Christopher leaned against the counter while he waited. Coming to the station had seemed like a good idea earlier, but, now that he was here, he could feel the blood pounding in his ears and he wanted nothing more than to leave. Suddenly, a door swung open and Joe Byrne stepped out.

Christopher stood upright. He wondered how to address this man he didn't know. Should he call him Joe, Mr. Byrne, Detective Byrne… or dad?

"What's the problem?" Joe said, taking a step closer to Christopher.

Christopher swallowed a lump in his throat. He hadn't expected Joe to be so brisk. He didn't even seem to recognise Christopher.

"I was in the shop earlier. My – my name is Christopher?"

"Do you want to report a crime?"

"I was with my – my mother?"

"I'm very busy."

"I was with my mother, Lisa O'Malley… in Tesco earlier…"

Joe's eyes narrowed. Christopher had his attention now. When he spoke again, his voice was colder.

"What do you want?"

Christopher swallowed. It was a struggle to make the words come out. His hands were shaking and so was his voice, but he'd come here for a reason, and he didn't want to leave without making his point.

"I – I just found out – when you saw my mum – she was, well, she forgot most of our shopping and – you know, we had a fight. Well, not actually a fight, but—"

Joe sighed. "What are you babbling about?"

Christopher took a breath.

"I think you're my dad."

"Excuse me?"

"I mean, you *are* my dad."

Joe didn't hold out his arms and say, *Come here to me, son.* He didn't smile and say he'd known the truth the moment he saw Christopher. He didn't get angry and blame Christopher's mother for lying for all those years.

What he did was drop a firm hand on the back of Christopher's neck and push him towards the door.

Joe opened it, pushed Christopher out, and said, "I don't have a son."

Then he slammed the door.

CHAPTER 14

Joe squeezed his eyes shut and leaned against the wall. Why did the teenager want Joe to think he was his father? Did Lisa say that? While Joe had been dealing with Donnelly, he'd managed to put her out of his mind. But that kid coming here tore the wound open.

It had been a long, long day. Joe still hadn't eaten. He'd left the chicken wrap in Tesco. The coffee too. He really needed them, along with half a dozen painkillers for his headache.

Joe hadn't seen Lisa in fifteen years, but she still had a strong hold over him. Even after what she pulled when he was in New York. How she stopped returning his calls.

Joe remembered complete sentences from the letter he wrote her, when he couldn't get through to her on the phone. He had thought of throwing himself in the Hudson when she cut him out of her life, but he'd been too much of a coward.

When he got back to Ireland, she'd avoided him. He heard that she had a baby. She'd dumped Joe and got knocked up. That was when Joe decided he'd follow his father's career path. He figured the force was a good place for a young man who wanted to be dead. He'd thrown himself in harm's way more times than he could count.

But here he was, still alive.

Joe pushed away from the wall.

Valentina was out there somewhere. For better or worse, he was the one tasked with finding her. That was what he had to focus on. Not ancient history.

He keyed in the door code, and walked down the corridor. Anne-Marie Cunningham sat at her desk in the DDU office.

"Donnelly is batshit crazy," she said. "Right?"

Joe slumped in his chair and looked at her. "I don't know."

"You think he's just lying?"

"I don't know."

"What do you think?"

"Jesus, I don't fucking know."

Joe leaned back in his chair and sighed. He was about to apologise to Cunningham when she stood up and walked out of the room.

What a day.

But it was about to get worse.

Joe's phone rang. It was Barry Wall. Joe had given Wall his number and the man had already called seven times to see if there had been any progress.

"I told you I'd advise you when there were developments," Joe said.

"What's going on?" Wall said. "What are you doing?"

"We're interrogating Aidan Donnelly."

"So what have you got out of him?"

"Mr. Wall, I appreciate your concern, but I'll let you know if I have anything. I'm doing all I can."

"I think you're sitting there with your thumb up your arse," Wall said. "You don't care about my wife."

Through gritted teeth, Joe said, "Goodbye, Mr. Wall."

Wall was still talking when Joe ended the call.

He sat back in his chair and pictured Valentina, bleeding from ten stumps on her hands, tied up somewhere in the dark, alone, terrified. Waiting for Aidan Donnelly to return and kill her. Maybe she was running out of time. She'd probably lost a lot of blood.

Joe thought of the hit-and-run that had killed his parents one night, when they'd gone for an evening walk. His mother had been killed at once, but his father had bled to death, slowly, at the side of the road. He could have been saved if he'd been found earlier.

Joe was determined not to let Valentina die.

He went to the holding cell where Cunningham had put Donnelly. Donnelly shifted when Joe unlocked the door. He was lying on the rubber mattress in the alcove at the back of the room.

There was a squat toilet in the corner on his right.

Aside from that the room was empty.

No DVD here. No one watching.

"Cut the UFO bullshit," Joe said. "Where is she?"

Donnelly sat up. "I couldn't tell you, pal. Honestly."

Joe could feel himself boiling with emotions that had no place here, but he didn't care. Donnelly was guilty. He was sure of it. He couldn't let Valentina die, the way his parents had. Waiting for help that would never come.

He walked over and grabbed Donnelly. The painter was wispy thin beneath his grip.

"Where is Valentina López Vázquez?"

Donnelly raised his eyes to the ceiling. "The ones above—"

Joe grabbed Donnelly's head and smashed his face into the wall.

And then he really lost control.

PART TWO

SIX MONTHS LATER

CHAPTER 15

The air in the courtroom was stifling on Thursday afternoon, and Barry Wall was starting to feel dizzy. Beads of sweat broke out on his forehead and upper lip. He wiped them away with the back of his hand, the movement making his muscles strain against the seams of his suit.

A gleaming modern structure housed the Criminal Courts of Justice, located near the entrance to the Phoenix Park. The circular building was world-class, according to the Courts Service website, but Wall felt there was nothing world-class about the heating, unless you wanted to be toasted like a marshmallow.

The maintenance staff seemed to be overcompensating for the freezing temperatures Dublin had experienced in the last few days.

Or maybe the heat had nothing to do with the courtroom at all.

Maybe it was him. He certainly felt feverish.

Barry Wall's brother, Ken, seated next to him in the courtroom's public area, looked composed. He'd been the only thing that kept Wall going through the hellish months since Valentina went missing.

If Ken hadn't forced home-made meals down Wall's throat, he might not have eaten anything for months. Wall had quickly got sick of eating Ken's chilli, but Ken was stubborn, and he insisted on feeding his younger brother, even watching to make sure he ate every bite.

Valentina's parents sat silently in the row behind, next to the family liaison officer and their translator. Her father held a metal crucifix tight in his hand. His knuckles were white.

In the witness box, Detective Sergeant Joe Byrne looked pink and sweaty. Perhaps he was feverish too. Martin Costello, the barrister for the defence, had been hammering him for half an hour. At this point, many people would have felt sorry for Byrne. Wall didn't.

Costello, a Senior Counsel who liked the sound of his own voice, said, "After the assault which we have discussed, you proceeded to coerce the accused into signing a confession. Is that not so?"

"I encouraged him to admit the crime," Byrne said.

"In the vernacular, you beat him black and blue," Costello said. "Did you not?"

"As I have already said, my eagerness to save a woman's life got the better of me. It was a lapse of judgement."

"In any case, my question related to your actions immediately following the assault, said offence having already been admitted. Accordingly, I am certain you would concur that the confession is inadmissible. Is that not correct, Detective Sergeant Byrne?"

Through gritted teeth, Joe Byrne said, "Yes."

"No further questions."

Judge Roberts nodded sagely and paused to consult his notes, while Byrne left the witness box so fast, it looked like he had used an ejector seat.

Costello sat down on the bench in front of Wall, who leaned forward, until he was on the edge of his seat and he could smell the barrister's cologne, a cloying sandalwood that wormed its way up Wall's nostrils.

"Asshole," Wall whispered.

Costello tilted his head to the side, as if assessing Wall in his peripheral vision. Then he turned his attention back to Judge Roberts, who was peering at the accused over his glasses.

If Wall had been within reach, he would have grabbed the judge and squeezed his windpipe shut.

But Wall was powerless.

Judge Roberts spoke in his high, reedy voice.

"In view of the evidence we have heard thus far, I must direct the jury to acquit the accused, Mr. Aidan Donnelly, whose rights have clearly been violated in a most grievous manner. The Director of Public Prosecutions had doubts about the soundness of this case, and I am satisfied that these concerns were well-founded. I am aware that Detective Sergeant Byrne has already been disciplined for his behaviour, and I trust that every possible action has been taken to ensure that no recurrence of these abuses is possible."

Journalists were already slipping out of the press area, eager to be first to report the verdict. As far as they were concerned, it was over.

Donnelly was free and Wall was left with nothing. Absolutely nothing. Donnelly had signed a worthless confession, saying he had attacked Valentina. He had given no details of what was done to her or where she had been taken. And as soon as Donnelly met his solicitor, the confession had been withdrawn. In the last six months, no progress had been made on finding out what had happened to Valentina.

Now Judge Roberts was saying that Aidan Donnelly was the victim here.

Never mind that Wall's wife was gone, that his plans for a new life in Spain were dead. And, of course, his fitness studio had not reopened after that awful day in June.

Wall locked his gaze on Donnelly. Sitting on the right side of the court, next to a prison officer, the young man seemed unemotional as the case against him was dismissed.

Wall got to his feet. He was aware that several detectives were nearby, and that they were watching him. There were uniformed officers too, standing at the side of the courtroom.

"This isn't right," Wall said.

Judge Roberts squinted at him, brow furrowed.

"Mr. Wall, please sit down."

It was all over, and nothing was going to happen. The little creep was going to return to his normal life. Wall had an empty home and a ruined life. Without a body, he wasn't even been able to give Valentina a proper funeral.

"Where is she?" Wall shouted. "Where's my wife, you bastard?"

Aidan Donnelly looked at Wall, his face as blank as an insect's.

"Look at him," Wall shouted. "You can tell he did it."

On the left side of the room, the members of the jury stared at Wall. One or two looked sympathetic.

"Mr. Wall," Judge Roberts said. "I appreciate that this is difficult for you. You have my deepest sympathies for your loss. However, I must ask you to remain silent until these proceedings are concluded."

Ignoring him, Wall rushed forward, past the barristers and solicitors.

"Stop!" the court clerk shouted. "Stop him."

Wall made it halfway to Aidan Donnelly before the prison officer next to him got to her feet. She was about a hundred pounds, average height and build. Wall was double her weight. Double her size. Moving fast. Her trying to stop him was like a tissue trying to stop a bullet.

Not going to happen.

He was three quarters of the way there now.

Guards were rushing over, but they wouldn't reach him quick enough. Panic flashed in Donnelly's eyes.

Time seemed to slow down.

Wall braced himself, ready to smash straight through the prison officer and tear Donnelly's head from his shoulders. He'd make the creep admit what he'd done with Valentina. He'd find the truth. Wall wasn't expecting her to be alive – he'd given up on that hope – but he had to find her body and give her the burial she deserved.

As Wall came within a metre of the prison officer protecting Donnelly, a blur appeared from the side and smashed into Wall.

Joe Byrne.

The bastard who'd messed up the investigation, who'd made it inevitable that Donnelly would get away with murder, wanted to mess this up too. Byrne tackled Wall hard, choosing his angle well. With his head lowered like a bull he charged into Wall's side. Under the arms. Byrne smashed Wall into the side of the courtroom.

They both went down.

Byrne recovered first, grabbing Wall by the collar of his shirt.

As Wall scrambled to his feet, he lashed out with his elbows, catching Byrne in the face with his right arm. Byrne fell backwards.

Immediately another officer threw himself on Wall. Wall punched him in the stomach. Then Wall's right arm was wrenched behind his back. His suit split apart at the seam. Joe Byrne pressed him down, shoving his face into the carpet.

"Take it easy," Byrne said.

Wall let out a howl of animalistic pain.

"This is your fault."

"Take it easy, Mr. Wall."

A dozen officers formed a tight circle around him. They pulled him to his feet. Straining in vain to tear himself free, he watched as the Judicial Assistant, next to the accused, looked around the room.

"All rise," she called out over the noise, as Judge Roberts stood up and strode out of the courtroom.

The jury were next to go. Then Wall saw Donnelly being led away. They were going to let him go.

Wall caught a glimpse of Valentina's parents. The family liaison officer and translator were talking to them. Explaining what had happened – and apologising. More empty words.

The injustice of it all was enough to make Wall crazy.

Byrne put a hand on his shoulder.

"Take it easy, Mr. Wall."

"You're dead," Wall shouted. "You're all so dead."

CHAPTER 16

The Criminal Court of Justice complex had a large central atrium, which was probably only appreciated by the building's staff. If you squinted, the interior looked a little like the Guggenheim Museum in New York, with its white balconies stretching around in a full circle.

Joe felt embarrassed and stupid as he walked into the atrium. His day at court couldn't have gone worse.

He was about to loosen his tie when he saw the journalists standing outside the main entrance. Dozens of them were clustered under the glass canopy, sheltering from hailstones, while they waited for comments and photo opportunities. The complex housed twenty-two courtrooms. There were always plenty of cases going on, but Joe had no doubt that, right now, the journalists only cared about the Donnelly trial.

He walked past security and headed outside. The journalists hit him before the cold did. An explosion of noise and camera flashes.

Joe ignored their questions and made for his Honda. He'd only taken a few steps when a lady stepped in his path and hit him in the chin with a microphone.

"Detective Sergeant Byrne, do you accept responsibility for the collapse of Aidan Donnelly's trial?"

"Get out of my way."

Keeping pace with him, she went straight onto the next question. "What do you have to say about the theory that a serial killer is at work here?"

Joe ignored her and pushed through the journalists. As quickly as they'd descended on him, they disappeared with a murmur of fresh excitement. Joe turned to see what had caught their attention.

Wearing a dirty tracksuit, Aidan Donnelly was scrambling into a taxi as the journalists chased him. Joe saw an older woman sitting next to him in the back of the cab. Donnelly slammed the door, and the taxi disappeared down the road.

Joe got behind the wheel of his Honda.

He didn't start the engine immediately. He wasn't ready. A few minutes to gather his thoughts was what he needed.

The serial killer idea that the journalist had mentioned had been floated in a number of the more irresponsible newspapers. The logic went like this: five young women had vanished from their Dublin homes over the previous four years; maybe the disappearances were connected to each other and to whatever had happened to Valentina López Vázquez.

Joe didn't buy it. There was nothing to say that any of those women were dead, let alone that they were the victim of the same person.

But what if he was wrong?

He was still sure that Aidan Donnelly was to blame for whatever had happened to Barry Wall's wife. If the other disappearances really were connected, and those women had all been killed, that meant that Donnelly was a serial killer. And Joe was responsible for him being released.

CHAPTER 17

In the back of the taxi, Aidan Donnelly struggled to breathe. The air was thick with apple-scented air freshener and the driver was listening to a pounding Bollywood disco track. Aidan felt like his air passage was shrinking to nothing. But at least his aunt Maureen was beside him, and that made him feel a little better.

"Aidan," Maureen said, hugging him to her with one arm. He turned in his seat and hugged her back. Maureen had always been there for him. She was more of a mother than his real one.

"Thanks for coming," he said.

"Don't be daft."

The driver turned in his seat.

"Where to, sir?"

"Could you turn down the music?" Aidan said.

"Certainly, sir."

Maureen gave the driver her address. Aidan stared out the window, needing a moment to catch his breath.

"How are you keeping?" Maureen said. "Did they feed you?"

"Yeah, I'm fine."

Maureen gave him a worried look but said nothing.

Aidan looked at the people and buildings as they passed by. Trying to be quiet, he breathed in and out slowly. Finally, his breath began to even out.

Aidan hadn't been interested in speaking to the prison psychologist while in custody, awaiting trial. But one day she approached him. Asked him about his breathing fits. She was a lovely woman with a soothing voice, and if she thought Aidan was a killer, she never showed it.

She said they were called panic attacks, the things Aidan got sometimes, when he felt like he was about to die.

"How did you know about them?"

"I've been watching you," she said.

She told him about breathing exercises. Stupid, really. Aidan already knew how to breathe. But he was desperate, so he gave them a try. And they helped a bit. He'd been having the attacks more and more often.

Fingers closed around Aidan's arm, above the elbow. It snapped him back to reality. The taxi. Maureen.

"You *are* alright, love, aren't you?"

He covered Maureen's hand with his own. Her skin was dry and warm.

"Yeah, I am."

She'd visited him often. Not like the rest of his family.

Maureen said, "God bless her, your mother is off on one of her benders. Drunk out of her mind, she is. Will you stay with me for the night?"

"That sounds great, Auntie."

"Good. I've lots of food for you. You must be sick of that prison slop."

"It wasn't so bad."

The taxi pulled up in front of her bungalow. She opened the door of the car.

Aidan said, "I'm just going to nip home and pick up some clothes. I'll be right back. Okay?"

Maureen looked concerned. She said, "That's fine, love, but I think I have an old T-shirt of yours and some tracksuit bottoms and—"

"No bother. I'll be back soon."

Maureen stepped out of the cab. Her little house stood behind her and Aidan felt so happy to see it. This place was like a beacon of light in his life. While in custody, he'd often dreamt of coming here, of coming to stay with Maureen. Now he finally could. He felt filthy, though. Stained by everything that had happened. He wanted to get cleaned up before he went inside her home.

He closed the door, rolled down the window, and said, "I'll just have a wash and get some clothes, alright? I'll be back in an hour."

Maureen smiled. "I'll have a pot of tea waiting for you." She pressed two twenty-euro notes into his hand.

"No need, Auntie."

"It's grand, Aidan. Take it. And don't worry. Now you've been proved innocent, people will stop being so nasty to you."

"Yeah," he said.

He waved goodbye and gave the driver his address. By the time the taxi pulled up in front of the block of flats where he lived with his mother, Aidan was again struggling to breathe.

There was a big difference between having your trial collapse and being proven innocent.

CHAPTER 18

Some days, Joe found Donnybrook Garda Station depressing, and this was one of them. The old cemetery next door was more inviting. He ditched his Honda in the car park and entered the station from the back. The corridor stank of disinfectant, a clear sign the holding cells had just been cleaned.

Joe strode down the corridor to the public office at the front, avoiding colleagues on the way. A handful of people stood at the counter, waiting to speak to the desk sergeant, who was familiar with Joe's habit of heading next door. He dug the keys out from under the desk and threw them over the counter.

The gate to the cemetery was kept locked, but the key was held in the station. Anyone who wanted could come and borrow it, but people rarely did. For that, Joe was grateful. The cemetery had become his thinking space.

He stepped outside, walked around to the gate and unlocked the padlock. He went inside, making his way up the steps to where the path began.

Unlike most cemeteries, there was nothing depressing about this place. The last person to be buried there was laid to rest in 1936, so there were never any mourners. No weeping, no fresh graves.

The place was small and beautifully overgrown. Lots of trees and bushes, and moss on the stone. A few benches were scattered around. A local historian gave tours of the cemetery in the summer, on Sunday afternoons. At the moment, Joe had the place to himself.

He sat down on a bench and let the cold from the damp wood seep into his legs, making him numb. Overhead the sky looked like grey cotton wool. A robin landed on the path in front of Joe. The little bird tipped its head at him quizzically. It brought a smile to Joe's face, and he needed that. He wasn't looking forward to telling O'Carroll what had happened in court.

Recent months had been bad.

The confession Joe got out of Aidan Donnelly was worthless. Donnelly didn't tell them where Valentina was, and he withdrew the confession when he finally consulted a solicitor. The case had fallen apart like an overripe banana.

The only surprising thing was that Donnelly didn't kick up more of a fuss about what Joe did to him. Anyway, Joe had been suspended without pay and made to take a dozen training courses to correct his behaviour.

He suspected that O'Carroll's intervention prevented him from being fired. Joe had explained to him how he had met Lisa and Christopher on that June day, the emotional strain he had been under. Joe don't know if O'Carroll included that information when he presented Joe's case to the superintendent.

The shock of becoming a father to a fifteen-year-old boy? Like that was going to get a lot of sympathy.

But Joe was still struggling to accept it. He and Lisa had talked a few times that week, after Christopher broke the news about Joe being his father. Those conversations were rough. Joe got angry. Lisa got angry.

For the last couple of months, they hadn't spoken at all. But she was always on Joe's mind. And Joe had decided to stay in Donnybrook.

Was he really a father? According to Lisa, yes. What did it mean? What was he going to do about it?

Joe looked at the looming clouds and wondered if it would snow. He decided to get indoors before he got an answer.

The District Detective Unit office was quiet when he arrived. Joe shared the room with four other plainclothes officers. It was tight. Especially with all the paperwork Joe had accumulating on his desk.

Anne-Marie Cunningham looked up when he walked in. Kevin Boyle did too, but he only smirked.

"O'Carroll wants to see you," Cunningham said.

She didn't ask any questions, so Joe gathered that she'd heard how things went in court. At least she had the decency not to say anything.

Boyle was different. He said, "How's Mr. Donnelly?"

Working with Boyle was a pain. Ignoring him, Joe backed out of the room, and climbed the stairs to O'Carroll's office. He rapped on the door and stepped inside.

"Acquitted," Joe said.

O'Carroll was sitting behind his desk, tapping away on his computer. He looked up when Joe entered.

"I heard," O'Carroll replied. "You're going to have to apologise to Aidan Donnelly."

"Are you kidding me?"

"But that can wait. What do you know about gelignite?"

Joe was thrown by the change of topic. "It's an explosive, right?"

"Right." O'Carroll glanced at his computer monitor. "Philips Construction contacted us."

Joe knew the company's name. He'd seen their vans all over the city. They were having a bonanza at the moment with all the offices, apartments and houses that were shooting up in Dublin. If they were calling about explosives, Joe guessed they had a sideline in demolitions.

"What did they say?"

"Forty pounds of gelignite was stolen from their depot last night."

"That sounds like enough to do some damage."

"It is. The company insists they had the material locked away securely. But someone got it."

"An inside job?"

"Unknown." O'Carroll narrowed his eyes. "That's why you're going to look into it, Joe. And fast. Go to their depot and check it out."

"Okay."

Joe had just left O'Carroll's office when an idea came to him. It was too crazy to be true. All the same, he knew he had to check it out, even if that meant ignoring O'Carroll's order to go to Philips Construction's depot.

He hurried downstairs. At the bottom, he ducked his head in the door of the DDU office. Cunningham was still there, piling bales of counterfeit cash three feet high on her desk. It had been used as a decoy in an operation, and she was tidying it away for future use.

"I need you," Joe said.

"What's going on?"

"Just a hunch. Probably nothing. But bring your gun."

CHAPTER 19

Barry Wall swung his car into the driveway of his house – the house he had once shared with Valentina. He killed the engine, jumped out and flung open the back-passenger door. The seat was empty. Aidan Donnelly lay strewn across the floor, hands tied behind his back with his own shoelaces. He was coughing and wheezing and struggling to breathe.

Wall ignored that.

He reached in and grabbed Donnelly by the scruff of the neck, then lifted him straight out of the car. As soon as Donnelly's runners hit the ground, he tried to make a run for it. Wall tripped him, and at the same time pushed Donnelly's head forward, enjoying watching him fall to the ground.

Wall pulled Donnelly to his feet and shoved him toward the house. It had been easy to grab him outside his block of flats. He'd been walking along like he hadn't a care in the world.

Now Wall would get the truth from him at last.

And he wouldn't waste months on it either.

Wall unlocked the door, then used Donnelly's head to push it open. The impact of skull on wood made a satisfying sound.

"This must be bringing back memories," Wall said. He stepped into the hall and shut the door behind him. The hall was now white. Wall had painted it himself after Donnelly was taken into custody. He couldn't stand to look at the peach colour Donnelly had applied months before. On that day…

Wall broke out in a sweat. Sometimes it happened like that. A flash of rage – or shame – overcame him at some memory. Like when he thought of how he'd been laughing and joking with that actress, Holly Martini, at the fitness studio, while his wife was here, being mutilated by this scumbag.

"Where is she?" Wall growled, pushing Donnelly towards the kitchen. "What did you do to her?"

His hands still bound behind his back, Donnelly lost his balance and fell to the floor.

"I don't know where she is."

"This time you're going to talk," Wall said.

Donnelly rolled onto his side and looked at Wall. "I don't *know* anything."

"You admitted killing her. You signed a confession."

"It wasn't true. They made me. That guy, Byrne? He forced me to confess. I signed it just to make him stop. You heard it yourself in court."

Wall crouched down on the floor. "You're a lying little shit. But now you're going to tell me everything. I want to bury my wife. Not just her…" Wall swallowed. "Not just… her fingers."

Donnelly tried to sit upright. He caught sight of the object on the island in the middle of the kitchen. The thick red sticks bound together and criss-crossed with wires and a digital display.

He swallowed.

"What's that?"

Wall admired the bomb. He said, "Mainly nitro-glycerine, with some kieselguhr mixed in. That's a sedimentary rock, in case you were wondering. A little basic wiring and a remote control for convenient detonation. Not bad, is it?"

He pulled a stool back from the island, lifted Donnelly and set him down on it. Then he went to the other side and took a stool himself.

There were three objects on the counter: the bomb, the detonator and a framed photo of Valentina and Wall, taken in Barcelona three years earlier. People say summer romances don't last, but Wall had wanted to be an old man with Valentina, decades down the line. He'd imagined children and grandchildren.

Now that was all gone forever.

Wall lifted the detonator. It looked like a crudely made remote control, which was exactly what it was. With his thumb he teased its red button.

"If you don't tell me what I need to know," Wall said, "I'm going to blow both of us to kingdom come."

Donnelly swallowed. "You wouldn't."

"You think I have anything left to live for?"

Donnelly's face grew paler.

"Please. I don't know anything."

"You're a liar."

"I didn't do it. I swear I didn't hurt her. Why would I?"

"I don't believe you. I bet you—"

The doorbell's chime interrupted him. Its cheery tone couldn't have sounded more wrong. Wall looked down the hall. The letterbox set in the front door opened slowly, with a *clink* as something metal was inserted.

Wall said, "Stay here, asshole. If you make a noise, I'll kill you."

He eased himself off his stool, and walked down the hallway, still holding the detonator. Something round and metallic hung out of the letterbox. As he got closer, he saw it was a pair of handcuffs. He eased open the door, but there was no one there.

He turned back towards the kitchen – in time to see the floor-to-ceiling window shatter at the impact of a golf club. Another blow and the glass smashed inwards and fell to the floor.

Joe Byrne dived into the kitchen through what had been a window, his steps punctuated by the crunches of broken glass underfoot.

Behind Wall, the front door crashed open.

A woman appeared.

Another plainclothes officer, with a gun.

She shouted, but Wall ignored her. He ran down the hall towards the kitchen.

Joe Byrne pushed the bomb away, off the side of the kitchen island, and grabbed Donnelly. Byrne dragged him off his stool and yanked him hard toward the garden.

No, no, no. They couldn't get away.

Wall lifted the detonator as he ran towards them.

The female detective was right behind him. She was screaming, "*Stop, right now.*"

Byrne and Donnelly were passing through what had been the window, and Byrne was dragging Donnelly around the corner, seeking the protection of the wall of the house.

Donnelly was getting away, slipping through Wall's fingers once more.

Wall brought up the detonator.

As he dived sideways, through the open doorway of the sitting room, and away from the path of the blast, Wall squeezed the red button on the detonator.

PART THREE

FIVE MONTHS LATER

CHAPTER 20

It was a hot May morning. It felt even hotter after Joe had been sitting in the Honda for two hours with the sun shining in his face. He wriggled out of his leather jacket and threw it on the passenger seat, next to the polymer case containing his pistol.

He was parked halfway down The Pines, one of a dozen tree-named roads in a middle-class housing estate in Deansgrange. Joe hadn't seen a single pine. Outside each house there was a strip of grass for dogs to crap on and a silver birch for kids to carve their names into.

You wouldn't have guessed that the four-bed semi-detached Joe was watching belonged to Ger Barrett. Nothing about it screamed *gangland*.

Barrett had a neat garden with one huge rose bush and a lot of daffodils that ran along the inside of the hedge.

The interior of the house was nice too. Joe had been inside it last week, when they raided the place.

Seven AM, and the street had been swarming. There were detectives like Joe, half a dozen uniforms, a few officers from the Criminal Assets Bureau, and a team from the Armed Support Unit, who made a breached entry. That's what it's called when they smash down the door with a battering ram.

They tried to work quietly, what with the time of day and the neighbourhood, but a raid is a raid. You get in and take the suspect by surprise.

Or not.

Ger Barrett's house was cleaner than a dentist's teeth. Nothing out of place. Absolutely nothing to tie him to the criminal empire they knew he ran. And Barrett's outrage at the raid sounded rehearsed.

Something was wrong.

He'd known they were coming.

Hence Joe sitting there, sweating it out on his day off. He took a gulp of water, trying to ignore the plastic taste of the bottle. His window was open an inch, letting in the sound of a nearby lawnmower and the faint smell of cut grass.

Net curtains hung from Barrett's windows, so Joe couldn't see what was going on inside the house. Barrett hadn't been out all day. The only thing Joe had seen was a few of Ger's buddies arrive in a black BMW. A 3 Series Sports Saloon. A year old, according to the plate. Polished like a mirror. They parked it behind another black BMW, same model as the first, but this year's model, and they went inside.

Since then, nothing.

Joe hoped he wasn't wasting his time.

His phone buzzed with a text message from Lisa.

Just to remind you, we're having cake at 6 pm.

Typical of her to think Joe had forgotten Christopher's birthday. His sixteenth. The first one Joe had been around for.

See you later, Joe texted back.

He rubbed his eyes and started to think about lunch. He was dreaming of grabbing a burger when the front door of Barrett's house opened.

A bodyguard emerged first. He looked around, then got behind the wheel of one of the BMWs. Ger Barrett followed. His thin frame and long, grey curls made him look like a hippy, but Barrett was as cold as they came. He got into the back seat.

Finally, some action.

Barrett's car pulled out of the driveway and set off down the road, nice and slow. Joe started the Honda's engine. When Barrett's car reached the end of the road, Joe began to follow. He turned on the AC, feeling a blast of cold air that brought a little relief from the heat.

Joe didn't try to predict where Barrett was going – just followed him on his leisurely drive, which seemed to be heading east. Donnybrook was some distance away, but Joe was helping colleagues in Cabinteely with this investigation. Every officer in South Dublin was happy to help, if it meant finally nailing Barrett.

It didn't take long before Barrett's car began to slow. Joe followed him down a one-way street.

Barrett pulled into a stubby cul-de-sac, just long enough for a couple of cars to park end-to-end.

A wasteland, surrounded by a chain metal fence, lay to one side. Weeds grew up through the cracked tarmac. It looked like a car park that had been deserted. Behind it, an ugly block of offices reared into the sky.

The other side of the cul-de-sac was bordered by a stone wall.

Joe drove on.

The road curved around to the left and there was nothing for a while but walls on each side. Farther down, he found a turn that let him do a loop. He circled back and found his way to the turn Barrett had made a couple of minutes earlier.

Instead of taking the turn again, Joe drove up onto the kerb and put on the hand break.

Now the turn Barrett had taken was ahead of him and to the right. Barrett, at his little cul-de-sac, lay just out of sight.

He was waiting for someone.

Joe waited too. He hated being unable to see what was happening, but he forced himself to be patient. He was glad he did.

After a couple of minutes, a sad-looking, grey Ford appeared from behind. Joe sank down in his seat while it passed, then sat up again. The car looked familiar, but it slipped around the corner, down towards Barrett, before Joe could catch the license plate.

He stepped out of the Honda and looked around. The area was quiet. Nearby houses had low walls, but they were topped up by hedges, which provided some privacy.

He took his 9mm Sig Sauer out of its case. The gun contained fifteen rounds, and he had another fifteen in his belt. He'd never needed to use it, but the familiar weight of the P226 was reassuring.

He jogged across the road, to the corner, pressed against the wall and peered around. He saw Ger Barrett get out of his BMW.

The man he was meeting got out of the Ford. Mid-thirties, with a smooth, round face, and short, dark hair gelled within an inch of its life. Downward sloping eyebrows, resembling an upside-down V. It was a face Joe knew well.

Detective Sergeant Kevin Boyle.

Boyle paused to light a cigarette. So much for looking after his health.

The failed raid on Ger Barrett's house made sense now. It wouldn't be the first time a detective had sold confidential information. Every police force in the world had a few rogue officers and Dublin wasn't any different.

Joe moved a little closer. He saw Barrett lean into the open door of his BMW and pull out a backpack. Barrett handed it to Boyle, who unzipped it and pulled out a wad of cash.

Then a second BMW came tearing up the road from behind Joe.

Barrett's friends.

The driver glared at Joe. He was a mean-looking bastard with floppy blond hair and a scar under his left eye.

The car's horn blasted, shockingly loud on the quiet road.

BEEP.

Ger Barrett looked up.

BEEP.

Kevin Boyle looked up.

BEEP.

Barrett and Boyle were suddenly tugging the bag of money back and forth.

So much for a subtle approach.

"Don't move," Joe shouted, coming around the corner, with the Sig raised, pointing it right at them.

Then everyone was shouting and running. Barrett gave up on the backpack and dived into his BMW.

The second BMW veered sideways and screeched to a halt across the footpath in front of Joe. He ran toward the back, but the car reversed, blocking him again, nearly hitting him.

Barrett's car was speeding away.

Boyle hurried to his car. He had nothing in his hands. No backpack. He got behind the wheel and pulled away.

Joe ran up to the driver's door of the BMW blocking his way. He was tempted to shoot the guy behind the wheel.

He didn't even get a look at him.

As he came alongside the passenger window, the car tore away with a screech of rubber, speeding the wrong way down the one-way street. Joe chased it for a short distance. The car slowed as it passed Joe's Honda. There was a bang and a hiss of escaping air as they shot his tire out.

CHAPTER 21

Christopher O'Malley was breathing hard by the time he neared home. The big red-brick on Belmont Avenue wasn't the prettiest house in the world, even if his Mum loved it. Christopher would have preferred a gothic mansion, far away from people. But this was home for the time being. Once he was behind the house's solid oak door, he would be safe.

He increased his pace, pausing only to look over his shoulder and check that no one was following him.

No, he was okay.

For the last two days, Christopher had stayed at school during lunchtime so he could fit in some extra violin practice. The Mozart recital was coming up on Friday and Christopher was struggling to master his part, first violin in The Hunt, String Quartet No. 17. Today, though, he'd forgotten to bring lunch, so he had to go home to eat.

Reaching his house, Christopher opened the door and stepped into the hall.

"Mum?"

He never knew when she'd be there. She often worked from home but some days she visited clients. She didn't drive a car, so the front driveway gave no clue about whether she was home.

Christopher walked down the hall to the kitchen. All was quiet. He glanced out the window. The door to the shed was closed, so maybe Graham wasn't around. Christopher didn't know why Mum let her boyfriend use the shed as a studio. Graham wasn't really an artist. He'd never sold a picture. Mum had hung up one in the hall, but only out of pity.

He opened the door to the American-style fridge freezer. As usual, it was well-stocked. Mum had started to order food online twice a week, and had it delivered on Mondays and Thursdays. It saved time. As a web developer, she was enthusiastic about automating stuff.

Christopher pulled out a packet of butter, a half-empty jar of mayonnaise and a plate with slices of cooked chicken, covered in plastic film. Setting them down on the kitchen table, he got a loaf of bread from the cupboard. Next, he got a knife out of the drawer. He was struggling to spread the hard butter when he heard laughter from upstairs.

People always talked about fight or flight, but Christopher had a third "f": freeze, and that was what he did now.

Upstairs a door opened and closed.

Was it a burglar?

Or Mum?

Holding his breath, he set down the bread knife and tiptoed out into the hall. Someone was peeing loudly into the toilet bowl. The toilet flushed and Christopher heard the door open immediately. No hand washing. Yuck. Christopher stepped back so he wouldn't be seen from the top of the stairs.

"Alright," Graham said. "Where—"

A door closed, cutting him off.

Christopher crept back into the kitchen. Was Mum up there with Graham? Were they having sex? If they found out he was here, it would be so embarrassing.

Could he just slip out without anyone seeing? No one had to know he'd been home. He only needed to hide the evidence.

He put away the loaf of bread, the mayonnaise and butter. The two slices of bread he'd already taken out were a problem. As quietly as he could, he eased open the drawer next to the sink. He took out a plastic lunch bag and dropped the bread inside. He took a few slices of chicken and dropped them into the bag too. There. He had a sandwich after all, or the makings of one, at least. He could eat it on the way back to school.

Upstairs, a door creaked open.

Christopher covered the remaining chicken with plastic wrap and put it back in the fridge, as footsteps started down the stairs.

He'd never get out in time – unless he slipped through the back door and went around the side of the house. He'd have to be quick.

Bringing the plate he'd dirtied to the sink, he rinsed it under the tap, running the water at low pressure so it would be quiet.

The footsteps were coming closer.

Moving faster.

Christopher felt his breathing turn shallow.

The footsteps reached the bottom of the stairs.

Mum was *humming*. Christopher had never heard her hum.

He quickly pushed the hall door shut, so she wouldn't see him, then grabbed his bag and hurried to the back door. He turned the key as quietly as he could. Wait. If he went out, how could he lock it again? They always left the key on the inside.

The footsteps were coming up the hall.

The humming grew louder.

He'd have to worry about the key later. He opened the back door. In his peripheral vision, he saw the door to the hall open behind him.

A high-pitched shriek stabbed his ear drums.

"Oh shit," Christopher muttered, as he tripped over the door saddle and fell out, tumbling down the steps to the patio. Just two steps, but that was enough.

He hit the ground hard.

A female voice shouted, "Graham, some creep is breaking in."

Christopher twisted around to see a young blonde standing in the doorway, wearing Mum's silk dressing gown. Through the gap in it, Christopher could see a bright red bikini.

"Hey pervert. Who are you?" she said.

"I *live* here. Who are you?"

Graham appeared, wearing a T-shirt and shorts. He was a big man, standing six feet tall, with a meaty head and thick arms and legs. He was brandishing a crowbar.

"Alright, you bastard," Graham said, stepping forward, ready to bring the crowbar down.

Christopher raised his hands to shield himself. "Stop, Graham, it's me!"

Graham hesitated. He said, "Chris? What are you doing?"

"T-trying to eat lunch."

"I never heard you." Graham lowered the crowbar. He rubbed his stomach thoughtfully with one hand. "So you've met Crystal."

Christopher got to his feet. His hands were cut and his legs felt like jelly.

"Who is she?"

"My model, of course. I'm painting her."

Crystal had found the belt of the dressing gown and was tying it shut. Christopher noticed she was chewing gum.

"Where's Mum?"

"She's out with a client." Graham turned to Crystal. "Why don't you go on out to the studio? I'll be there in a minute. You can do your meditation stuff for a while."

"Fine. But don't keep me waiting."

Crystal gave off a strong strawberry scent as she walked past.

"You want lunch? Come on, let's order a pizza," Graham said. He ushered Christopher into the kitchen, as if rescuing him from a sinking boat.

Christopher said, "I can't. I have to be back to school soon. I don't want to get into trouble."

"You worry too much," Graham said. "Come on, what do you fancy?" He dug out a take-away menu from on top of the fridge and set it down on the kitchen table. Christopher didn't need to look. He often browsed the digital version of the menu on his phone while he lay in bed at night.

"Pepperoni with jalapeños," he decided.

"Good choice." Graham rang the take-away place and placed the order. He asked for a Hawaiian for himself. "All done," he said, ending the call. "Be here in fifteen minutes. You'll have enough time."

"Cool."

"How's school?"

"Okay," Christopher said. He hadn't told his mum about the bullying, so he certainly wasn't going to tell Graham. He got himself a bottle of lemonade from the fridge.

Graham said, "Do me a favour."

"What?"

"Don't mention Crystal to your mother. I don't want her to get the wrong idea. Know what I mean? She's awful sensitive."

"Oh," Christopher said.

"I didn't tell her Crystal would be posing in her swimsuit."

Christopher didn't like the sound of that. He said, "It's a secret?"

"Not really," Graham said thoughtfully. "I'll show your mother the painting when it's done. You see, I asked your mother to pose for a beach scene, but she didn't want to stand around with her bits hanging out. So I'm going to use Crystal for the body."

"Does Crystal know you're not using her face?"

Graham winked.

"Not yet. Let's keep that between you and me too, alright?"

"I guess," Christopher said slowly. But he felt a stab of unease. What had the two of them been doing upstairs?

"Good man," Graham said.

"Are you coming?" Crystal called. She was standing at the door to the shed, down at the end of the garden. "I'm bored."

Graham sighed.

"Give me a second, Chris," he said.

He stepped out into the garden.

Christopher went to the drawer by the window to get some antiseptic. He looked out the window as Graham reached the shed. His artist's studio. Crystal jabbed Graham's chest with her index finger. Half playful, half accusing.

"Come on," she said. "Let's go."

Christopher rinsed his cuts under the tap and dried himself with a tissue. Then he got the antiseptic out and dabbed it on his wounds. It stung like hell, but he had to do it. Only then did he look out the window again.

Crystal looked angry now. She was arguing with Graham.

Christopher stopped breathing. That was part of his normal reflex when faced with something that made him anxious. Freeze and hold your breath. Pretend not to exist.

Graham was looking to the side while Crystal talked. When she jabbed him in the chest again, Graham gave her a shove that sent her reeling back into the shed.

Graham closed the door.

Then he slipped the padlock on and clicked it shut.

CHAPTER 22

After the cars sped away, Joe scoured the area for the backpack. Boyle hadn't taken it, and Barrett's hands had been empty when he dived into his BMW. Joe figured the backpack had been ditched somewhere nearby.

It hadn't been thrown over the chain mail fence, so Joe turned to the concrete wall on the other side of the road. Seven feet tall. No grip, except the top. Joe took a running jump. Lucky he was tall. He grabbed the top and pulled himself up.

The garden on the other side was so overgrown it could have passed for a forest. A house lay at the top of the garden, but Joe ignored that. He only cared about the backpack caught in a bush.

He snapped a couple of photos of it on his phone, then dropped down to the ground. Pulling a pair of gloves from the pocket of his jeans, he walked over to the spot where the backpack had landed. Slipping on the gloves, he looked inside, and saw cash in neat bundles of fifty-euro notes. Joe wasn't sure exactly how much the backpack contained. Maybe ten or twenty thousand euro.

He jumped the wall again, and brought the backpack to the Honda. He returned his pistol to its case, put the backpack into an evidence bag and threw it on the back-seat.

Time to call this thing in, get some uniforms after Ger Barrett and Kevin Boyle.

Before he could do that, his phone rang. The screen said it was Detective Inspector David O'Carroll. Curious timing. Joe hit the green button and placed the phone to his ear.

Joe said, "I want to put out a bulletin for Kevin Boyle's arrest—"

He didn't have a chance to explain what had happened because O'Carroll cut him off.

"Kevin just called."

"What?"

"He's on his way to the station and he's making very serious allegations about *you*."

"I'll be there as soon as I can."

Stewing, Joe ended the call.

He'd almost forgotten about his front right tire, the one Barrett's pals had shot out as they got away. He popped the boot open. His spare tire lay under a sheet of rough plastic which he used to line the boot, protecting the interior of the car from his dirty boots.

He worked fast, getting more irritated as he thought of how much time he was losing.

After five minutes, he felt like smacking Boyle around. After ten, he felt like killing him. But after eleven minutes, the tire was on. It was a personal best.

He stowed everything away, slipped behind the wheel and got moving. Fast. He turned on the lights and the siren.

Boyle was on the take. Now he was trying to drag Joe down.

Not going to happen, Joe thought.

CHAPTER 23

Barry Wall shuffled out of the building, the cuffs biting into his wrists as he walked. The thick beard he had grown during his time in prison was itchy in the heat. He rubbed his face with the back of his hand and peered at the ambulance waiting at the kerb.

Mountjoy Prison's population gave everything a nickname, even the ancient ambulance the prison service used to transport inmates to the hospital. Wall wasn't sure if it had been dubbed "Death on Wheels" because it was so close to the end of its own mechanical life, or because you were taking your life in your hands when you travelled in it.

He didn't much care. He was going to give the name a new meaning in the next five minutes.

His escort consisted of Lauren Fairview, who walked ahead of him, and Timmy Martin, who was behind.

A clear, blue sky reared up overhead. For a second, Wall closed his eyes and savoured the warmth of the sun on his cheeks.

Then he continued to follow Lauren to the ambulance. He moved slowly, as if he were in great pain. Not that Timmy was going any easier on him. The little rat-faced man had insisted on cuffing Wall. Standing up to him, Lauren had insisted they do it at the front, not the back. Wall was glad of that. The back was a lot more uncomfortable.

He decided that Timmy deserved to die first.

Lauren was part of the sham justice system, so she deserved to be punished too. It was a pity. Wall had almost grown fond of her. He'd even taught her to play chess, though only on paper.

As they reached the ambulance, Timmy Martin leaned in close and hissed in Wall's ear.

"I know you're faking it, Barry, you piece of shit."

Wall said nothing.

No one here called him Barry.

He'd earned a nickname the afternoon he arrived in Mountjoy. A belligerent junkie walked into him and tried to knock him down.

It was a stupid idea.

Wall, at the time of his arrival, had consisted of 230 lbs of muscle. The junkie bounced off Wall's chest and hit the floor like he'd slammed into a tonne of bricks.

Wall picked the guy up and landed three sledgehammer punches before the prison officers pulled him away. Messed the guy's jaw up badly. His brain too. As far as Wall knew, the guy was still in a coma. After that, his name was "Brick Wall".

Timmy Martin held the chain cuff in his hands, jingling it as he walked. They planned to use that in the hospital. Either Timmy or Lauren would cuff themselves to Wall once they were inside. But they'd never get that far.

In four minutes, Wall would be free and they would be dead.

"Does it still hurt?"

Wall looked up. Genuine concern showed in Lauren Fairview's eyes. He nodded. Said nothing.

He'd done a pretty good impression of pancreatitis, he thought. Even going so far as to plant an empty bottle of booze in his cell and skip the last two meals.

He knew he didn't have to go to such lengths. Anyone who complained of chest pains was sent to the Mater Hospital, directly across the road from the prison. No prison officer wanted to be responsible for failing to help a prisoner who might be having a heart attack.

If a prisoner complained of an injured wrist, he wouldn't even be cuffed. But the officers would watch him extra carefully, especially if he had a long sentence still to serve, like Wall did.

Lauren helped him into the ambulance.

"It's probably not worth lying down on the stretcher," she said. "Sitting might be easier. What do you think?"

This would be a very short journey. They only needed to head around the block to the emergency department entrance.

Wall nodded. "I can sit."

"Okay."

Two seats were attached to the side of the ambulance. Wall eased himself into one, resting his cuffed hands on his knees.

Lauren sat next to him. The fine hair on her arm brushed against Wall's arm. They were very close but he couldn't help the way he filled the seat. Six months in Mountjoy's gym had only made him bigger.

Timmy shook his head.

"You're too soft, Lauren," he said, then slammed the door shut.

As far as Wall could tell, it was four in the afternoon. But the exact time didn't matter. Whatever time it was, there were three minutes to go. The clock would start ticking as soon as they went out the gate.

Timmy got behind the wheel, started the engine, and they got moving towards the gate. Wall could see nothing from where he was sitting, but he could picture what was happening, every step of the way.

Waiting for the gate to open, then passing the guard box. The Mater Hospital was dead ahead, while Mountjoy Garda Station was just to the left. Everything was close together, making it an extremely unlikely place for an escape attempt to succeed. But succeed it would.

Timmy tackled the first corner the way a rally driver might.

Lauren sighed. "Christ, Timmy, learn to drive."

Up front, the other officer sniggered.

"I know you love it when I take corners with gusto."

"Gusto. Right."

The prison gate would be closing behind them.

Now they were taking another corner, the left turn onto Berkley Road, a pretty little thoroughfare, still skirting the perimeter of the hospital.

The interior of the ambulance was thick with early summer heat.

Without meaning to, Wall conjured up an image of Valentina. He often pictured his wife the way she looked on the day she went missing. Her big brown eyes and playful smile. She'd been wearing light grey shorts that day, a black top, her father's mahogany cross, and the necklace he'd bought her the previous Christmas. The one with a bright yellow sunflower.

Obviously, the authorities would never find out what happened to her. They simply didn't care. The whole sham justice system was a joke, from the judges and barristers to the solicitors, detectives and prison officers.

Well, they could all die.

"We're nearly there," Lauren said.

Two minutes.

Wall wasn't going back to jail. Why should he? His wife had been taken, and the sham justice system had done nothing about it. They'd *forced* him to take things into his own hands. And then, when he did try to get Aidan Donnelly to talk, they threw *him* in prison. Where was the justice in that?

"Are you okay?" Lauren said.

Wall realised that he was breathing as loud as a bull.

"Yeah. Just sore."

"You poor creature."

The ambulance lurched forward again, then pitched hard to the left, into the hospital grounds, and accelerated to the Emergency Department.

"Any opportunity to mess around," Lauren muttered.

She called up to the front, "Quit it, you jerk. He's in a lot of pain."

Timmy Martin said, "My heart bleeds for him."

The ambulance came to a shuddering halt. Timmy turned in his seat to look back at them, through the small opening behind his seat. He held his fist up to his mouth and cleared his throat, as if preparing to speak into a microphone.

Lauren said, "Could you please not give the landing speech?"

"I'm going to pretend you didn't say that," Timmy said, before assuming his best pilot's voice. "Welcome to Dublin, Ireland. Local time is four oh one pm. Thank you for flying with Martin Air and we look forward to welcoming you on your next journey. Please remember to take your belongings with you when you disembark. And don't be shy about sucking my dick on the way out, if you like. It's not going to suck itself."

Lauren rolled her eyes.

Wall figured the last part was directed at her rather than him.

"Let's go," Lauren said.

"Alrighty then."

Timmy jumped out, slamming his door behind him.

If this was going to work, two men should be approaching Timmy Martin at this precise moment.

Wall waited. Lauren waited.
Finally, she said, "What's keeping that idiot?"
A dull thump came from outside. Then another.
Lauren frowned.
"What the hell was that?"

CHAPTER 24

Once Joe got back to the station, he headed straight to David O'Carroll's office, taking the stairs two at a time. The door was closed. He knocked and went in without waiting.

O'Carroll stood behind his desk. As always, it was bare, and Joe detected the faint scent of furniture polish. Detective Sergeant Kevin Boyle sat in front of the desk, looking like a kettle on the brink of boiling.

Joe put the evidence bag behind his back so that Boyle couldn't see the backpack inside it.

"Go and have a cup of coffee, yeah?" O'Carroll said to Boyle, coming around his desk as Boyle stood up. O'Carroll guided him toward the door with a hand on his shoulder.

"Wait a minute," Joe said, stepping in the way. "He should be in a cell. He should be suspended, for a start. You have no idea what he's been up to."

"Joe, I'll talk to you in a minute."

"You're sending him to Starbucks?"

O'Carroll's eyes narrowed.

"I said I'll talk to you in a minute." He turned his attention back to Boyle. "Go on, Kevin. Take your time."

Boyle gave Joe a dirty look as he walked past, but he said nothing. It was all Joe could do not to reach out and smack him one. He manged to hold it together until Boyle had shut the door.

O'Carroll walked back around his desk and slumped in his chair. Joe placed the backpack on the desk.

"Dirty money," he said.

O'Carroll looked at it for a moment, then picked up his desk phone.

"Jessica, come to my office, please."

When he hung up, Joe said, "What's Boyle's story?"

"He said he stopped and searched a vehicle, as he recognised that it belonged to Ger Barrett, a person of interest in multiple investigations. He noticed a suspicious bag in Barrett's vehicle. He was conducting a search of the bag when some lunatic appeared waving a gun, causing Barrett to flee the scene."

Joe shook his head. Boyle's gall was hard to credit.

"You want to hear what really happened?"

O'Carroll sighed. "Go on, then. Give me an executive summary."

Joe told him in a few sentences. The phone rang as he finished. O'Carroll picked up the receiver and listened. His scowl deepened.

"Send him up."

"What?" Joe asked.

Slamming the phone down, O'Carroll combed his hair with his fingers. "Ger Barrett's solicitor is here, complaining that his client has been harassed."

"That was fast."

O'Carroll nodded. "Very bloody fast."

A knock came on the door.

"Yes?"

Jessica Nolan, a young Garda, stepped into the room. Nolan was a fitness fanatic who always seemed to be trying some extreme new diet, and pairing it with an intensive new training regime in the gym. Joe could see why O'Carroll liked her – the two of them loved rules. She gave Joe's T-shirt and jeans a surprised look, then turned her attention to the inspector. O'Carroll handed her the backpack.

"Evidence," he said.

It would be logged in in the usual way. Given a barcode, lodged on the Property and Exhibits Management System, and filed at the Property and Exhibit Management Store.

"Sir," she said. "Unfortunately, the store is closed to evidence."

"Pardon?" O'Carroll said.

Nolan cleared her throat. "There's been a sewage leak at the store. They've asked that no more evidence be sent until they've… um… cleaned up the situation."

O'Carroll sighed. "Then take this and lock it up in your office. Guard it with your life."

"Yes, sir."

"You're responsible for minding all evidence until the store reopens."

"Yes, sir."

She left, closing the door behind her.

"I've warned you about Boyle before," Joe said at once.

"You've made repeated, unsubstantiated *allegations*."

"Has anyone done anything about them?"

O'Carroll jumped up from his seat like there was a pin in his backside. His complexion deepened to a tomato-red, making it hard to see where his skin ended, and his gingery hairline began.

"What are you saying?"

"I'm trying to understand why nothing has happened."

O'Carroll grabbed the back of his swivel chair and slammed it against his desk. His computer monitor wobbled precariously.

"You've made your complaint. Now leave it."

"Has Superintendent Kavanagh been told?"

O'Carroll glared, clearly irritated by Joe's mention of his boss. "No, and you're not going to tell him."

"Why?"

Another knock came on the door. O'Carroll fixed his tie and ran his fingers through his hair again.

"Don't worry about that. What I want from you is a detailed statement about this morning's events. Record *everything* – every piece of gum you chewed, every bad pop song you hummed."

"What about Boyle?"

"He'll be doing the same. For the moment, you're both under investigation."

There was no point saying anything more. Joe walked out of the office and found Barrett's solicitor standing right outside the door. Probably eavesdropping. Joe brushed past him, making his way downstairs. There was no sign of Boyle in the District Detective Unit. Joe slumped at his desk.

Anne-Marie Cunningham glanced at him, and adjusted her hearing aid. The explosion at Wall's house had left Joe more or less unscathed, but Cunningham had lost seventy percent of the hearing in her left ear.

"Kevin's very upset," she said.

She talked louder now. Even with the aid. Joe gave her his cheesiest smile.

"He'll be more upset soon. I'm only getting started."

CHAPTER 25

Wall could have strangled Lauren Fairview as she stared at the door of the ambulance. She had her back to him and her neck was exposed. He could have slipped his wrists over her head and choked her with the cuffs. There would have been some kind of justice in that.

But Lauren reminded him of Valentina. Those warm brown eyes.

He would have preferred to strangle that little shit, Timmy Martin. The world would be better off without him. That was for damn sure.

Fifteen seconds.

Muffled noises outside.

The door opened suddenly. Two men appeared. Wall could see the hospital behind them. Thankfully the ambulance was not parked in front of the doorway, so no one inside would know what was happening.

The two men were kitted out in baby-blue surgical scrubs, complete with face masks.

Wall recognised Buzz's nasty little eyes, the only part of his face that wasn't hidden by the mask. Lauren would recognise his face, if she saw it. He'd only been released from prison three weeks earlier.

"Where's Timmy?" Lauren asked.

"He had to go to the toilet," Buzz said.

Lauren winced. "I'm sorry about that."

"You want to get out? It feels like an oven in there."

"Tell me about it."

Lauren turned to Wall.

"Are you alright getting out on your own?"

"Yeah. You go ahead," he said.

Five seconds to freedom.

Lauren shuffled to the back of the ambulance as Buzz pulled an axe from behind his back. Lauren's gaze was lowered, watching her feet as she stepped down onto the ground.

"No!" Wall shouted.

But Buzz was already swinging the blade. It arced down and lodged itself in Lauren Fairview's chest. With blood bubbling from her mouth, she dropped to the ground. Buzz tore off his surgical mask.

"Holy shit," he said. "I always wanted to fuck that bitch up." His eyes were wide with glee, as he stared at the fallen prison officer.

No longer pretending to be unwell, Wall moved swiftly to the back of the ambulance.

"Get these cuffs off me," he shouted. "And don't touch her again."

"Take it easy, pal. I need to get my blade."

Lauren's eyes were closed. She didn't react when Buzz tried to pull the axe out of her chest.

Handsome, another recent release, appeared beside Buzz. He held up his index finger, from which dangled Timmy Martin's keys.

"Shall we?" the Englishman asked.

"Hurry," Wall said.

Once the cuffs were off, he jumped to the ground, trying not to look at the gory mess that was Lauren Fairview's chest. Buzz was still trying to retrieve his axe. Nearby, Timmy Martin lay motionless on the ground. Wall stepped over him, pausing only to kick him once, hard, in the mouth. In case he was still alive.

Wall looked around, but no one was watching.

Time to move on.

A white Range Rover with no licence plate was parked at the end of the row of ambulances.

Paramedics, doctors, nurses, visitors and security staff constantly came and went through the entrance a few metres away. Wall had been lucky not to be seen so far, but there was no telling when someone would appear.

"Come on," Wall called. "I'll drive."

Handsome was watching with fascination as Buzz struggled with his axe.

"We can take her with us, if she's still alive," Handsome said.

"Leave her," Wall shouted, feeling nothing but disgust. He got behind the wheel of the SUV. Handsome shrugged and sat in the front passenger seat.

Buzz was last to reach the vehicle, and he had to settle for the back. He ran a hand over the bloody blade of the axe, brought the blood to his lips and licked it.

"Pity," Handsome said. "We could have had fun with her."

Buzz grinned. "I *did* have fun with her."

Wall started the engine and pointed the car towards the exit ramp.

They'd been exposed for less than a minute and, as far as he could tell, no one had seen them.

CHAPTER 26

Joe's workspace was the opposite of David O'Carroll's. While O'Carroll's desk was bare, Joe couldn't even *see* his desk under all the clutter. Everywhere around him, there were files and notes, witness statements and warrants.

On the floor, he had a stack of boxes which he was preparing to send to the Director of Public Prosecutions. It was so tall that, if he added one more box, the tower was going to block the light switch on the wall.

No space was left unused in the station. It was old, not built for today's policing. But they had to manage with what they were given.

Joe turned to Cunningham. He said, "Boyle is going down."

"He's done nothing wrong."

"Either you're wrong or you're lying," Joe said. "Everything's going to come out. All his dirty little secrets. And yours too, if you're involved."

Cunningham blanched. Joe didn't think she was dirty, but it annoyed him that she always took Boyle's side. Maybe the two of them had a romantic history. Joe didn't know, but it was something he'd wondered about.

He could tell that she wanted to give a witty reply, maybe tell Joe to go screw himself, but, casual as they kept things in Donnybrook, he was still her superior officer.

She said, "You always think you're right."

"I usually am."

Cunningham gave an eye-roll as she turned away.

Joe set to work writing up his statement detailing the morning's events. He'd just finished when Boyle came in the door. He held a take-out coffee from the shop down the road.

Joe took out his wallet and removed a crisp ten-euro note.

He said, "Without the bribe, you must be a little light. You want to borrow a tenner?"

Boyle gave a shake of the head and pursed his lips.

"That cash was nothing to do with me," he said, sitting down at his desk, and leaning back as if he hadn't a care in the world. He took the lid off his coffee and took a sip, the cappuccino leaving a foam moustache on his upper lip. "You acted like a nutter though. Amazing you didn't kill a civilian. I suppose it would make a change from beating them up."

Joe's phone buzzed with a text message from Lisa.

If you haven't bought Christopher a birthday card yet, I have a spare one you can use.

Joe wrote back, *No need*. He made a mental note to buy a birthday card on the way to her house.

Joe wondered what Lisa would say if Joe asked her out. Since getting back in touch, he'd only ever seen her around her son. Their son. Whatever. The whole idea of being a father hadn't fully sunken in yet, but he was glad that they were starting to get along.

Maybe Lisa and Joe could meet up some time, just the two of them. That was why he'd bought tickets for a gig at the end of the week. A rock band they both used to listen to. Joe decided he'd suss her out this evening, see if she might be interested. He tapped his pocket, making sure the printouts of the tickets were still there. He wanted to have something physical to hand her. A digital ticket wouldn't be the same.

Boyle said to Cunningham, "I just saw on Facebook: a lad I know got a rat as a pet. Can you believe that?"

"What for?"

"He says it's good company. Affectionate."

Cunningham's eyes widened in disbelief. "Affectionate? Are we talking about vermin?"

Boyle nodded. "*Vermin*. That's exactly right. My mate says this fucking piece of vermin is intelligent."

"Intelligent? A dirty rat?"

"A filthy fucking rat."

Joe was still thinking about Lisa, and it took him a moment to realise that they were talking about him.

Boyle took a sip of cappuccino. "Why buy a rat, anyway? There's plenty of them around here. You could have one for free."

Cunningham grinned.

Joe tried to ignore them, but the room was small. He felt his skin prickle.

Boyle said, "Someone should do something about these rats."

"You mean, get an exterminator?" Cunningham asked.

"Right." Suddenly Boyle leaned forward, pressing his stomach against his desk. "You know what I'd like to do?"

"What's that?"

"Forget the exterminator. I'd like to take care of them *myself*."

"Now you're talking."

Boyle made a machine gun out of his hands, and moved it from side to side as if spraying Joe's side of the room with bullets. "Rat-a-tat-tat!"

Cunningham grinned. "Wipe them out."

"That's what happens to rats."

Enough was enough.

Joe got to his feet and walked over to Boyle's desk. He slapped Boyle's cup off the desk with the back of his hand, splashing scorching hot coffee over Boyle, who let out a shout and jumped to his feet.

Joe said, "You threaten me again, and I'll knock your block off." He turned to Cunningham. "You too," he said.

Boyle shook coffee off his hands and looked down at his ruined shirt.

"Joe, you bastard."

Just then, Joe's phone rang. He returned to his desk and sat down. His swivel chair allowed him to turn his back on Cunningham and Boyle. That was about as much privacy as he could get.

"Byrne," he said.

Joe was smiling. Pleased with himself. Ready for whatever was on the other end of the line. But he wasn't ready for this.

CHAPTER 27

Even with the driver's window open, and fresh air blowing on Barry Wall's face, the Range Rover stank of marijuana. How many joints could Buzz have smoked? The car had only been collected that morning.

Wall heard the click and hiss of a lighter. He glanced at the rear-view mirror and saw a fresh joint between Buzz's lips.

In the front passenger seat, Handsome, the thin young man from Liverpool, kept shifting his position and looking around. Before going to prison, he'd been a taxi driver. He used to work the night shift, picking up young girls when they were too drunk to put up a fight. Sometimes they were so drunk that they hadn't even been able to tell him where they lived. Didn't matter. Handsome always found a place to stop for some fun. Wall had heard all the stories.

Wall turned his attention to the road ahead. He was careful to keep to the speed limit. No point getting pulled over.

"There you go," Buzz said. "I bet you're a happy fellow now, aren't you, Bricky Boy?"

A cold rage spread across Wall's chest, but he said nothing.

He eased the Range Rover into the car park of a large auto-repair shop. Cars were parked all around, gleaming in the sun, but nobody was within sight. He parked next to a sparkling red Mazda and checked the time on the watch Handsome had brought him. In Mountjoy, there had been no clocks. Prisoners weren't allowed to wear watches.

Part of Wall was surprised that the plan had worked, that he was free. He'd had his doubts about Handsome and Buzz. That was why he'd kept the plan simple and trusted Handsome to be the responsible one, like he had been back in Mountjoy's kitchen.

Handsome opened his door and got out. He looked around, making sure no one was watching. The young man wasn't actually good-looking, but he took care of his appearance. Wall watched him slip into the unlocked Mazda.

So far, so good.

In the back-seat of the Range Rover, Buzz began to strip.

Buzz's friend owned the shop, and he was lending them the Mazda. The friend would keep the Range Rover out of sight until the Gardaí no longer cared about it.

Friends were useful.

It had taken a month of incarceration before Wall realised he'd need help to escape, and that other prisoners were his best chance. That was when he became interested in a job in the kitchen. You didn't have to work when you were locked up, but it passed the time, and there were perks. For Wall, it was all about getting to know prisoners who'd be released soon, and who wanted to make some money.

Wall squeezed his massive frame between the two front seats and clambered into the back of the car next to Buzz. He stripped off and passed his shirt and jeans to Buzz. Buzz handed Wall his clothes in return. Wall ignored the stench of sweat that Buzz's deodorant failed to beat. Each of them began to get dressed again.

Buzz had worked in the kitchen too, until he was caught one breakfast time, snorting a jar of nutmeg in the hope of getting high.

"I don't like this," Buzz said. "I've only finished doing my whack. I'm not going back to the Joy."

Wall said, "You won't. I guarantee it."

"How can you guarantee that?"

"Trust me. You won't go back to jail. And think of the money."

Wall reached under the seat and found the hair clippers. It only took a minute to shave off his beard and give himself a skinhead on top, just like Buzz's. The two men were the same height. Buzz wasn't as muscular as Wall, but he was close enough, to the casual observer.

Buzz had acquired a fake beard. When he finished dressing, he put the beard on. It was thick and brown, like Wall's. Not a perfect likeness, but good enough.

"I look stupid," Buzz said.

"So what?"

A distraction – that was what Wall needed.

Buzz would go into a petrol station and make a nuisance of himself. Someone would call 999. When the Gardaí heard the description of Buzz, they'd think he was Wall. Then Buzz could lead the police on a merry chase, while Wall got away.

That was the plan.

At least, it was what Wall had shared with these two. The real plan had a different ending.

Buzz didn't like the idea of leading the Gardaí on a chase. No one wanted to end up behind bars again. Five thousand euro was a great persuader, though. Especially to Buzz, who'd once killed a man for twenty.

Now wearing Buzz's black T-shirt, faded grey jeans and white runners, Wall got out of the Range Rover. He slipped on Buzz's sunglasses and sat in behind the wheel of the Mazda. He ran a hand over his shaved head and beardless face. The car's interior had an apple air-freshener smell that was almost as bad as the marijuana in the previous vehicle.

Buzz got in the back, and they pulled out of the car park. The road led north-west, to a petrol station Wall knew, which lay ten minutes away.

Its forecourt was quiet when they arrived. A young woman was pumping up the air in her bicycle tires. As they arrived, she finished and cycled away. The only other vehicle at the pumps was a white Ford Transit van.

Wall pulled in on the other side of the pump.

"Alright," Buzz said, flexing his shoulder muscles. "I'm ready. How's my beard looking?"

Handsome looked back and nodded. "Gorgeous, mate."

"Shut up," Buzz said and punched him hard on the arm.

"I'll be watching," Wall said.

Buzz nodded. "Yeah, whatever."

Wall turned and looked at him. "Do you remember what you're to do later?"

"What?"

"The route you're going to take?" Wall said.

"Of course. I'm not stupid."

"Tell me."

Buzz scowled. "Come on, pal."

Wall reached behind him. The angle was awkward, but his fingers were quick and strong and he had long arms. Once he found Buzz's throat, he squeezed it until Buzz's windpipe was about to collapse.

"Tell me."

"Okay, okay," Buzz gasped. His hands clawed into the back of Wall's seat. Wall eased the pressure a little. Buzz said, "I drive north."

"North where?"

"To Drogheda."

"Where don't you go?"

"Near Aidan Donnelly."

"Why?"

"Because you'll be going there."

"Right."

As soon as Wall released his grip, Buzz broke out in a fit of coughing and rubbed his throat. His eyes flashed murder, but he could do nothing until he'd been paid.

"What the fuck?" Buzz said.

"Just helping you get into the right frame of mind."

"I'm getting in the frame of mind where I'm going to kick your bollocks up into your tonsils."

"Go on," Wall said. "Piss off inside."

Buzz got out of the car and began walking towards the shop. He was geared up for a fight, exactly as Wall wanted.

Another man came out of the shop as Buzz approached it. Dressed in black jeans and a tight burgundy T-shirt. A baseball cap covered his eyes. Buzz deliberately bumped shoulders with him, but the man seemed untroubled.

The man glanced at the Mazda they were sitting in and tilted his head ever so slightly. Then he got into the van on the other side of the pumps.

"Is that him?" Handsome said. "Your ride?"

He'd always been the smarter one.

Wall said, "Yes."

"You trust him?"

"Of course. He's my brother."

It was weird to see Ken in a T-shirt and jeans, instead of one of his usual Hugo Boss shirts.

A shout came from inside the shop. Through the glass, twenty metres away, Wall saw Buzz knocking wine bottles off shelves and shouting at the alarmed shop assistant. Wall and Handsome exchanged a look. Then Handsome's gaze passed beyond Wall.

Wall turned and followed his gaze.

A patrol car was coming down the road.

CHAPTER 28

The Mater Hospital loomed in Joe's windscreen, huge and grey. His stomach had been churning during the whole way from Donnybrook, as he thought of Barry Wall escaping custody. He had mixed feelings about Wall. On the one hand, he was a dangerous man who had nearly killed Aidan Donnelly – not to mention Joe himself, and Anne-Marie Cunningham. On the other hand, Wall wouldn't have needed to take the law into his own hands if Joe had handled the investigation into his wife's disappearance better.

A patrol car was parked outside the Emergency Department, next to a line of ambulances. A couple of uniforms stood near the hospital entrance. The patrol car's lights were flashing, but they were barely visible in the sunshine.

Joe parked across the lot from them, so he wouldn't be in the way of the medics. It was only when he removed his hands from the wheel that he realised how tightly he'd been gripping it.

He blinked quickly, then got out of the car. Bringing his laptop case with him, he walked over. Two young officers from Mountjoy Garda Station were cordoning off the scene, a man and a woman. The woman was thin as a beanpole and had the bright eyes of a five-year-old. Her colleague suffered from the worst adult acne Joe had ever seen. The two of them made Joe feel old.

Once Joe had showed them his ID, Beanpole filled him in. She got to the part about the prison officer, Lauren Fairview, being attacked by one of the accomplices.

"Did you say an axe?" Joe said, just to make sure he'd heard her right.

Beanpole nodded. "She's in surgery now. Massive trauma. A lot of blood loss. As you can see."

She pointed to a pool of red liquid on the ground.

Joe couldn't believe it. Most prison escapes were short-lived, and they didn't involve anyone getting hurt. This thing just kept getting worse.

It was only four in the afternoon, and it was still Joe's day off.

"Where's the witness?"

Acne Man replied. "Inside, getting in the doctors' way."

"Okay." Joe glanced around, spotted a camera on the wall. "CCTV?"

"There is," he said. He turned behind him and shouted, "Hey, Petyr? You still there?"

A stocky, middle-aged man with thinning hair emerged from the hospital entrance. He was wearing a fluorescent yellow vest with SECURITY emblazoned across it. His watery eyes looked lively and not entirely unkind.

"Detective Sergeant Joe Byrne."

"Petyr Kowalski. I'm in security here. I came out and found the lady officer there." He pointed to the puddle of blood.

"What about the other officer?"

Kowalski pointed a few metres away. "He was there. When I found him, he was disoriented."

"You've got CCTV footage?"

"Yes."

"Did you get the licence plate of the getaway car?"

"No. The car didn't have one. Nevertheless, the vehicle is a white Range Rover with blacked-out windows."

One of thousands driving around the city. This didn't sound promising.

"I'd like to see the footage."

"Of course."

A Garda Technical Bureau van pulled in next to them. Scene-of-crime-officers in spacesuits got out. Joe waved and stepped back out of their way. An examination of the scene might provide some clues regarding the identity of the accomplices, which might help him figure out how to find Wall.

That was the best Joe could hope for.

He left the SOCOs and uniforms and followed Kowalski into the hospital, to a small room lit by a bank of flatscreen monitors. Pushing aside a can of Coke, Kowalski played Joe the footage.

The whole thing lasted one minute and thirty-seven seconds.

Joe didn't much like what he saw. The way Wall sprang out of the van, he didn't look like the man Joe had put in jail. He looked a thousand times more dangerous. The beard was new and it made him look like some kind of zealot.

What had those months in prison done to him? And who were the accomplices? Clearly, the guy who buried an axe in Lauren Fairview was also extremely dangerous.

Joe downloaded the CCTV footage onto his laptop, thanked Kowalski and then went to find Timmy Martin, the second prison officer.

Martin was pacing in the corridor outside an operating theatre, a young man with three-day stubble and long greasy hair. His eyes were set close together. Blood was caked down the side of his neck. The fluorescent light over his head was flickering, and in its jarring illumination, Timmy Martin looked more like a prisoner than a prison officer.

Joe introduced himself, then gestured towards the operating room. "How's Ms. Fairview doing?"

"I don't know," he said. "The doctors haven't told me."

"But she's alive?"

"She was, last I heard. She's a mess though."

"I'm sorry to hear that."

"They're probably still trying to put her spleen back in her abdomen."

"I'm sorry," Joe said again. He didn't much like the guy's tone, but he had to cut him some slack. Joe took out his notebook and pen. "Can you tell me how it happened?"

Martin shrugged.

"We arrived. A doctor met me. At least, I thought he was a doctor. Someone else hit me on the head."

"Did you recognise the men?"

"No, I didn't get a good look at them."

"Why didn't you request a Garda escort?"

It was standard procedure when transporting a dangerous prisoner for the prison officers to be accompanied by an armed detective. But they had received no request for one.

"Lauren thought we didn't need an escort."

"Why's that?"

"We weren't expecting any trouble. Barry isn't part of a gang. He doesn't have criminal contacts. Or at least, he didn't before he came to Mountjoy. Who's going to break him out?"

Joe had been asking himself the same question.

"Plus," Martin said, "the prison medic said Barry had pancreatitis. Apparently, it's usually pretty incapacitating."

The skin on Joe's cheeks prickled. Pancreatitis. Joe knew first-hand how incapacitating the condition was. Joe had suffered from a bout of it a year and a half earlier, after he'd nearly drunk himself to death. You don't do anything when you're crippled with that kind of pain, certainly not break out of jail.

Clearly Wall had been faking it.

The stale, hot air here reminded Joe of his own time in hospital. He didn't think that Wall's choice of pancreatitis was a coincidence. Somehow, Wall had discovered what Joe had gone through.

He's mocking me.

Joe said, "Was Wall close to anyone inside?"

"Who'd be close to a prick like him?" Martin said.

"Where was he was housed in the prison?"

"C Wing."

"I'd like to get the contact details for his A.C.O."

Joe figured the Assistant Chief Officer, the senior prison officer in C Wing, would be able to tell him who Wall had spent time with. He could think of no other place Wall would have found accomplices. Joe wrote down the name and number Timmy Martin provided.

"Okay," Joe said. "Let's get back to the incident. They knocked you down. Then what?"

"I was kind of dazed by the blow. Dizzy, you know? I think I blacked out. When I came to, I saw Lauren. She was covered in blood. Her face was… she didn't look right."

Martin rubbed his eyes roughly. Joe took this as a sign that he didn't want to talk more right now. He put his notebook back in his pocket.

"Have you let the doctors check you out?"

"I'm okay," Martin said.

Joe was looking to the matted blood on the side of his head.

"Seriously, have yourself checked. Thank you for your help."

He was about to leave when Timmy Martin looked up.

"Lately, Barry was quiet. At the start, it was different. For the first month he was crazy angry."

"And then?"

"It was like he chilled out. He came to terms with being where he was." Timmy Martin paused, stared at Joe. His eyes narrowed. "Have we met before?"

"I don't think so. Did Wall talk about what he wanted to do when he got out?"

"Sure. He said he was going to get the guy. The one who abducted his wife."

"Aidan Donnelly?"

"Right. Barry was going to make him talk. Tell him what happened. You know they never found Barry's wife?"

"Did he say anything else?"

"I *do* know you," Timmy Martin said. His eyes lit up. "I mean, you said your name, but I didn't make the connection before. You're the one who caught Barry, aren't you?"

Joe said nothing.

Timmy Martin nodded. "Barry talked about you, those first few weeks."

Joe felt his pulse quicken.

"What did he say?"

"That he was going to kill you and everyone you love. So you'll know how it feels."

"I hear guys say shit like that every day of the week."

"Me too." Martin smiled. "But most of them don't mean it."

CHAPTER 29

Like most properties on Clyde Road, the Highfield Academy was a red-brick Victorian structure. It would have made for a large house, and that's what it had been many years earlier, but in its current incarnation it was an elite private school. Only eighty students were enrolled, but Highfield's sizeable fees made up for its small student body.

For the last class of the day, Christopher O'Malley and seven other students were scattered around the Hibiscus Suite, which was what they called the front room on the ground floor.

Christopher liked the ground floor the best, because of the high ceilings, and the ornate chandeliers hanging in every room, each one of them unique.

The neighbours included embassies and fancy white-collar firms, though there were also some residences. Mum made plenty of money, but she said they couldn't afford to live here. She was struggling enough to pay the tuition fees. Christopher didn't know why she bothered. It wasn't like he *wanted* to come here.

Finally, the bell rang to mark the end of the period. Mrs. Dresden, the music teacher, was speaking to Clara Fry, a cello prodigy from the west end of London. She'd arrived in Dublin the previous year after her mother's job in financial services was moved.

Christopher hated the stupid Highfield uniform, with its pretentious navy blazer with the school crest, but he thought Clara looked pretty good in hers. Her haircut was a complicated up-style. For Christopher, there was nothing more beautiful or fascinating on earth. He couldn't keep his eyes off her.

"Are you alright, Mr. O'Malley?"

Mrs. Dresden's voice cut through his daze. Christopher blushed, realising that she was talking to him.

"Oh, y-yes, Mrs. Dresden."

"Good." The teacher looked around. "Alright, class. You may go."

Christopher packed up his violin and his sheet music. He walked out the door, past the secretary's desk, and outside.

He hurried down the tall flight of granite stairs to the ground, his steps a little unsteady, as he was getting used to his new glasses. He hitched his violin case over his shoulder as he crossed the gravel driveway.

Once out the gate, Christopher turned left, headed for home. Belmont Avenue was a short walk away through the park. He hoped Graham wouldn't be at the house.

Christopher hadn't stopped thinking about Graham and Crystal. He kept repeating in his mind that moment when Graham had locked Crystal in the shed.

It was the weirdest thing ever.

Graham came back into the house as if nothing had happened. Then the pizza arrived. Christopher couldn't eat, and Graham didn't seem to know why.

"Is she okay?" Christopher had finally said, glancing at the shed from which banging sounds were coming.

"I'm only messing with her," Graham said, winking. "Women need a firm hand. They enjoy it. That's a rule you can live by."

Christopher nodded, feeling sick to his stomach.

After eating two slices of pizza, Graham had gone outside and unlocked the shed. He'd somehow calmed Crystal down, and, after a little coaxing, he got her smiling again, then finished eating and dropped Christopher to the school.

Things seemed okay.

Sort of okay.

But Christopher hadn't been able to shake the uneasy feeling he'd had since he'd heard that lock click shut.

He pushed those thoughts from his mind. He had to hurry. John Kavanagh might be just steps behind him. The thought made Christopher's blood turn icy. Kavanagh was two years older than Christopher, a foot taller, and mean as hell.

Christopher turned onto Pembroke Park, a broad road lined with tress, and hurried past the big houses. Though it was mid-May, some cherry blossoms were still blooming and light-pink petals stuck to the soles of his shoes.

Why did Kavanagh have to live near him? Every day Christopher struggled to get home unscathed. Even when Kavanagh didn't lay a hand on him, he still made Christopher's life hell.

Christopher felt the sun on his cheeks as he walked along. Vitamin D, he thought. That should help his skin. He should try to soak up more sun. When Christopher was in his twenties, he would be clear-skinned. Or perhaps he'd grow a beard. He'd have a beautiful girlfriend and they'd drive around in a red Lamborghini. Maybe his girlfriend would be Clara, with her long legs and her London accent.

Christopher would be a professional musician by then. Clara could meet him at the National Concert Hall after his violin practice. Everyone in the orchestra would see them together and be insanely jealous.

Christopher would work out. He'd develop bulging biceps and a well-defined six-pack. He'd be untouchable, able to outrun or outfight anyone. In his fantasies, Christopher would jump in the sports car with an easy grace. Clara would lean over, put a hand on his rock-hard chest and kiss him. That would be nice. That would be—

Bam.

Christopher slammed into someone.

His head jerked back, and his hands shot up. The violin case flew through the air and skidded across the footpath.

He blinked in confusion and surprise. A larger boy was standing in his way, at the corner of Pembroke Park and Herbert Park.

Of course, it was John Kavanagh.

The older boy turned around and a malicious grin stretched across his lips when he saw Christopher. Somehow, Kavanagh and his lackey Colin Harrison had managed to get out of school ahead of Christopher.

"You dipshit," Kavanagh said. "You walked into me."

"Sorry," Christopher said, bending forward to pick up his violin. Kavanagh stood on the case before Christopher could take it.

"That's mine now," Kavanagh said. "As compensation."

CHAPTER 30

A cluster of pyjama-clad smokers stood outside the doors of the hospital. Joe pushed past them. He was shaken after his conversation with Timmy Martin – and the hospital was stifling. Joe needed a minute alone to collect his thoughts.

Outside, the sun beat down relentlessly.

Joe opened the Honda's door to let the hot air out, and stood beside the car. He was sweating more than the heat alone could explain.

Somewhere nearby, Barry Wall was sweating under the same sun. Joe thought of his conversation with Timmy Martin about Wall.

What did he say?

That he was going to kill you and everyone you love.

He checked his notebook. Breda Murray was the name Timmy Martin had given for Wall's ACO. Joe dialled the number and tried to tune out the wail of approaching sirens. The phone just rang and rang. He hung up.

Joe couldn't see Mountjoy Prison from where he stood, but it was nearby, on the other side of the hospital. He'd have to pay it a visit.

The longer Barry Wall was free, the harder it would be to catch him. And the more of a danger he'd be. It was safe to assume that Aidan Donnelly would be Wall's number one target, so Joe wanted to get eyes on him soon. Joe would probably be the next target.

What if Wall was able to do what Joe had failed to do? What if he was able to find out what had happened to Valentina?

Joe's phone buzzed with a text message from Lisa.

Can you get birthday candles on your way?
Sure, he texted back.

Joe had forgotten Christopher. Maybe if he hurried, he could still make it back to Donnybrook for six o'clock. But he had things to do first.

The Honda hadn't cooled much, but Joe couldn't wait any longer. He jumped in and drove around the block to the prison.

An ominous red-brick wall surrounded Mountjoy. The country's most serious male offenders were housed here. Bad vibes radiated off the place.

Joe felt it, even out here.

He drove up to the big metal gate, showed the security guard his ID and explained that he wanted to speak to Breda Murray. He stressed that it was urgent, that he was investigating Wall's escape. The security guard got on his walkie-talkie. After a bit of to-and-fro, he raised the barrier and pointed to a parking space in front of a building.

Joe parked there and got out. He was wondering where to go when he heard a woman's voice.

"I don't suppose you've found him yet."

Joe spun around to see a grey-haired lady in a navy uniform. She looked a bit like KD Lang. She smoked a cigarette as she walked towards Joe.

"Not yet."

"Breda Murray."

"Joe Byrne."

"I know who you are."

Joe sighed. Everyone seemed to know who he was.

An irreverent twinkle shone in Breda Murray's eyes.

"Let's talk inside."

She flicked her cigarette butt away and set off for one of the prison buildings.

"Wouldn't it be easier to talk here?"

"My break's over," she said without looking back.

Joe followed her inside the building. He presumed they'd talk in her office. Instead she led him through a series of locked doors. Joe found himself in front of a security guard, manning an X-ray scanner. Joe didn't like leaving his gun behind, but he wasn't allowed take it in. He wasn't even allowed to bring his phone in. He left it there and followed Murray.

She said, "You might see some old friends here."

Joe realised she was taking him onto the block, past the cells. The place was on lockdown, so no prisoners were roaming free. That was probably a good thing. Still, he didn't like being paraded in front of them. After you've caught a criminal, you never really want to hear from them again.

"Hey, Joe," someone shouted.

"Fuck off," Joe said.

Murray flashed a smile, then led him down a flight of stairs.

Joe said, "Barry Wall had help escaping. Two accomplices. I thought it might be some of the men he met here."

"Don't you think that's a little judgmental?"

"Being judgmental saves time," Joe said. "Half of prisoners re-offend within three years of being released."

"Forty-seven percent," she said.

"Whatever. I'd be surprised if Wall didn't source his accomplices here."

"It's possible," Murray said. "He didn't get a lot of visitors."

"Who came to see him?"

"Just his brother."

"Ken?" Joe said after a moment. "Is that the brother's name?"

"Think so."

"Do you think he could be involved?"

"I doubt it. Doesn't seem the type to get his hands dirty. Too fond of his nice clothes. And he didn't visit often."

"Was Wall close to any of the other prisoners?"

"At the start he kept to himself, but you can't survive here like that. After a few months he got a job. In here."

They passed through a doorway. Joe found himself in a big industrial kitchen, where a prisoner was mopping the floor. He must have had special privileges, not to be on lockdown like the others.

"That's why you brought me here, through the cell blocks?"

"Why else?"

"I thought you were pulling my chain."

The ACO smiled. "I have better things to pull than your chain, Detective. Brick Wall got transferred to C Wing where all of the kitchen workers have their cells. If he was close to anyone, it must have been someone from the kitchen."

"Brick Wall?" Joe sneered. "That what they call him here?"

Murray nodded. She turned and called over the man mopping the floor. "This is Toby O'Neill."

"Alright?" O'Neill said, approaching the counter from the other side, like he was about to serve Joe dinner. He was middle-aged, average looking. Didn't look like a criminal, but they often don't.

"Toby, this is Detective Sergeant Joe Byrne."

"You're the fella Brick blew up." It took Joe a moment to realise that the man was talking about the explosion in Wall's house. His grey eyes looked Joe up and down. "I thought you'd be bigger."

CHAPTER 31

Christopher stared at John Kavanagh and his friend, Colin Harrison. Kavanagh still had his foot on Christopher's violin. Christopher realised that Kavanagh really wasn't going to give the instrument back to him.

Christopher said, "I need it."

"*I need it*," Kavanagh echoed.

Christopher felt himself blush. Did his voice sound whiny like that?

Harrison said, "The little pussy needs it."

"Well, he can't have it. Because he's a blind dope. Even now that he has four eyes, he still can't see a thing."

Harrison said, "Don't worry, Chris, you're too fat to play violin anyway."

"Yeah, he is," Kavanagh said with a laugh. "A fat piece of shit like him is never going to be any good at the violin. His fingers are too thick. Look at those fat sausage fingers."

Christopher swallowed. He tried to think of a way to get his instrument back. Not only did he need it for school, but it was a family heirloom.

"You know what else?" Kavanagh said. "He really doesn't need those glasses. They don't seem to work so good."

"That's true. We should take them too."

Kavanagh came forward. His fingers reached out, ready to pluck the glasses right off Christopher's nose.

Christopher started running, around the two older boys, down the road towards the park. His black leather shoes slapped the road's surface harder with every step.

He heard footsteps behind, but the older boys soon stopped chasing him. Kavanagh's voice followed him though.

"Hey, thanks for the violin."

Christopher ran for as long as he could. Herbert Park's thirty-two acres opened up on both sides of him. The park was cut in two by the road, and the bulk of the park lay on the right side. That was the way Christopher walked to get home.

At the gate, he stopped. He had a stitch in his side from running, and he tasted pepperoni from the pizza he'd eaten for lunch, as it threatened to come back up.

He entered the park and walked a little way down the path, before sitting on the grass with his back pressed against a hawthorn tree. His chest heaved as he caught his breath. After a minute's rest, he forced himself to his feet. He had to get moving again. His breath was ragged as he hurried down the path, leaves overhead fluttering in the warm breeze.

He walked past a pedestrian gate and on by the side of the club house, next to the sports fields. The whole way, his heart was racing.

How could he explain the loss of the violin to Mum? He'd have to make something up. And what would happen tomorrow? Would Kavanagh take his glasses? How could Christopher explain that?

As he came to the edge of the park, he stopped. The tears came quickly, so quickly they took him by surprise.

He couldn't take it anymore.

The fear, the stress, the humiliation. It had been going on for so long. He squeezed his eyes shut.

And his stupid dreams… Clara was never going to gaze in awe at Christopher as he jumped in a Lamborghini. More likely, horrible people like Kavanagh would enjoy such a glamorous life. Just look at Kavanagh's dad, who was some bigshot in the Gardaí. People said he was a jerk too.

More tears came.

And with them, a decision.

Christopher pulled himself together, then walked out of the park and headed to the nearest pharmacy, on Morehampton Road.

He bought a pack of pills. Twenty-four tablets, each containing 500 mg of paracetamol.

Then he went to the next pharmacy, down the road, for a second pack. Sanjeev, the pharmacist behind the counter, smiled at Christopher when he entered the shop. Mum had built the pharmacy's website last year.

"Happy birthday, Christopher," Sanjeev said. "Sixteen? Today you become a man."

"How did you know?"

The pharmacist tapped his nose, giving Christopher a conspiratorial smile.

Mum must have told him. Maybe this was where she had bought that meal-replacement shake the other day, the one Christopher insisted on trying, so he'd slim down before his birthday. But the shake had tasted horrible, and he was hungry again an hour after drinking it. After two meal shakes, he'd gone back to eating normal food. In fact, he'd eaten more than normal to make up for the shakes.

He thought of Kavanagh and Harrison.

A fat piece of shit like him is never going to be any good at the violin.

Christopher hurried out of the shop. He was afraid he'd cry again if he didn't keep moving, and that would be pathetic. He just needed to hold it together a tiny bit longer.

Forty-eight pills.

Christopher figured that ought to be enough to do the job, even if he was a fat piece of shit.

CHAPTER 32

Joe couldn't tell exactly what age Toby O'Neill was, but the prisoner's face was more weathered than Tommy Lee Jones's. Beneath heavy brows, his pale grey eyes peered at Joe.

Joe said, "Barry Wall escaped custody today while being taken to hospital. Do you have any information that might help us find him? He had help from two men. Perhaps former prisoners."

"I don't know anything about that."

"He worked here?"

"Yes."

"Was he close to anyone?"

"I wouldn't say close, if you know what I mean. But he hung around with a few of the lads."

"Were any of those men released recently?"

O'Neill put his hand to his chin.

"Well, Buzz was released a few weeks ago. He worked here. Handsome too. And, last month, Leech."

Joe took out his notebook.

"Real names, please."

O'Neill listed them off. *Gar "Buzz" Butler. Johnny "Handsome" Westfield. Larry 'Leech' Beech.*

"Oh, and Dinky," O'Neill said. "William 'Dinky' Talbot. Big lad, him. Joyrider. I can't think of anyone else. But why would they help him escape? They were already on the outside. Why risk it?"

It was a good question. One that Joe had been asking himself.

"What do you think he'll do now?"

The prisoner stroked his chin. "Go abroad? He mentioned Spain before."

"His wife was from there," Joe said, almost to himself.

"Yeah. He wanted to go there."

"If you think of anything that might help, please let Ms. Murray know, and she can contact me. Parole hearings look kindly on prisoners who've made themselves useful."

"Yeah, no bother."

Murray said, "Go ahead and finish up, Toby."

The prisoner nodded and walked away.

Joe turned to Murray and said, "Could you check if any of those men visited Wall here after they were released?"

"I can tell you right now. They didn't. As former prisoners, they wouldn't have been allowed to visit."

"Could they have phoned him?"

"They could, but we listen in on all calls, so they'd hardly have plotted his escape that way. And I don't actually remember Brick getting any calls."

He must have been planning this for some time.

At least Joe had some names to look up.

Murray led him back the way they'd come, up the metal staircase. On the landing, she paused, took out her cigarettes and slipped one behind her ear. Then she continued walking.

Joe said, "That's a filthy habit, you know."

"Thanks for the newsflash."

"And I thought your break was over."

Murray smiled. "The next one is just around the corner. Good luck catching him."

"You don't think we'll get him, do you?"

Murray shrugged. "He's a tough man. A personal trainer. And smart too. Did you know he's a chess whizz?"

"So what?"

"That makes him a smart man."

"If he's so smart, then why did he end up in prison?"

"Have you ever made a mistake? Do you really think the men in here are so much different from you and me?"

Joe shrugged. Time was running out. He didn't have time for hypothetical questions.

"How do I get out of here?" he said.

Murray smiled. "That's what I thought."

CHAPTER 33

The petrol station's forecourt was quiet. Just the white van on the other side of the pumps. Ken Wall had got into it and the van was sitting there. Engine off. Barry Wall and Handsome sat together in the Mazda, facing the petrol station's shop.

There was nobody else around.

Except the two officers in the patrol car.

Wall watched it crawl down the road toward the petrol station. A young female Garda was at the wheel. A young male Garda sat in the passenger seat. The girl looked thinner than a skeleton. The guy had a horrible pizza face. They looked young and alert. Eager to make names for themselves. Promotion, power, money.

Wall's fingers dug into the steering wheel.

They could be trouble.

The patrol car came alongside the forecourt, fifteen feet from where Wall sat. Wall stared hard at the driver. She had a sharp face and small, dark eyes.

Her attention was focused on the road, until she looked Wall in the eye.

"Oh no, mate," Handsome gasped, lowering himself in his seat.

Wall stared at the Garda and she stared at him. He was sure that she saw right through him and knew who he was. Fifteen feet away or not. Even with Wall's shaved head and beardless face.

She recognised him.

She *knew*.

His pulse started to race.

If she so much as glanced at the shop, she'd see Buzz inside, causing mayhem.

What if she needed petrol?

Wall breathed through his nose. Like a bull.

Then he noticed the shadowy form of a passenger in the back-seat. A suspect. Wall blew air out of his mouth. They weren't going to stop, not with a suspect in the car. Not unless they saw something serious.

The driver looked at Wall for another second, then turned her attention back to the road ahead of her. The car passed by and was gone.

Handsome sighed.

He said, "I think I just soiled myself."

Wall could see Buzz at the counter. He had the shop assistant by the collar and he was looking out the window. He gave a shrug like, *Enough?*

Wall held out his hand.

"Phone," he said.

Handsome handed over his mobile. Wall took it and called Buzz. Inside the shop, Buzz dug his phone out of his pocket.

"Yeah?"

"Hit him."

Wall hung up.

He handed Handsome his phone. They turned to watch. Buzz landed a neat blow on the shop assistant's chin. The young man crumpled onto the floor.

"Gorgeous," Handsome laughed.

"I'll go get the money," Wall said.

"Sounds good, mate."

Handsome was expecting five thousand, the same as Buzz. They'd get nothing.

They thought they were going on a merry chase. They were going nowhere.

Wall opened the door and got out. He checked that Handsome wasn't watching, then he lifted the pump and poured petrol onto the ground around the Mazda's back wheel. When the concrete around the sedan was a pool of petrol, Wall hunkered down and slashed the back-left tire. Just to make sure. Then he walked to the Ford Transit on the other side of the pump.

The front passenger door was already open. Ken sat behind the wheel. Leech sat in the passenger seat. He nodded at Wall.

"Alright, Brick?" Leech said.

Wall hated that stupid name. He was glad Leech was going to be dead in sixty seconds.

The two brothers looked at each other. They didn't need words.

Ken started the engine while Wall went around the back of the van. The doors were open. A bag was sitting in the back. Wall took it out, closed the doors, went back to the front of the van and handed the bag to Leech. He nodded to the sedan in which Handsome sat.

"They'll want to count it. Let them. It's all there. Your cut too. Leave a couple of minutes after us. I'll see you later. When it's safe."

The man nodded. He got down from the van, took the bag from Wall and walked to the Mazda. Wall watched him. If Leech looked down at his feet, he'd see the petrol. But he didn't because he was so eager to get at the cash. He got straight into the sedan.

Buzz came running out of the shop.

He had taken the opportunity to rob the cash register, though Wall had told him not to. Now bank notes were flitting in the breeze, as Buzz ran over to the sedan and jumped in.

Buzz, Leech and Handsome. All in one place. Going nowhere.

Wall got into the van, next to Ken.

"Good to see you."

"You too," Ken said as he peeled off a pair of latex gloves.

The two brothers hugged.

"Did Leech ask why you're wearing those?"

"Yeah." Ken smiled. "I said it was to avoid leaving fingerprints."

"He believed you?"

"Sure. I don't think he knows anything about explosives."

Ken wouldn't have handled the contents of the bag without gloves. It would have been absorbed through his skin and it would have given him a hell of a headache.

"This is a blind spot," Ken said, pointing above. "No one will know you got away. There's no camera here. Or rather, there is one, but it's out of order. I checked."

Ken handed Wall a new phone and the bomb's detonator.

A car pulled into the petrol station, a silver Nissan that had seen better days. A man in his thirties was driving and a girl of about ten sat in the back. The father was easing the car towards the sedan containing Buzz, Handsome, Leech and ten pounds of gelignite.

"Stop that car," Wall said.

"Are you sure?"

"You want to kill a little girl?"

"Of course not. But it's a delay."

"So hurry up. They won't see our faces. They'll be too surprised."

"Alright, fine."

Wall and Ken fastened their seatbelts. Then Ken accelerated straight at the Nissan. It was a short distance and Ken closed the gap quickly. Wall braced himself as they approached. The driver was distracted, talking to his kid.

They hit the Nissan with a crunch of crumpling metal, the impact hard enough to trigger the other vehicle's airbags, and to snap Ken and Wall's necks back as the van jerked to a halt.

"You okay?" Ken said.

"Of course. Let's go."

Ken reversed a few metres, then took off fast, ignoring the traffic on the road outside the petrol station.

A call came on Wall's phone. He put it to his ear. "What?"

"What the hell was that about?" Handsome said. "Why did you crash into a car?"

"Don't worry about it."

"Okay, well, there's a lock on the holdall. I want to check the money before we lead the cops away. What's the code?"

"517," Wall said.

He could hear Buzz's voice in the background. As usual, he was impatient. "Where's the money?"

Handsome said, "Alright. It's open."

Buzz's voice was getting louder. "What's that? Where's the money?"

Handsome said, "It's not here. What's this thing?"

Wall smiled. He said, "Gelignite."

"What the fuck is that?"

"It's mainly nitro-glycerine, with some kieselguhr mixed in. That's a sedimentary rock, in case you were wondering."

He thought of Aidan Donnelly. He'd sat in Wall's kitchen and Wall had almost got the truth out of him. Then Joe Byrne ruined everything.

He'd get Donnelly.

And he'd get Byrne too.

Soon.

"Oh shit," Handsome said.

Buzz, in the background, said: "I'll kill you, you fucker. Where's the money?"

Leech was shouting too. "I have no idea. I thought it was here. They told me—"

"*I'll kill you!*"

Ken eased the van's speed now that they were in traffic. Wall ended the call and slid the phone into the pocket of his jeans. He looked in the rear-view mirror. He could still see the petrol station.

The Mazda full of ex-cons began to move, then lurched to a stop on its deflated tire.

Wall teased the detonator's button with his thumb, readying himself to squeeze it.

Ken said, "I doubt the underground tanks will ignite."

"Me too. But let's see."

Ahead the sky was blue and clear. Wall rolled down his window so he could taste the air. With his thumb, he pressed down the button on the detonator.

Behind them, the sedan exploded in an immense roar, and the sky burst into flames.

CHAPTER 34

The lot at the back of Donnybrook Garda Station was almost empty when Joe arrived. The station was already closed to the public for the night. He headed straight up the stairs to O'Carroll's office, but found it empty.

He continued up the next flight of stairs and made his way to the incident room – the place where the team investigating Wall's outbreak would meet and talk through leads, collate information, and figure out everything that needed to be figured out.

Detective Inspector David O'Carroll was standing at the front of the room looking at a white board. Someone had written BARRY WALL on it and drawn lines to ACCOMPLICE 1 and ACCOMPLICE 2. A few times, places and other pieces of information were scrawled on the board.

It took Joe a second to realise that O'Carroll was not alone. A fresh-faced blonde in a crisp blue blouse and a charcoal skirt stood next to him. Joe figured she was in her late twenties. With the outfit and her severe ponytail, she looked like an ambitious solicitor. The woman turned her hazel eyes on Joe. She didn't look particularly happy to see him and neither did O'Carroll. Joe wondered if she was connected to Ger Barrett. Another one of his legal representatives? That whole scene with Ger Barrett, Kevin Boyle and the backpack of cash felt like it had happened years ago.

"Ah, Joe. So there you are," O'Carroll said. "Meet Detective Garda Alice Dunne. She's just been transferred here from Cork. I was going to make the introductions in the morning, but since you're here…"

Dunne held out her hand. Her skin felt warm and soft. She didn't blink as she gazed at him.

"Pleased to meet you, sir."

Joe said, "I'm not sure how you talk in Cork, but things aren't very formal in Donnybrook. We're mostly on first-name terms."

Except me, Joe thought.

He rarely used anyone's name at all.

Dunne smiled. "It's the same in Cork. But I didn't want to presume anything. You know how that can rub people up the wrong way."

Her face, which had seemed somewhat plain at first sight, became animated when she talked, taking on an almost magnetic quality. Joe realised he was smiling back at her involuntarily.

O'Carroll raised his hands, as if embracing both Dunne and Joe, without actually touching them.

"Joe, I want you to take care of Alice while she gets settled in. I've given her the bare facts about Barry Wall. You can tell her the rest."

"Of course."

"Alice, I want you to work closely with Joe on this case."

She said, "I'm looking forward to it."

Some Cork accents are thick, but Dunne's just gave her voice a melodic lilt, so her words seemed to float in the air.

O'Carroll gestured to the coffee machine. "Still hot if you want it."

Joe did. He poured himself a cup and knocked it back, though it was bitter. Probably it had been stewing for an hour or two on the hot plate. Better than nothing though.

He told them what he'd learned from visiting The Mater Hospital and Mountjoy Prison. Dunne's eyes burned into him as he spoke. O'Carroll didn't bat an eyelid when Joe mentioned Timmy Martin, how he'd said Barry Wall wanted Joe dead.

"The usual bluster," O'Carroll said.

Maybe he was right.

When Joe mentioned the names of the men Wall had worked with in the prison kitchen, and who had been released recently, O'Carroll wrote them on the white board. He wrote PERSONS OF INTEREST over the names.

He listened to the rest of Joe's report, then said he'd already put out a bulletin for Wall's arrest. Every officer in the country was looking for him. There would be no getting away. Officers downstairs were poring over CCTV footage. Forensics people were working on fibres recovered from the crime scene. Uniforms were scouring the streets.

O'Carroll said, "Mark my words. He's going to turn up at the airport or a ferry port with a fake ID and a ticket to Spain, just like that prisoner told you. That's when we'll catch him. We just need to keep a watch out for him."

Joe said, "I'm not so sure about that. Wall wants revenge on Aidan Donnelly. I think we should put surveillance on him."

"That's not in the budget," O'Carroll said, "and it's unnecessary. Look, you've had a long day. Go home and get some rest. Tomorrow you can take a shift watching the airport, if Wall hasn't turned up by then."

Arguing with him was pointless, so Joe didn't.

"Go on, get out of here," O'Carroll said, showing an uncharacteristic amount of selflessness. Joe was pretty sure he was doing it for Alice Dunne's benefit rather than his.

Dunne followed Joe out onto the corridor and they walked downstairs together. "Do you know where I could get a bite to eat?" Dunne asked.

"What did you have in mind?"

"Something spicy."

"There's a Chinese place down the road. They do Thai food too. They'll make it as hot as you can handle."

"Sounds great," Dunne said with a smile that lit up her whole face. "Which way is it?"

"Are you driving?" Joe asked.

"Not today."

"I can drop you at the restaurant if you like."

"That would be great."

She touched his upper arm, just for a second. It was enough to send a quiver of excitement through Joe's body. He led her out to the car park, unlocked the Honda and got in. Dunne eased herself into the passenger seat. Her movements were smooth and efficient.

"Do you know Donnybrook?" he said.

"Not really. I've heard it's a good area, though."

"It's not bad."

"Where are you from? You sound like a Dubliner. But your accent is light."

Joe nodded. "I grew up not far from here."

He pulled out of the lot and swung out onto Morehampton Road. The radio was on, turned to the news. When Joe heard the word "explosion", he turned up the volume. Something had happened at a petrol station on the north side of the city.

Dunne cocked her head to the side as she listened.

"How hungry are you?" Joe said.

"I can hold off for a while, if you want to see what that explosion was about?"

"You read my mind."

Joe pointed the Honda towards the city centre.

An explosion.

He thought of that day at Barry Wall's house. How he'd made his way around the side and seen Aidan Donnelly through the kitchen window. Joe remembered the sight of the bomb. He remembered the sound of it when it detonated, shredding Wall's kitchen and throwing Annie-Marie Cunningham out the front door. In the aftermath of the blast, Joe had found Wall out cold. He'd cuffed him while he was still unconscious. Then he'd called it in. That day, Wall's house had turned into a circus of emergency-service vehicles for the second time.

All this passed through Joe's mind in a flash.

He turned on the car's lights and siren, and stomped on the accelerator.

CHAPTER 35

Lisa O'Malley was filling the dishwasher. As usual, she ran the plates under the tap before loading them neatly into the machine. Separated from her by the dishwasher, Graham popped the lid on a bottle of Budweiser and leaned back against the kitchen counter. He shook his head, baffled. "Why'd you clean them first?" he said.

"I don't want food to clog up the machine."

"Don't you care if it clogs up the sink?"

Lisa shot him a look.

"Sorry, it's just that the kid's giving me a headache," Graham said.

"You know how upset he is."

Graham nodded. "Joe was never going to come. That's just the way he is. Chris shouldn't get so worked up about it."

He could hear the little bastard stomping around in his bedroom. Was he sixteen or six? What a baby. He'd hardly said a word since he got home from school, and he'd barely touched the birthday cake Lisa made. Graham had enjoyed it though.

Lisa glanced at Graham's beer. "You said you were going to cut the hedge tonight, right?"

"Oh yeah." He took a sip and rubbed his chin thoughtfully. "I can do that. I just want to chill out for a few minutes first. Get rid of this headache."

"Why don't you do some painting?"

Lisa's garden shed was practically a house. Made of brick, with two large windows, the shed was plumbed and wired for electricity. When Graham and Lisa started dating, she'd said he could use the shed as his artist's studio, if he wanted, as she never used it, and Graham said he had nowhere to paint. She'd given him his own key to the side gate, so he didn't have to go through the house to get to it.

"That's a good idea," Graham said. "Maybe I'll paint for half an hour. If you don't mind, that is."

"That's fine. Why don't you start now? Then it will still be bright when you finish. You'll be able to do the hedge before dark."

Graham set his beer down on the counter. He went around behind Lisa and placed his hands on her shoulders.

"Are you upset?"

"I'm just disappointed that Joe let Christopher down again."

"Yeah, well, he's not really father material, is he?"

Lisa shook her head. "I shouldn't have invited him."

"Don't be so hard on yourself. It's not your fault."

"Yeah, it is."

Graham hugged her tight.

"You know you could join me in the studio for a while. I know how to help you relax."

He pressed his crotch against her backside.

Lisa pulled away. "Christopher could see," she hissed.

"He's upstairs."

"And I'm really not in the mood to fool around right now. I'm sorry, Graham."

"Okay, no problem. I get it."

"You go and relax for a while," Lisa said. She inserted a washing capsule and started the machine.

"You sure?"

"Yeah."

"What are you going to do?"

"I have to work. I'm updating my parents' website."

"So they're still making you work for free, are they? All the work you do for them? You should send them a bill. It's not like they're short of cash."

"What? Why would I want to do that?"

"Your parents are loaded," Graham said.

"Well, they're comfortable."

"But they don't want to spend a cent on their website. They're taking advantage of you."

"It's not like that."

"Are you sure?"

"I am." Lisa smiled. "They're family, Graham. They're not trying to exploit me."

"Okay then."

He pulled another beer from the fridge and took it out into the garden, shutting the door behind him. He liked how spacious the garden was. Every square foot cost a fortune in Donnybrook.

He lit a cigarette and looked up into the still-blue sky. He felt like having some female company. If Lisa was too busy to spend time with him, that was okay. He could find someone else. He dug into his pocket for his phone.

He dialled Crystal's number. The phone rang as he walked down the garden path. Crystal picked up after a couple of rings.

"What do you want, Graham?"

"What's up with you?"

"You locked me in a shed, you bastard."

"Are you still mad about that? It was only for half a minute."

"It freaked me out."

"I thought you liked a laugh."

"That wasn't a laugh, Graham."

"Okay, okay. Now I know." He stepped into the studio and closed the door behind him. "So are you busy?"

"Now?" Crystal asked.

"Yeah, I have some free time."

"Where are you?"

"I'm at the studio."

"You mean the shed you locked me in?"

Graham grinned. "How about I lock us both in it this time?"

"I don't think so."

"Why not? You can come around the side. No one will see."

Crystal giggled.

"I can't. My sister is here with me. We made spaghetti."

"Come on. You're not going to leave me with my dick in my hand, are you?"

"We're in the middle of dinner. Can I ring you back? How about later, when my sister goes?"

"Come now. You can bring your sister too."

"Graham. I'm not doing that."

"Prick-tease," Graham said.

He ended the call and looked around the shed. An easel was set up in the middle of the room. Paints rested on a workbench, beside which stood a sink. The place was cosy. Lisa had even put a spare kettle there, and left an armchair in the corner.

Graham didn't feel like painting right now. He lowered himself into the chair and closed his eyes.

CHAPTER 36

The drive to the scene of the explosion gave Joe a chance to fill Alice Dunne in on the Barry Wall case. From the passenger seat, she gazed at him with those big hazel eyes while he told her about Valentina López Vázquez's disappearance, and how they arrested Aidan Donnelly. Joe was surprised she hadn't seen it all on the TV. The media had made a big enough deal out of the story.

Dunne said, "So in the end, you couldn't secure a conviction against Donnelly?"

"No, it's hard to secure a murder conviction when there's no body."

"Her body has *never* been found?"

"No."

Joe rolled down the window. The acrid smell of smoke wafted on the evening air, tainted by plastic, metal and petrol. Ahead, traffic was slowing. It must have been chaos earlier in the evening.

Dunne shifted in her seat. Her skirt had ridden well above her knees, and Joe caught a glimpse of shiny black tights before forcing himself to look away.

He said, "That night, when I brought Aidan Donnelly into custody… I was later accused of violating his rights."

"Did you?"

"I was trying to save a woman's life. I hoped she might still be alive somewhere. I thought every second's delay might mean her death. I did everything I could to get Donnelly to tell me where he put her."

"You slapped him around?"

Joe blinked quickly a couple of times. "His legal team accused me of a lot of things. Questioning him while he was under the influence of alcohol, keeping him in custody too long, assault… The Director of Public Prosecutions had big issues with the case. Very reluctant to prosecute. Finally, they did, but the judge threw it out. Directed the jury to acquit him."

Dunne nodded. "So that's why Wall hates you."

"Because of me, his wife's killer went free."

Joe told her what happened after the trial. Wall kidnapping Donnelly, trying to make him talk, the bomb he had rigged up. The explosion. And what happened afterwards – Barry Wall being sent to jail for his attempt at vigilante justice.

Dunne shook her head when he was finished. "Donnelly kills the guy's wife but gets off. Then Wall tries to get justice and *he's* sent down? That's messed up."

"I get that, believe me."

"What would you do?"

Joe glanced at Dunne. "What do you mean?"

"If you were Wall, would you have taken the law into your own hands?"

Joe shrugged. "I think I've learnt my lesson. Better to stick to the rules as much as possible."

They turned a corner, and the wreckage of the petrol station came into view. The forecourt roof was lying drunkenly on its side. Twisted metal poked out of the debris like skeletal limbs. The shop was ruined too. The glass there was all blown out and the walls were blackened and crumbling. A car, out on the road, was covered in debris. There was little trace of the vehicle that had been the centre of the explosion. Its remains must have been scattered all over the place.

Four fire engines were on the scene, and fire officers swarmed around, putting out the last of the flames. Uniforms were keeping the crowd well back. Several ambulances were dotted around, and an army bomb-disposal van was jammed in between the ambulances, its olive-green paintwork ominous.

Joe ditched the Honda at the side of the road. He and Dunne walked through the crowd of onlookers, up to the nearest uniform who was manning a barricade. Even though the flames were now out, Joe could feel the heat radiating out from the centre of the fire. The air was dense with petrol-scented smoke.

Joe flashed his ID at the officer, then shouted to him over the noise. "Do you know what caused the explosion?"

"We don't know the details yet, but we believe it was a bomb of some kind."

"Anyone hurt?"

"Six people. The poor kid who worked behind the counter has been taken to hospital for some minor injuries. A man and his daughter were a little battered and bruised, but they'll be okay too. And three men were killed."

"Three men? Together?"

The officer nodded.

"Are you aware of the Barry Wall situation?"

"I am."

"Tell me Wall was one of them."

The officer stepped closer. "A man matching his description was seen getting into the car just before it exploded. We'll have to wait for the forensics to know for sure. If they can even find pieces of the men."

Explosives matched Wall's previous form. Perhaps he'd been playing with another bomb. But he'd got sloppy and blown himself up.

"Thanks," Joe said.

He and Dunne headed back to the car, as there was no use hanging around, getting in the fire brigade's way. Joe sat down behind the wheel and dug out his mobile. He had a dozen missed calls and texts from Lisa. He sighed.

"What is it?"

"I forgot about my son's birthday."

"You have a son? Are you married?"

"No, it's not like that. We're not together."

Not at the moment, anyway. But he had the tickets for that gig. Maybe Lisa would want to go with him.

He'd deal with Lisa in a minute. First, he phoned O'Carroll on his mobile because he'd want to know immediately. O'Carroll answered after one ring.

"This better be good, Joe. You're disturbing me in the middle of the news."

O'Carroll was religious about watching the news. In the background, Joe heard a man's voice, shushing O'Carroll. It must have been his husband.

Joe said, "Anything on the news about a petrol station explosion?"

"Yes," O'Carroll answered slowly. Joe could picture him sitting up in his chair. "Terrible thing that. Why do you ask?"

Joe said, "It might not be so terrible."

CHAPTER 37

The hideout was a semi-detached house in north Dublin, with cream-painted walls and brown PVC windows. The roof was covered in sombre brown tiles, which was nice, but the front lawn had been dug up and covered over with crazy paving, which wasn't.

It was like the owners had woken up one day and thought, *Enough cutting the grass. Screw this place.*

"The owners were a couple. They separated," Ken said as they pulled into the driveway. "They were in such a hurry to unload that they would have taken a jar of pickles as payment. I'm going to make a hundred and fifty k selling it on. As soon as we're finished with it."

A trickle of blood ran down Wall's arm. He'd been digging his fingernails into his palm for the last mile – so hard, he'd cut himself. This should be his moment of triumph. And Ken was messing everything up.

Wall said, "I want to go there now."

There meant straight to Aidan Donnelly's flat.

Ken killed the engine, stepped down to the ground and turned to look back at his brother.

"That's an awful idea, Barry. Use your head. We have to wait for dark."

"I can go alone, if you don't want to risk it. They think I'm dead."

"And we want to keep it that way. They're not going to learn any different in the next few hours. In real life, that CSI stuff takes time. We'll get Donnelly later. I know you've waited a long time, but you can wait a little longer, alright? Let's just stay out of sight until the sun goes down. Then we'll pay him a visit."

It was true. Wall *had* waited so long. Every day in prison, he'd thought of Aidan Donnelly. Whenever he closed his eyes, he pictured him.

He got out of the van. He made a promise to himself as he followed his brother up the driveway.

Aidan Donnelly will pay. And Valentina will get the burial she deserves.

That was important to her family. They were religious enough to go to church just about every day. Valentina believed in God, heaven, hell. The whole deal. Wall had never been able to credit that stuff. He was never going to be reunited with Valentina. It was important to him, though, that he honoured his wife's beliefs.

When they went inside, William "Dinky" Talbot appeared at the top of the stairs. He was one of the better men that Wall had met inside.

"My man." Dinky took the stairs two-at-a-time and threw his arms around Wall. "Alright, Brick? I saw it on the news. It worked."

"Don't call me that," Wall said, disentangling himself. "That was prison bullshit."

"Sorry, man. You got it." Dinky grinned. "We've got food, we've got beer, we've got weapons. This place is like a holiday camp." Wall glared at him. Dinky said, "Sorry, man. I didn't mean it like that. I'm just glad to see you. You look different without the beard."

They followed Dinky into the kitchen.

"I set up a dart board for you," he said, gesturing to the back of the kitchen door. Three photos were pinned to the board. On the outer circle, there was a photo of Judge Roberts, who'd told a jury to acquit Donnelly. Wall stepped closer, staring at the man's solemn face.

"The learned judge erred," Wall whispered.

Closer to the centre of the dart board was a photo of Detective Sergeant Joe Byrne. Wall poked Byrne's eyes out with his fingers.

And right in the centre of the board was Aidan Donnelly.

The photo was taken outside the Criminal Courts, right after the acquittal. Donnelly wore a black and grey tracksuit. Unshaven, he ran towards a taxi. That scumbag had made a mockery of them all.

"The sham justice system," Wall said, touching the dartboard.

"Everyone is here," Dinky said.

"Not the barrister," Wall said. He hadn't forgotten that prick, Costello.

Ken said, "How do you feel?"

Wall looked into the sitting room, peered at the two couches and TV, and continued down the hall.

"Impatient."

"No, I mean, about those lads from the prison?" Ken followed him. "You don't feel bad?"

Wall turned. "Why should I feel bad?"

"Not saying you should. But they're dead."

"It wasn't any great loss. Handsome liked to rape girls in his taxi. Buzz was an absolute nutjob. And Leech stole his own mother's pension for three years. He broke her collar bone when she tried to stop him. That's why he was in prison."

"But taking a life…"

Wall shrugged. "They deserved it. Simple as that."

Handsome had been a friend to him in prison, but Buzz was an asshole. And he hardly knew Leech at all. He didn't even remember the man's face.

"Everyone dies," Wall said. "It's just a matter of when."

Before Valentina was taken from him, Wall would never have been able to kill three men in cold blood, would never even have been able to contemplate such a thing. He wasn't a bastard like some men, like his father, who used to discipline the young Barry and Ken by wrapping them up in a rug and beating them with a plank of wood. When he was really mad, he'd roll them down the hill at the back of their garden. They'd lived in a farmhouse at that time, and there had been a rocky stream at the end of the garden. It was a six-foot drop from the garden level. Sometimes Wall still thought of that moment of terror, when he rolled off the last inch of grass and fell through the air, never knowing if he would dash his brains out on a rock (if the water level was shallow), or remain stuck in the rug and drown (if the river was full). It was a miracle he'd even survived.

But that was ancient history. These days, Wall rarely thought of anything except Valentina, and whatever it was that had happened to her.

"I'm going to make some food," Ken said. "Any special request, Barry?"

"No," Wall said flatly.

He was thinking of Valentina, not food.

He remembered coming home that day. The upside-down clock, mocking him from the mantlepiece. The upside-down fruit bowl in the kitchen.

And the fingers.

The fingers.

Wall followed Ken back to the kitchen. While Ken heated oil in a frying pan, Wall slumped in a chair to wait for darkness.

CHAPTER 38

Joe and Dunne headed back towards Donnybrook after leaving the scene of the fire. Along the way, Joe spotted a McDonald's. His stomach rumbled loud enough for Dunne to hear.

"Let's grab a burger," she said with a smile.

They went inside and loaded up on hamburgers and chips. The restaurant was cool and quiet. A reassuringly typical McDonald's.

Joe felt better thinking there was a chance that a very dangerous man was no longer on the loose. O'Carroll had certainly sounded pleased when Joe told him.

"This isn't exactly the restaurant I planned to show you," Joe said between mouthfuls.

"Don't worry about it. You can show me that place another time."

"Will do."

"So, you have to hurry home to your son?"

Joe washed down some chips with a mouthful of Coke. She was right. He'd have to get to Lisa's house soon.

"It's not my home. He lives with my ex. Like I said, I'm not with her."

"When did you split up?"

"Nearly seventeen years ago."

"Wow," Dunne said. "How old is your son?"

"Sixteen."

"So you left her as soon as she got pregnant?"

Joe snorted. "You ask a lot of questions, you know? Offensive ones."

"You don't seem like the type to take offence easily." Dunne grinned. "What age are you? You can lie if you like."

"Thirty-five. You? Since you seem so comfortable asking me personal questions."

"Twenty-seven."

Joe nodded. "I remember being that age."

"How was it?"

Joe shrugged. "For me, not great. But young enough that you don't think about lying."

According to his watch, it was well after eight, but the sky was still bright. That had fooled him into thinking it was earlier.

"Where are you living?" he asked.

Dunne finished her burger and dabbed her lips before replying. "I'm crashing at my friend's place at the moment. It's so hard to find a place to live in Dublin. Rent is crazy."

"Where does your friend live?"

"Ranelagh."

"That's handy. Not too far from the station."

"Yeah. Where are you based?"

"Rathmines. That's pretty close to Ranelagh."

"I know where it is. Maybe we'll see more of each other."

"Maybe. At the local take-away." Joe wiped his hands again. He was eager to get moving. Lisa was going to be furious. "Ready to go?"

Dunne finished her drink. "Yeah. Thanks for dinner. I owe you."

They left the restaurant and headed back to the car.

"I can get a taxi," Dunne said. "If this is taking you out of your way."

"No. It isn't."

On the way to Ranelagh, Dunne told him a little about her time being stationed in Cork. It had been in her home county, but far from the town where she grew up. That was just how it was. The force transferred you all over the damn country. Everywhere except where you were from. O'Carroll had worked some magic to get Joe in Donnybrook, and Joe was starting to wonder if he should feel grateful. Getting to know Christopher had been good.

"This is me," Dunne said, pointing to a terraced house just off the main street. Joe pulled over right outside her door.

"See you tomorrow," he said.

She got out, gave a wave, and closed the passenger door. Joe set off for Lisa's place, bracing himself because he was very late.

CHAPTER 39

Detective Garda Alice Dunne stood on the footpath and watched as Joe Byrne's car disappeared from view. It had been fun to meet him. She thought he was more handsome in real life than in the photos she'd seen in the media. She liked the way his suit fitted him, liked the look in the blue pools of his eyes.

Interesting that he had a kid and an ex. Of course, he didn't seem like the father type. What a nightmare it must be to have children. Dunne certainly wouldn't have been interested in raising one.

When Joe's car had gone, she took out her phone and dialled a number. A man answered. She listened while he spoke.

"Of course not," Dunne replied. "He didn't suspect a thing."

Dunne listened for a few more seconds. She ended the call, then glanced up at the house that Joe had dropped her outside. It was a nice building. Dunne wondered who lived there.

She turned and started walking down the road to her own apartment, which was a ten-minute walk away.

CHAPTER 40

Joe eased the Honda onto Belmont Avenue. For these mature red-bricks, property prices started in the seven figures, which was about six figures more than he could afford. Lisa's parents owned the O'Malley's chain of souvenir shops, but Joe reckoned that she didn't need help buying the house. Over the years he'd Googled her more often than was healthy. She'd been good at computers when they met, and Joe wasn't surprised to see her emerge as a successful web developer. She had a freelance business but also helped out her folks at O'Malley's.

Anyone who had walked around Dublin city centre in the last twenty years had probably passed a dozen branches of O'Malley's, and they'd have known all about it too. The shops were hard to miss, what with the fluorescent green leprechauns screaming from the window display, and traditional Irish music blaring from the speakers. Tourists seemed to like it.

As Joe parked at the curb outside Lisa's house, he noticed a handyman standing on a stepladder, trimming the garden hedge. The man turned his head as Joe approached. He looked to be a few years older than Joe, pushing forty and with a slightly flabby face and a belly that strained tight against his pink polo shirt.

"How much are you being paid?" Joe asked.

The guy squinted at him, the evening sun in his eyes.

"What?"

He was doing a terrible job. Just terrible.

"Whatever Lisa's paying you, it's too much."

"She's not paying me anything," the man said. "I offered to help."

"Yeah, right."

He watched as Joe walked up the driveway. The door stood open, the wire from an extension lead disappearing down the hall. Joe rapped his knuckle against the doorframe. Down the hall in the kitchen, Lisa stuck her head out.

"Come in," she said after a moment.

Joe walked down the hall, past pictures of Lisa and Christopher.

There was a painting on the wall too, one Joe hadn't seen before. An original work, by the look of it. He wondered if Christopher had done it. He figured only a mother would want to hang up such an eyesore.

"Hey," Joe said as he entered the kitchen.

"Give me a minute," Lisa said, typing furiously on her laptop.

He took a seat beside her at the kitchen table. Lisa guided a loose strand of hair over her left ear and continued working.

When they'd first met in the college library, she'd worn her hair longer. Now, it only came to the top of her shoulders, and it was curly. Joe preferred the old look. At least she hadn't dyed it, though she'd said a few times that she was sick of her natural toffee colour.

Joe was still getting used to the fact that she was back in his life. Still trying to balance out the mixture of hope and resentment. The last few months had been weird. The awful fallout from messing up the Aidan Donnelly case, the abject failure to find Valentina López Vázquez's body. But there had also been the gradual acceptance of the idea that he had a son. There had been the tentative encounters with Lisa, who still seemed to make a point of keeping her distance.

A streamer hung over the window.

HAPPY SIXTEENTH BIRTHDAY!

A pleasant aroma hung in the air, like she'd made Christopher's birthday cake herself. If Joe hadn't eaten, he'd be drooling.

He said, "Something smells delicious."

"It's all gone."

"Are you kidding me? Nobody ever finishes a birthday cake on the day of the birthday."

"Yeah, well, you're two and a half hours late. I guess you forgot the candles?"

Joe winced. He'd completely forgotten her text message. And he hadn't got Christopher a present yet either.

"I'm sorry, but it's not my fault."

"It never is."

Lisa slammed her laptop shut and turned her icy gaze on him at full blast. The temperature in the room dropped by about ten degrees.

Joe poked his thumb towards the front garden. "Where did you find that idiot, by the way? He's making a mess of your hedge."

"Graham? He lives just down the road. Haven't you seen him before?"

Joe searched his memory banks. Maybe he had seen him, but he didn't remember.

"I'm not sure."

"Graham Lee? I think I told you about him before." Lisa lowered her voice. "His wife left him last year. Remember? I told you she just walked out the door one day and left him. He was very upset."

The story sounded vaguely familiar.

He said, "All I know is, you should find someone who can actually use a hedge trimmer."

An indignant voice came from behind.

"I know how to use it just fine."

Graham lumbered into the kitchen. It was his belly that Joe noticed first, at eye level. Then his sweaty pink face.

He leaned down next to Lisa and kissed her cheek. She turned away.

Joe was on his feet at once.

His chair banged back against the fridge.

"What do you think you're doing?" Joe said.

He gave Graham a shove, and the other man returned it.

"What do *you* think you're doing?" Graham said.

Joe slammed him back against the fridge.

Then Lisa was beside him. Her hands were on Joe's shoulder. "Joe, stop it!"

"Give me one reason I shouldn't beat the living shit out of this asshole. You think you can just go around forcing yourself on women, huh, Graham?"

Joe was just about choking with rage.

"We're dating," Graham hissed. "She's my girlfriend."

"You wish."

"Joe, stop. It's – it's true," Lisa said.

"What?"

"Graham and I are going out."

"What?" Joe repeated, not quite believing what he'd heard.

"Seeing each other. Dating. You know."

Joe loosened his grip on Graham, who pushed Joe away. It was tempting to punch him, but Lisa's words had broken the spell. "You're *dating*? You're dating *him*?"

"Yeah. Graham and I have been seeing each other lately. I was going to tell you."

"Are you crazy?"

"What do you mean?" She put her hands on her hips. "It's not like it's any of your business. You think I should run my dating choices past you? Maybe you could vet them at the station?"

"I didn't mean that. I just thought—"

"You had to be dragged here just to spend five minutes with Christopher."

"That's not true."

"And you didn't bother to come on time, despite me reminding you literally a dozen times."

"It's not like that." Joe had let his voice get too loud. He regretted it at once.

Lisa said, "Please don't shout at me."

"Yeah, Joe. Cool it," Graham said.

The handyman put an arm around Lisa.

"I don't believe this," Joe said.

He felt like he had to get out of there. But he'd only arrived, and he still hadn't seen Lisa's son. Their son. Whatever.

"Where's Christopher? What does he think of this?"

"Up in his room," Lisa said. "He kept asking when you'd get here."

"I was working. I'll explain that. Can I talk to him?"

"You can try."

"Make sure you knock on his door," Graham added.

Joe said, "Shut up, Graham."

He made his way out to the hall and started up the stairs. Graham and Lisa's voices carried up to him as he climbed the steps.

"That guy's a real jerk."

"He's just surprised."

"You saw how he assaulted me. I should sue the arse off him for that," Graham said. "But I wouldn't. It would be too much for Chris."

Sanctimonious prick.

At the top of the stairs, Joe headed down the hall on the right.

KEEP OUT, said the sign on the door.

He knocked.

"Christopher, it's me."

There was no reply, so he knocked again.

"Sorry I'm late. I got held up at work. Can I come in?"

Nothing. Only silence.

He reached for the knob, turning it slowly.

"I'm coming in."

Joe pushed the door open. For a second, he thought the room was empty. But then he saw Christopher was on the floor on the far side of his bed.

"What are you doing over there?" Joe asked.

When he stepped closer, he saw. Christopher was kneeling on the floor beside his bed, stuffing pills down his throat.

CHAPTER 41

Aidan Donnelly let himself walk slowly along the bank of the Grand Canal, enjoying being close to the gentle flow of the water. He watched mallards bobbing on the water's surface. Sometimes one of them would dive for food, submersing its head and leaving its hindquarters and legs pointing at the sky. Then it would resurface with a dignified expression on its beak and look around to see what it had missed. Aidan loved watching them.

His tracksuit was loose and his runners hung from his fingers, with his socks rolled up inside them. He was far from home. No one would ever know that he was walking barefoot along the canal. No one except strangers, the happy young ones lounging on the grass verge next to the canal, and the motorists passing by on the nearby road.

Aidan liked to go for long walks, ones which lasted two hours or more. If he went a day without taking one of these walks, he found it difficult to get to sleep.

More difficult.

As he got to the bridge at Dolphin's Barn, Aidan spotted a bare strip of grass where he could lie down. Many people were sitting on the canal's banks, enjoying the sun. Most were clustered in groups.

Aidan took a can of cider from his backpack and set it down on the grass. Then he took out his wildlife guide. He lay down, using the backpack as a pillow. His jumper inside the bag, useless on such a hot evening, gave Aidan some cushioning.

He had brought a few slices of stale bread for the swans. He'd give it to them when no one was looking. Even though his family would never know what he was up to, Aidan felt ashamed. His family were not swan-feeders or barefoot walkers.

They *would* have approved of, or at least understood, the can of cider. That, at least, was a bit more normal.

But what on earth was normal anymore?

It was shaping up to be another week without work. Before the Spanish lady went missing, Aidan had been busy from morning till night, painting, decorating, assembling flatpacks, fitting out homes. Now no one wanted to hire him. When he offered to do a paint job for half the going rate, there were no takers.

What was he supposed to do?

He rubbed his eyes and looked around.

Two girls sat nearby on a beach towel. One of them got up and walked off, leaving her friend alone for a moment. The girl's outfit was real vintage stuff: baggy, dark trousers and a loose white shirt, plus a waistcoat. It was like something Buster Keaton wore in old movies.

Aidan sat up.

"How are you?" he said.

The girl squinted at him. "Okay."

"You're a lovely-looking girl."

"Oh Jesus. Go away."

"What's wrong? I'm only trying to pay you a compliment. I mean I like your style. Your fashion sense. I wasn't making personal remarks."

"Please stop talking to me."

"I didn't mean any offence. I'm not trying to be an arse or anything."

The other girl came back and joined her friend. They exchanged a few words, glanced at Aidan, and began folding up their towel, preparing to leave.

"Ah, don't go," he said. He rubbed the centre of his upper lip, where the skin was beginning to irritate him. He'd started chewing his lip during the trial, and a round section of skin was now constantly regrowing and being chewed off. He said, "I hope you're not going because of me. I didn't mean any harm."

Neither girl replied.

When they were gone, Aidan's breathing got tight. He could feel a panic attack coming. His first of the day, thank God, but one was more than enough.

He started doing the breathing exercise, the thing the prison psychologist taught him. In and out, nice and slow. Stupid, really. He already knew how to breathe. He didn't need a psychologist to tell him. But it helped. And sometimes, if he did it enough, he felt like he might survive the attack.

CHAPTER 42

Over the previous months, Joe had got to know Christopher a little. Once he had processed the idea that he was a father, Joe had taken Christopher out for pizza a couple of times, and they'd gone to the cinema once. They'd begun to develop a rapport. But Joe never realised that he'd developed an attachment to Christopher until that moment in his son's bedroom, when he saw Christopher trying to end his own life.

There, surrounded by posters for bands Joe had never heard of, and video games Joe had never played, it hit Joe so hard it scared him silly.

Christopher had a bottle of mineral water in his hand and two packets of paracetamol open on the floor in front of him. He was stuffing pills into his mouth while trying to pour water in, frantically chewing and swallowing at the same time, his eyes wide as he stared at Joe.

Joe ran around the foot of the bed and grabbed Christopher by the scruff of the neck. It wasn't easy to drag him to his feet – he was a big boy – but Joe did it. He knocked the pills out of Christopher's hand and dragged him down the hall to the bathroom.

He kicked open the door and hurled Christopher at the toilet.

Christopher started to crawl away, but Joe wasn't about to let that happen. Dropping to his knees beside him, Joe stuffed his fingers down Christopher's throat until the teenager was coughing and spluttering and retching, and the contents of his stomach were spilling into the bowl.

When there was nothing more to come up, Joe collapsed back against the bathtub.

Footsteps pounded up the stairs.

"What's going on up there?" Lisa called.

"Cool it, Joe," Graham shouted.

Joe didn't answer.

He couldn't.

The cool ceramic of the bathtub pressed against his back. He focused on that as he caught his breath. When he looked up, tears were rolling down Christopher's face.

"You idiot," Joe said.

Then Lisa burst into the room.

*

The four of them sat around the kitchen table. A bare bulb hung overhead. Darkness had fallen all at once, like a light switch had just been flicked.

Lisa wanted to take Christopher to the Accident and Emergency Department at St. Vincent's, but Joe told her they'd be waiting all night to see a doctor.

They went back and forth about it. It was Lisa's choice. In the end she decided not to go.

They figured Christopher hadn't swallowed many pills, and those that had been swallowed had been quickly brought up. He told them he'd only taken a few by the time Joe found him. Joe went up to Christopher's room and counted the number that were missing from the packets. The boy was telling the truth.

"Why did you want to do that?" Joe asked when he came back downstairs.

It was baffling. The kid had his whole life ahead of him.

Christopher cried while he told them about the bullying, but Lisa cried even more. Her love for him was so strong, Joe could feel it radiating off her.

Joe didn't know why Graham was there. He looked bored. If the decision had been up to Joe, he would have kicked Graham out, but this wasn't his house. And Joe had seen three toothbrushes in the bathroom.

"What's that kid's name?" Joe said. "The bully?"

"John. John Kavanagh."

Joe was aware of another bully with that surname. He didn't know the man really, but there were rumours that his son was a real troublemaker. "I don't suppose his dad is a Garda here in Donnybrook?"

Christopher's eyes widened. "How did you know?"

"He's not your boss, is he?" Lisa said.

"No," Joe said. "No, he's not."

"Good."

"He's my boss's boss. Superintendent Michael Kavanagh."

Lisa shook her head. "Great. That's just what we need."

"His old man is supposed to be a nasty piece of work," Joe said. "Anyway, I'll talk to the kid."

"Please don't," Christopher said. "That will only make things worse."

"What are you talking about?"

Lisa sighed. "Joe, if you want to help, maybe you should just talk to the school principal. Leave the boy alone."

"Sure," Joe said. "I'll do that tomorrow. It won't be a problem, will it? I mean, the people at the school don't know me."

Christopher said, "I can tell them you're – I can vouch for you."

Lisa nodded. "If they still have doubts, they can call me."

"Okay," Joe said. He thought for a moment, then leaned forward in his chair. "Christopher, I think you need to talk to someone."

The boy looked horror-struck. "You mean a psychiatrist?"

"Maybe, but it doesn't have to be. I just mean some kind of professional."

Joe wasn't expecting Christopher to get some miracle cure. But maybe it would help for him to talk to someone about his feelings, someone trained to not pass judgement.

"I'm not crazy," Christopher said.

"Of course, you're not. I didn't mean that."

"And I didn't really want to die. I love you, Mum. I just – I felt so bad. I'm sorry."

Lisa hugged Christopher so tightly, it practically counted as assault. "Don't ever do that to me again. Promise me."

"I promise. I'm sorry."

"You're alright. That's the important thing."

Joe reached across the table and took Lisa's hand in his. Graham shot him daggers, but Joe didn't much care. Especially not when Lisa seemed glad of the support. He held out his other hand to Christopher, who took it tentatively.

"It's going to be alright," Joe said. "You're a teenager. You're full of hormones that will make you crazy. It happens to everyone and it's nothing to be ashamed of. It won't last forever."

"Joe's right," Lisa said. "And you should talk to someone. I'll find a doctor for you to see tomorrow."

"I'm not going to a shrink."

"You're going, and you're going tomorrow."

"Listen to your mother," Joe said.

Christopher hung his head, defeated.

Graham piped up. "Is seeing a shrink really going to do any good?"

"Why don't you piss off back to wherever you live?" Joe said. He turned back to Lisa. "Tell me he hasn't moved in."

"Our living arrangements are none of your business," Graham said.

"What do you do for a living, Graham?"

"I'm an artist."

"Of course you are."

"Oils." Graham smiled at Lisa. She tried to return the look. "Lisa lets me use the shed outside as a studio. I've always known I had a creative talent, but I was never able to develop it before. I didn't have the space to work. That's all changed now. I'm sure I'll start to sell some pictures soon. I can give you a tour of my work some time if you're interested."

"I'm not."

"Okay, fine. Not everyone appreciates art."

"Is that your picture hanging in the hall? The piece-of-shit portrait of a naked girl?"

Graham sighed and shook his head, as if answering Joe would be beneath him.

Joe squeezed Christopher's hand. Though it was time for him to leave, he didn't want to go. He had to force himself.

"I'll talk to you tomorrow, Christopher."

"Okay."

"I'll show you out," Graham said, as everyone rose from the table.

Joe felt a fresh stab of irritation.

"Show yourself out. I want a word with Lisa."

Lisa ruffled Christopher's hair. "You go on up to bed," she said. "I'll be up in a minute to say goodnight."

"Okay. Good night, Joe."

"Night, Christopher."

Graham pulled out a cigarette and a lighter and started for the back garden. It looked like he had no plans to go home. As he opened the back door, he smiled and waved Joe goodbye.

CHAPTER 43

Christopher plodded up the stairs and ducked into his bedroom, where he kicked off his runners. With all the stealth he could muster, he then sneaked back out onto the landing and hunkered down. The door to the kitchen was only open a crack and Christopher strained to hear what Joe and Mum were saying.

Mum had sent him to bed, saying she would be up to say goodnight. That hadn't happened since Christopher was ten, but he couldn't argue. He'd given her a scare. It was true what he'd said, though: he didn't want to die.

The realisation of the pain he had caused her gave him a fresh bout of anguish.

He wondered if they would throw him into a mental hospital. Would they feed him drugs to make him less suicidal? His imagination began to run wild, but he soon realised that Joe and Mum weren't talking about him at all. They were talking about some guy named Wall.

An escaped prisoner?

Christopher wondered if he'd heard correctly. What did an escaped prisoner have to do with them? Wait, was that Barry Wall? Christopher had heard of him.

"I'm sure you're not in any danger," Joe said. "But just take extra care. We have reason to believe that Wall has a grudge against various people, including me."

"How worried should I be?"

"You shouldn't be at all worried. Like I say, he may have been killed in the explosion. We need to wait for the DNA testing. Even if he's alive, I don't expect him to target you, but I just wanted to let you know."

Mum asked something about protection, which made Joe snort.

"Anyway, I should go," Joe said.

Christopher scooted up to the top of the stairs as Joe and Mum came out into the hall. He kept out of sight. Even without seeing it, Christopher could tell that the goodbye was awkward. He found it hard to picture them ever being a couple.

Once the door had closed, Christopher waited until Mum went into the sitting room. Then he sneaked back downstairs and made his way into the kitchen. A quick look out the window confirmed that Graham was still outside.

Christopher made his way over to the knife block. He was glad that Mum was so obsessed with quality. These knives were the sharpest ones Christopher had ever touched. There were five in the set, all different sizes. They had razor sharp blades and bright orange handles. He tried to figure out which one to take. The big one looked too large for his schoolbag, and the smallest one didn't look threatening enough.

Christopher took the middle-sized knife. He figured the blade was probably fifteen centimetres long. He hurried back upstairs with it, being careful not to trip and impale himself. That would really be too much for Mum.

He made his way back to his bedroom. Unzipping his schoolbag, he hid the knife inside his history book.

Christopher needed to protect himself. He wasn't going to let anyone bully him anymore, whether it was John Kavanagh or an escaped criminal. With a knife, he'd be able to defend himself.

He got into bed and lay there, waiting for Mum to kiss him goodnight.

CHAPTER 44

Joe's stomach churned as he walked to the end of Lisa's driveway. He hoped Christopher wouldn't do any other stupid stuff. Joe would talk to the principal in the morning and do whatever he had to in order to sort out the bullying situation.

But other things were playing on his mind too – like Barry Wall.

Joe had put him to one side while he dealt with Christopher. Now Wall came back into focus.

He got behind the wheel of his Honda and pointed the car towards home, which was a second-floor apartment in a big old house, just off the main street in Rathmines. Rathmines was more affordable than Donnybrook, and Joe had been lucky to find a place to live there the previous summer, when he had decided to stay in Dublin.

The building contained eight other units, but Joe met no one as he passed his bicycle in the hall, and made his way up the stairs to his door. His apartment was spartan. Joe had filled the bookshelf inside the door with some non-fiction paperbacks and put his aloe vera plant on top. That was about all he had done with the place since moving in. Not that there was a lot of room to do anything.

The place consisted of a small sitting room, leading through an open doorway to a kitchen. The bedroom was next to that. Joe had always been a lousy sleeper. At night, he often lay in bed listening to the hum of the fridge on the other side of the bedroom wall. For variety, he sometimes came out and sprawled on the couch in the sitting room, where he could bathe in the glow of the street light outside, as he waited for dawn.

Once Joe got inside, he stripped and showered. Under the hot water was where he did a lot of his best thinking, so he didn't rush. Afterwards, he towelled himself off, then slumped on the couch.

He opened up his laptop and typed Graham Lee's name into Google. He didn't find anything about Lisa's new boyfriend, as an artist or otherwise. No website. He wondered about Graham's history. Did he have a criminal record? Joe wanted to check. Technically, he was not supposed to use the Pulse database for personal reasons, but someone had to protect Lisa and Christopher. He decided to look into it the next day.

He closed the laptop and sat for a minute. If he went to bed, he knew he'd just lie awake thinking, after all that had happened during the day. It was pointless.

He thought about Barry Wall again.

If Wall had blown himself up, it would certainly make life a lot easier for Joe. But the optimism he'd felt when he rang O'Carroll and told him about the explosion had faded while he was at Lisa's house, and faded even more since he got home. Something about it just felt too neat.

Imagine if Wall was alive. What would he do? What would Joe do if he was Wall?

I'm fresh out of jail. The guy who killed my wife is out there. He's never explained what happened, never revealed where her body is. The cops think I'm dead so I have time...

Would he really go to the airport, like O'Carroll thought?

If it was Joe, he'd want to go and beat Aidan Donnelly fifty shades of purple. He'd want to find out what had really happened to Valentina.

Joe had been so busy during the day, his attention divided between Boyle, Barrett, Lisa, Christopher, and Wall, that this was the first time he'd managed to clear his head and think. The more he thought about it, the surer he felt that the explosion was a distraction. If that was the case, then Wall would want to use this time to accomplish his task: getting Aidan Donnelly and making him talk.

Joe grabbed his car keys, slipped his shoes on, and went out into the night. He still remembered where Aidan Donnelly lived.

He hoped he wasn't too late.

CHAPTER 45

Barry Wall stared out the windscreen of the Ford Transit van. Orange street lamps glowed along the narrow inner-city street. A block of flats loomed into view. It was an ugly place. Everything grey and cold and merciless. The place where a monster had been born. A killer. St. Stephen's Green was only a few minutes' walk away, but this was another world, far from the beautiful park and the luxury shopping of nearby Grafton Street.

Ken found a parking space and pulled in at the side of the road. Barry Wall oriented his gaze, looking up to the top floor, to the place where Aidan Donnelly lived.

Apartment 508.

Wall jumped out of the van. As he did so, two junkies were shambling down the footpath, a man and a woman.

"Got any change, bud?" the man said.

Ignoring him, Wall cracked his knuckles. His throat was dry. He was so close. An ambulance screamed past, sirens screeching, lights flashing.

Wall set off across the road.

"Wait," Ken called.

"Hurry up, then."

They bustled up the path, through a gap in the wall surrounding the complex, and headed towards the enclosed stairwell. It looked like a round tower stuck onto the side of the blocky building.

The stairwell smelled of piss and its walls were covered with graffiti. They passed a woman with two young kids, heading down the steps. She took a drag on her cigarette and looked at Wall out of colourless, dead eyes.

"We could have waited a little longer," Ken said nervously, once they were past the woman.

"I couldn't."

"We might be seen."

"You can go if you like. Wait in the van."

"I didn't mean that, Barry."

They emerged on the fifth-floor landing. 508 was down the end of a long balcony which looked out onto the street. Ken took up a position on the left side of the door, Wall stood directly in front of it.

Ken looked around one more time and gave his brother a nod.

Clear.

Wall kicked the door in. It was made of light wood and secured by a single flimsy lock. Wall's boot separated the metal from the wood.

He pushed the door open and went in fast.

Ken was right behind.

A sitting room lay inside the door, with a kitchen off to the side. Both areas were empty. At the back, two more doors. Both of them closed. A bedroom and a bathroom, Wall figured.

He stepped forward quickly, moving towards the room on the left first. The door opened when Wall pushed it. He found himself almost on top of a squalid-looking toilet. A shower stall stood next to it. No sign of Aidan Donnelly.

He backed out. Together, he and Ken approached the other door.

Twitching with adrenaline, Wall kicked open the door of the final room. The only possible place Donnelly could be hiding. The door swung in to reveal an empty bedroom.

Ken said, "He's not home."

"Shit," Wall shouted, looking around, as if Donnelly might be hiding somewhere. He dropped to his knees and looked under the bed. Nothing there but dust. "Where is he?"

"We'll get him later," Ken said.

"No."

"We have to."

"We can wait here for him."

"No," Ken said. "We can't. Someone will notice the damage to the front door. And if Aidan Donnelly comes home and sees that, he's not going to come inside. He'll walk away."

Wall knew that was true, but he had psyched himself up to see Valentina's killer and he wanted to do it now.

"Come on," Ken urged. "We'll get him. I swear we will. Just not now."

Wall walked around the sitting room, looking for any clue about where Donnelly might be. There was nothing. Ken grabbed his arm.

"Okay, okay," Wall said.

He let himself be dragged back out. Ken shut the door behind them, while Wall stepped over to the balcony and scanned the street below, hoping Donnelly would appear.

"Barry? Come on. Let's get out of here."

Wall jogged to the stairwell and started down the steps after Ken. At the bottom, Ken stopped and pressed himself against the side wall.

A Honda was slowing down near a parking space four spaces up from Ken's van, on the other side of the road.

"What is it?" Wall asked.

Ken held his brother back with an outstretched arm.

"Cops."

"What?"

"Joe Byrne."

Wall stepped forward. "I thought he wasn't supposed to be here."

"Well, he is." Ken scowled.

"Let's take him."

"Are you crazy? That's not the plan."

"I don't care about the plan."

"We need to get him alone. There might be more of them around."

Wall was irritated by his brother's lack of enthusiasm. "I don't see anyone."

"His partner might be getting coffee. We need to go, while he's distracted," Ken said.

They sprinted past the low wall, out onto the footpath and over to the van. Wall pressed himself against the van and waited to see if they'd been seen. There was no shouting. No running. Nothing.

Ken unlocked the van. He got in and watched to make sure his brother did too. Wall got in, but he didn't fasten his seat belt.

"We could take him," Wall said again.

Ken shook his head. "He doesn't know you're alive."

"Then why is he here?"

"He's just suspicious. We don't want to confirm it for him. We still have time to get Donnelly, while we're under the radar, right?"

"*Are* we under the radar?" Wall gritted his teeth. "Check with your contact."

Ken took out his phone and dialled the number. Wall listened as his brother and the contact exchanged a few words. Ken hung up. "It's like I thought. The cops all think you're dead. Byrne is off-duty."

"What a bastard."

Ken started the engine. "We'll get him later. We'll get both of them later."

Wall nodded.

"That's for sure," he said.

CHAPTER 46

Detective Sergeant Kevin Boyle arrived home late. He could smell the shit as soon as he opened the door to his ground-floor apartment. He groaned as he stepped inside. This wasn't the kind of greeting he liked.

"Babe?" he called.

Boyle's golden retriever was sixteen years old and even sicker than he was. Sometimes she couldn't hold off until Boyle came home. On those occasions, she tended to let loose on the rug in the sitting room. Thankfully it didn't happen very often, and when it did occur, Boyle thought Babe felt worse about it than he did. She looked mournful for hours.

"That's all I need," Boyle muttered, stepping inside. "I should have got a rat. Shouldn't I, Babe?"

No answer.

He stepped into the kitchen and set down his bag of groceries on the counter.

Boyle had moved here after his bout of pneumonia the previous year. His last flat had required him to climb four flights of stairs. He was weak and the damn steps had nearly killed him. He was also in debt, and he suspected things were going to get worse. So a cheap flat on the ground floor suited him.

Around the time he moved here, the doctors had finally diagnosed him with vasculitis. That his blood vessels were inflamed went some way to explaining why he was so tired all the time, why he had a rash, and joint pain, not to mention all the other health issues he'd suffered lately, which had probably been caused or exacerbated by his condition. The corticosteroids the doctors put him on had helped a bit, but Boyle had spent a fortune trying to recover his health, and he still felt like crap a lot of the time.

Boyle walked into the sitting room.

"Babe?"

She was in the sitting room, like Boyle expected, lying on the floor with her back to him. A pile of faeces sat on the rug in front of the TV.

The dog wasn't moving, and Boyle had the terrifying thought that she was dead.

Murdered.

"Babe," he shouted.

The dog lifted her head, pricking up her ears and looking around, trying to determine where the sound had come from. When she caught sight of Boyle, she struggled to her feet on arthritic legs, wagging her tail.

Boyle breathed a sigh of relief.

The stupid dog was getting deaf as well as incontinent. He hunkered down and hugged her to him.

"You had me worried, girl."

Babe wagged her tail and licked Boyle's face. He stroked her under the chin, so happy she was alright that for a moment he forgot that he was meant to be mad at her. He pointed a finger at the pile of dirt on the rug.

"Who did that?"

Babe flattened her ears to her head and looked up at Boyle with big sad eyes. He couldn't stay mad at her when she gave him those eyes.

"Alright, alright. Never mind who did it."

He patted her on the head.

Boyle wasn't supposed to have a pet here, but his girlfriend had dumped him when the steroids made him gain weight, and he was damned if he was going to live without his dog as well as his partner.

He got to his feet as his phone started to ring. Boyle swallowed when he saw the number displayed on the screen.

Ger Barrett.

He hit the green button and held the phone to his ear. The voice on the other end of the line was cold and business-like.

"You picked the wrong man to screw over."

"I didn't. It wasn't—"

"You think you can take my money and then turn on me when it suits you?"

"No, it was Byrne. He was acting alone. I didn't know."

"You've made your bed. Now you're going to sleep in it."

The line went dead.

CHAPTER 47

The next morning, Joe set a big pot of coffee brewing while he took a shower.

At six thirty, he'd woken up in the Honda with a sore back and a sour taste in his mouth. He'd driven home, feeling like he'd wasted the night. It had been uneventful. Joe had watched Aidan Donnelly's building for hours. There was nothing to see. Nothing at all. He'd been tempted to go up to Donnelly's flat and warn him that he was in danger, but O'Carroll had told Joe not to go anywhere near Donnelly, and that was a reasonable request, given their history.

When Joe stepped out of the shower, the smell of coffee from the kitchen cheered him up. He found a fresh shirt and a clean pair of trousers, and left them on the bed.

There was half a quiche in the fridge. Ham, cheddar, leek. Joe polished it off while he drank his first coffee.

Once he'd poured his second cup, he gave Christopher a call. He wanted to catch him before he left for school. Christopher answered after two rings.

"Hi Joe."

"You okay? How are you feeling?"

"Fine."

"Were you able to sleep last night?"

"It took a while. Mum kept checking on me. Asking me if I was dizzy or felt sick or whatever. I thought she'd keep me awake all night but eventually I drifted off."

"Good." Joe smiled. That sounded just like Lisa. "I'll talk to your principal today."

"You probably need to make an appointment. He's always busy. He might not have time to see you."

"Don't worry about that. He'll find time for me."

"I should go. I didn't get my history homework done last night because of... you know, everything. I'm trying to finish it now, but it's really not my best subject."

"You don't like history?"

"I prefer music."

"Maybe I could give you a hand with that some time. Did your mother ever tell you I'm a history buff?"

"No. She never mentions you."

"Oh. Well, anyway I can help you sometime if you like. I better let you go. Just avoid that boy for the moment."

"I always avoid him."

Joe ended the call and returned to his coffee. He replayed the conversation in his mind.

She never mentions you.

He realised he still had the tickets he'd planned to give to Lisa the previous evening. What a stupid idea that had been. He tore them up and dropped them in the bin on his way out the door.

*

Joe found Anne-Marie Cunningham at her desk in Donnybrook Garda Station. Kevin Boyle was at his. Boyle glanced at Joe but said nothing. If he was worried about yesterday's fiasco, he was doing a good job of hiding it. And he ought to be worried. Joe planned to get him.

Joe tried to focus on the Barry Wall case, which had taken precedence over everything else.

They still didn't have any definitive identification of the men killed in the explosion.

Joe rang the Technical Bureau to remind them he was waiting for the DNA test results, but they already knew that. Someone was always waiting for results, and it was always urgent.

Joe figured everyone hoped the test would come back positive, telling them that some of the remains at the site of the explosion belonged to Wall. Case closed. Onto the next. It would be nice and easy that way.

And as the morning went on, Joe became more and more convinced that it wouldn't work out like that.

He spent some time revisiting his original case notes. Once he was done with that, he decided to take a field trip. If anyone who knew where Barry Wall would be, Joe figured it would be Wall's brother or the former prisoners Wall had come into contact with. O'Carroll already had a couple of uniforms trying to contact the recently released prisoners, so Joe decided to pay Ken Wall a visit. At this time of day, he figured Ken would be at work.

Dunne appeared at the door just as Joe was throwing on his jacket. She wore a navy trouser suit today, with a pale grey blouse. Her hair was straight like a ruler. Her eyes looked more green than hazel today.

"Mind if I tag along?" she said.

Joe didn't mind at all.

*

Ken Wall's company had an office in the city centre. Joe parked in front of a gleaming sign saying *WK Partners*. It was a small office, set on the corner of a busy street.

"What are they?" Dunne said. "Estate agents?"

Joe nodded. "Lettings, sales, all kinds of stuff."

The windows were spotless, all the better to show off the cards displaying properties for sale.

"Ken must know of some vacant properties. Places where his brother might hide."

Joe turned to Dunne.

"You're almost as cynical as me."

"I'm sure I'm worse."

Grinning, Joe got out of the car and crossed the footpath. Dunne followed as he pushed through the gleaming glass door. The only person he could see was a receptionist, a pink-haired girl with pink nails and pink lipstick.

In his experience, estate agents usually had big, spacious places, painted white and decked out with lots of expensive computers. There were usually plenty of chairs for potential buyers to sit and chat. There was a welcoming, informal atmosphere.

Not here.

The room was stubby and bare. The only place to sit was a leather couch positioned in front of the desk where the punk sat playing with her phone. Joe walked up to the desk.

"Can I help you?" she said.

From her manner, Joe took it she'd never had any customer service training.

"Is Mr. Wall here?"

"No."

"Good," Joe said.

He showed her his ID. Her eyes widened. Her grip on her phone slackened, but she didn't put it down.

"Oh my god, yeah. I read about his brother on the news." She lowered her voice. "Did you find him yet?"

"Not yet. What's your name?"

"Clarissa."

"Clarissa, do you know Barry, Ken's brother?"

"No, I've never met him."

Dunne said, "How is Ken Wall as a boss?"

Clarissa blinked. "I haven't worked here very long. Only a month. He's okay, I guess. Wears too much aftershave."

Joe nodded.

"Was Ken here yesterday afternoon, say from 3pm to 5pm?"

"Yeah. I remember he went out and grabbed a bagel for lunch. He actually bought me one too, which was kind of nice. Then he stayed in his office for the rest of the afternoon. He had a conference call with a client."

"Do you know who that was?" Dunne asked.

Clarissa tapped away on her keyboard.

"Give me a second.... No," she said at last. "His diary doesn't list a name."

Joe said, "Okay. And when did you see Ken again?"

"I guess he was still on the call when I left? I finish at five, but Ken is often here later. He comes and goes a lot."

"I wonder if you'd be able to give us a list of properties you're handling?"

"Sure. I mean, most of them are on the window and on our website."

She pointed a pink fingernail at the displays.

"What about unlisted properties? New ones maybe?"

"I can get a printout—"

A door swung open behind Clarissa. Joe recognised Ken Wall right away. He'd last seen him in court. Ken wore a crisp green shirt and tight pants. Joe had never seen such shiny shoes as the pointy-toed black leather ones that he was wearing.

"What's this?" Ken said,

His voice was clipped, authoritative, and surprisingly deep for a man who stood an inch shorter than Joe.

Clarissa said, "These are officers – I was – they're from—"

"Thank you," he said. "I'm surprised you're still on the force, Joe."

"How's Barry doing?"

"I haven't heard anything from him."

"Sure. I was asking Clarissa if she could give us a list of all your properties."

Ken smiled. "Do you really think I'm concealing a fugitive in a company property? That wouldn't be very smart."

"People have done stupider things," Joe observed.

"They certainly have. Like botching murder investigations."

Joe let that one go. Ken looked preoccupied, like something important was on his mind. Joe deliberately slowed his speech to annoy him a little.

"So help us out," he said. "Give us a list."

"It would be of no use to you. And it's commercially sensitive information. Now, I'm busy, so if you'll excuse me."

"Do you have somewhere to be?"

"I have work to do," Ken said. "You should try it sometime."

Joe smiled. "Thank you for your time."

Ken glared at them, then disappeared through the doorway.

They stepped outside.

"Well, that was fun," Dunne said.

She headed for the Honda, but Joe walked down the road and around the corner.

"What are you doing?" Dunne called.

"Clarissa said Ken wasn't in the office." Joe peeked around the corner, then joined Dunne at the car. "The office has a side door. Looks like it leads to a back office. I guess Ken can go in and out as he pleases without Clarissa noticing."

"Huh," she said. "That's pretty handy if you want to go visit your brother on company time."

"My thoughts precisely. And it means his alibi is worthless."

CHAPTER 48

Barry Wall made his way up the driveway to the bright blue door of the huge house called Glenavogue, where Mr. Justice Paul Roberts lived with his wife Maria.

There was something imposing about a house that had its own name, rather than a number. Especially when the name was as portentous as Glenavogue, which was engraved on an oval of ceramic next to the door.

Wall looked up at the white stucco house with its bay windows, and at the freshly cut grass, fringed by lilacs, on both sides of the garden. It was nice, very nice. The spoils of the sham justice system.

Ken had had an encounter with Joe Byrne an hour earlier. He said he was fine, though he looked a little shaken. Ken stayed at the front, while Wall went around the back, followed by Dinky Talbot. The back garden was lovely. It had a little fountain, surrounded by a rockery, and a wooden bench lay at the end of the garden, next to an apple tree.

And, at one side of the garden, there was a thriving lavender plant, with bees buzzing around it. It was exactly like the one Valentina had planted in their garden. Wall stared at it. He had to tear himself away.

He went up to the back door and looked through the glass. No one seemed to be home, not on the ground floor anyway. He saw no movement.

Taking a step back, and looking up, Wall squinted at the box mounted to the wall, emblazoned with the name of a security company.

"Do you know them?" he said, turning to Dinky.

The man looked at the box and smiled. "Indeed I do."

"How long will it take to get around it?"

"About a second."

Dinky picked up a stone from the rockery, and threw it through the glass of the door.

Wall braced himself but there was nothing. No shrill siren. No phone call from an alarm company.

"It's a bluff," Dinky said. "The box is empty. More popular than you'd think, especially with cheapskates."

Wall couldn't believe that the judge used a dummy alarm. He, of all people, should have been aware of the risks. Judge Roberts must have thought no one would dare break into the home of someone of his status.

Wall reached through the broken window. He unlocked the door with a turn of the key on the inside.

"See?" Dinky said. "Easy."

Wall stepped inside. Dinky walked down the hall to let Ken in the front door, his steps sounding heavily on the wooden floor.

"Is no one here?" Ken said.

A wisp of steam rose from a half-filled electric kettle. A cup sat on the counter next to the kettle. There was a tea bag in it, which was brewing. Wall touched the cup, found it hot.

"I don't think he'll be long."

"Let's have a look around," Ken said, heading upstairs.

Wall walked around the ground floor in a slow circle, beginning in the sitting room and examining each room as he went.

Photos of Paul and Maria Roberts were scattered around the tables and sideboards of the room, often pictured with what appeared to be their adult children, and their grandkids.

Dinky drew back his foot, the kicked out at a huge TV. The screen shattered and the TV fell onto the hardwood floor. Dinky took off up the stairs after Ken.

Wall continued to explore the ground floor. He paused in the sitting room to look at the ruined TV. He was about to head upstairs too when the front door opened. The door to the hall was closed, so he listened. He waited as the steps went up the hall to the kitchen. Then Wall went back the way he had come, through the dining room.

Mr. Justice Paul Roberts was peering at a newspaper, which he had laid out on the kitchen table next to a gourmet sandwich that could have fed half of Mountjoy Prison's population.

"You can afford a decent security system," Wall said, stepping through the doorway into the kitchen. "You really should have got one."

The judge's body jerked in surprise. He turned around, his eyes narrowing as he recognised Wall.

"What are you doing here? How dare you? Get out!"

Wall took a step towards him. "The learned judge forgets himself."

Roberts peered over his glasses.

"Mr. Wall, what do you—"

"I said you forget yourself, asshole. You're not in court anymore."

"I thought you were dead."

"You thought wrong. It wouldn't be the first time. But it *will* be the last."

The judge turned, but his escape route to the front door was blocked. Ken and Dinky blocked that route.

"I'm not going to be intimidated," the judge said, standing straighter and looking Wall in the eye.

Wall stepped closer, the wooden floor groaning beneath him with every step. He walked into the older man's personal space. The judge's eyes were level with Wall's chest. Wall took another step, until he could smell the judge's sour breath. Wall lowered his massive head until his mouth was next to the judge's ear, until the hairs on the older man's ears tickled his lips.

"You will be."

Wall smashed his fist into the judge's stomach. It was a monster blow, a devastating car crash of an impact. A single blow would have been enough, but Wall hit him three times, rapidly, with all the strength of his left arm, which was his weaker arm. The last blow was greeted by a crunch of bone – the ribcage shattering.

The judge collapsed on the floor.

Ignoring Dinky's laughter, Wall stepped closer to the pathetic form on the floor beneath him.

The judge tried to speak. Wall didn't feel like listening.

He unleashed a kick that damn near took the judge's head off. The click of teeth on teeth, a drip of blood down his chin. Then Wall stomped on the judge's head until there was no need to check his pulse.

CHAPTER 49

Joe and Dunne grabbed lunch on the way back to the station. It was just sandwiches, which they picked up in a shop. Joe still hadn't taken Dunne to the Chinese restaurant. This time Dunne paid.

They ate in the car, parked outside the station. Dunne's eyes again seemed to be a different colour. The hazel had changed to brown. She told Joe a little more about her career. Some of the drug cases she'd been involved in. She said she was glad to be in Dublin, that her previous boss in Cork had an unhealthy interest in her.

"Did you report him?"

Dunne shook her head. "I took care of it myself. I made my feelings known and he got the message."

Joe didn't want to push her, so he left it at that.

After eating, they headed inside. Dunne made for the toilet. Joe went up to the incident room. O'Carroll had scheduled a meeting for 1:30 pm to discuss the case. This time, he was leading the investigation himself as the Senior Investigating Officer.

Joe wondered if he'd ever be given a chance to lead an investigation again, after what had happened with Aidan Donnelly.

He made his way to the back of the room and poured his third cup of coffee of the day. The position gave him a good vantage point to survey his colleagues. There were fifteen of them packet into the room. Annie-Marie Cunningham and Kevin Boyle were conniving on one side. O'Carroll was speaking with some uniformed officers by the white board. Their voices were hushed.

Dunne came into the room a moment later. Joe brought his coffee over to a seat at the back of the room. He rested his hand on the seat next to him, saving it for Dunne. She walked up to O'Carroll and they shook hands. As everyone else took their seats, O'Carroll turned to address the room.

"Alright, first of all, if you haven't met her yet, please welcome Detective Garda Alice Dunne, who's just been transferred here from Cobh, County Cork. Alice has worked on a number of serious crimes, particularly drug cases. Alice, welcome to Donnybrook."

A round of applause broke out.

Dunne nodded. "Thank you very much, Detective Inspector O'Carroll."

She glanced around the room. Her eyes ran over Joe briefly, but they didn't linger on him.

O'Carroll said, "Please call me David. Now, have a seat and let's see where we are with this thing."

Dunne didn't look Joe's way. She lowered herself into the seat next to Boyle.

Joe watched in amazement as Boyle leaned over and whispered something in her ear. Dunne laughed like it was the funniest thing she'd ever heard.

"Joe," O'Carroll said. "Would you mind bringing everyone up to speed?"

After clearing his throat, Joe made his way to the front of the room, and summarised what they knew about Barry Wall's escape. O'Carroll stood at the side of the room, watching.

O'Carroll nodded enthusiastically when Joe got to the bit about the bomb. "So we might have caught a lucky break."

Joe took a breath and prepared to disappoint him.

"I think he's alive," Joe said.

O'Carroll gave him a look like he'd just been handed a turd pie.

"What was that?"

"I've thought about this a bit more, and I think it's unlikely that Wall is dead."

O'Carroll crossed his arms. "That's not what you said last night. We have witnesses placing Wall in the vehicle that exploded."

"Yes, but nothing conclusive. Upon further reflection, I think this might have been part of his plan. He's too smart to blow himself up minutes after escaping from custody. The bomb was waiting for him on the outside. His accomplices must have prepared it for him."

"That doesn't change anything," O'Carroll said. "So what really happened? A lookalike coincidentally got blown up in the same area?"

"No coincidence," Joe said. "It was a diversion. Or a way to get rid of the guys who broke him out.

Or both. I think we need to be watching Aidan Donnelly. I think Wall faked his own death so he'd be free to go after him."

"Alright," O'Carroll said. "That's one theory. Take a seat." His brow furrowed with thought. "So if it was a diversion, he would have got to Donnelly by now?"

"Yes," Joe said.

O'Carroll looked around the room.

"Where is Donnelly? Anne-Marie?"

Cunningham cleared her throat. "I tried to contact him this morning, but he didn't answer his phone."

"Okay," O'Carroll said. "Locate Aidan Donnelly immediately. And keep me posted."

Cunningham nodded and touched her hearing aid. When stressed, Joe had noticed that she did this more often.

O'Carroll said, "Joe, I want you and Alice at the airport. If you're right about Barry Wall being alive, then I don't want him to escape the jurisdiction."

"He's not going to run for it."

O'Carroll ignored Joe. He said, "I have a feeling Wall is going to try to get to Spain. Right out in the open. This guy thinks he's smarter than we are. That arrogance makes him brazen."

"I don't think so."

"Just fucking do it," O'Carroll snapped. "Excuse my French, Alice. I rarely have call for such foul language. Only Joe is able to bring it out."

Dunne smiled. "French duly excused."

O'Carroll strolled over to the desk and gestured to a pile of papers sitting there. "Alright, everyone, take a set of notes. I've assigned you all locations to watch, and provided photos of Barry Wall and some background notes on the case."

Once Joe had drained his coffee, he got up and took a sheaf of papers. He flicked through it, then turned to O'Carroll.

"Am I missing something? No one is assigned to watch Aidan Donnelly's home?"

"You heard what I said a minute ago. Anne-Marie is going to contact him, to warn him of the very unlikely event of Barry Wall targeting him. We certainly can't afford full surveillance."

Joe was about to argue when he sensed someone close by. He turned his head and saw Dunne. Sunlight from the window fell on her face, making her eyes glow like fish tanks.

"Ready to go?" she said.

"I am."

Joe walked out of the room, hurried downstairs and out the back door. Dunne followed close behind. He heard her legs working quickly as she struggled to keep up.

"Will we both use your car?" she said.

"No, you go ahead." Joe unlocked his Honda and pulled the door open. "I have something else to take care of."

"You heard O'Carroll's instructions."

"Which are bullshit," Joe said, getting in the driver's seat. "If Wall is alive, he's not going to the airport."

"You're sure he's after Donnelly?"

"Of course."

"Then I'll go with you."

Joe closed the door. He rolled down the window.

"You don't want to get into trouble. You might as well go to the airport, like O'Carroll said. I'll catch up with you later. Or you can hang around with your new friend, Kevin Boyle."

Dunne gave him an incredulous look.

"You sound jealous."

"Just watch yourself around him. He's dirty."

Dunne started to say something, but Joe was already accelerating. He pointed the Honda out of the car park and towards the inner city.

*

Once he got to Aidan Donnelly's building, where he'd spent the night, Joe parked in the same place, and sank down low in his seat. Just like last night, nothing seemed to be happening.

After an uneventful half hour, watching the block of flats, a knock on the window startled him. Alice Dunne was leaning over the front passenger window. Joe opened the door.

"Get in quick."

"Alright, alright."

She sat down and closed the door.

"Do you want to blow my cover?"

"Blow your cover? How could I blow your cover when no one knows who I am?"

"You're drawing attention to me."

"Well, you shouldn't have left me like that," Dunne said. "It was unprofessional."

Joe still felt annoyed that she had snubbed him in the incident room. He knew it was childish, and that made him feel even worse.

"So I'm not very professional. Stay away from me."

"You think you're a rebel, don't you?"

"I think I'm trying to get results."

"No, you imagine you're Bruce Willis or something."

Before Joe could reply, his phone rang. It was Lisa.

It was half three already. *Christopher.* Joe was meant to talk to the school principal today.

Dunne said, "Is that David?"

"No." Joe answered and pressed the phone to his ear. "Hello?"

"Joe?" Lisa said. "I didn't hear anything from you. I wanted to check how you got on at the school."

"I haven't got there yet."

There was a long pause before she spoke. "Why?"

"I was kind of busy."

"I truly thought you were going to do what you said this time." Lisa laughed bitterly. "God, I'm stupid."

"No, you're not. I'm going to do it."

"Do you even care? Have you forgotten last night? Do you remember our son trying to end his own life?"

"I remember, believe me. I'll go to the school now."

"Forget it. Christopher has probably left already. I hope he gets home safely."

"I'll catch up with him," Joe said, but Lisa had already ended the call. "Shit," he muttered. He turned to Dunne. "I guess you heard that."

Her face was blank. She said, "I guess I did."

"I have to go. You better go back to your car. I guess you'll have to make your own decision about whether to stay here or go to the airport."

Dunne got out of the car. As soon as she'd shut the door, Joe pulled away from the kerb. Fast.

CHAPTER 50

Christopher was late getting out of school, because class didn't finish on time and then Mrs. Dresden, the music teacher, asked him to stay back. Christopher watched the other students file out, chatting as they went. Clara didn't even glance at him as she passed.

Mrs. Dresden had questions about why Christopher had sat out practice for the concert. Where was his violin?

"It's a long story," Christopher said. "My dad is meant to be talking to Mr. Littlewood today. He can explain."

Mrs. Dresden raised a single eyebrow when she heard the principal's name.

"I hope that's true," she said.

Why does she think I'm lying?

"It is true."

Where was Joe? Had he talked to Mr. Littlewood already? If so, Christopher had heard nothing about it. Maybe Kavanagh was in the principal's office, getting his head shouted off right now? Getting expelled, with any luck.

"Go on, then," Mrs. Dresden said. "I'll see you tomorrow. I'd tell you to do your practice, but it seems that you can't."

"Not right now. But I'll imagine practicing in my head. I read in a magazine that imagining practicing is almost as good as actually practicing. Actually, that study was about exercise, but I figure the same should apply to music."

Mrs. Dresden gave Christopher a wary glance as he got to his feet. He lobbed his schoolbag over his shoulder and made his way out of the room, down the corridor and out the door of the school.

He checked the time on his phone as he made his way down the steps. He'd lost a few minutes. With any luck, everyone would have gone by now.

Christopher ambled down Clyde Road. The wonderfully bright summer day had receded into cloud.

A misty rain began to fall.

At the corner of Pembroke Park and Herbert Park, he stopped dead. He could hear the familiar sound of two boys' voices. They were around the corner, just out of sight.

He'd nearly walked into Kavanagh again.

He pressed himself against the hedge outside the house on the corner.

Kavanagh and Harrison were talking about football. They clearly hadn't been spoken to by the principal. Or if they had, they didn't care. They sounded completely carefree. Christopher would have to wait for them to go on ahead. Otherwise they'd torment him again.

All the despair and fear that Christopher had felt the previous day came rushing back.

He was alone.

Joe had promised that he would sort this out, but he hadn't. He had done nothing because he didn't care.

After a while, Harrison and Kavanagh parted ways. It took a long time for the two bullies to say goodbye, as if they missed each other already. Maybe they were better company than whatever awaited them at home. Christopher smiled bitterly at the thought.

Finally, Harrison took off, heading for his house. When he was gone, Christopher glanced around the corner and saw Kavanagh walking towards Herbert Park.

Christopher had to do something.

He wasn't going to harm himself. Disappointing Mum was something he never wanted to do again. He'd never take pills again. But he had to do something.

He unzipped his school bag. He felt the reassuring solidity of the kitchen knife, still there. Its cold, sharp blade looked brutal in the dull light.

He left the knife where it was and closed the bag again.

If he wanted to give Kavanagh a scare, now was the best time to do it. There was no one around. The rain, which was growing steadily heavier, ensured that Herbert Park would be quiet. Maybe even empty.

Except for Kavanagh.

He would be alone.

People always said bullies were cowards when they were alone. Christopher hoped that was true. How would Kavanagh fare without backup? He was bigger and stronger than Christopher but maybe he was also more of a coward, if that was possible.

Kavanagh entered the park.

Christopher waited a full minute and then set off after him.

The rain began to fall faster, the droplets becoming fatter, hitting harder. Christopher stopped at the entrance gate to the park.

Looking around again, he saw no one.

This was his chance.

The long path stretched ahead, cocooned on both sides by trees. Ahead was a club house, next to a football pitch. The duck pond, where Christopher had spent many early mornings and late afternoons thinking about ending his own life, lay to the left.

Kavanagh didn't seem to notice the rain. He just kept walking along, not even increasing his pace. Christopher had a raincoat Mum had got him. It rolled into a ball to save space when not in use. He unzipped his school bag and pulled it out. He slipped it over his shoulders, then closed his bag most of the way. It was still partly open so it would be easy to get at the knife.

Christopher couldn't wait to see the look on Kavanagh's face.

He took a breath and hurried forward, closing the distance to Kavanagh, while trying to keep his footsteps silent.

Now approaching the clubhouse, Kavanagh seemed not to hear Christopher's footsteps. He had his earbuds in.

Christopher was two metres away from Kavanagh and his heart was thumping at an insane pace.

Kavanagh's head moved in time to the beat of his music. He looked just like a pigeon. Christopher might have found it funny if he wasn't so scared.

The previous day's humiliation came back to him. And a hundred days like it before that. Could he really threaten Kavanagh? What if Kavanagh's revenge was worse than anything Christopher had suffered so far?

Christopher was right behind Kavanagh when he decided that this was a mistake.

He needed to get out of there.

Before he could slip away, Kavanagh turned his head and saw Christopher out of the corner of his eye.

Christopher reached into his bag. He pulled the knife out and brandished it in Kavanagh's face.

Kavanagh wheeled around. He saw the blade but punched Christopher in the face. The blow knocked Christopher backwards.

The knife disappeared into the wet grass.

Kavanagh grabbed Christopher by the scruff of his neck and lifted him to his feet, then began to pummel him with his fists.

"You little shit. You thought you were going to cut me, did you?"

Christopher tried to wriggle free but Kavanagh held his jumper tight.

"I'm sorry. Just, please, let me go."

"No way," Kavanagh said. "This time, you're dead."

CHAPTER 51

Joe drove as fast as he could, but other motorists seemed to take a perverse delight in slowing him down, and every traffic light seemed to work against him. He was tempted to turn on the siren and the flashing lights, but the circumstances didn't call for that. After all, he was only going to talk to his son's principal.

As he approached the Highfield Academy, it began to rain, and he flicked on the windscreen wipers.

He wanted to show Lisa and Christopher that he meant what he had said about taking care of this. He hoped the principal would still be there.

As he drove down Clyde Road towards the school, he passed the turn onto Pembroke Park and saw a boy in the Highfield Academy uniform heading for the park. Christopher? Joe figured the principal could wait a few minutes. Joe should talk to Christopher first. Check how his day went and see if anything had happened.

There were multiple entrances to Herbert Park, and Joe was familiar with them all. The park was only a couple of minutes away from the station, so he had been here often. He went back out onto Morehampton Road, and then turned down Auburn Avenue, a narrow road lined with small red-brick houses.

Joe wanted to talk to Christopher before he got home. Aside from the whole bullying thing, Joe wanted to ask him more about Graham. He didn't trust that man.

At the end of the cul-de-sac, the road opened up into a small circle where a car could turn. Joe brought the car to a stop next to a pedestrian gate into the side of the park. He could see two figures coming towards him through the rain.

Christopher… and another boy?

The rain grew heavier. To his right, Joe saw a woman run into one a nearby house, out of the downpour.

Joe looked towards the park again and saw the two figures drawing closer. He'd wait for Christopher to get closer before he called out to him.

Joe's phone rang. It was Dunne.

"What is it?"

Dunne said, "I thought you'd want to know that Lauren Fairview has died."

The Irish Prison Service officer had done well to last so long, considering the injuries she suffered. Though Joe had never met her, he pictured her as one hell of a fighter.

"When did it happen?"

"Half an hour ago."

Joe's blood boiled as he thought of Wall hurting her like that.

"Hold on," Dunne said.

Joe could hear talking in the background. He waited impatiently.

"What is it?"

"Just a second, Joe. I'm back in Donnybrook. We might have a lead."

She must have driven even faster than him. He sat up straighter in his seat. "Tell me."

"This is big… We've got *two* crime scenes. A house in Monkstown and one in Booterstown."

"What kind of crime scenes? What does this have to do with us?"

"There's a dead male at the Monkstown house. The wife found him beaten to death. It's the judge who presided over Aidan Donnelly's trial."

This had to be Wall's work.

Joe felt no satisfaction that he had been right and O'Carroll had been wrong.

"And the other scene?"

"Another dead male. Found outside his house. Also attacked violently. The house belongs to a Martin Costello."

"Aidan Donnelly's barrister," Joe said to himself.

"A motorcycle was seen leaving the house in Booterstown."

"Where's the suspect now?"

"Driving north. Heading this way. Where are you?"

"Just outside Herbert Park," Joe said.

"The Garda Traffic Corps are on a path to intercept the biker. I'll meet you on Morehampton Road. Let's bag this fucker."

"See you in a minute."

He ended the call, his head spinning. Joe had seen deaths on the job, but they had rarely been violent. Most were traffic accidents. The Aidan Donnelly case was completely different. Joe had never encountered anything like it.

It took him a moment to remember what he'd been doing before Dunne called. *Christopher.* He looked to see if his son had walked past yet but could see no one, so he turned off the engine and stepped out of the car. He could taste the early summer rain as it fell on his face.

He jogged around the back of the car and made his way through the pedestrian gate into the park. Shielding his eyes from the rain, he scanned the vicinity. For a moment nothing caught his attention.

Then Joe saw it.

A body lying in the grass. Motionless.

Joe recognised the pretentious Highfield Academy uniform.

He sprinted over.

As he got closer, he saw the blood.

CHAPTER 52

Aidan Donnelly woke up feeling like a turkey in an oven. He found himself lying in a single bed, covered by layers of blankets. He was drenched with sweat and had a headache.

Where was he? What had happened?

The aroma of fried bacon seeped into the room.

Aidan reached out his arm, feeling around on the bedside table for his phone. Its display told him it was well into the afternoon already, which wasn't a surprise. Staying up late, until he felt like dropping, had become normal, just like the long walks had.

The text messages were a surprise though.

Mate, you're so screwed!!! read one. It was from a lad who had been his friend before the trial.

You okay, bud? read another message. *Best stay clear of your usual haunts.*

There were two missed calls from his mother.

What was all that about?

He could hear his auntie bustling about beyond the bedroom door.

Aidan threw off the smothering blankets. He slipped on his tracksuit bottoms and opened the door. His auntie's house was cosy. The bedroom led right into the combined kitchen/sitting room, where his auntie stood before the cooker, frying rashers and sausages.

"Morning, auntie."

"It's not morning anymore, love," Maureen said with a smile. Despite the room's warmth, she was wearing a yellow cardigan over her long, flowery dress. Aidan returned her smile.

"Oh yeah, I know. Sorry."

"I thought the rashers might wake you up. You always did love a fry. Will you have a few eggs and sausages too?"

"I will, yeah. Cheers."

Aidan began to remember last night. He'd walked so far, he decided not to go home. Instead, he'd headed for Maureen's house. His mother's sister lived alone, and she never minded him visiting.

"Thanks for letting me crash here, auntie."

"You know you're always welcome, love."

Aidan scratched his head and tried to get his brain working. The bungalow had only one bedroom.

"Did I take your bed, auntie?"

"Don't you worry about me." Maureen cracked two eggs into the pan, then dropped bread into the toaster. Aidan was mortified.

"Ah, I'm sorry. Where did you sleep?"

She waved him away. "I'm fine."

"Were you on the couch? Why didn't I take the couch?"

"The couch is more comfortable anyway. You were tired. You'd drunk a can or two, hadn't you?"

Aidan lowered his head. "I had a few cans of cider by the canal. It was the weather for it."

He thought of the two girls who'd gone away to avoid being near him. He'd had a few more cans after they left.

"You know you're a lightweight," Maureen teased. "You've never been able to handle your drink."

"I'm so sorry, auntie. You should have made me sleep on the floor."

"It's fine, love. Don't you worry."

"Yeah, but that's not right."

She shook her head and tipped the fried food onto a plate. She gave him a smile as she brought it over to the couch. Her house didn't have a kitchen table. There just wasn't enough room for one. Normally, Maureen ate with her plate on a tray, resting on her lap. She was usually watching reality TV or one of the English soaps.

"You eat up now."

Aidan sat down on the couch, and Maureen placed the tray on his lap.

"I'll make you a nice cup of tea."

"Cheers, auntie."

Once she had poured them both a cup, she sat beside Aidan. She flicked on the TV but kept the volume low. He became aware that she was shooting nervous glances at him.

"Are you okay, auntie? You look like you want to say something."

"I don't know how to say it, love." She gave a chuckle.

"If it's about the cider, you know, I don't really drink a lot. I might have been a bit dry what with the weather being warm"

"No, it's not about cider."

"What is it? I had some missed calls last night from Ma. Is it something to do with that?"

Maureen nodded. "I called her and told her you were with me, and not to worry. Nothing bad happened to you."

"Why would they think something bad happened to me?"

She nodded to herself. "I thought you hadn't heard, from the way you were talking last night. You didn't say anything about him."

"About who?" Aidan said.

"About your man, Barry Wall."

"What about him?"

"He escaped from The Joy."

Aidan flinched, slopping tea over the side of his mug.

"What?"

"The Guards are after him, though. You don't need to worry, love. It's just that when you didn't answer your phone last night, your mother was worried. But I called her up, I said Joanna, Aidan is here with me. Don't you worry about him."

Aidan put down his fork.

"What are you going to do?" Maureen asked. Just then a phone rang. "Oh, wait. Here's your mother again." Maureen answered her phone. "Yes, yes, he's up. Hang on a second. I'll pass him over."

She handed Aidan the phone.

"Hello?"

The voice of the other end of the line was harsher than normal.

"Aidan, are you trying to give me a heart attack? Why don't you ever answer your phone?"

"Sorry, Ma."

He held the phone back from his ear while she ranted at him.

"Come here to us, where you'll be safe, will ya?" she said at last.

His mother had moved out past Blanchardstown with her new boyfriend. Aidan hated both the boyfriend and the place, so he wasn't about to go there now.

"Listen, Ma. I'm going to stay with my mate. I'll be safe. Don't worry about me. I'll talk to you later."

She began to say something, but Aidan ended the call, and handed the phone back to Maureen.

"I don't like that look on your face," she said.

"Don't worry. Everything's going to be okay," he said.

CHAPTER 53

Joe threw himself onto his knees on the wet grass, feeling the moisture soak through his trousers. The swollen sky over Herbert Park seemed to be getting darker every second, the rain heavier.

Joe turned the body over. The boy's shirt was soaked with blood and his eyes stared sightlessly into the sky. Obviously, he was dead.

And he wasn't Christopher.

Thank God, Joe thought. He knew it was selfish, but a boy was dead, and Joe was only glad that it wasn't his son.

What had happened? Christopher had been here, with this boy, just minutes earlier. There had been no one else around.

So where was Christopher?

Joe looked around but saw no one.

He thought he knew who the teenager was. He had the same muscular build and Neanderthal forehead as the Superintendent.

This had to be John Kavanagh.

The bully.

This looked bad for Christopher. Seriously bad.

Motive? The Kavanagh kid was bullying him so badly, Christopher had tried to kill himself. Which meant Christopher had a motive to kill Kavanagh.

Opportunity? Christopher just been alone in a deserted park with the victim. Joe had witnessed that much himself.

Evidence? Once crime scene tape had been set up around the body, the forensics people would go to work, turning up all kinds of trace evidence.

This was an unlawful killing and it had been done by Christopher. There could be no other suspect. It was an open and shut case. Joe let the realisation sink in – Christopher had killed someone.

That was what all the evidence said, but it couldn't be right. Christopher wasn't a killer. He didn't have a mean bone in his body. Whatever happened to John Kavanagh, he must have brought it on himself. Perhaps there was a struggle? Christopher must have been defending himself.

Still, if this wasn't murder, it was certainly manslaughter.

Joe jogged back to the car. He sat down in the driver's seat, and steeled himself to call the crime in. He could picture the scene in twenty minutes. The place would be swarming with people, with his colleagues. Joe would have to tell them everything he knew.

Christopher would be in a holding cell before dinner.

And that would be it. He'd be put away for life.

Joe raised his phone and took a breath. He prepared himself to say the words. Then he made the call.

"Go ahead," said the professional voice at the other end of the line.

Joe opened his mouth – and no sound came out.

That was when he realised he couldn't do it.

This wasn't right.

Christopher was a good kid. Joe didn't know exactly what had happened, but his son wasn't a danger to society. It wasn't fair to send him to prison, to ruin his life before it had even started. There was a chance to prevent that from happening, but the odds were against it, and Joe would have to work fast.

"Apologies," he said. "False alarm."

"No problem."

He ended the call, then stepped out into the rain again. He looked around at the dozens of neat little houses. This was a densely populated area, but the rain was keeping people indoors. Though Joe didn't see anyone, someone could appear any second.

Joe popped open the boot of the car. His muddy wellies, flashlight, umbrella and other tools of the trade lay there on a sheet of plastic. So did the heavy black case containing his Sig.

He grabbed the gun case and wellies and threw them in the back seat. Then he grabbed the sheet of plastic and pulled it out from under the remaining bits and bobs.

He brought it with him as he ran back into the park. There was still no one around. Joe rolled the body onto the plastic sheet, wrapping it up like a burrito.

Once he had Kavanagh wrapped up, he flung him over his shoulder and ran as fast as he could back to the car. Joe lowered the body into the boot and slammed it shut. The damn thing wouldn't close. It was caught on Kavanagh's legs. Joe lifted them up, then shoved him farther into the boot.

Then it shut fine.

Joe got behind the wheel and closed the door. He'd been as quick as he could, but there was no way to guarantee that had been quick enough. He could only hope that no one had seen him.

Did anyone see Christopher do it?

Joe felt a chill as he thought about that.

Then his phone rang and he had to snap out of it.

"Yeah?"

"Where are you?" Dunne said. "I've been calling."

Joe could see the little icon indicating missed calls.

"Oh, yeah… sorry…"

"What are you doing? Are you still near Herbert Park?"

"Never mind," Joe said. What had they been talking about before? He shook his head, trying to remind himself. Wall. "Where's the motorcycle now?"

"Nearly here."

"I'll be there in a second. Like we agreed."

Joe ended the call.

His fingers were sticky. In the overhead light, he could see that there was blood on his hands. Not metaphorical blood. Fresh red blood from a murder victim, whose corpse was now concealed in a police vehicle by a detective, whose son was the killer.

If things could have gotten any messier, Joe couldn't have imagined how.

He dug out a packet of tissues he kept in the glove compartment. He grabbed a handful of them and did his best to clean his hands.

His phone began to ring again.

Dunne.

"Fuck off," Joe snapped.

He tried to keep a cool head and take stock of where he stood.

There was a corpse in the boot and it was a timebomb. He'd have to get rid of it as soon as possible. And he had now created a trail of evidence, from his door handle to his phone to his glove compartment, to the bloody tissues with which he was trying to clean himself. Every one of these things was trouble.

Joe avoided thinking of them as *exhibits*. He could never let these items be logged as evidence.

The phone stopped ringing.

Then it buzzed with a text message.

Hurry up, Joe.

Dunne knew where he was. The phone records would be able to confirm that. The time and the place.

Panic began to swell in his chest.

He adjusted the mirror and checked himself for any visible signs of blood. There was some on his jacket, so he wriggled out of it and dropped it on the floor. Aside from that, his hands were the only problem. The tissues hadn't really done the job. But

Joe had a bottle of water in the back seat. He poured water onto a fresh wad of tissues and wiped his hands.

The phone began ringing again.

Joe rejected the call, then wiped the phone with a wet tissue. He dumped the tissues at his feet, on top of his jacket.

The evidence was multiplying like rabbits and the crime had only happened minutes ago. Joe had to get rid of all the evidence as soon as possible.

His phone buzzed again.

Dunne was on the other side of these red-brick houses, just a minute's drive away. Joe started the engine and pulled away from Herbert Park. He wanted to get to her before she came looking for him.

The last thing he needed was a suspicious detective after him.

CHAPTER 54

Christopher staggered in the door of his house. He was home. Safe.

Everything was shaking, the whole house, or maybe that only him, his shoes slipping on the bare wood floor, the blood pounding in his ears, rain and wind lashing against the window. He tore off his raincoat, and then Mum was in front of him.

"Christopher? Oh my God. You're bleeding," she said.

"No, no, I'm not."

"Yes, you are. You're cut."

She sounded as alarmed as Christopher felt.

"It's nothing. It wasn't... it's nothing."

Mum's face was pale.

"What happened? Why are you bleeding?"

"I fell down. That's all. I fell down when I was in the park. It's nothing."

Mum's panicked face reflected his own. "Christopher, don't lie."

"I'm fine," he said. "I swear."

"We need to be honest with each other."

He swallowed. "I know that."

She stared at him for a moment. "I'll get a plaster for you, and some antiseptic."

Her hand on his arm reassured him.

"I should get cleaned up first," Christopher said. "I'm covered in mud."

His voice, which sounded strangely calm, seemed to be coming from a long way off, as if it belonged to someone else.

"Okay," Mum said. "Go and have a shower."

She ducked into the kitchen. Christopher heard the fridge door open. Then she was back beside him, opening a bottle of smoothie and pushing the drink into his hands.

"Drink this. You'll feel better."

"Why?"

"It's good for you. You'll feel better."

She wasn't making a lot of sense, but Christopher did as she said, his fingers clumsy. He just about choked on the thick fruit drink. After he'd swallowed it, he did feel a little better.

Mum took the bottle from him.

"Go ahead." She nodded to the stairs. "Go and have a shower."

"Okay. I'll be back in a minute."

He stumbled up to the bathroom where he washed his hands.

He looked in the mirror.

Maybe he lost himself in his reflection, because suddenly Mum was in the doorway, asking if he was okay.

"I'm fine," he said, blinking quickly.

She went away, still looking concerned.

He went into his bedroom, where he stripped, dumping his clothes in the laundry basket and grabbing a pair of boxers and a T-shirt from the wardrobe.

He brought the clean clothes back into the bathroom, turned on the shower, and stepped under the water. It was only when he'd been under the shower's spray for five minutes, that he began to think about Kavanagh.

The way Kavanagh had turned and seen the knife.

The way he knocked Christopher to the ground.

Christopher shuddered.

Pushed those thoughts away.

He'd got away from there. He'd scrambled to his feet and run. Maybe he should consider a career in athletics. Running seemed to be his thing. His coach would just need to put a bully on the starting line, and Christopher would outrun anyone.

He laughed, his mouth filling with water.

Then he stopped himself, because the laughter sounded crazy.

CHAPTER 55

The nose of Joe's Honda jutted out onto Morehampton Road. There was no sign of Barry Wall's motorbike yet. He accelerated into the thickening traffic. Rush hour was approaching, and they were close to the city centre. The road would get clogged soon.

Joe drove past the station. A little further down the road, he saw a silver Lexus stalling. The flash of a blonde ponytail confirmed that Dunne was behind the wheel. Joe pulled in just in front of her.

His phone rang.

"What the hell is going on, Joe?"

He was beginning to regret being so familiar with Dunne from the start. The whole first-name thing was not helping. A little formality might have reminded her that he was the more senior officer.

"Nothing."

"What were you doing? Is everything okay?"

"Yeah, fine." He could hear sirens in the distance. "Get ready," he said.

"I've been ready for ten minutes."

Joe ended the call. He watched in the rear-view mirror as a motorcycle approached.

Barry Wall, all in black leather, with a black helmet, shot past on a black motorbike. Two white motorbikes were right behind him, lights flashing, sirens blazing. The Garda Traffic Corps used Honda Deauvilles, which could get up to 200 km per hour, even with all the equipment typically loaded onto them. There was no chance of Wall getting away this time.

Joe flicked on the lights and siren and fell in behind the traffic cops. A quick look in the mirror told him Dunne was right behind.

They shot up Morehampton Road. The sirens did their job, making motorists pull over to the side to let them pass unobstructed. Wall's bike kicked up water from the wet street, but the traffic cops stuck on him, while Joe stayed in their slipstream.

They passed onto Upper Leeson Street, very close to the city centre now.

Joe had always liked the way Dublin city was bounded by two canals and cut in half by the River Liffey. There was something appealing about that symmetry. The Royal Canal enclosed the north inner city while the Grand Canal enclosed the south, and that lay just ahead of them now.

He could already see the hump of Leeson Street Bridge, rising over the water.

The street they were on went straight across the bridge before branching at another junction. Ahead was St. Stephen's Green, Grafton Street, Trinity

College and Temple Bar. In other words, tourist central.

Cutting across Leeson Street was another busy road running along the south side of the canal.

As they approached the bridge, the traffic lights changed to red. Joe slowed and so did the traffic cops.

Wall didn't stop.

He didn't slow down.

He shot straight through.

Immediately, cars began to pass from right to left and left to right, blocking the way. The two traffic cops went ballistic, waving and shouting over the wail of their sirens. Soon the traffic stopped, but it had cost them time. Joe accelerated forward as soon as he could.

Wall had cut in around the far side of the bridge, and was driving down a cycle lane parallel to the canal. Joe couldn't follow. He beeped his horn and pointed Wall out to the traffic cops, but they'd already seen him, and they set off in pursuit.

Joe had to content himself with turning left and drive down Adelaide Road, past the Eye and Ear Hospital. He checked his mirror, but Dunne was nowhere to be seen.

Down a road to the left, Joe catch a fleeting glimpse of Wall, powering along on the bike path. Unfortunately, Joe still couldn't follow him, and Adelaide Road began to curve away from the canal.

Ahead, another little road turned in to the left. As Joe was turning to look that way, Wall shot towards him from that direction and passed right in front of him, almost close enough to touch the Honda's front bumper.

Joe jammed on his brakes, then turned to the right and followed Wall towards the National Concert Hall. The two Traffic Corps motorcycles shot past him.

The thumping sound of a helicopter came from overhead. A quick glance confirmed it was a Garda Air Support Unit.

Wall really wouldn't get away this time. He was done for. The roads ahead would be packed. It was nearly rush hour in the city centre, and it was raining. Put those ingredients together and you get gridlock.

Motorcycles, cars and a helicopter.

It was game over.

As Wall's motorbike approached the next junction, Dunne's Lexus shot out in front of him. He braked hard and skidded on the wet tarmac. The bike toppled onto its side, then skidded along the road.

Joe slammed on the brakes, bringing the Honda to a screaming halt. He got out of the car and ran forward.

Wall twitched, and managed to stagger to his feet.

Tough guy.

"Don't fucking move!" Dunne shouted, as she got out of her Lexus.

The helicopter was right overhead now, hovering just above them, its noise deafening, its blades creating a furious gale.

Wall turned in Joe's direction. His hand began to reach into his jacket.

"Stop or I'll shoot," Dunne shouted. She pulled out her 9mm Sig Sauer and stepped forward, pointing the gun at Wall. With a quick movement, Wall reached into his jacket.

Dunne called, "Get down, he has a weapon."

She fired her Sig three times into Wall's chest, knocking him to the ground.

"Stay down," she shouted.

Joe hurried over. Wall was lying motionless on his back. Joe reached for his helmet. Working carefully, in case he was still alive, Joe began to ease the helmet off his head.

The traffic cops crowded around. One of them was on his radio calling for an ambulance.

Dunne stepped closer, gun still raised.

"Is he dead?" she shouted.

Joe finally eased the helmet off completely. He looked down.

"Is he dead?" Dunne said again.

"Oh shit," Joe said.

CHAPTER 56

The rain began to ease off at five thirty. At five forty, it stopped completely and by a quarter to six, the sky cleared to reveal a canvas of clean blue.

Christopher lay on his bed, wearing a T-shirt and his boxer shorts, the afternoon's events running through his head.

Clara Fry. Mrs. Dresden. Hurrying out of school. The light rain turning hard. Following Kavanagh, his heart racing. The deserted park.

The knife.

Struggling with Kavanagh. Shouting. Falling.

Running away.

I must be a loser, Christopher thought, watching a spider cross his ceiling. *I'm not normal. Why else would Kavanagh haven chosen to bully me?*

When the spider began to descend from its web, Christopher roused himself. He stood on the mattress and prodded the spider with a sheet of A4 paper until the spider clung to it. He took it over to the window, lifted up the glass, and dropped the paper and spider together down into the garden.

He closed the window and started pacing the room.

He could hear the shower running in the bathroom. Mum had gone in there after Christopher finally finished. By the time Christopher was done, his skin was as wizened as that of a hundred-year old.

The bedroom door opened.

"Alright, pal?" Graham said with a smile. He wore a brown polo shirt today – a little more subdued than his usual style. "I thought I might go to the chip shop, get us some dinner. What do you think? I don't think your mother has anything planned."

"No. Yeah. That sounds alright."

"Good man. What do you fancy?"

"Chicken burger and chips," Christopher said. "And a battered sausage. And curry sauce."

"You have some appetite on you tonight."

"Sorry," Christopher said, and blushed. But he didn't change the order.

"No reason to be sorry about a healthy appetite." Graham gave him a smile and stepped into the room. "Everything okay?"

"Oh, yeah. I'm fine."

"Everything okay at school?"

"Yeah."

"Did your dad talk to the principal?"

"I don't think so."

Graham shook his head, then gazed at Christopher. "You seem jumpy."

"No, I'm fine."

"Look," Graham said, putting a hand on Christopher's shoulder. "I know we haven't known each other that long. But I really like your mother. She's a classy bird. And I hope you and me can get on well too. You know what I mean?"

"Um, I guess."

"I just want you to know that you can talk to me whenever you want. About anything. Alright?"

Christopher nearly let go then. He almost told Graham what happened. Maybe he'd feel better if he did.

He opened his mouth to speak.

But the shower fell silent. Mum would be out in a minute. Christopher looked up at Graham. The stocky, older man gave him another smile.

"Thanks," Christopher said. "I'll let you know if I want to talk."

The sound of Mum's footsteps came from the hall. She was padding into her bedroom in her bathrobe.

Graham said, "Let's talk later, alright?"

"Sure."

"Good man."

He squeezed Christopher's shoulder before backing out of the room and closing the door.

Christopher heard Graham go down the hall. He heard the sound of a slap, and Mum gasped in surprise. She hissed, "Not now," and Graham said, "The usual fish and chips? No problem. Back soon."

When Graham was gone, and Mum was dressed, she came and knocked on his door. Her wet hair was wrapped in a towel.

"Mind if I sit down?" she said.

"Go ahead."

She began to towel her hair dry as she spoke.

"I meant to ask you earlier. What do you think of Graham?"

"Not much," Christopher said. A flash of guilt hit him. He thought of the way Graham had spoken to him a minute ago. "But I guess he's not the worst."

"I've been thinking we should go our separate ways. I wanted to know what you thought of that."

"Will you marry Joe?"

She stopped drying her hair. "What? Why would you ask me that?"

Christopher shrugged.

"I don't know. I just wondered."

She shook her head. "I don't think Joe and I have a future together."

"But you love him, right?"

A long pause.

"I did," she said. "A long time ago."

"Not anymore?"

"Let's talk about Joe another time. I was only wondering if you'd miss Graham."

"I wouldn't miss him at all. When will you dump him?"

"Maybe tonight. He's spending more and more time here. I'm starting to feel suffocated."

Christopher gave a nervous laugh that turned into a sigh of relief.

"Me too," he said.

Mum finished drying her hair, and threw the towel into Christopher's overflowing laundry basket.

"Hey," he said.

"I think I'll put on a wash," Mum said, and took the basket out of the room with her.

CHAPTER 57

At nine o'clock, Donnybrook Garda Station closed to the public. The front door was locked. The public desk was abandoned. You might have been forgiven for thinking that the building was empty. It wasn't. The station was full of activity. Two dozen officers swarmed around.

Half of them were in the incident room. Joe included. He was still full of adrenaline. On a high from the chase, and queasy from the other stuff that had happened.

The murder.

Upon Joe's return to the station, he'd written up a statement about the chase and the shooting, and he'd now been waiting twenty minutes for David O'Carroll to start the meeting he'd called. So far, he hadn't even shown up.

Anne-Marie Cunningham and Kevin Boyle were chatting like they were having a casual natter in a pub. Alice Dunne was right there with them, laughing at their jokes like they were best friends. It turned Joe's stomach.

If she could be taken in by Boyle, then Joe wanted nothing to do with her. He'd thought she was smart. Of course, he'd also thought his son was incapable of murder… maybe he wasn't such a good judge of character.

He made a coffee run to the back of the room. Dunne came over as he retook his seat.

"Everything okay, Joe?"

He decided to be civil.

"Fine. You?"

"I'm good."

"Feeling upset?"

Dunne looked confused.

"Of course not. Why would I be upset?"

"You killed a man this afternoon."

Dunne gave him a look, like Joe was being silly.

"A bad guy," she said. "Why would that bother me? I thought he was going to shoot you. Aren't you glad I put him down?"

"Yeah. I am glad you had my back."

It turned out that the man hadn't been carrying a gun. He seemed to have been reaching into his pocket for his phone.

More to the point, the man wasn't Barry Wall.

Dunne took a step closer and leaned over Joe, so close he could feel the warmth of her breath. "What were you doing earlier?"

Joe took a sip of coffee.

"What do you mean?"

"You went AWOL at Herbert Park. You still haven't explained why you ignored my calls and hung up on me."

"Nothing. I was on my way."

"You were so eager to catch Wall, but something—"

"Dunne, are you always such a pest? I told you, it was nothing. Why don't you let it go? Just go and sit with your new friends."

Dunne stared at him for a second.

"That doesn't work for me," she said. "Letting things go."

A chill ran down Joe's spine. He had the feeling that she meant it.

"Too bad," he said.

She went and took a seat next to Cunningham.

Joe didn't need an ambitious, pissed-off, trigger-happy detective poking into his business. He tried to gauge how worried he should be.

John Kavanagh's body still lay in the boot of his car, wrapped in plastic. The thought made him sick.

He was doing something terrible. Or was he? Was protecting his son the right thing to do? Joe rubbed his eyes. He couldn't afford to get tangled up in the ethics of it. Not now. Getting rid of the body was his number one priority. Every second that it lay in Joe's car, the forensic evidence linking Christopher and Joe to the murder might be increasing, getting out of control.

Joe pictured microscopic fibres from Kavanagh's uniform, hair from his head, droplets of blood from his wound. He imagined them attaching themselves to Joe's clothes and skin, being carried with him wherever he went, contaminating his office and home… and being found later by a Technical Bureau team.

He wondered if anyone had seen what happened. Pointless to torture himself, but he couldn't seem to help circling back to that question.

David O'Carroll finally bustled into the room.

"Alright. Let's have a little quiet please."

The chit chat was already subdued. It died completely as everyone took a seat around the conference table. O'Carroll made his way to the front of the room, and took up position next to the white board.

"Alright, so, our leather clad friend – as you know, he is not Barry Wall."

When the chase ended down by Harcourt Street, and Dunne put three rounds into the suspect, Joe couldn't wait to see Wall's face. But when he removed the helmet, he'd seen at once that it wasn't Wall.

Joe had no idea who the motorcycle rider was. Another decoy?

"We've now ID'd him as William 'Dinky' Talbot," O'Carroll said. "Released from Mountjoy Prison in February. Worked in the kitchen with Barry Wall. Now, we're not going to cry any tears over Dinky's death. He wasn't a very nice man. We've established that three motorcycles departed from the scene of the crime in Booterstown simultaneously. They each went in a different direction."

"So it was a lottery?" Cunningham said. "And we didn't get Wall."

She adjusted her hearing aid. Joe could understand how badly she wanted to catch Wall after him blowing her halfway to hell in the bomb blast at his house.

O'Carroll paced across the front of the room. "Unfortunately, the motorcycle we were able to follow was not our primary suspect. Barry Wall is still out there, as is one other accomplice, who also got away. I've spoken to the superintendent and he's agreed that we need to escalate our response."

"What about the victims at the two houses?" Joe said. "Have we confirmed who they are?"

O'Carroll nodded. "As you may recall, Roberts was the judge who directed the acquittal of Aidan Donnelly. He's dead. Very dead." O'Carroll let that sink in before he continued. Many detectives knew Roberts. Despite the Donnelly acquittal, Roberts was generally tough on crime, and that attitude went down well in the station. "Many of you will also be familiar with barrister Martin Costello, the second victim today. His death was also extremely violent. Clearly, Barry Wall is on the warpath. Now, I've just got some overtime pay approved. We are going to be working flat out until Wall is recaptured. Call your wives, husbands, drinking buddies. Let them know."

"What's the plan?" Joe asked.

"Surveillance." O'Carroll glanced around the room, looking every officer in the eyes. "Wall is out for revenge. So, as of this moment, the key targets are going to be under 24/7 surveillance. Teams of one or two watching at all times, depending on who I have free."

Joe felt his stomach sink.

"Who are the key targets?"

O'Carroll frowned. "You identified them yourself already, Joe. There are two targets left. Aidan Donnelly is one."

A cold sweat broke out on Joe's upper lip.

"And the second?" he asked.

"Yourself, of course."

All eyes turned to Joe. He wiped the sweat away with the back of his hand. But he could feel more trickling down his sides, from the armpits.

The timing couldn't have been worse. Joe couldn't afford to be watched. Not when he had a body to dispose of somehow.

"I don't—"

"No need to worry, Joe. You will continue to work on this case, along with everyone else. You will just happen to be under surveillance. And Aidan Donnelly will be under surveillance the whole time too. But just to be clear, Joe, given your history with Donnelly, you will not go anywhere near him and you will not be part of any surveillance team on him."

"Sure."

"And I promise you, Joe, that you will be perfectly safe too. We're going to make sure you're not alone for a second until Barry Wall is caught."

A team of detectives watching every move he made, every second of the day, would make it impossible for Joe to get rid of Kavanagh's body.

"The surveillance on me is not necessary. I can take care of myself," Joe said.

O'Carroll shook his head. "It's not just about whether you can take care of yourself. It's also about catching Wall when he tries to get to you, whether that's at your home in the middle of the night, or out and about during the day." O'Carroll smiled grimly. "You are now officially bait."

CHAPTER 58

Barry Wall had arrived back at the house first. Ken followed a few minutes later. They'd got away without any problem, but there was no sign of Dinky. They waited for him in the kitchen, Ken checking the news on his phone.

It reminded Wall of his father's bank-robbing days. His father, and whoever was doing the job with him, held post-robbery meetings in the garage attached to the Wall family house, because the property was isolated. The activity had peaked when Wall was in his early teens. Despite being afraid of what would happen if he was caught, Wall was compelled to hang around outside the garage and eavesdrop. Sometimes there was jubilation in the men's voices after a job. Sometimes fear, hate, rage. Always excitement. Until the day his father didn't come home. Neither did his 'friends'. They'd taken two thousand euro from a credit union in Raheny, and on the way home had plunged their car into a school bus at 140 kmh. They'd all died on impact.

Wall had always told himself, and anyone who would listen, that he was nothing like his father. That he was not a violent man. But here he was, with blood on his hands, and his father's voice ringing in his ears.

I'm gonna roll you down the hill, Barry…

"Here's something," Ken said.

There was an article about a traffic disturbance in the city centre. Ken kept refreshing the screen, waiting for more details. After half an hour, the phrases "shots fired" and "motorcycle rider" appeared in the updated article.

"They've killed him," Wall said.

"Damn," Ken said, still staring at his phone. "I think you're right."

Only the two brothers remained.

"I doubt Dinky had a chance to tell them anything," Wall said. "Not if he was shot on the street. All the same, it will be better if we move to a different location."

Ken nodded. "It says here they're looking for two motorcyclists. They're appealing to the public."

"Some of the neighbours might have seen us," Wall said.

"We should go to my place."

"Let's do it."

Ken's phone rang.

"Yeah?" he said.

Wall watched him.

"Okay," Ken said and hung up.

"What is it?"

"Our contact says they're putting surveillance on Aidan Donnelly and Joe Byrne. They know your plan."

"Shit."

"We'll find a way to get them. Don't worry. Our contact will help. But for now, we should move."

Wall took a frustrated breath, nodded. He looked out the kitchen window. Into the infinite sky.

I promise I'll find you, Valentina. I'll do whatever has to be done. Whatever it takes.

"Let's go," he said.

It didn't take long for them to clear out. Wall took the dart board Dinky had hung in the kitchen, with the photos of Judge Roberts, Joe Byrne and Aidan Donnelly pinned to it, and threw it in a holdall.

When Wall had collected everything, he went outside to find that Ken had already loaded the motorbikes into the back of the Ford Transit. Wall helped throw the makeshift wooden ramp into the back of the van too. Then they shut the doors and got in the front.

Wall didn't see any neighbour watching, but you never knew. In any case, the licence plate on the van couldn't be traced back to Ken.

As Wall got into the passenger seat, Ken's phone rang again. He listened for half a minute, then ended the call. He smiled.

"What is it?" Wall asked. "Was that your contact again?"

"Yes. He said he found out that Aidan Donnelly is not under surveillance yet because they haven't been able to find him."

Wall's eyes lit up.

"Where is he?"

"I'm not sure." Ken smiled. "But our contact has an idea."

*

Lisa jumped when she heard a key slide into the lock. Graham pushed open the door, two grease-stained paper bags in his hands.

"Hey, babe."

He came into the kitchen and kissed Lisa on the cheek.

She'd been leaning against the washing machine, her glass of Chardonnay untouched on the kitchen table. She'd fallen into a daze and lost track of time.

"You were a long time gone," Lisa said, straightening up.

"Sorry. There was a queue in the chip shop."

Lisa opened the cupboard and took out three plates. Even if they were going to eat a take-away, she wanted to have a bit of decorum about it. She wasn't going to eat from the bag.

She called up the stairs to Christopher while Graham ripped open one of the bags. Chips spilled out onto the tabletop, releasing the sharp smell of vinegar. Lisa sighed and gathered up the fallen chips. She got a bowl and poured them into it.

Tell him, she thought. *Tell him right now that he's out of here. Screw him and his chips.*

Instead she sat down in her usual place at the table. She'd never been good at break-ups. She wasn't even able to dump Joe, except by not talking to him. And that had nearly killed her.

Christopher came down the stairs. He grabbed a soft drink and sat down in his usual place. They began to eat.

Tell him, she kept thinking. *Just tell him.*

Instead she ate. Graham babbled on, but she had no idea what he said. When they'd finished eating, and Christopher had disappeared back upstairs, she finally worked up the courage.

"Graham," she said, at the same time as he said, "I have some news."

Lisa laughed nervously. "You go first."

"No, you."

"You," Lisa insisted.

"Good news. I called my landlord," Graham said.

"What for?"

"I gave him my notice. Since we've been spending so much time together, I think it makes sense that I move in. You know, I practically live here anyway."

"You gave up your house?"

"It's a needless expense," Graham said. "You're happy, aren't you?"

"I am," Lisa said blankly.

"Good. Now we'll be able to spend more time together."

She forced a smile. "Great."

Graham said, "What did you want to tell me?"

Lisa was wondering what to say when the doorbell rang.

CHAPTER 59

Bait. The word echoed in Joe's mind as he drove to Lisa's house. The evening was milder than Joe would have liked, and though the rain had stopped falling, everything was wet. Damp and warm – ideal conditions for bacteria.

It was impossible to forget even for a second that John Kavanagh's body lay behind him in the boot of the car. It had been there since Herbert Park. Even as Joe chased Wall's accomplice through the city, the body had been there. Even as Joe sat in the station, working on the Wall case, it had been there.

And it would have to stay there for the moment. Because Dunne's silver Lexus was right behind him. His security detail. First shift.

Joe arrived at Lisa's place, pressed the doorbell. The hedge circling the garden looked like it had been cut by a blind man on a rollercoaster. Lisa opened the door an inch.

"Hello Joe."

"I didn't get to speak to the principal today. I'm sorry."

Lisa looked distracted, haggard even. Or maybe Joe was picking up on how disappointed she was at him for letting her down again. It had happened so often, she must have become tired.

Joe said, "I'll do it tomorrow. Or did you do it yourself?"

"No, it was too late."

"How did Christopher get on today? I'd like to have a word with him."

Lisa said, "He's tired."

"Tired?"

"He needs to rest."

"Why does he need to rest?"

She sighed. "Joe, he just does. I don't have time to explain everything to you."

"Explain what?"

"That he had a long day at school, and he's tired. He's upstairs playing a computer game."

"It sounds like he's alert enough for a quick conversation with his father."

Lisa scoffed, "Father?"

"Did I say something funny?"

"Never mind." She opened the door a little wider and stepped aside. "Okay, then. Go ahead."

"Thanks," Joe said, stepping into the hall. Two huge pieces of luggage sat just inside the door. "Are you going somewhere?"

Graham appeared in the doorway of the kitchen.

"Joe? You're interrupting an important conversation. Not that I mind, but Lisa might not be so—"

Ignoring him, Joe turned to Lisa. "Is this asshole here all the time?"

"Hey, hey, hey," Graham said.

Lisa really did look tired.

She said, "Play nice, Joe."

He made his way up the stairs and knocked on Christopher's door. The *KEEP OUT* sign stared back at him. From the other side of the door, he could hear the engine sound from a racing game.

He opened the door.

Christopher was sitting on his bed, propped up by a pile of pillows, holding a controller in his hands and staring at the huge TV screen mounted to the wall.

"Alright, Christopher?"

The boy's face looked puffy and pink, and a bruise was developing around one eye.

"Hi," Christopher said in a small voice.

"Can I sit down?"

"Alright." He paused the game.

"How was school?"

"Fine." Christopher shrugged. He began to play with his fingers, pulling at a loose piece of skin next to the nail on his thumb.

"You didn't have any problems?"

"Not really."

"I planned to go and see your principal today, but I got held up at work." Christopher nodded like this was not news. "I actually did go to your school, but it was a little late when I arrived. You'd already left. But I saw you walking home."

Christopher looked up.

"Yeah?"

"I saw you heading into Herbert Park. Is that right?"

"Well, that's the way I usually go."

"I thought so. It's got to be the quickest route."

"Yeah."

"You were with another boy. Is that right?"

Christopher's face clouded over. "Um…"

Just then, Lisa appeared in the doorway. "What's going on?"

"I was telling Christopher how I went to meet him earlier. I saw him heading into the park with another boy."

"I wasn't, like, *with* anyone. There – there may have been another boy in the park."

Joe nodded. "Alright. Who was that?"

"I don't know," Christopher said.

He was a terrible liar.

"Tell me who it was."

Lisa said, "Who cares who it was?"

"I'm just trying to build up a picture."

"Of what?"

Joe didn't answer. Instead, he reached out and put a hand on Christopher's leg. "Tell me what happened this afternoon."

Lisa crossed her arms. "Joe, I don't know what you're going on about, but I've had just about enough of it."

"This is important."

"What's important is that Christopher goes to bed now. Tomorrow is a school day."

"It's not late yet."

"Not for you, maybe. Christopher, turn the PlayStation off."

Joe lowered his voice and leaned over so he could speak directly into Christopher's ear. "Did something happen in the park?" Joe asked. "Who did that to your face?"

His son's eyes darted about the room.

"I – I fell," Christopher stammered.

Lisa said, "Alright, Joe, that's more than enough. It's time you left."

Joe kept his eyes on Christopher.

He said, "What happened?"

"I – I – I…"

Lisa raised her voice. "Joe! Have you gone mad? I want you to leave. Go now."

"What happened in the park, Christopher? Tell me."

"Graham? Joe is leaving. Can you show him out?"

Joe heard Graham coming. He straightened up as Graham entered the room.

"Alright, Joe, time to go home," he said. "Don't make me use force."

"Try it, dickhead."

"If you're going to be rambunctious, I'll call the Gardaí and ask them to remove you."

Joe decided he wouldn't be able to get anything out of Christopher with Lisa and Graham standing there. He'd have to leave it for now, and try again later.

He trudged downstairs, with Graham two steps behind him. Graham said nothing as Joe opened the door. But when he paused on the doorstep, Graham gave him a shove. Joe lurched off the step and staggered a couple of paces down the driveway. The door closed before he could retaliate.

What a day.

Joe trudged to the end of the driveway, where Dunne was sitting in her Lexus, watching him.

CHAPTER 60

On his way home, Detective Sergeant Kevin Boyle stopped off at a pub just down the road from his flat. He only wanted a pint, to take the edge off. He hoped Babe wouldn't make another mess on his rug before he arrived home.

Just one drink, he had thought.

Here he was, finishing his third.

The place had an old-time feel to it. There was a bar on one side of the premises and a lounge on the other. Boyle sat in the bar. It was darker, which suited his mood. There was no live music to annoy him.

Boyle punctuated his drinks by stepping outside and smoking a cigarette after he drained each glass. Here he was lighting cigarette number three. He looked around wearily with every inhalation. When he'd finished it, and flicked the butt into the street, he went back inside and ordered his fourth pint.

While the Guinness was settling, he went to the toilets. Empty, thank goodness. The urinals here had bullseyes painted inside them. Made it more fun, Boyle supposed.

He was finishing up when the door to the bar opened. Boyle looked around, but he wasn't fast enough.

Someone grabbed the back of his head and smashed his face against the wall.

Boyle was dazed.

The man pulled him back.

Boyle brought his hands up in front of him in time to prevent a second impact. That just provoked the man, and he punched Boyle in the side. Hard.

Boyle turned, piss flying all over the place. The blond man in front of him had a scar running from below his left eye down to the corner of his mouth. Boyle had never learnt his name, though he had met him a few times when meeting with Ger Barrett. The scarred man pulled a pistol out of the waistband of his jeans.

"Hey, hey, hey," Boyle said holding his hands up.

The scarred man said, "You fucked us."

"No. Ger knows I would never do that to him."

"Then what happened?"

"Byrne must have followed Ger."

The scarred man gave Boyle the ugliest smile he had ever seen. "Maybe he followed you."

"No. I checked."

"You work with this guy?"

"Yes. I didn't sell you out."

"What's his name?"

Boyle hesitated. The blond man slapped him across the face.

"Joe Byrne is his name," Boyle said.

A dirty fucking rat.
Vermin.

The words he had used to describe Joe came back to him. He gritted his teeth. Now Boyle was the rat.

"Mr. Barrett is in trouble because of you."

"I'll sort it out. Ger will be fine."

"How?"

"It's my word against Byrne's. The money is untraceable, right?"

"It's clean."

"Good. There's nothing to worry about. I'll make this go away. I'll get the money back. It's my money anyway. Ger isn't out of pocket."

The scar-faced man sneered.

"Not anymore. Because of this trouble, Mr. Barrett wants the money back."

"What? I did what he paid me for."

And Boyle hadn't been particularly happy about doing it. At the start, he'd just been selling low level information. He didn't feel guilty about it, because it could cause no damage. And Boyle had really needed the money. He had bills to pay. Big ones. But once Ger Barrett had got his claws into Boyle, he kept asking for more and more information. More sensitive information. Like the stuff about the planned raid on Barrett's house. That had been invaluable. It had given Barrett time to get rid of any evidence that might cause him trouble.

The scarred man shook his head.

"Mr. Barrett feels that you've failed in your duties. You let Joe Byrne become suspicious of you. You must retrieve the money and give it back to Mr. Barrett."

"I can't. It's locked up in evidence."

"Any problem?"

Boyle sighed. Obviously, it was a problem. But he said, "No. No, I guess not."

"You'll make the problem go away? It's your word against Joe Byrne's?"

"Yes. I'll persuade them. There's no evidence."

"You must get rid of Joe Byrne."

Boyle's eyes widened. "Hold on. Get rid of Joe? I can't do that."

"You will get rid of him, or I will get rid of him *and you*. It's your choice."

He put the pistol to Boyle's head and started to apply pressure to the trigger.

"Okay, stop," Boyle said. "Fuck. I'll do it."

The scarred man looked at Boyle's crotch and sniggered.

"You might want to put your little worm away."

Boyle realised his penis was still exposed. He zipped up his fly.

The man tapped his pistol against Boyle's cheek. Then he replaced the gun in the waistband of his jeans and walked out of the toilets.

As soon as he had gone, Boyle stumbled into a stall and collapsed on the filthy seat.

Could he really do it? Passing on a bit of info was one thing. But murdering a fellow detective in cold blood?

It seemed there was no choice. If Boyle did nothing, he'd end up dead.

He had to kill Joe.

CHAPTER 61

There were some beautiful old houses in Rathmines, just off the main street. A lot of them were subdivided into apartments. Some were cheap and grotty; others were high-end and expensive. Joe's place fell somewhere in the middle.

He parked and sat in the car for a moment, thinking again about Christopher.

Obviously, he'd got into a fight with John Kavanagh. Joe imagined it had gone bad and somehow Kavanagh had ended up with a lethal wound. He tried to imagine how things had played out. There had been a struggle of some sort, he guessed. Someone had been carrying a blade. Kavanagh got stabbed.

It was an accident.

Joe was keenly aware of John Kavanagh's body in the car with him. It pulled his attention to it constantly, like a black hole.

Soon the corpse would start to rot, to decay.

It would reek. Maggots would begin eating it.

Joe breathed out through his nose.

Were John Kavanagh's parents wondering where he was? Several times over the years, Joe had seen first-hand the anguish that parents suffered when a child went missing. He had no desire to inflict that on anyone.

On the other hand, if he hadn't hidden the body, Christopher would already be in a cell. There was no way Joe was going to allow that to happen. He was a bad enough father as it was, without sending his son to prison.

He stepped out of the Honda and into the mild night. Once he had retrieved the case containing his gun from the back seat, he crossed the road.

Dunne was already standing outside his building.

She had kept a medium distance as she followed him home. She did a good job. Even though she was close enough to keep an eye on him, her presence hadn't been obvious.

Now she seemed to have thrown out covert surveillance altogether.

"What are you doing?" Joe said. "Someone might see you."

She glanced at her watch. It was a tiny thing with a silver dial and a rose gold bracelet. It looked good on her.

"My shift is over."

"So what? You should keep out of sight."

"I want to check your home. Make sure there are no threats."

"I think I can handle it."

"Two heads are better than one, right?"

Joe shrugged. "Okay, come on."

He jogged up the steps to the door, and let himself in.

"I hope you like steps," Joe told her, and started up the staircase. When he didn't have the inclination to go to the gym, he comforted myself with the thought that he was at least getting a little cardio climbing up to his flat.

He unlocked the door to his apartment and pushed it open.

"Do you want to do a search?"

"Sure," she said.

Joe had been joking, but, honest to God, she had her 9mm out, and she entered the room the way the instructors teach you in Templemore. She remembered all that Garda Training College stuff better than Joe.

"Clear," she said, emerging from the bathroom.

"That's a relief."

Joe closed the door and took off his jacket. He put his gun case down on the coffee table.

"You want a coffee?" he said.

"You're going to have coffee at this time?"

He shrugged. "Not going to sleep anyway."

He had a lot on his mind. He wanted to think about finding a way to evade his surveillance escort. Also, he wanted to see if he could find anything more on Graham Lee, Lisa's new boyfriend. Joe hated the bastard more every time he saw him. There was dirt somewhere and Joe wanted to find it.

"Okay," Dunne said. "I'm game. But just give me half a cup. I can't stay."

She followed him into the kitchen and draped her jacket over the back of a stool that was pressed in against the side counter. It was a cramped space, but it suited Joe, given the amount of cooking he did.

He made a French press full of coffee and they drank it in the sitting room. Dunne looked sleek and at ease on Joe's couch. Joe used a folding stool. He could have sat on the couch too, but then he and Dunne would have been pretty close.

Her gaze moved slowly around the room.

"You like living alone?" she asked.

"Most of the time."

"Me too. You ever get lonely?"

Joe pointed to the bookshelf. "If I do, I can read. Every one of those books is like an old friend."

Dunne squinted, trying to make out the titles. "Are they all history?"

"Almost. I'm interested in explorers. Conquistadores, the scramble for Africa, that kind of thing."

"Accounts of ambition, power and exploitation." Dunne nodded to herself. "Books are good. Sometimes people need real company, though."

"What I need is a miracle," Joe said, and laughed bitterly. "Or maybe a good luck charm."

He meant it too. He had absolutely no idea how he could get out of his current situation.

"I should go," Dunne said.

She got up, and made for the door, pausing in front of Joe's bookshelf.

"Here you go," she said, taking off her watch. "Your good luck charm." She placed it carefully on the top shelf of the book case.

"You're leaving your watch here? Don't you want it?"

"Of course, I do. You can return it later."

"Are you sure?"

"Yes." She squeezed Joe's arm and smiled. "Good night, Joe. I'll make my own way out."

When he had closed the door, he picked up Dunne's watch. It was still warm from being next to her skin. It was Cartier and each hour was marked by a diamond. If it was the genuine article, Dunne's watch could have paid Joe's rent for a year or two. He wondered how she could afford it on a Garda's salary. Or had someone given it to her?

He replaced the watch on the shelf and went over to the window. Anne-Marie Cunningham's car was outside. A shadow lurked under the tree next to the car. Joe saw the glowing red dot of a cigarette. Then a man's face came into view.

Boyle.

Joe had thought Boyle was off duty now. He closed the curtains. Then he went to his gun case and checked that his Sig was loaded.

CHAPTER 62

Orange streetlights lined the road by the old canal.

Inside Ken's van, everything seemed to be in motion. Wall's heart was thumping in his chest. His knees were shaking. The motorcycles in the back were rattling. Only Ken was still, as he stared at the road ahead.

They were moving westwards, following the information received from their contact. Wall scanned the footpath beside the road. A barefoot man came into view. Runners in his hands, a backpack slung over his shoulder. Tattooed arms exposed to the air. Wall felt a rush of excitement.

"There!" Wall shouted. "There he is."

"Barry, wait."

Wall was already halfway out the door of the moving van. He tumbled to the ground, then scrambled to his feet, and sprinted to the tow-path next to the canal.

Aidan Donnelly turned as Wall reached him.

There were a few people around. Potential witnesses. Not many, but a few.

Wall didn't care.

He knocked Donnelly down with a sledgehammer punch to the jaw. Behind him, brakes screeched. Wall crouched down over the fallen figure, brought his face close to Donnelly's.

"I've got you now, Aidan."

Ken caught up with his brother.

"Let's get him in the van," he hissed. "Quick."

They bundled Donnelly into the back of the van, next to the motorbikes. Wall jumped in after him.

"I've waited a long time for this," Wall said.

He slammed the door.

The van began moving.

*

Ethel Kavanagh was ironing a pair of John's school trousers when her husband arrived home. She liked to do ironing in batches. A week's supply of shirts, trousers, and jumpers, all sorted for the week ahead. It was reassuring to be prepared like that. Sometimes she ironed more than that if she was at a loose end or feeling stressed. It was a great way to take her mind off things.

She was doing a little extra tonight.

John made fun of her for ironing his boxer shorts, but Mrs. Kavanagh had been taught that by her mother, and she couldn't leave them crumpled, the way they came out of the dryer. All laundry should be ironed. That was how she liked it, everything from tablecloths to bedsheets.

Her husband shot her a scornful look when he saw the Pierce Brosnan movie she was watching on the TV. She lowered the volume.

"Did you only get out now?"

"Paperwork," Michael replied with a nod. "You know how much paper superintendents have to push around. It never ends."

"John hasn't come home."

"Did you call him?"

"He didn't answer."

Michael scowled. "I'll give him a slap he won't forget when he gets home."

"Don't."

"You're too soft on him."

"You're too hard."

Ethel stopped. Talking always ended in argument these days. She watched her husband disappear into his study.

She looked around. The room was full of piles of freshly ironed laundry.

There must have been something else to iron. She went upstairs to look.

*

There was pain in the van. A lot of pain.

As soon as they got moving, Barry Wall threw Aidan face down on the floor, knelt on his lower back and twisted his right arm behind him so hard, Aidan was sure it would pop out of its socket. He squealed like a pig.

Wall was crazy with anger. He banged Aidan's head against the floor until Aidan felt himself slipping into darkness, punctuated by white flashes behind his eyelids.

Sometime later, he woke up.

There was noise, lights.

Grabbing. Lifting.

Spinning around. Rough hands dragging him.

Aidan opened his eyes. They were in an open space. Aidan caught a glimpse of pine trees in the darkness. He sucked in the night air like a swimmer coming up for breath.

"You're going to tell us everything," Wall said.

Then Aidan was dragged into a building and thrown on a concrete floor. Even as he drifted into unconsciousness again, he felt the clink of metal and realised that he was being chained up.

CHAPTER 63

Joe woke on the couch. He'd stayed up all night, and had only nodded off thirty minutes earlier.

Friday. Another warm morning.

Joe pulled open the curtains and looked down onto the street. Anne-Marie Cunningham's car was still parked across the road. Joe had kept an eye on her and Boyle during the night. He'd left his lights on and kept his gun next to him. Boyle being on his security detail was outrageous. Joe intended to complain to O'Carroll as soon as he got to the station.

He made his way to the kitchen, dog-tired. No one loved coffee more than Joe, but it couldn't compensate for a good night's sleep. All the same, he made a pot. Drank all of it. Fried some bacon and eggs, and made them vanish too.

When he was done, he called Graham Lee's wife, Philippa. He'd managed to get her name after making a couple of calls. With a few seconds' online sleuthing, he'd managed to find out where she worked and get a phone number. Lisa said that

Philippa had walked out on Graham. Joe wondered what she had to say about him.

He phoned her but got no answer. Was she alright, or had something happened to her? He decided he'd try to contact her again later.

He threw on his leather jacket, made his way downstairs, past the bikes in the hall, and walked outside to Cunningham's car.

Her forehead rested on the steering wheel. She was snoring louder than a coal train. He rapped on the window.

"Wakey wakey."

She jumped, then saw Joe and rolled down the glass.

"I was just resting my eyes for a second."

"Yeah. Glad to know you care so much about my safety."

"Seriously," she said. "I just put in some eye drops."

"Whatever. Why the hell was Boyle here last night? I don't want him outside my home."

Cunningham cleared her throat. "He just came to say hi and see how I was doing. He said he had nothing better to do. I'm sorry. I know he wasn't supposed to be watching you. You're not going to make a fuss, are you?"

"I don't know. Let's see," Joe said. He turned to walk away.

"Where are you going?" Cunningham called.

"I guess you'll see, if you manage to keep up."

His pace slowed as he reached his own car. Joe could hardly believe the previous day's events had been real. But they were. And John Kavanagh's body still lay in the car, wrapped in plastic.

If he'd known Cunningham was napping, he could have sneaked to the car. But Boyle might be lurking somewhere nearby too, and getting away from the surveillance was only part of the solution.

What the hell was he meant to do with the body? He'd spent the previous night wracking his brains, but had come up with nothing solid.

Forensic science has come so far that it was hard to get away with anything anymore. From invisible fibres to DNA sequences to omnipresent CCTV. Joe was usually thankful for such advances, but not today.

Not when Christopher's life hung by a thread.

And Joe's too.

He took a breath and got behind the wheel. He was headed for Donnybrook, but he took a longer route than normal, as he felt like passing Lisa's house. He wondered if it was too early to try again with Christopher. Maybe, and maybe it would be better to talk to him when Lisa wasn't around.

Down the road from Lisa's house, Joe saw a group of men standing outside a house. The ringleader was a man in his sixties, dressed in a faded T-shirt, with a sagging belly pressed tight against the material. The two younger men were big brutes. Maybe his sons. Or employees. They looked like thugs for hire. The older man banged on the door.

He shouted, "Open up, you bollocks!"

Joe stopped the Honda and got out.

Behind him, Cunningham's car stopped.

"What's going on?" Joe said.

The old man turned around.

"None of your business."

Joe pulled out his ID as he walked up the driveway. "You're making a racket."

"Is that a crime now?"

"Maybe," Joe said. "You want to break the door down?"

"I'm the owner," the older man said. "So no. I'd prefer not to break down the door."

"You rented the place out?"

"That's right."

"Don't you have a key?"

The man held up a keyring with about two dozen keys jangling on it.

"I do indeed. I planned to let myself in, but the bollocks of a tenant has changed the locks. Open the door, Graham."

Joe felt a prickle of excitement. "What's his name?"

"Graham Lee."

"Graham Lee lives here?"

"Not anymore. He hasn't paid rent in four months. Can you help us?"

"Call the station," Joe said. "My colleagues will be happy to help you." Joe was already getting back in the Honda. If Graham wasn't home, Joe had a good idea where the bastard was.

He eased the car a short distance down the road. Stopped in front of Lisa's place. Behind him, Cunningham stopped again.

Joe made his way up to Lisa's door and rang the bell.

Lisa took a minute to open up.

"Joe," she said. She squinted at him. "Why do you look like that?"

"Like what?"

She thought for a moment. "Smug."

Joe shrugged. "That's just my face."

"No, it's not."

"Is Christopher here?"

She scowled. "Of course he's not. He's at school. And I'd like you to leave him alone."

"What do you mean?"

"I mean you acted crazy last night."

"Me? What about you? You made such a big deal out of nothing and then you asked that stupid 'painter' to—"

"I was upset."

"Is Graham here?"

"He's asleep."

"Well, you might want to tell him his landlord is up the road, evicting him."

"What?"

"The guy said he hasn't paid rent in four months."

She shook her head. "I'm sure there's been some mistake. He was only talking to his landlord yesterday. He told me. It's a misunderstanding."

"Oh, I don't think so, Lisa. By the way, do you know where his wife went?"

"His former wife."

"Aren't they still married?"

"Only technically."

"Being married is a technical thing, is it?"

Lisa gave an exasperated sigh.

"Joe, what are you going on about? Why are you here?"

"I've been trying to contact Graham's wife. I haven't been able to."

"Okay," she said slowly. "So what? And why are you trying to contact her?"

"I have a bad feeling about Graham. And his landlord just confirmed it."

Lisa leaned back against the doorframe and actually laughed. "So you're having a fit of jealousy sixteen years too late."

"What? No. It's not about that."

"I think it is. You see me with someone else, and suddenly you feel wronged."

Joe felt blood rush to his face. The accusation was so unfair.

"That's not why I feel wronged."

"Why then?"

"If you want to know, I feel wronged because you lied to me and abandoned me and broke my heart."

The words came out in a rush. He'd never meant to say them, and now that he had, he felt like a fool.

Lisa must have agreed. She closed the door in his face.

CHAPTER 64

After closing the door, Lisa squeezed her eyes shut.
Stupid, stupid, stupid. She turned, and, with purpose, strode up the stairs. *No fighting*, she reminded herself. She wanted to be in a good mood for Christopher's recital.

Graham was snoring loudly as he lay in her bed. She looked at him, sprawled out topless, one leg splayed across her side of the bed, his mouth hanging open. A worn pair of boxer shorts the only thing that gave the scene a scrap of decorum, though one testicle peeped out the side like a baby mouse.

What had she ever seen in him? She couldn't understand it. It was as if she'd had cataracts, and during the night they'd cleared. She went and pulled the curtains, then opened the window. Graham shifted in the bed.

"All right, love?" he said.

He stretched and yawned.

"We need to talk," Lisa said.

"Now?"

"Now."

"About what?"

Lisa hesitated. Maybe she was being a bit unreasonable. He wasn't even awake properly yet. "I'll make breakfast," she said.

"Thanks, love. Give me a shout when it's ready, will you?"

She went downstairs, and got out a bowl, thinking she'd try a pancake recipe she'd seen recently. It used cream of tartar to make the pancakes fluffy. Should she make bacon too? Or would Graham prefer fruit on top? Bacon, of course. He was never going to be a vegetarian. She got out the flour, and a carton of eggs, and was reaching for the milk when she froze.

Lisa was meant to be *confronting* Graham. But here she was spoiling him with culinary treats.

Alright then. No fancy breakfast.

She took another look in the cupboard and found some small packets of cereal. The kind that contained enough to fill a tiny bowl. There were a variety of flavours. Lisa picked the plainest one she could find – cornflakes – got out a bowl, and was about to pour the cereal into it, when she stopped herself again.

Let Graham do it.

She threw the unopened carton of cereal into the bowl and put it on the table.

"Breakfast's ready," she called.

She heard nothing back. Maybe Graham had gone back to sleep. That would be just like him. The life of an artist.

"*Breakfast,*" Lisa shouted.

His voice, sleepy and surprised: "Okay, love."

She sat down at the table to wait. Coming into the kitchen, Graham glanced at the cereal. He came over and kissed Lisa's cheek.

"Good morning. Any milk?"

"In the fridge."

"Lovely."

He got it out and sat down, shooting furtive looks at Lisa.

"Everything alright?" Graham said.

Lisa sighed. "Are you behind on your rent?"

"What? Why do you ask about that?"

"Can you just answer the question? Is that why you decided you want to live with me?"

Graham looked appalled. "What's with the interrogation?"

"Joe was here. He said your landlord is outside your place." Lisa jerked her head sideways, in the direction of Graham's house. "Evicting you. Accusing you of not paying rent for months."

Graham pushed back his chair and stood up. "What? That's disgraceful. I've always been a model tenant. There must be some mistake."

"Let's go and talk to your landlord then."

"Good idea," Graham said. He sat back down. "I'll do it first thing. I just need some food in my stomach first. You know I wouldn't be surprised if this is something to do with Philippa."

Lisa sighed. She watched Graham shovel food into his mouth.

For some reason, she wasn't surprised to find him bringing up his ex-wife. Or wife. Or whatever she was.

"Philippa hasn't been around for ages, right? So how could she be involved?"

"I'm not sure." He spoke through a mouthful of half-chewed cornflakes. "But I wouldn't put it past her. She was always on the phone, talking to the landlord about this and that. She probably put him up to this."

"Graham, stop."

"What?"

"Have you paid your rent or not?"

"Of course I have," he said. "Every cent. What kind of person do you think I am? I told you I gave my notice anyway, so this is bull. He's probably annoyed he has to find a new tenant. It's impossible to find one as good as me."

Graham finished his cornflakes and brought the bowl over to the sink. He gave the spoon and bowl a cursory rinse under the cold running water, then dumped them on the draining board.

"Maybe we're moving too fast," Lisa said. "Maybe we should slow down. Spend some time apart."

Graham gave her a hard look.

"I don't think so," he said.

CHAPTER 65

At the station, Joe was following up leads that might help him catch Barry Wall. Anne-Marie Cunningham and Kevin Boyle were following up on trying to contact Aidan Donnelly, who still hadn't turned up. Other officers were checking out CCTV and digging up potential witnesses. Alice Dunne was at a counselling session with a psychologist after discharging three rounds into the suspect on the motorbike the previous afternoon.

Joe decided to go next door to the cemetery to clear his mind. He'd just got to the front desk when a well-dressed lady in her late fifties walked hesitantly in the door of the station. She looked nervous and clutched her handbag to her chest. She swallowed as she approached the desk.

"Hello, I – I'd…" She closed her eyes for a second, as if taking a moment to compose herself. "I'm sorry. I'm not sure I should be here."

"That's alright," the desk sergeant said, as he handed Joe the key to the lock on the cemetery's gates. "What's the matter?"

Joe walked around the back of the desk, heading for the door. He was just about to go outside when the lady spoke again.

"My son didn't come home last night."

"Okay," the sergeant said. "What age is he?"

"John's seventeen." Joe froze as the woman gave a humourless laugh. "My husband told me not to come. He said it was nothing. I'm just – I'm worried."

"That's very understandable. Now, if you could give me some—"

Joe placed his hand on the sergeant's shoulder.

"I'll take care of this," he said.

The sergeant looked at him in surprise.

"Okay," he said. "Detective Sergeant Byrne will assist you."

"Thank you very much," the lady said.

She was small and birdlike, and Joe felt like hugging her.

He led her down the corridor to his office. There was no one else around, so he was able to borrow Cunningham's chair. He pushed it over to his desk.

John Kavanagh's mother sat down on it.

"Would you like a cup of tea?" Joe asked.

A pathetic gesture, but he wanted to do her some kindness.

"Oh, no, thank you."

Joe didn't know exactly what he expected Michael Kavanagh's wife, and John Kavanagh's mother, to be like, but he didn't expect her to be like this. The lady smelled faintly of rose water. She was wearing a floral blouse over white trousers. Her hair was neatly brushed and hung down to her shoulders. She looked like she was dressed for a special occasion.

Even now, she clutched her handbag tight, as if afraid of letting go of it.

Joe felt himself choking up. He blinked quickly and took a breath.

"May I take your name?"

"Ethel Kavanagh."

Joe wrote it down, and her address too. The house was a ten-minute walk away. Close to Lisa's place.

"Maybe you could tell me everything from the start."

"Of course. My son, John, didn't come home from school yesterday."

"Where does he go to school?"

"The Highfield Academy on Clyde Road. I called him at about six o'clock, but he didn't answer. I kept some dinner warm for him but he never came home. I called him again and again after that and I called his friend's mother, Ann Harrison. She hadn't seen him either. He wasn't with her son."

"Does your son usually come home on time?"

Mrs. Kavanagh squeezed her bag tighter. "Not always. John's not a bad lad, you understand. But he's… he sometimes stays out a little late. You probably know how teenagers are."

Joe nodded. "So he didn't come home last night? And you heard nothing from him?"

Mrs. Kavanagh shook her head. "I stayed up all night, waiting, but he never showed."

Joe cleared his throat. He was struggling to keep it together.

"Has that ever happened before? Could he have stayed over at another friend's house?"

"It's possible. He sometimes stays over at his friend's house without telling me. But usually if I call his phone, he'll answer eventually, or at least send me a text. If he's not at the Harrison house, I don't really know where he'd be. I'm afraid he's had an accident. Maybe he had something to drink... Once he went to the beach and fell asleep there. I just don't know. I'm worried. Could you help me find him?"

The woman's trembling voice shook Joe, reminded him that the boy wasn't a vicious bully to Ethel Kavanagh. He was her son. A young man struggling through the hardest years of his life, just like Christopher. It took all the willpower Joe had not to tell her the truth.

He said, "I'll do all I can to see you right."

It was the only sincere thing he could say. Joe couldn't bring her son back to life, but he could do his best not to draw out her suffering.

He resolved there and then that he couldn't just dump Kavanagh's body. He would let it be found somehow, so it could be buried, so this woman would know John was dead, and at least have some closure.

Joe was about to ask for a few more questions, when he heard raised voices.

Mrs. Kavanagh looked startled.

"It's okay," Joe said, raising his hand. But she knew better than he did. They turned in unison to see Superintendent Michael Kavanagh march into the room.

"Ethel, I told you not to come," he said. From his dismissive tone, he might as well have been rebuking a new recruit, rather than speaking to his wife.

"John hasn't turned up yet."

"You're embarrassing me," Kavanagh said. He turned to Joe. "Forget it. My wife is overreacting."

"With all due respect," Joe said, "I think she's right to be worried. If he's missing, he might be in danger."

"That's enough. He's only had a few beers and fallen asleep in a hedge somewhere. Stop arsing around, and do some real work."

Mrs. Kavanagh got to her feet. She looked at Joe.

"Thank you," was all she said. But it was a *thank you* that sounded like *help me*.

Then she was walking out the door.

Superintendent Kavanagh turned to Joe.

He said, "Your job is to catch Barry Wall. Don't get confused."

Then he turned and followed his wife out the door.

"Shit," Joe muttered.

He leaned back in his chair and closed his eyes. When he'd composed himself, he opened them again and looked at the notes he'd written down.

John Kavanagh, missing since…

He tore the page off the pad, scrunched it up, and threw it in the bin.

When he looked around, he realised that Alice Dunne was watching him from the doorway.

CHAPTER 66

Gravel crunched under Barry Wall's boots. The legs of his jeans were dusty and his T-shirt was wet around the armpits. The noon sun was out, baking dry the path and showing up every stone on the ground in sharp relief.

He'd spent the morning walking around Ken's property. Ken already had a house in Wicklow, but he said he liked this one better. He'd bought it the previous year, and this was the first time Wall had got a chance to see it.

The patch of land was a sprawling place, with a big house in the middle, pine forest on both sides, and a steep slope up to the back of the property. At the front end, there were disused stables, where they were keeping Aidan Donnelly, and a driveway that led out onto a narrow road.

The place was isolated.

Not a neighbour for many kilometres.

Wicklow was handy like that. Unforgiving. Sparsely populated. Its landscape had been shaped by the last Ice Age. It was characterised by valleys, forests, lakes and the predominantly granite mountain range that extended down to the suburbs of south Dublin.

Aidan Donnelly had spent the night hovering on the edge of a coma, and Wall hadn't been able to question him much. Wall had shown too much enthusiasm when they got Donnelly there the previous night. He'd started beating on him, unleashing all the rage and pain he'd carried inside since Valentina's disappearance, and he just couldn't stop. Ken had pulled him away, but it was too late.

Donnelly remained unresponsive. Unconscious. But not dead. Wall needed the bastard to *talk*. So he was forced to wait.

Ken walked ahead of Wall, up the steep dirt path to the back of the property.

"Here," Ken said. "Stop and take a look."

Wall did, once he had reached the top of the hill. Squinting in the sun, he looked down on the house, the top of which was maybe two storeys below them.

"There's another road behind us," Ken said after a moment. "Good for a quick escape."

Wall scowled. His face felt hot from the sun.

"This reminds me of—"

"Home? Yeah."

The house they had grown up in was isolated too, though not as much as this, and it had lain over the county line, in Dublin.

"I'm going to check on Donnelly," Wall said.

"Whoa, wait for me. We don't want you losing it on him again, do we?"

Wall set off down the path, with Ken trotting behind. The door to the disused stables creaked when Wall pulled it open. A shaft of light fell across Aidan Donnelly's pathetic form. He was where they had left him, shackled to the wall. He flinched in the blinding light.

Wall walked over to him. "So you're not dead."

Donnelly said nothing. Wall crouched down in front of Donnelly.

"Ready to tell me the truth?"

"I don't *know* the truth."

"You're going to talk. And I don't mean some day. I mean, now."

Donnelly shook his head.

"I never hurt your wife."

The man's insistence that he was innocent was infuriating. "Then who did?"

"I have no idea."

"I'm going to kill you, if you don't tell me. What do you think about that?"

Donnelly looked Wall in the eye. His voice trembled, but he spoke firmly all the same. "I still don't know what happened to Valentina."

"If you tell me, I'll let you go."

"I don't think you will."

"Fair enough. But I'll make it easier for you, at least. I'll tell you what. I'll release you. Yes, I will come after you again. But I'll give you a head start. One hour. How does that sound?"

"I don't *know* anything."

Wall smashed his huge fist down in a brutal arc. It hit the side of Donnelly's face. His head snapped to the side with a crunch, and blood shot out his mouth.

Ken grabbed his brother.

"Hey, hey. Take it easy, Barry. Let's give him a minute. You don't want to kill him."

No, Wall didn't want to kill him.

Yet.

CHAPTER 67

Joe found a parking meter on Clyde Road and paid for twenty minutes. The small car park at the front of the Highfield Academy was taken up by a flashy sports car and a slightly less showy Mercedes. Joe was admiring them in passing when he heard Dunne's voice.

"Are we in the wrong line of work?"

Joe spun around. Dunne was standing behind him. Today her hair was in a ponytail. She was wearing shades, a crisp black blouse, and dark grey trousers that clung to her body. The sun lit her up like she was on fire. She looked spectacular.

Joe guessed that Cunningham's shift had ended and Dunne had taken over his security detail again.

"You seem to be doing okay. I mean, a Cartier watch?"

"Pretty, isn't it?"

"Anyway, I thought you were meant to be doing surveillance," Joe said. "Are you *familiar* with surveillance?"

Dunne smiled. "I like close surveillance. What are we doing here?"

Joe wanted to talk to Christopher, but he searched for another excuse for his visit to the school.

He said, "Ethel Kavanagh said her son goes to school at the Highfield Academy."

"The superintendent said to drop it, right?"

"I will. I just want to see if the kid turned up. Stay here. I'll be back in a minute."

Joe started towards the door. Immediately, Dunne followed. She said, "I'm here now. I might as well come in."

She started up the big granite steps.

Joe had never been there before. It looked more like a grand old house than a school. He could imagine them carving out a small exclusive graduate list, headed for law, finance and government. Christopher was a smart enough kid when he wasn't trying to OD, but it was hard to imagine him in such a group.

The middle-aged lady at the reception desk greeted them with a scornful glance. Joe thought maybe only he got the scornful glance. Dunne looked like she belonged here, and wherever else she wanted to be, for that matter.

Joe introduced them.

"Identification please," the receptionist said, checking it briskly. "Very good. How may I assist you?"

"John Kavanagh's mother, reported him missing this morning."

"John Kavanagh. A fifth year," the receptionist said.

"Has he come into school today?"

"No," she said. "I have already phoned Mrs. Kavanagh to let her know."

Dunne turned to Joe. "Do you want to talk to his teachers?"

"Not at the moment," he said. He turned back to the receptionist. "But, while I'm here, I'd like to speak to another one of your students. Christopher O'Malley."

The woman peered at him suspiciously.

"Is this about John Kavanagh too?"

"No," Joe said quickly.

"May I enquire as to the matter to which it *does* relate?"

"You may. I just want to have a word with him. I'm his father."

She looked Joe up and down again, as if to confirm her initial assessment. "I thought your name was Byrne."

"He doesn't carry my name."

"Do you have any proof that you're his father?"

"Twenty-three chromosomes, all of them full of DNA. Ask Christopher, if you're so dubious."

She scowled like that was an outrageous request, but rose with laboured grace and strutted down the hall. She was wearing towering heels and a long skirt that prevented her feet from straying more than an inch apart.

Dunne broke her silence. "Your son goes to school here?"

"Yeah."

The receptionist was back in a minute, accompanied by Christopher. He looked worried.

"Mr. O'Malley has confirmed your bona fides. You have five minutes until the next period begins. I would ask you not to delay him."

"Understood," Joe said. "Is there a garden out back?"

"The botanical education space is at the rear."

"Dunne, I'm going to the botanical education space. At the rear."

"Gotcha," Dunne said. She sank into a rickety antique chair, placed between the front door and the reception desk. Her impassive face watched Joe.

When Christopher managed to tear his eyes away from Dunne, he led Joe down the hall and out the back door. The garden opened up in an explosion of colours and shapes.

"Lisa would love this," Joe said. The back garden was full of all kinds of plants, some outdoors and others in a greenhouse to one side. All labelled.

"She does. She's seen it."

They sat down at a bench. Out in the light, his face fully illuminated, Christopher appeared even queasier than he had indoors. Joe wasn't sure how to start, so he just launched into it.

"John Kavanagh's mother came to the station and reported him missing this morning."

"Oh?"

Christopher stared at his feet.

"It's important that you tell me what happened."

"I don't know what you mean."

"You're an awful liar," Joe said. "Look, I'm not trying to blame you for anything. Whatever happened."

That caught his attention.

"What do you mean?" Christopher said slowly.

"Let me tell you what I think. I think you walked home with John Kavanagh."

"No. I didn't."

Joe took a breath. "Not arm in arm, best buddies, but you were in Herbert Park at the same time as him. And something happened."

Joe looked deep into Christopher's eyes and let the silence between them grow thick. Christopher began hyperventilating.

"Whoa, whoa, take it easy," Joe said. He put his hand on the boy's shoulder.

"I was there," Christopher said, "and he was there, yeah."

"Okay. What happened?"

"I thought I'd… tell him to… leave me alone. I'd brought… this is going to sound stupid."

"Keep going. What did you bring? Tell me."

"I brought a knife… so that I could scare him."

Joe wanted to say that had been an awful idea, but he stopped himself. No point making things worse. "Then what happened?"

"He saw me coming and he took the knife off me."

"Did you stab him?"

Christopher looked up. "What? No. He took the knife off me, and he said he was going to kill me."

The bell inside began to ring. Joe guessed the period was over.

Time up.

"What then?"

"I have to get to class."

"You're not going anywhere until you answer my question. What happened?"

"I ran home."

"You didn't fight him?"

"No, I'm not good at fighting. I ran away."

An impatient call came from inside the building. "Mr. O'Malley?"

"You didn't hurt him?" Joe said.

"I *wanted* to," Christopher said, looking at his feet. "But no, I didn't."

The receptionist came and stood just outside the door, looking down on the garden like it was her personal fiefdom. She said icily, "Mr. O'Malley. Class is commencing."

"Okay." Christopher got to his feet. "I better go to class."

"Okay."

"Are you coming to the recital today?"

"Recital?" Joe said.

"Didn't Mum tell you? We're performing Mozart for the parents."

"I don't know. I'll try," Joe said.

He watched Christopher head back inside. He was pretty sure that Christopher was telling him the truth. He hadn't killed Kavanagh. But if he didn't do it, then just whose crime had Joe covered up?

He started back into the building, walked along a corridor lined with the qualifications of the school's teachers and awards in excellence which the school had received.

His phone buzzed.

There was a text message from an unknown number.

It said, *Thanks for taking care of the body.*

CHAPTER 68

The old stables were cool and dark. A horsey smell still permeated the air, now joined by the coppery tang of blood. Barry was breathing heavily with the exertion of questioning Donnelly for an hour.

Donnelly didn't look like he was breathing at all, and it was hard to tell whether he was still alive, behind the mask of blood.

Ken took a hand mirror from the shelf on the wall and held it in front of Donnelly's mouth. After a few seconds, the glass misted slightly. He gave his brother a thumbs-up.

"Breathing."

"Good," Barry said.

"The little bastard is tougher than he looks."

Barry scowled. "He's not tough. He's nothing. What kind of man would pick on a woman?"

"I just mean, he's holding out pretty well."

Ken's phone rang. He pressed the green button and pressed the device to his ear. An older lady's voice spoke: "Please hold for Charles Pennington, Governor of Mountjoy Prison."

What an unexpected pleasure. He listened to elevator music as he waited.

"Good morning, Mr. Wall."

"Call me Ken."

"Good morning, Ken. This is Charles Pennington from Mountjoy Prison. Is this a convenient time for you to talk?"

Ken looked at Donnelly, chained to the wall, beaten half to death, the dried blood on his eyes now drawing flies. Barry stood beside him, eager to finish the job.

"Now is fine."

"I'm sure you know why I'm calling."

"Because of Barry."

"That's right, Ken. Barry escaped custody on Wednesday afternoon at approximately four o'clock, Ken."

Ken stifled a chuckle. This pencil-pusher thought he'd get on his good side by using his name a lot. Not a bad trick, but goofy when overdone.

"I know that, Charles."

The Governor cleared his throat. "Yes, well, I wanted to let you know, Ken, that we're eager to place your brother in custody again, for his own safety and the safety of the public."

"How exactly does his own safety come into it, Chuck?"

"We think Barry is in a fragile frame of mind. He might not be thinking very clearly, Ken. We all know he's had a tough time over the last year."

Barry had just opened the door and was standing in the doorway, looking out. His bulky frame silhouetted against the early summer light. Blood dripped from his knuckles onto the door saddle beneath his shoes. He didn't look fragile.

Ken said, "I hear you, Charlie. So what do you want from me?"

"You may not believe this, but I'm trying to help your brother. Ken, if he tries to make contact with you, I would urge you to inform the Gardaí or myself immediately. Perhaps, Ken, you could try and contact him. That would be best for him."

"You're right, Charlie."

"So you'll help us contact him?"

"No, I mean that I don't believe you."

Ken ended the call. He doubted they were trying to trace it. According to his source, no warrant had been issued to that effect. They were just fishing, and they were going to go home hungry.

Ken walked to the doorway and clapped his brother on the shoulder.

He said, "I better go take care of some business."

Barry looked around.

"What was that about?"

"Charles Pennington says hello. He wants you to go home."

CHAPTER 69

Joe felt dizzy. The phone slipped from his sweaty hand. He caught it before it hit the floor. Around him, the Highfield Academy's beautiful corridor, with all its impressive certificates, seemed to twist. Joe was suddenly dizzy, plunging, reeling with vertigo.

He closed his eyes and forced himself to take a deep breath.

Then he looked at the text message again. It didn't read any better the second time.

Thanks for taking care of the body.

Someone knew.

And Joe figured that that someone was the real killer. The one who had sunk a knife into John Kavanagh's side and left him dead in the grass. They couldn't have been expecting an idiot like Joe to come along and take the corpse, but that was what had happened.

Christopher hadn't killed anyone. Someone else had, and Joe had helped them get away with it.

It was all over. Joe had hoped to find a way out of this mess, but it was never going to happen now.

He looked at the unfamiliar phone number. There was nothing to lose by calling it. He hit the green button and waited as it rang. His body flooded with adrenaline. More and more. He couldn't keep still, couldn't stop shaking. The phone just rang and rang. Joe ended the call.

He tapped out a text message. *I think you have the wrong number.*

"Excuse me?" A woman's voice. The secretary was standing next to her desk. She was peering down the corridor at him. "Detective Sergeant Byrne? May I assist you with something?"

"I don't think so."

He began to walk towards her. At that moment, his phone buzzed. He could feel the secretary staring at him, willing him to leave the building, but he stopped to read the new message.

No mistake, Joe.

Then another message.

I see you still have poor John in your boot. Does he smell bad yet?

"Oh, fuck," Joe said.

He sensed rather than saw the secretary put her hands on her hips.

"Detective Sergeant Byrne, kindly refrain from such profane language while on the grounds of this—"

"Shut up," Joe said.

"Excuse me?"

He slipped the phone into his pocket and walked to the door. Dunne was standing there.

"What's up?" she said. "You're sweating."

"It's hot," Joe said.

"Did you tell that woman to shut up?"

"Let's get out of here."

Joe brushed past her, wiping the sweat off his brow while he went. He felt like he could barely breathe.

"Aren't you going to introduce me to your son?"

"Christopher had to go back to class. I barely got to speak to him. Anyway, it doesn't matter."

They walked out into the sun. Dunne started down the steps. Joe traipsed after her.

I shouldn't have moved the body. That was a mistake. Now I'm going to pay for it.

He was about to be exposed. Blamed for covering up a murder. Maybe he'd even be blamed for *carrying out* the murder.

How could he have been so stupid?

The best thing to do now was turn himself in. Admit what he'd done and face the consequences. Because that was the only way he could point the investigation into John Kavanagh's disappearance in the right direction – and start looking for the real killer. Joe thought of Ethel and Michael Kavanagh, waiting for John to come home.

"What now?" Dunne said without looking back. Her feet crunched on the gravel of the driveway. Should he let Dunne do it? Slip the handcuffs on and take him to the station?

They reached the end of the driveway. Dunne stopped next to her car. Only then did she turn and see his face.

"Joe, what's wrong?"

She touched his arm. It was almost more than he could take.

"Joe?"

He turned away from her and wiped his face with his sleeve. Dunne grabbed his shoulder, pulled him around.

"You can tell me. Whatever it is. I won't judge, okay?"

Joe snorted. She'd judge alright if she knew what he'd done. Anyway, there was no point drawing out the inevitable.

"I like you, Dunne."

"Thanks," she said slowly, looking a little taken-aback.

"You know, I've always tried to be a good person."

"Okay," she said. "Maybe you have a fever. You want to see a doctor?"

He took a long breath and let it out. "No, I don't."

"You sure? I'm getting a weird vibe here."

Joe took out the key fob for his Honda. He pushed it into Dunne's hands.

"The boot," he said.

"What?"

"Go to my car. Look in the boot."

She gave him a quizzical look, then turned and started walking to his car.

CHAPTER 70

Maureen didn't get many callers, so she was normally cautious about opening her door. Today was an exception, though. When a knock came, she opened the door eagerly, sure that it must be Aidan. She'd called him to make sure he was okay, but he hadn't answered his phone. His mother couldn't say where he was, though there was nothing new about that. It would be just like him to appear at her door, though.

However, when she opened up, a stranger stood outside. A man, about forty, with a shiny bald head, in a sharp shirt and trousers, and well-shined leather shoes. Maureen thought she knew him from somewhere.

"Oh, hello," she said.

He took out his ID and held it up so that she could read it. The man was a Garda.

"What's wrong?" Maureen asked. Even before Joe Byrne had brutally attacked her nephew, her family didn't have much love for the police. Now that one of them was standing at her door, she felt worried. Was this officer here to tell her that something had happened to Aidan? "Is it about my nephew?"

The Garda nodded grimly.

"I'll need you to come with me," he said.

She was right. Something terrible had happened.

"Let me get my cardigan," she said.

CHAPTER 71

Alice Dunne walked to Joe's Honda, glancing back at him as she did so. He watched her, saying nothing. His life was just seconds away from ending. Everything he'd worked for, all his hopes and dreams – dashed. He'd sleep in a cell tonight, and for many more nights to come.

Joe's phone buzzed. He took the device out of his pocket and checked it. Another text from the anonymous number.

Get me €100,000 in cash. Not traceable. You have six hours. Instructions will follow. If you do what I say, your secret is safe with me.

The demand was impossible. Completely impossible. But Joe had a sudden feeling of elation. The person texting him wanted something and that meant there was hope. Joe could walk away from this. That is, if he could find the blackmailer in the next six hours, before his deadline expired, it might still be possible to walk away from this.

Dunne was at the back of the Honda, feeling for the button to open the boot. She was seconds away from finding John Kavanagh's corpse.

"Wait," Joe called.

But Dunne had just found the button. She pressed it and the lid of the boot popped open a centimetre.

Joe sprinted to the car.

"What?" Dunne said, starting to lift the lid of the boot with one hand. Joe caught a glimpse of the plastic wrap covering the body.

He reached her just as the top of the boot was reaching her line of sight. He grabbed it, pushed it down. Made sure it was shut.

"Never mind," Joe said.

She gave him a quizzical look.

"Come on," she said. "What's in the boot?"

Joe said, "I have something I wanted to show you, but it doesn't matter."

"What is it?"

Think fast, Joe.

"A present for Christopher, but you know what? I'll show you later."

"I don't understand."

"That's okay. Forget it."

Dunne still looked confused, but she said, "Where are we going now?"

"Good question."

Another text message. Joe checked it.

Catch you later, Joe.

Not if I catch you first, he thought. He had about fifty euro in his bank account, so he wasn't going to be able to get the money. But he had six hours to track this bastard down.

Joe said, "I don't know about you, but I need a coffee."

"Are you sure you're feeling alright?"

"I'm starting to feel better."

*

He took Dunne to Bean Machine, a café on Upper Leeson Street. The place was a regular haunt of Joe's. He knew Derek and Iris, the couple who owned the place. There was only room for ten small tables. The glass counter was at the back, where Iris displayed her freshly baked pastries.

They served strong coffee in generous cups, always accompanied by a dark chocolate with mint filling. The menu was full of crepes and omelettes.

Derek was behind the counter today. Joe gave him a wave and sat down. After a moment, Derek brought over a couple of menus. He was a tiny man with jet-black hair and small, pink features.

"Hello," he said, drawing the word out as he looked at Dunne, flirting even though his wife was on the other side of the room. Joe made a quick introduction, then asked for a pain au chocolat with his Americano. Dunne ordered herbal tea, then went to use the bathroom.

While she was gone, Joe started thinking.

If Christopher didn't kill John Kavanagh, then who did? Barry Wall had to be top of the list. He was just out of prison. If he'd found out that Joe was a father, he might have gone after Christopher, seen him walking through the park, then killed the wrong boy by mistake.

Since Joe had no other ideas for the time being, he'd have to think of Wall as his number one suspect. In that case, Joe's primary goal hadn't changed, merely intensified. He still needed to recapture Wall, but now his motivation was personal. Even more personal.

But was the killer the same person as the blackmailer? Would Wall really be looking for money? The questions were mounting.

Joe was so deep in thought that it took him a moment to realise that Derek was at his side with the order.

"Your friend is gorgeous," Derek said as he put Dunne's pot of tea down on the table, along with Joe's coffee and pastry.

"Derek."

"I'm just saying. She looks like just what you need."

Joe rubbed his eyes. "I was thinking of trying again with Lisa."

Derek straightened up, put his hands on his hips. "Forget about Lisa."

Joe nodded. "Turns out she's dating someone. A real asshole too. But I keep—"

"Forget Lisa. She had her chance with you. For goodness sake, Joe, it's been *sixteen years*. How can you still be hung up on her? After what she did to you? You could have had a thousand girlfriends since then. You're wasting your life."

"But there's Christopher."

"So what? He grew up without you. She never even told you about him until you came back here."

Joe nodded, remembering that evening in Tesco the previous summer.

"Keep the change," he said, handing over ten euro.

Derek slapped him on the shoulder and walked off to look after another customer. Joe took a sip of coffee and began munching on the pain au chocolat.

He turned his mind back to the blackmailer.

Maybe the money was an excuse, a way to lure Joe to go somewhere. Perhaps Wall just wanted to torture and kill him.

Wall must have killed John Kavanagh, then hurried away when he realised that the dead boy wasn't Christopher. Then Joe had come along, like an idiot, and hidden the crime. Wall had probably been hiding somewhere nearby.

Joe took out his phone. He sent a text to the blackmailer's number. *Who is this?*

Unsurprisingly, there was no reply.

The bathroom door creaked as it opened. Dunne appeared in the doorway.

Joe forced himself not to stare at her. Instead, he tapped out another text message to the blackmailer.

This is bullshit. You've got the wrong number.

If only he could get rid of Kavanagh's body, and clean out his car, there'd be nothing to tie him to the crime, even if someone made allegations to the contrary. Especially if it was Barry Wall telling people Joe had hidden a crime. Who'd believe him?

Dunne took her seat, her movements as graceful and economical as those of a puma.

"I'll get this," she said, nodding at their order.

"I already paid."

Joe poured tea from the pot into her cup.

"A gentleman." She smiled. "It's unexpected to come to the big city and find a gentleman. I guess it's one of those weird things that happens in life. You know what I mean?"

Joe laughed. "Not really."

Dunne leaned forward. "You know, sometimes something unexpected happens. Like you crash your car, but walk away from it in one piece, and you feel this *thrill*. You feel so alive."

"Okay," Joe said slowly, still not sure he got her point.

"Something surprising and beautiful. Like the kindness of…"

She broke off.

"The kindness of what?"

"Never mind." An enigmatic smile played at the corners of Dunne's mouth. "You'll understand what I mean when you experience it." She took a sip of herbal tea. "So what's next?"

"We need to find where Wall is hiding."

"Nothing new about that," she said.

"I'm thinking of Ken Wall."

"He's not exactly cooperative."

"Maybe we could try his office again. Maybe he won't be there this time."

"Try his punk secretary?"

"She was nice. We could have another crack at her. Or maybe there'll be another member of staff there this time. If you have a better idea, I'm listening."

She shrugged. "That stuff's all going to be on a computer, right? The company's holdings?"

"Right," Joe said. "On a computer hard drive or on the cloud."

"Wherever it is, it's going to be in digital form."

"Obviously."

"We could see if there's some way to get at that information."

"No judge is going to give us a warrant. We don't have grounds for one."

Dunne shrugged. "Maybe the information isn't very secure."

She took a sip of tea.

Was she suggesting that they should find someone to hack into Ken's computer systems? The only person Joe knew who might be able to do that was Lisa.

He gobbled down the last bite of pastry, finished off his coffee, brushed the flakes out of his lap and wiped his hands on a napkin.

His phone buzzed.

There was no text in this message. Just a photo. It was a little dark but Joe realised what he was looking at pretty quickly. It was a photo of Joe, rolling John Kavanagh's body up in plastic.

A second photo arrived. The next shot in the sequence. Joe stuffing Kavanagh's body into the boot of his car.

The photos weren't great quality. It looked like maybe whoever took the pictures had been standing far away and zoomed in.

Joe texted back, *Who is this?*

He waited half a minute for the reply. *Never you mind.*

Another buzz.

Your deadline has been brought forward. Now you have two hours to get the money. That's what you get for pushing me.

Joe broke out in a sweat.

He wrote, *That's not enough time.*

A reply came.

I'll give you instructions in one hour.

Joe looked at the photos again. They weren't great, but they were good enough to ruin his life. He deleted them.

Dunne leaned forward in her chair. "Who's texting you?"

"What?"

"Is that O'Carroll?"

"Um, yeah."

"What did he say?"

"He said…" Joe swallowed. "He said time is running out."

CHAPTER 72

The Highfield Academy's room called the Geranium Addendum reminded Christopher of an oversized cupboard. It was the school's "green room" for the purposes of the day's recital, the area where hushed Highfield Academy students preened before mirrors and prepared for performances, which always took place in the Orchid Suite. That was another small room, but it was the largest one in the building so by default became the Highfield Academy's amphitheatre.

Clara Fry sat in the corner of the Geranium Addendum tuning her cello. She glanced up when Christopher came in.

"Hey," he said.

"Hey."

Christopher went over to a seat on the other side of the room. He opened up the case of the violin. The instrument was borrowed from one of his Mum's friends. It wouldn't be the same as playing his own instrument, but of course it was better than nothing.

And he had no choice. Kavanagh had probably thrown Christopher's violin in a bin when he took it off him.

Clara gazed out the big bay window onto the road.

Just talk to her. There's no one else around. This is the perfect time. Say something.

"Are... are your parents coming to hear you?" Christopher asked.

"No," Clara said. Her London accent crisp as a peach.

"Why not?"

"My mom is busy working. My dad is travelling for work. I think he's in Brazil this week. Or maybe it's Mexico. It's hard to keep track."

"Oh, cool."

"Not really. He just arrives at the airport, and then he's driven to an office and has meetings. And then it's back to the airport. Then he's home for like an hour. And then he has to go away again."

"Oh. That sucks."

"How about you? Are your parents coming?"

"My Mum is coming."

"Nice." Clara said.

Silence.

Think of something. Say something, for god's sake.

Christopher thought desperately. Before he could come up with anything, Clara got up and walked out of the room. Christopher watched her go.

What the hell kind of crappy conversation was that? She'd never talk to him again. That was for sure. The door opened again. Christopher was surprised to see the secretary poke her head in.

"Mr. O'Malley, there's someone here to see you."

Someone. Not Mum. Not Joe. Not a teacher. Then who was it?

The secretary backed away and a man stepped into the room. He wore a sharp shirt and very shiny shoes. His bald head reflected light from the chandelier overhead. Christopher could smell his aftershave from across the room. The man fixed Christopher with a hard stare. He slowly removed his aviator sunglasses, tucked them into his shirt pocket, and walked over. His steps were firm, decisive. He stopped in front of Christopher. Quite deliberately, he looked Christopher up and down.

"Are you Christopher O'Malley?"

"Y-yes."

"Christopher, I'm here to talk to you about something very serious."

"Is it Mum? Is she okay? What's happened?"

The stranger held up his hands in a conciliatory gesture.

"Your mother is fine, as far as I know. I work with your father."

"Are you a detective?"

"Yes, I am."

"Can I see your identification?"

The man shot him a surprised smile.

"Yes, you can, and I'm glad you asked that. Very sensible of you."

He took a badge out of his pocket. Christopher just had time to glance at it before he put it away again.

He said, "You're in danger, son."

"What?"

The man held up his hands.

"But it's okay. I'm going to take you somewhere safe."

CHAPTER 73

Joe pressed the doorbell three times before Lisa opened up. He'd driven straight back to her house, after leaving the café. He needed to ask Lisa something. It was about money. Joe figured that Lisa was the wealthiest person he knew. She and her parents had a lot of money padding their bank accounts. He wondered if he could borrow some.

Enough to keep the blackmailer happy, and buy himself more time. If she didn't, Joe didn't know where he could find that kind of money.

Lisa opened the door, showing eyes that were bloodshot and cold. She crossed her arms as if to give herself support. Her voice was steady, though.

"What are you doing here again?"

"You okay?" he asked.

"Yes. Why not?"

"You look …"

Lisa crossed her arms. "I had an argument with Graham."

"What?" Joe said, suddenly distracted.

"No, not an argument. It's just... Who's she?" Lisa said, squinting past Joe, to where Dunne was parked.

"Surveillance."

Lisa tilted her head to the side, and took another look at Dunne. "What do you mean?"

"Barry Wall is still out there. My boss thinks he might target me."

"So they're using you as bait?"

"That's not why I'm here."

"Why then? I don't have much time. Christopher's recital is going to begin shortly."

"I have a personal question. Can I come in?"

Lisa stood aside. Quickly Joe stepped into the hall.

She said, "Go on into the kitchen."

"Are you working?" Joe asked as he made his way down the hall. He noticed another one of those awful paintings hanging on the wall. Another naked lady.

"Yes, I'm trying to work."

"Sorry for interrupting."

He sat down at the kitchen table. Lisa sat across from him.

"So what's up, Joe?"

"Was Christopher upset when he came home from school yesterday?"

"Why do you ask?"

Joe shrugged. "I wondered if there were any more bullying incidents."

"You already asked him about that."

"I know. But I have to ask again. John Kavanagh has gone missing."

Lisa's eyes widened. "What do you mean, missing?"

"He never went home last night. His mother came to the station this morning. She's worried something may have happened to him."

"Oh my god."

"Christopher said he doesn't know anything about it. But I feel like he might be holding out on me."

"He would never hurt anyone. You don't think he has *anything* to do with it, do you?"

Joe felt a flash of shame at his earlier suspicion. "I know he wouldn't hurt anyone. But I feel like he knows more than he's saying."

"He wouldn't lie to you."

"No."

You're the liar of the family, Joe thought. *You never told me I had a son.*

He wondered if Graham was upstairs. A bitter smile spread across his face.

"What?" Lisa asked.

Joe shook his head.

Just ask for the money.

Now.

"I thought you had a personal question," Lisa said.

For some reason, Joe was momentarily consumed with anger at her. It happened like that sometimes – thoughts of the past hit him from out of nowhere, and knocked him for a loop. This was one of those moments.

She'd gone and had Joe's kid and never told him. Never answered even one of the letters he sent her when he found out she was pregnant. And she just let him believe that the baby was someone else's. She never told him the truth. He had to wait so many years for his own kid to tell him he existed.

"How are your parents?" Joe asked. "The company is doing well?"

"They're fine. Why?"

"The money is rolling in?"

A bitter, mocking tone had crept into his voice.

"What's wrong with you?"

Joe needed a lot of cash, and this was the only place he could get it, so he struggled to put his feelings aside. To swallow his pride and ask for the money that would save him. But when he looked at Lisa, and her indifferent expression, he couldn't do it. He'd been running around trying to save her son. But did she care at all about him?

He stood up, the chair screeching as he pushed it back.

"You know what?" Joe said. "Never mind. You go and patch things up with your new boyfriend."

He walked down the hall, went out and slammed the door behind him.

CHAPTER 74

In the Highfield Academy's "green room", the bald detective held up his hands, a peaceful gesture that somehow alarmed Christopher.

He said, "I don't mean to scare you, okay? But I want to be straight with you."

"What's happening?" Christopher whispered, his mouth dry.

"We think you're in danger, but Joe sent me here to protect you."

"Where is he?"

"He's hard at work."

"I just saw him half an hour ago."

"I know." The detective scowled. "There have been developments in the case your father is working on."

Christopher swallowed. "You mean the prisoner? Barry Wall?"

"How much do you know about that?"

"A little."

"Then you know how serious this is. We think they might target you to get to Joe."

"Oh my god. Why do you think that?"

"We've received a tip-off. But don't worry. I'm here to make sure nothing happens to you."

"Can I still play in the concert?"

The man shook his head.

"Sorry, son. We need to get out of here right this minute."

CHAPTER 75

Joe sat at his desk in Donnybrook Garda Station. His phone sat in front of him. He was keenly aware of the other officers nearby. Cunningham was staring at her monitor. Boyle was away from his desk somewhere, which was a small mercy. Meanwhile, Dunne had claimed the spare desk in the corner as her own. She had followed him back to the station without a word. She was sitting there now, speaking on the phone to Ken Wall's secretary.

Pride is a terrible thing. That thought kept repeating in Joe's head.

Lisa might have loaned him the money if he'd kept calm and explained. Not explained exactly why he needed to borrow it, but to explain that he really did need it. If she didn't have a lot of cash around the house, she could have withdrawn some from the bank or else approached her parents. They must have had a lot of cash in the safes at O'Malley's offices.

But Joe hadn't asked.

He had nothing. And time was running out.

Pride is a terrible, terrible thing.

He pretended to read a document on his computer, but actually he stared into space, and waited as his panic surged.

In half an hour, if he wasn't able to produce the money, those photos would be released. The ones showing Joe and a very dead John Kavanagh together.

Then: an investigation.

Joe was already under investigation for the whole Ger Barrett/Kevin Boyle thing on Wednesday. He hadn't been worried about that before. But combined with a suspicion that he was involved in the murder of Christopher's bully? Plus the whole Aidan Donnelly/Barry Wall thing being basically his fault? A colossal weight was about to crush him.

It didn't bear thinking about.

Suspension. Arrest. Holding cell. Trial. Prison.

And, oh, would prison be fun for a detective. Maybe he'd end up under ACO Breda Murray's care.

He felt like shooting himself in the head.

Dunne hung up the phone.

"I wasn't able to get anything from the pink-haired punk. Ken obviously told her not to say a word to us."

Joe said nothing.

"You okay?" Dunne kept glancing his way, like he might make a run for the door.

"Never better."

"Let me know when you want to go out again."

Joe got the hint. *Don't go anywhere without your security detail.*

"Sure," he said.

Dunne gave him a doubtful look, as Joe's phone buzzed.

Have you got the money?

Joe thought for a second. Then tapped out a reply.

Yes.

Put it in a bag. Leave it at the south east corner of Anglesey Bridge in 45 mins.

That bridge ran over the River Dodder. It was just down the road.

Okay.

Don't try anything. We'll be watching.

Shooting himself was starting to seem like a better and better idea. But then an idea struck him. He remembered the counterfeit cash Cunningham had used as a decoy in an operation. It had cluttered the DDU office for months. Joe wondered if it was still around. He got to his feet and went to the locker in the corner. No sign of the money.

"What are you looking for?" Cunningham said.

"The counterfeit cash you had ages ago. Is it still here?"

"What?"

"Those bales of cash you had sitting here for half a year?"

Cunningham laughed. "No. I finally cleared that stuff out."

Joe kept his expression neutral but it was hard. His only idea had just gone down the toilet. Cunningham leaned back in her chair and yawned.

"Yep, the only bales of cash around here are the ones you confiscated from Barrett."

Joe sat down in his chair and sighed. Then he realised what she'd said. Could the money Ger

Barrett had planned to give to Boyle still be in the station?

"That money is still here?"

"Yep."

"Hasn't it been taken to PEMS?"

The dirty money should have been logged in as evidence and taken to the Store as soon as it reached David O'Carroll. Joe remembered O'Carroll calling Garda Jessica Nolan, asking her to take the money away. He remembered her reply. That there was a problem at the Store. Nolan had said they had a sewage leak, that they were unable to accept evidence. Joe had assumed that the issue had been resolved, but maybe it hadn't.

"No," Cunningham said. "They're still fixing up the Store."

Joe nodded thoughtfully while Cunningham returned to her work.

A possible solution – though it was far riskier with real money involved, especially money that was evidence in an investigation.

Still, a solution was a solution.

And it was all thanks to Boyle. Because of him, Joe might be able to get at a bag full of money. It wasn't €100,000, as far as Joe knew. He didn't know how much money it was. A third of that? Maybe more. But in the short term, it ought to be enough to convince the blackmailer that Joe was complying with their instructions.

He didn't plan on letting them keep the money. No one was going to get rewarded for blackmailing him. That was for sure.

The only problem was that the bag of money was probably locked up in Jessica Nolan's office. Joe would have to change that. He walked over to the door. Dunne looked up.

"Toilet," Joe said. "I doubt I'll meet Barry Wall there."

"I'll let you go alone then."

But he didn't go to the toilet. He went upstairs and found an empty room. From there, he phoned Jessica Nolan's desk. He made his voice as annoying as possible and said, "Hey, sugar buns."

"Jesus, Kevin. Is that you? What do you want?"

"Thought you might have come to your senses, Jessica. You feel like a drink later?"

Boyle's mannerisms came far too easily.

Nolan said, "Like hell I do."

"You sure? Because I could sweeten the deal and spring for a pizza?"

"Fuck off, Kevin."

"Fine," Joe said, trying not to laugh. "Then I'm glad your car is being burgled."

"What?"

"The alarm is going off. I hope your car gets stolen."

He ended the call, and grinned. He thought he had done a pretty good impersonation of Boyle. Now to see if she took the bait. He started down the stairs, just as Jessica Nolan came storming up the corridor. She nodded briskly before continuing towards the car park. Joe headed to her office.

There was a big fireproof safe with six drawers. It was meant for storing papers, but it was the only place Nolan could have locked up the backpack. The safe was secured by a simple lock. Why not? It wasn't meant to be used for storing evidence.

When Joe's father had been a detective, storing evidence around the station had been the norm, but standards had grown more stringent in the intervening years.

Joe slipped on a pair of latex gloves, and started looking for the key in the drawers of the desk. He worked through the top one quickly, then the second. Finally, he got to the third. There was nothing.

When a uniform walked past the open doorway, Joe thought his heart would jump out of his chest. But the guy went straight on down the corridor without looking in.

Joe felt around in case the key was taped to the underside of one of the drawers but it wasn't. Where the hell was it? Nolan would be back as soon as she realised her car was fine, which had to be a matter of seconds. Joe was taking too long.

He walked out into the corridor – and froze as Jessica Nolan appeared at the end of the corridor. She looked pissed. He quickly stepped away from her doorway, and pretended to be walking down the corridor.

"You seen Kevin?" she asked. "Sir," she added quickly.

"He's floating around somewhere. Upstairs, maybe?"

Joe figured this might buy him an extra half a minute to find the key.

Nolan shook her head. "Is there any chance you could mind my office for a moment sir? While the

Store is out of action, I'm not technically supposed to leave the evidence unattended."

Finally, some good luck. "No problem," Joe said.

He watched Nolan as she started up the stairs. As soon as she was gone, Joe ducked back into her room. He looked around – and saw a biscuit tin. As far as he knew, Nolan didn't eat biscuits. She was a fitness addict. She'd rather put heroin in her body than sugar.

He grabbed the tin and opened it up. Not only did he find one key, but the tin was full of keys. Maybe two dozen of them.

He brought the tin over to the safe and tore through it, trying every key until one finally unlocked it.

Nolan was guarding many plastic evidence bags, including the backpack full of money. There was a log inside too, for recording any interactions with the evidence. Joe scrawled Kevin Boyle's name in the log, next to the Exhibit Number corresponding to the bag of cash.

Then he replaced the key, grabbed the backpack, and headed for his Honda.

CHAPTER 76

Christopher stared at the detective.

"There's no time for my concert?" he said.

The man frowned. "I'm afraid not. It would be safer to move you to a secure location without delay."

"Please. My Mum is out there."

A phone rang. The detective reached into his pocket and took his out. He held up a finger to Christopher and stepped out of the room.

Christopher stared at the closed door as if the answers to his questions were written on it.

Who was coming after him? Was it this guy Wall by himself or did he have a gang? What would they do? Where was Joe? Where was his mother? Could he talk to her?

He'd been okay for a minute after hearing that a criminal might target him, but now he was starting to feel overloaded with stress.

This man was a *murderer*. Even worse than John Kavanagh.

He swallowed and ran a hand over his violin. It was nearly time for the concert to begin.

The detective burst through the door.

"They're coming," he said. "We've got to move you. *Now*."

He grabbed Christopher's shoulder and bundled him out the door, and past the secretary's unattended desk.

"Can I tell my Mum?"

"Later," the detective said. "For now, just run."

Christopher ran like he'd never run before, his hard, leather shoes crunching on the stones in the driveway, as he hurried after the detective, past the principal's sports car and out onto the road.

"Here," the detective said, pointing Christopher to a white van.

CHAPTER 77

Joe ran up the steps to his apartment, the backpack full of cash slung over his shoulder.

The lucky break he'd got finding the cash and been countered by an equal stroke of bad luck. Dunne had seen him getting into his car, and she had followed him.

He'd driven like a maniac all the way from Donnybrook, but he hadn't been able to lose her. He needed Dunne off his back so he could get to the drop-off with the blackmailer. So he had gone home. He had an idea that might work, but he needed to get something from his apartment.

Taking the stairs two at a time, in case Dunne decided to come in after him, Joe reached his apartment and let himself in. He immediately started tearing through the drawers in his sitting room. Nothing. He moved to the bedroom. He couldn't find what he was looking for there either. He took the whole drawer out and emptied it out onto his bed.

Then he found it. An old phone he'd stopped using because it had been running slowly. Aside from the slowness, the phone had been fine. He hoped it still was. He held his breath as he tried turning it on. The phone buzzed and warned that only 3% of the battery charge remained.

Joe found the charger and walked over to the kitchen table, where he plugged it in. Then he brought over his laptop and booted it up. He tried turning the phone on again. Once it was up and running, Joe activated the phone's GPS and logged onto Google on his laptop. He checked that he was able to track the phone's location.

It worked. A little blue dot appeared on the laptop screen, showing Joe's current location in Rathmines. The map automatically zoomed in on the area.

Joe checked the time. He was already running late and he had to let the phone charge a little or this would all be worthless.

He texted the blackmailer.

I'm on my way but I'll be five mins late.

A reply came back straight away.

Don't be 5 seconds late you cheeky bollocks.

The blackmailer wanted to play hardball. Or were they just saying that? If the money was coming, would they really blow the whole thing just because Joe was a little late? Probably not.

Joe tried to remain calm while he waited for the phone battery to creep up to 10%. That was still poor. Once a phone was below 30%, he didn't trust it much. But he couldn't wait all day. 10% would have to do. He'd just have to hope the phone would stay on long enough to do its job.

He shut off the laptop, unplugged the phone and stuffed it in the middle of a bundle of cash in the middle of the backpack. Then he moved to the window and peered out. Dunne's Lexus was on the street below, parked right behind his Honda. As expected, driving wasn't going to be an option.

He'd have to cycle. He hurried out the door, pausing only when Dunne's Cartier watch caught his eye. It was still sitting on his bookshelf, where she had left it. For some reason, the sight of it unnerved him.

He went racing back down the stairs. In the hallway, he grabbed his bike and wheeled it towards the back of the building, out the door and to the end of the garden, where a gate led out onto the lane behind.

He got in the saddle and started peddling like hell, headed for Morehampton Road, with the backpack full of dirty money strapped to his back.

He felt his phone buzz, and pulled over to the side of the road.

The blackmailer: *Where are you?*

Nearly there, Joe replied.

I'm going to release the photos. You and John...

I'll be there in 2 mins.

I should release them anyway, to teach you a lesson.

Joe texted back, *Do what you want but I have the cash.*

Don't try to be clever. It doesn't suit you.

Joe slipped the phone back into his pocket and got peddling even faster. He had the bike in the hardest gear and was urging it forwards with every ounce of strength he had. Finally, Anglesey Bridge came into view. At the south east corner, Joe stepped off the bike and peered over the side. A heron, still as a mountain, stood in the water of the Dodder, six or seven metres below. The branches of a tree, growing out of the river bank, reached up over the top of the bridge.

A text message arrived.

Leave the money on a branch.

Okay.

We're watching you. Three sniper rifles are pointed at your head. As soon as you drop the cash, leave the area.

Joe doubted that there were three sniper rifles pointed at his head. But what did he know? If this was Barry Wall, then anything was possible. He looked around but there were no pedestrians nearby, just cars passing, the drivers paying him no attention whatsoever.

He eased the backpack over the side of the bridge, and let it snag on the branch of the tree.

Leave, read the next text message.

Joe was very close to Donnybrook Garda Station and the irony was not lost on him. He would have loved to have some backup there to watch the blackmailer collect the bag. But he couldn't trust anyone to help him. They'd want to know what kind of mess Joe was in. And once his colleagues started asking that, he'd really be done for.

So he had to go it alone. And he had to leave the bag.

He mounted his bike, kicked off from the kerb and cycled back the way he had come, not racing the way he had on the way here, but not loitering either. He stopped a short distance away and looked back.

Buzz. Another text.

This is your FINAL warning. Leave the area or we WILL release the photos. Everyone will know what you did.

They were still watching him.

Joe turned around and headed back towards Donnybrook. He hadn't really expected that he'd be able to watch the blackmailer collect the bag. That would have been wishful thinking. He'd have to rely on his old phone. It was probably down to 8% already.

Joe cycled on, halfway back to Rathmines. There was no chance the blackmailer was still watching him. He pulled over.

He used his current phone to track his old one, concealed in the backpack full of cash.

When the map came up, Joe saw that the backpack was already moving. Fast. It must have been collected by someone in a car.

He turned and headed back to where he'd made the drop-off, but the blue dot marking the bag's location was moving away too quickly. He couldn't keep up. There were cars all around, and it was impossible to guess which one the money was in.

Joe needed a car. He tried to stop a passing taxi. No good. It sailed right past.

He'd lost the cash and he'd lost the blackmailer. He thought he could make this right, but only if he acted very quickly.

CHAPTER 78

At the Highfield Academy, Lisa took a seat in the back row and waited for the recital to begin. She wanted to be at the front, but the best seats were already taken. She'd been late, delayed by the men in her life.

Graham had scared her earlier, when she tried to dump him. The cold expression on his face – she hadn't been able to get it out of her mind. And when he'd said no, that they shouldn't spend some time apart, she'd been too surprised to argue. He'd turned charming a moment later, told her he loved her and Christopher, and suggested that they talk later. Then he'd gone out, saying he wanted to clear things up with his landlord.

Then there was Joe, with his questions about money, and his anger at her for breaking his heart. She hadn't thought he could still hang onto such pain after all these years.

Lisa tried to push those thoughts out of her mind as the principal walked out onto the stage.

"Ladies and gentlemen, proud parents, you're in for a treat this afternoon," he said.

Lisa took a breath. She was here to support her son. This was a big moment for him. She'd enjoy the recital and she hoped he did too, despite everything that was going on.

When the principal stepped aside, students with instruments walked out onto the stage. Not one of them was Christopher.

CHAPTER 79

Joe cycled home at a frantic pace. With every second that went by, the backpack of money was moving away from him. He needed a car so he could follow it.

His phone rang as he reached the lane behind his house. It was Lisa. He ignored her and jumped off the bike. He wheeled it up the garden path and in the back door. In the hallway, he stood the bike up against the wall, the place where everyone in the building left their bikes.

His phone rang again.

Lisa again.

He ignored the call. As soon as it stopped ringing, Joe used his phone to check the GPS tracker, which showed that the money was still moving.

He walked to the front door of the building and pulled it open. Dunne's Lexus was parked right outside, in the same place as it had been when he left. Dunne saw Joe and stepped out of the car. He didn't like the fact that she looked furious.

His phone rang again. Lisa again.

This time he answered.

He said, "I'm a little busy. Can I call you back?"

"Joe? Did a detective go to the school to talk to Christopher?"

"What? No. Why?"

"I can't find Christopher. They say someone came to talk to him, and now we don't know where he is."

Joe's stomach fell. "But he was doing his recital, right?"

"He didn't show up. He's – he's gone."

"I'll be right there."

Joe ended the call and ran outside. Dunne was standing on the footpath. She tried to talk to him.

"Not now," Joe said.

He got in the Honda and headed straight for the Highfield Academy. He needed to track down the blackmailer before the phone battery died, but Christopher came first. Hopefully there was an innocent explanation. But what if there wasn't? What if something had happened?

Clyde Road was packed with fancy cars belonging to Highfield Academy parents. Joe parked down the road and ran up to the school, pushing through clusters of parents standing around inside the door. Everyone had a glass of wine and was munching on nibbles. Joe found Lisa standing at the reception desk, leaning over the secretary.

"Hey," Joe said. He saw panic in Lisa's face. He squeezed her arm lightly, hoping to reassure her. "Anything new?"

"Joe, this woman won't tell me anything. She insists they did nothing wrong."

"Excuse me, Ms. O'Malley—"

Lisa jabbed her index finger at the receptionist. "You let someone talk to Christopher and now you can't find him. You have no idea what happened."

"Please lower your voice, Ms. O'Malley. We're looking for your son. Please take a seat for a moment."

Lisa slammed her fist on the desk. Joe had never seen her look so angry.

She said, "I've been waiting for fifteen minutes. This is a small building! Are you fucking defective? Where is he?"

The receptionist gaped at her in silence.

Joe said, "Have you tried his mobile?"

"Of course, I have. I guess he turned it off before the recital."

"Maybe one of his classmates knows something. Who's his best friend?" he asked.

Lisa said, "A boy named Peter."

"Is he here?"

"I don't know. I think I saw him earlier, in the garden."

Joe followed Lisa as she hurried down the corridor to the garden. Dozens of parents stood around, reflecting on the recital, chatting to each other and to the teachers.

"Him," Lisa said, pointing to a teenage boy.

She led Joe over to him. Joe caught the suspicious look the boy's mother gave as Lisa approached.

"Is everything alright?" the lady said icily.

"My son is missing," Lisa said.

"What do you mean?"

Lisa turned her attention to the boy.

"Peter, do you know where Christopher is?"

The boy looked at his feet. "I saw him with some man."

"Some man?" Joe said. "Who was he? Did they go somewhere together?"

Peter shrugged. "I don't know."

Lisa said, "This is important."

The boy's mother frowned. "Take it easy, Lisa."

"What did the man look like?" Joe said.

"I only saw him for a second. He was bald."

"Was he a big man?"

Peter said, "Average." He thought for a moment. "Maybe he wasn't with Christopher. I'm not sure. But I saw Christopher near the door. There was a bald man near him."

Lisa took Joe's arm and pulled him aside. She said, "Who's this man? Do you think it's Barry Wall?"

"No, Wall is as big as a mountain."

"Then what?"

"What if the man has nothing to do with it?" Joe said, "What if Christopher left voluntarily? Where would he go?"

Lisa said. "Home?"

"Let's take a drive."

Joe gave the receptionist his number as he passed her desk, and told her to call if Christopher turned up. Lisa followed Joe out to his Honda.

He pulled away from the kerb with a screech of rubber. Dunne's Lexus appeared in the rear-view mirror, right behind him.

"Let's check around here," Joe said.

He did a loop of the block, but there was no sign of Christopher, so he continued driving around, thinking about where the boy might have gone. He drove to the road separating the two sides of Herbert Park. Ignoring the beep of the car behind, he slowed down so they could scan the area.

Lisa said, "Joe, what if someone did something to him?"

The thought sent a pulse of panic through him. Wall wasn't able to get to Joe because of all the surveillance. But he might target Joe's son. Could it have been one of his accomplices? Could it have been Ken Wall? He wasn't the kind to get his hands dirty, but maybe he'd make an exception to help his brother exact revenge.

Lisa said, "That boy, John Kavanagh."

Joe tensed. "What about him? I don't think John Kavanagh did anything to Christopher."

"He couldn't have. But what if someone else wants payback?"

Joe stared at her.

"Payback for what? And how do you know John Kavanagh *couldn't* have done anything?" Joe said slowly.

Lisa's eyes darted around.

"I mean – I mean, he's missing too… so…"

Joe brought the Honda to a stop at the side of the road.

"As of this moment, John Kavanagh is missing," Joe said. "That doesn't mean he couldn't have hurt Christopher."

"Yeah. You're right," she said quickly.

"Unless you have reason to believe that John Kavanagh is more than just missing."

She was just inches from Joe, her face turned towards him. Her eyes were big like a deer's. Joe could practically hear her brain squirming as she tried to find a convincing explanation for what she'd said. She knew more than she was letting on.

Had Christopher put that knife in John Kavanagh's side, after all?

Lisa started crying. Her scrunched-up face turned red. Watery snot dripped from her nose. The tears were almost as shocking as her slip of the tongue. Lisa O'Malley wasn't a crier. Sensitive, yes. Emotional, yes. But not tearful. She struggled to get a tissue out of her pocket, then held it in front of her mouth as if she didn't know what to do with it.

"Take it easy," Joe said. "Slow, deep breaths."

She nodded, and looked down at her hands, which were resting on her lap. "Okay."

"Slower." Joe waited a minute for her to calm down. Then he said, "Do you know what happened to John Kavanagh? Did Christopher kill him?"

"No," Lisa said quietly. "I did."

CHAPTER 80

Lisa watched Joe's face. He was reeling from the realisation. Lisa could see that. She was reeling too. And yet, there was a sense of relief once she started talking. She'd been keeping it all bottled up, and she wasn't sure she would have been able to keep it to herself much longer. Joe listened in silence as she told him what had happened.

It started after she'd talked to him on the phone, when Joe told Lisa he hadn't spoken to the principal. She'd been so disappointed, so angry. It was as if he was unwilling to do even the smallest thing for Christopher.

She was alone at home. She phoned the Highfield Academy and got put through to the principal's office, but the principal didn't answer. Lisa left a message, probably sounding like a crazy person, venting to the answering the machine that Christopher was a sensitive boy, fragile, and that someone was bullying him so badly he'd tried to end his own life. The machine cut her off before she finished speaking. She hadn't even got around to mentioning the bully's name yet.

That made her feel so helpless. Like no one was listening to her. She walked into the kitchen to pour herself a calming glass of Cabernet Sauvignon when she noticed that a knife was missing from the block on the counter.

Christopher had attempted an overdose the previous night. He had promised he'd never do anything like that again, but who knew? Like Joe said, teenagers acted crazy sometimes. What if Christopher planned to slit his wrists this time? Maybe he'd do it at school. Or after school, somewhere quiet. Somewhere like Herbert Park.

Lisa grabbed her raincoat and ran out the door, hurrying towards the park. She took the route Christopher usually walked, hoping to meet him on the way. She slipped into the park near the playing fields. By then the rain was getting heavy and visibility was low.

She made out a form through the rain. A Highfield Academy boy, in that distinctive, pompous uniform. She hurried towards him, but slowed when she saw that it wasn't Christopher. This boy was taller, older.

Then she saw Christopher behind the first boy. Through the rain, she saw him pull out a knife. The older boy, John Kavanagh, turned around. There was a struggle. Kavanagh knocked Christopher down. The knife went flying.

Lisa shouted, but the rain drowned out her voice.

So she ran through the grass.

When she reached the two boys, Christopher was flat on his back in the wet grass. Kavanagh was standing over him. Christopher's eyes widened when he saw Lisa there.

"Mum?"

Kavanagh turned. He looked taken aback for a second, but his face then twisted into an ugly smile.

"You brought your mommy to help you? Huh, you fat piece of shit?"

Kavanagh sat on Christopher's chest, then started pummelling him.

"Stop it!" Lisa screamed. She ran over, grabbed Kavanagh, and tried to pull him off her son, but he was big and strong. And he wasn't scared of her. With one arm, he pushed her away.

She fell onto the ground. In the wet grass, her hand touched against something cold and sharp. Her kitchen knife.

"Mum," Christopher called.

Kavanagh turned and stood over her. The look in his eye was blank, dead.

"Maybe I should fuck your mother," Kavanagh said. He smiled. "How about that, fat boy? You can watch if you like. Then I'll slit both your throats."

The bully was as sick and depraved as Christopher had said. Lisa could see it in his eyes.

He took a step closer to her.

"You're a bit old for my tastes. I'm not a big fan of crow's feet."

Christopher struggled to his feet. He grabbed Kavanagh from behind. But he was no match for the larger boy, who wriggled easily out of his grasp, then punched Christopher in the gut. A devastating blow that made Christopher double over, and which tore Lisa's heart to shreds.

"Stop it, stop it!" she screamed.

She watched Kavanagh hit her son again. And again.

Christopher's eyes closed.

A hot rage came over Lisa, sending flickers of fury through her body, down to her fingertips. She hardly knew what she was doing, but suddenly she was standing, and the knife was in her hand.

She tugged at Kavanagh, trying to pull him away from Christopher, but he was too strong. He punched Christopher a few more times, then turned his nasty little eyes on her. Slowly, he licked his lips. Then he launched himself at her.

Lisa panicked and sank the knife into his side. The blade passed through his flimsy shirt and through his flimsy skin, between two ribs and, Lisa thought, probably right into his lung. A wave of panic washed over her. Kavanagh reached out as if he wanted to touch her face. She pulled out the knife and stabbed it into him again.

For a couple of seconds, Kavanagh opened and closed his mouth like a fish. Then he toppled face-first to the ground. Soon, he stopped moving.

Christopher's eyes were wide with shock.

"Run," Lisa said.

"What?"

"Go home. Run. Now."

Christopher looked at Kavanagh uncertainly.

"What about you?"

"Christopher, go," she screamed.

Slowly, hesitatingly, he began to run.

Lisa bent down beside Kavanagh. He was dead, she thought. There was nothing she could do.

Someone would be along any second. Only the rain was keeping people away. Christopher had not gone far. Lisa hurried after him, grabbing him and dragging him away from the scene.

She put up her hood, zipped the jacket shut and made Christopher do the same. There was blood on his jacket, but Lisa wiped it away and the rain helped too.

She hurried him home, making sure they kept their hoods up and their heads down. No one could know about this. No one could ever know.

When they arrived home, Lisa took a look at her son.

"Christopher? Oh my God. You're bleeding," she said.

"No, I'm not."

"Yes, you are. You're cut."

Christopher looked like he might be in shock.

"It's nothing. It wasn't… it's nothing."

"What happened?" she asked. "Why are you bleeding?"

She was almost hysterical. Had Kavanagh cut him?

"I fell down. That's all. I fell down when I was in the park. It's nothing."

"Christopher, don't lie."

"I'm fine. I swear."

"We need to be honest with each other."

"I know that."

"I'll get a plaster for you, and some antiseptic."

Christopher looked down at himself.

"I should get cleaned up first. I'm covered in mud."

"Okay," Lisa said. Her head was spinning. "Go and have a shower."

He needed to get cleaned up. What else? Hadn't she heard that people who had suffered a shock needed sugar? Or was that a myth? She ducked into the kitchen and found a smoothie in the fridge. Back in the hall, she pushed the drink into his hands.

"Drink this. You'll feel better."

"Why?"

"It's good for you. You'll feel better."

Christopher choked down the drink. Lisa had no idea why she thought a smoothie would help, when the problem was that she'd killed a boy.

CHAPTER 81

Joe said nothing while Lisa spoke. The sun shone through the front windscreen and lit her up like God was listening to her confession too. When she was done, they were both silent for a while.

Lisa blew her nose while Joe let what she'd said sink in. He found it incredible that she could have stabbed John Kavanagh, even during a struggle. Lisa was the gentlest person he'd ever known. But he knew how fiercely she loved Christopher, and it sounded like John Kavanagh had been a nasty piece of work, a bit like his father.

"I know what you have to do," Lisa said. "I won't blame you."

Joe blinked, looked at her. "What are you talking about?"

"I need to find Christopher. Make sure he's alright. I know you have to arrest me, but, please, let me make sure Christopher is okay first."

"Lisa—"

She blinked and said, "It's a relief to let all this stuff out. That I'm responsible for the boy's death. I've been waiting to hear that the body had been found. It feels like I've been waiting forever. Hasn't it been found, Joe? Surely someone has found the body by now?"

He took her hand, and she let him. He felt such tenderness for her at that moment that it almost overwhelmed him.

He said, "Listen to me. You can't tell anyone else what you just told me. No one. Ever."

"But I did it. I killed him."

"No, you didn't. Not if anyone asks. I'm not going to arrest you."

"But Joe—"

"I was there."

"What?"

"I went to the park too, so I could meet Christopher as he walked home. I parked by the gate, and I saw Christopher and Kavanagh in the park."

She put a hand to her mouth. "Did you see me?"

Joe shook his head. "I had to take a phone call. I wasn't paying attention. When I was done on the phone, I went into the park and found Kavanagh dead."

"Oh my god."

"First I thought it was Christopher who was hurt. I mean, I was worried about him after what he did with the pills. Then I saw it was someone else. I thought Christopher must have done it. So I…" He swallowed. "I hid the body."

Lisa's eyes widened. "You hid the body?"

"Yeah."

"That's crazy. Why did you do that?"

"To protect Christopher."

"You care that much?"

"He's a good kid."

"You don't cover up a murder just because someone is a good kid."

Joe shrugged. He said nothing.

"So that's why the body hasn't been found," Lisa said. "Where is it?"

"Not far from here," Joe said, and looked towards the back of the car.

It took a moment for her to catch his drift.

She put her hand to her mouth. "I think I'm going to be sick."

And she was. She flung open the door and vomited on the road.

Joe passed her a bottle of water. "Did anyone see you leaving the park?"

Lisa rinsed her mouth out. "Aside from you? No."

"No one saw you? No one could identify you or Christopher?"

"No, because of the rain. There weren't many people around. We were both wearing raincoats, with the hoods up."

Joe leaned back in his seat and sighed.

"But someone saw me. And they have photos to prove it."

"Who?"

"I don't know. I went to Christopher's school and asked him about Kavanagh. He said he didn't harm Kavanagh, and I believed he was telling me the truth. Then I started to wonder if Barry Wall murdered

Kavanagh, to get revenge on me. And then tried to blackmail me, while he was at it."

"I don't follow. How would killing Kavanagh be revenge on you?"

"It would be, if he thought he was killing Christopher. I thought it might be a case of mistaken identity. Wall killed the wrong boy. But now I know he didn't kill Kavanagh."

"This Wall guy? You really think he would hurt Christopher to get back at you?"

Joe nodded slowly. "Yes. We have to find him fast."

Lisa made a small sound of despair. He knew it was a lot for her to take in.

"Wait a minute. You said someone is blackmailing you."

Joe rubbed his eyes. "That's right. They saw me putting the body in the boot."

"Did this person make any demands?"

"They asked for money."

"Is that why you asked me those questions earlier? You didn't explain anything!"

"I know. Forget it. I borrowed some money, and made the drop."

"Jesus. I think my head is going to explode. Now what?"

"I'm tracking the person who collected it. The blackmailer."

"Then maybe you're tracking whoever has Christopher."

"It's possible."

"Then what are we waiting for? Let's go. Let's find this person. Call backup."

"I can't call backup."

"What? Why?"

Joe thought of the bag of cash, stolen from evidence. The illegal tracking. The fact that the blackmailer had evidence implicating Joe in a murder.

"It's a delicate situation," Joe said. He started the Honda's engine, and got moving, pointing the car towards Lisa's house. "I'm taking you home," he said.

"What? No. We need to track the blackmailer."

"I'll do that, but you're not coming. It's too dangerous."

"Bullshit, Joe."

"I have something I need you to do. I want you to hack into Ken Wall's company. Can you do that? I'm trying to see if his company owns any property where his brother might be hiding out."

"But you have the tracker."

"The battery is very low. About to die if it hasn't already. You need to work this angle in case I lose the signal."

Which was true. But Joe also wanted to give her something else to put her mind on. He pulled up in front of Lisa's house and waited as she got out of the car. She closed the door, then bent down. Joe rolled down the window.

Lisa said, "Promise me you'll find Christopher. That you'll bring him home safe and sound."

"I promise you I'll do everything I can. I need you to focus on the properties."

He told her the name of Ken Wall's company, gave her a wave and dug out his phone. He was still getting a signal from his old phone, located in the blackmailer's backpack. It was no longer moving. And it had stopped at an interesting location.

Joe hit the accelerator and got going.

CHAPTER 82

Lisa's hands shook as she slipped the key into the lock of her front door. This was the time to be strong. Her son needed her, and she was damned if she was going to let him down. Once inside, she went up the stairs to her home office.

She ignored her main computer and went straight to the laptop which was loaded with the Kali Linux operating system, perfect for an attack machine.

This was the computer she used to test the websites she built for clients, and for penetration testing on other sites, where clients were worried about security.

She booted it up and went straight to Ken Wall's company's website, where she began digging.

CHAPTER 83

Though a new hotel, the Melford on Stephen's Green had already established itself as exclusive, about as exclusive as Irish hotels got, with its elegant canopy and rotating door, its concierges in designer uniforms and its focus on detail. For the last couple of years, some of the richest and most famous visitors to Dublin had stayed there.

Despite having passed the place dozens of times, Joe had never once been inside, not even to the bar. He'd always imagined the prices were eye-watering, and he didn't feel like sitting at the bar with a cup of tea and an empty wallet for company.

He parked around the side of the hotel. After stepping out of the car, he grabbed his Sig, slipping the gun into the holster at his hip. Joe untucked his shirt a little so it would conceal the gun. Then he checked his phone. The GPS signal was definitely coming from inside the Melford.

Was Barry Wall living it up in a luxury hotel between murders?

Joe went in the side door and cut through the bar. The signal wasn't coming from there. He dodged a waiter with a tray of cocktails and continued to the lobby, where an elegant staircase rose above him. He started up the stairs.

He looked at the phone while he climbed. There was no way to tell what floor the signal was coming from. He only knew that it was coming from somewhere to his right. On the first-floor landing, he headed down the corridor to the right, with its vivid red carpet and sparkling chandeliers overhead. Joe's pace slowed as he approached the place where the signal was coming from.

Looking at the map, it seemed like he was in the right place – close to the blue dot that marked the location of his phone. But in reality, he was staring at a bare wall. There was no entrance to a guest room. Joe wondered what was on the other side of the wall. Maybe a staff area.

He retraced his steps to the stairs and headed up again. On the second-floor landing, he set off in search of the blue dot again.

This time the GPS led him to room 206. That might have been the source of the signal, or it might not. Joe pressed his ear to the door and listened. When he heard nothing, he rapped on the door and waited. No sound came from inside. The occupant might have been out. Joe knocked again.

He decided to check out the floor above, so he made his way back to the stairs and headed up again.

Laughter was coming from room 306. Joe rapped on the door.

A man's voice came from within. "What is it?"

"It's your complimentary champagne, sir," Joe said.

"More?" said a woman. "I won't say no to that."

Giggles. Footsteps. Joe stepped to the side of the doorway.

The door swung open.

A man leaned forward. His head extended out into the corridor like a turtle peeking out of its shell. He looked to his right, down the empty corridor, then flicked his head to the left and looked right at Joe.

It was Graham Lee.

Joe grabbed his head and shoved him sideways, so that the right side of his skull smashed into the door frame. Graham bounced off the doorframe and fell backwards into the room. Joe followed him in.

Lying on the expensive navy carpet in his boxer shorts, Graham looked dazed and confused.

A woman who looked to be in her twenties lay under the covers in the huge bed. She squealed and pulled the sheets up to her neck.

Joe closed the door behind him and stepped into the room.

The woman said, "What are you doing? Get out."

Joe took out his gun. That shut her up.

"What's your name?"

"C-Crystal."

He turned to Graham, who was now halfway to his feet. "What does she know?"

"I don't know anything," she said.

"I didn't ask you."

Graham said, "Nothing. She knows nothing."

"Tell her to scram."

"Go on, get out of here," Graham said, adjusting his boxers. He picked up a Hawaiian style shirt from the floor and put it on.

Crystal slipped out of the bed, wearing only a t-shirt and a thong. She pulled on her jeans and slipped her feet into a pair of shoes with sky-high heels.

While she was dressing, Joe took her phone off the nightstand.

"Hey!"

Ignoring her, he looked through her messages, the photos in her gallery, and her e-mails, but he didn't see anything relevant. He handed her the phone.

"Bastard."

Graham stood watching from the other side of the room.

"Keep your mouth shut," Joe said. "Or I will find you and shut it for you."

He pushed her toward the door, opened it and watched as she trudged out. She gave Joe the finger, then set off down the corridor.

As soon as Joe had closed the door, he turned around to see that Graham had come up behind him. He looked like he was about to make a grab for him.

"Not so fast, asshole."

Joe hit Graham in the face with the butt of the Sig. Graham stumbled back until his ass hit the writing desk at the side of the room. It was a beautiful writing desk and a beautiful room. It must have cost a fortune.

Joe slipped the Sig into his holster, walked over and grabbed Graham's throat. He sized up the soft area in Graham's side, just under his ribcage, and pounded his fist into that spot. Graham shouted in pain and surprise. Joe hit him again, and again, and again, harder each time, until Graham crumpled to the floor, wheezing and pink-faced.

"I'm done playing nice," Joe said. "Where's Christopher?"

CHAPTER 84

In the passenger seat of the van, Christopher clutched the borrowed violin close to him. His school bag sat in the footwell. He squeezed it nervously between his feet. The car smelled like chewing gum, and the detective was chewing gum as he drove. He offered Christopher a stick. Christopher thanked him and popped it in his mouth. He scrunched up the wrapper and held the little ball of paper in his hand.

The man said he worked with Joe. He was going to take Christopher to the station, because they thought he was in danger.

"So it's him? That Wall guy? He's the one who wants to hurt me?"

The man nodded. With his shiny cranium, strong cologne, and unblinking eyes, he looked more like a fashion designer than a cop.

"We believe so."

"Just because Joe is my dad?"

"Afraid so."

"That's not fair."

"You got that right, son."

Christopher watched as the car drove past the station.

"I, um, I thought we were going there."

Christopher glanced back at the station, receding behind them. The man put a thoughtful finger to his chin as Anglesey Bridge flew by.

"A safe house might be, well, safer."

"A safe house?"

The man nodded. "Wall might have help. Maybe even someone in the station."

"You mean a corrupt Garda?"

Christopher felt his chest constrict. He'd never even thought of such a thing. The man turned his head sideways and smiled sadly.

"It happens once in a while. You get a bad egg. But don't you worry, son. I'm going to take you somewhere no one will ever find you."

CHAPTER 85

"Where's Christopher?" When Graham didn't reply immediately, Joe pulled him to his feet. No easy task, given his size. But Joe did it all the same. He pushed Graham back against the writing desk. "Where is he?"

"What are you talking about?"

"Don't mess me around."

"Okay, okay," Graham said, holding up his hands. "Take it easy."

"Where's Christopher?"

"Is he missing? I don't know anything about that. I swear."

Was he telling the truth? Hard to tell.

"What do you know? I'm running out of patience."

Joe formed a fist and drew back his hand. Graham flinched.

"Wait, I know about the kid. The one who died."

"What do you know?" Joe shouted, shaking him.

"It was Lisa."

"What about her?"

"That day, she must have realised a knife was missing from the kitchen. I guess she thought that Christopher took it, that he might harm himself again. God knows why he'd want to do that. Anyway, she ran off into the rain. She didn't know I was in the house at the time. I decided to see what she was up to."

"Why?"

Graham shrugged. "I was curious."

"You mean she seemed upset so you smelled an opportunity. What happened?"

"I followed her to the park. It was pretty wet so I couldn't see much, but I saw Lisa go up to Christopher and that other boy. They struggled."

"And you didn't help."

"I was too far away."

"I bet."

"I saw Lisa struggling with the kid, saw the kid go down. Christopher and Lisa ran off. I walked a little closer, trying to see what had happened. And then you came along, so I hid."

"And, again, you didn't offer to help. Instead, you decided to exploit the situation."

Graham shrugged. "I'm sorry. I was annoyed at you. You'd been pretty nasty to me at Lisa's house the day before. I wasn't in any mood to do you a favour."

"So you took out your phone and started snapping pictures."

"Well, yeah. You were putting the body in your car. I thought I might as well take a few photos."

Graham shrugged as if his behaviour was the most natural thing in the world.

"Then what?"

"The next morning, I bought a phone. I texted you from the new number. I thought you might be able to find some money. Maybe from Lisa or her parents. They don't like me much. They seem suspicious that I'm a gold digger."

"How unfair," Joe said, his voice dripping with sarcasm.

"Yeah, well. That's all."

"When I dropped off the money, you said you had three snipers watching me."

"Obviously, I didn't. It was just me."

Joe said, "Now Christopher is missing, and I guess you don't care about that at all."

"Sure, I do," Graham said. "I don't want anything bad to happen to him."

What a mess. Joe tried to figure out what to do. He looked around the fancy hotel room.

"How much money did you spend, Graham?"

"Nothing. I just booked a room and ordered some refreshments."

"How much, asshole?"

"Only about two thousand."

Joe whistled. "Fast work."

He walked to the bed, where Graham's jacket had been flung. He found two phones in the pocket, plus a wad of cash.

"Where are the photos stored?"

"Just on the phone."

Joe looked through each phone. He found five photos from Herbert Park on what he took to be

Graham's main phone. He deleted them and checked Graham's e-mails and online storage, but he didn't seem to have backed them up on the cloud. The second phone had the photos too, plus the text messages exchanged with Joe earlier.

Joe deleted the photos and texts, then did a factory reset on each phone, wiping the memory. After that, he took out the SIM cards and smashed them to pieces with the butt of his gun.

He slipped the phones into his pocket, together with the cash. Then he went over to the backpack and checked that the rest of the cash was still there. It seemed to be.

Joe took his own spare mobile phone out of the backpack and brought the screen to life. 1% battery remaining, it said. And then a message appeared, saying that the phone was shutting down. It had done its job, just about.

He still had no idea where Christopher was, but he'd least got rid of those incriminating photos. There was still the problem of what to do with Graham.

Joe said, "I'm going to make this real simple."

"Alright."

He took out his Sig and forced the barrel of the gun into Graham mouth.

"You didn't see anything. You don't know anything. Nod if you understand."

Graham nodded.

"You certainly didn't see me in Herbert Park, and trying to blackmail me was a stupid mistake."

Graham nodded again.

Joe said, "I played along with your demands just to see who was trying to blackmail me. That's all. Now I know it was you. You're not going to talk about this to anyone."

An eager nod.

Joe forced the barrel to the back of Graham throat. He heard the awful sound of metal on teeth, and Graham started to gag.

"You're never going to see Lisa or Christopher again. You're not going to text, phone or e-mail them. You're not even going to collect your belongings from their house."

When Graham nodded, Joe eased the gun out of his mouth.

"What about my passport? I need that."

"Tough titties, Graham. It's mine now. You're going to leave Dublin today. Within the next hour. A selfish prick like you will probably find some way to sponge a living off someone else."

"I'm not so bad. Despite what you think. I know blackmailing you was a shitty move, but my art isn't paying yet. I needed some cash to hold me over."

"Shut up. I don't give a shit about your bullshit fucking art. If you tell anyone anything, I'll find you."

"You wouldn't really hurt me."

Joe laughed. "Try me. I'm doing things I never would have thought I'd do."

Graham stared at Joe for a few seconds, as if deciding whether he meant it. Then he gave a little nod, like he'd made a decision.

"I think I'll do what you suggest – leave Dublin tonight. I'd like a break from the city, actually. It's a good idea."

"Not tonight. In one hour. I'll swing by later. Check your house and Lisa's. If you're around, if you've even visited there, I'll put a fucking bullet in your head."

"Okay," Graham said, nodding slowly. "I can do that."

"And forget about Crystal."

"Already forgotten." He smiled. "I'm glad we could part as friends, Joe."

It took all the restraint Joe could muster not to shoot Graham right then.

CHAPTER 86

The detective drove the van for a long time, the best part of an hour. He and Christopher passed out of the suburbs and into hilly countryside. They were in Wicklow now, having left Dublin behind. Christopher grew more nervous with every minute that passed. He'd tried to turn his phone on, so he could call his mum or Joe, but the detective said that, for security reasons, he needed to leave it off.

Christopher nodded as if he agreed, but he felt something was wrong, and he was trembling by the time the van pulled into an isolated driveway. A wooden fence extended both left and right. A big house lay ahead. Past it, the land sloped up into a hill. The detective turned off the driveway and parked next to a dilapidated building that looked like old stables.

"Is this the safe house?" Christopher asked, eyeing the pine forest stretching away on both sides of the property.

"Safest place there is. No one will find you here. Let's get you inside."

Christopher pushed open the car door and stepped out.

Something was wrong. He was sure of it.

He had to do something.

He pulled a long breath into his lungs. Then, as he exhaled, he forced his body into motion and set off running down the driveway.

His legs worked harder than they ever had before, carrying him away from the strange man and the creepy stables.

He thought he might make it.

If he could just get out onto the road, a passing car might stop. Someone could help him. He would be able to call Joe.

As he was thinking this, he heard the man come up behind him. The sound of fast, hard footfalls on the dry ground.

Then the man tripped him.

He fell to the hard ground, banging his head.

When he opened his eyes, the man was crouched next to him, and he was smiling.

"I can't let you go," he said. "I'm sorry."

The man pulled Christopher to his feet. There was a ropey kind of strength in his slim arms. Dragging Christopher to the stables didn't seem to take much out of him.

"I'll introduce you to the other guest," the man said, unlocking the door with one hand while the other gripped Christopher's neck like a vice.

The door creaked open.

Christopher recoiled. He was in a long room with rough stone walls. Stumps of interior dividers showed that the room had been gutted some time before, and it didn't look like a very good job had been made of it. A number of rough wooden shelves lined the walls.

A man – Christopher thought it was a man – was chained to the wall. He was such a mess of blood that Christopher could hardly make out what he looked like. He didn't move when the door opened.

Maybe he was dead.

Christopher dug his feet in. He tried to resist the man, but he wasn't strong enough.

"Please let me go," he said.

"I may not have been entirely straight with you," the man said.

"You're not a detective."

"No shit, Sherlock."

He pushed Christopher toward the man chained to the wall. In a moment, Christopher's wrists were cuffed too. Like the man, he was chained to the wall.

Christopher said, "Why are you doing this?"

"Blame the sham justice system," the man said. "Blame Joe. He ruined my brother's life."

The man took Christopher's phone, then made his way to the door. Christopher was terrified by the idea of staying here with this bloody mess of a man in these dark stables.

"Wait," Christopher said.

"Don't worry," the man said. "Aidan will keep you company when he wakes up. Anyway, I'll be back soon."

The door slammed shut.

Aidan? Christopher knew that name from the news articles he'd looked up about Joe. He squinted through the darkness. Christopher could not have recognised Aidan Donnelly. His face was too much of a mess.

The chains were long enough to allow Christopher to sit on the stone floor. Would he die here? His heart hammered in his chest. He thought it couldn't beat any harder until Aidan spoke.

"Get out of here," he said, his voice sounding low and wet and broken.

"I can't. I'm chained to the wall too."

He groaned. "Who are you?"

"I'm Joe Byrne's son. That's why I'm here."

Aidan raised his head and looked at him. "You're just a kid."

Christopher shrugged, affecting a nonchalance he didn't feel. Barry Wall – the huge mountain of a man who'd escaped from prison and killed those people – must be around here somewhere.

"Why did he hurt you?" Christopher asked at last, though he thought he knew the answer. He just wanted to break the silence.

Aidan said, "They think I know where that woman is."

"Who?"

"Barry Wall's wife. Barry and Ken want me to tell them."

"D-do you know where she is?"

The man shook his head. A tiny, defeated shake. "But they don't believe me."

"Joe – my dad – he doesn't believe you either."

The man gave a humourless laugh. "No one believes me."

"Do you think they'll let us go?"

Aidan laughed. In the darkness, the sound was terrifying.

"Never."

CHAPTER 87

Joe rang Lisa's doorbell. He was coming to her empty-handed and he hated that. The air on the street smelled of barbecued chicken. It was Friday afternoon, segueing into evening. Most people were chilling out, enjoying the weather. Barbecue, beer, friends.

Not Lisa and not Joe.

Brakes screeched behind him. He turned to see Alice Dunne jumping out of her car. She ran over. Joe had almost forgotten she was tailing him. There hadn't been a thing he could have done about it anyway. He'd had to follow the tracker. He wondered what she'd seen.

"What are you up to?" she said. "Why were you at that hotel?"

"Checking a lead," Joe said. "It didn't pan out."

He hoped she hadn't seen the backpack slung over his shoulder as he left the hotel. It was now sitting in the back seat of the Honda. And John Kavanagh was still in the boot. If anyone looked in his car, he'd be done for. There was enough evidence to put him away for a thousand years.

Dunne said, "What was the lead?"

Joe decided to level with her more than he had, especially now that the blackmail angle was taken care of. He could afford to have official resources behind him now.

"Listen to me. My son is missing. We need to find him."

"What?"

"He disappeared from his school."

"Maybe he's playing truant?"

"No. The school said a detective arrived and took Christopher away for his own protection."

"I'm sure that's not true."

"I think it was one of Wall's cronies."

The front door opened. Lisa appeared in the doorway.

"Did you find him?" she said.

"No, it was a false lead," Joe said. "Have you got anything?"

Lisa glanced warily at Dunne.

"She's okay," Joe said. "You can talk in front of her."

He hoped that was true.

Lisa said, "Not yet."

"Got anything?" Dunne said, arching one eyebrow. "What does that mean?"

"Can you call this in?" Joe said. "Get everyone looking for Christopher? I'll fill you in, in a minute."

"Of course."

Dunne jogged back to her car. She got behind the wheel to get on the radio to Control while Joe followed Lisa into the house. He left the door ajar so Dunne could follow.

Lisa led him to the kitchen, where her laptop was plugged in. She slumped in front of it. Joe remained standing.

"I used my attack-computer, upstairs, and got into the company server," she said. "I've been looking at their list of properties, but I haven't found anything interesting. They're the same ones that are listed on the website. I don't know what to do now."

"Keep looking," Joe said. "There must be more information. Something hidden."

"It's not there."

Lisa's voice was tight, and a vein bulged on her forehead. This was all because of him. If he wasn't in Lisa and Christopher's lives, no one would ever have taken Christopher. No one would ever have thought of hurting him. Of killing him.

Joe said, "Maybe it's not in the name of this company."

"What do you mean?"

"These smart business people, they like to set up lots of companies, right? Maybe companies within companies?"

She nodded. "This company could have subsidiaries."

"Or it is a subsidiary?"

"Or it has a sister company. How are we supposed to check every possibility?"

Lisa began pounding furiously on her laptop. Joe pulled out his phone and began to search the Companies Registration Office, looking for businesses Ken Wall might be involved in. After a minute, he found something.

Joe said, "VLV Holdings?"

"I'm way ahead of you."

"Got anything interesting on it?"

Joe was eager to get moving.

"Give me minute, for God's sake."

"Sorry."

He looked down the hall. Through the crack in the door, he could see that Dunne was still on the radio.

He got a phone call on his mobile.

"Yes?"

It was the station. The desk sergeant was letting Joe know that Philippa Lee had returned his call. Graham's ex-wife had left a message, saying she wanted nothing to do with her ex-husband and had nothing to say about him.

"Fine," Joe said. He ended the call. He'd wanted to talk to her to see if she could tell him anything about Graham. But Joe had already learned enough by himself. Bad as he was, Graham wasn't a killer or a kidnapper. Joe had no interest in wasting anymore time on him.

Joe closed his eyes and refocused on the task at hand: finding Christopher. VLV could stand for Valentina López Vázquez. If so, Ken and his brother were rubbing Joe's nose in it. The initials were a reminder of why they hated him. Because he'd let Aidan Donnelly walk free, even though they all knew Donnelly had killed Wall's wife.

Joe turned to Lisa. "Got anything?"

Her shaky hand was jerking the wireless mouse around like it was a boiling kettle.

"I think I have," Lisa said.

There was excitement in her voice.

"What?"

"This company doesn't have much to it. Maybe it was just set up to own property. Anyway, they don't have much in the way of security."

"So what have you got?"

"VLV Holdings owns an office in the city centre and a car park in Booterstown."

"They don't sound promising. Anything else?"

"One more. Let's see… a property in the Wicklow mountains."

Joe felt a rush of excitement.

"That could be it. Where?"

"Hold on," Lisa said. With a few clicks she brought up the map. Then photos of it. Joe looked at it over shoulder. The property was perfect. A large piece of land with nothing close to it.

"On my way," Joe said.

"I'm coming with you," Lisa said.

But he was already running for the door.

"Tell Dunne the address," he called over his shoulder.

He didn't want her with him in case things got nasty. And he had a feeling that they would.

CHAPTER 88

Barry Wall stepped out of the house and started off for the stables, with a pair of garden sheers gripped tight by the handles. The sky over him was blank and dead. Ken met him when he was halfway there, emerging from the treeline like a ghost.

"I took a walk around the perimeter," Ken reported. "Nothing."

Wall nodded, quickened his step.

The anticipation was murderous. Aidan Donnelly was tougher than Wall ever would have expected. He'd seen men break during his time in prison. Physical violence helped, obviously, but it usually wasn't enough. What usually made people break was a thought, an idea. The idea of more pain to come. The idea of something worse.

Wall gripped the garden shears tightly.

The idea of loss was incredibly powerful.

He unlocked the stables. The narrow building was dark inside, the only light coming in pouring through a small window near the ceiling. Too small for anyone to escape through.

He flicked on the light.

Christopher O'Malley looked up at him with big doe eyes, wet with tears. Wall wasn't sure Ken should have grabbed him, but he was here now. Ignoring the boy, Wall crouched down next to Donnelly and lifted his chin.

"I'm going to ask you one more time."

The painter opened his eyes.

"I know nothing."

"Tell me what you did with my wife."

Donnelly simply shook his head.

"In thirty seconds, I'm going to start taking your fingers. You better think about that."

"I don't know anything!"

Wall exchanged a look with Ken, who pulled Donnelly's hand forward, immobilising it under his armpit. Donnelly squealed and tried to pull his hand away, but Ken held it tight.

Wall opened the blades of the shears and lined them up with Donnelly's thumb.

"Sure you have nothing to confess?"

"No… please…"

He brought the blades together and squeezed, lopping off the digit. Donnelly screamed as the thumb dropped to the floor. Blood spurted from his wound.

"Shut up," Ken shouted.

Donnelly's screaming echoed around the building.

Christopher brought his hands to his ears to block out the sound. He placed his head between his raised knees.

Wall said, "Are you ready to tell me the truth? What happened to my wife? Where's her body?"

"I know nothing," Donnelly screamed. "You crazy idiot. I didn't do it."

Wall shook his head. "I'm going to take your left index finger. Then I'm going to ask you another eight times."

Over the next few minutes, they sheared off Aidan Donnelly's fingers, one by one. Donnelly screamed and begged and cried, but he gave them nothing. Not a word. He stuck to the line he'd held all along. He knew nothing and had done nothing.

After the tenth finger, Ken bandaged the stumps so that Donnelly wouldn't bleed to death.

They left him to his screams and his insistence that he hadn't hurt Valentina.

Outside, Wall closed the door. He exhaled loudly and looked around.

"I don't understand. He didn't give in. He didn't tell us anything. Why not? He has nothing to lose by talking now." Wall frowned. "Something's wrong."

"Don't worry," Ken said. "We haven't shown him his surprise yet."

*

Maureen woke in darkness. Not complete darkness, though. Light came from above. Or from the side? She was disoriented. Where was she? What had happened? She tried to remember. Her back was sore and something rough pressed against her.

She tried to move her head, but her neck was very stiff, and she was held in position. Something was pressed against her whole body. A carpet? A rug? Yes, that was it. She was wrapped in a rug and lying on the ground.

She was outdoors somewhere.

Light came in at the top and the bottom of the rug, several feet beyond her head and feet. Her arms were stuck by her side. She couldn't get them up.

Maureen felt sick.

She began to remember.

The man at the door. The detective.

He'd had his van outside. He talked to her for a minute, looked up and down the road, and then pressed a cloth against her nose. She remembered nothing after that.

"Hello?" she called. "Can anyone hear me?"

*

In Donnybrook Garda Station, Detective Sergeant Kevin Boyle was hanging around the radio, drinking a lukewarm cappuccino, when the news came in. He was in a rotten mood. Jessica Nolan had just come up to Boyle and more or less assaulted him. All kinds of crazy shit came out of that woman's mouth. Something about car alarms and evidence lockers.

What the fuck?

Boyle had no idea what she was talking about. But he quickly grasped that Ger Barrett's cash was missing.

That caught Boyle's attention.

Barrett was breathing down Boyle's throat as it was, and Boyle had got no closer to killing Byrne. There just hadn't been an opportunity. Boyle didn't even know where Byrne was. The slimy rat had gone AWOL.

Ten minutes earlier, Alice Dunne had reported Joe Byrne's son, Christopher O'Malley, missing. Boyle was tense, waiting for something more.

A crackle came over the radio. It was Dunne again, reporting an address where Christopher might be found.

Boyle memorised it, then left the radio room. In the corridor he ran into Detective Inspector O'Carroll.

O'Carroll scowled at him.

"Kevin, I want to see you in my office in five minutes."

"I was just going out to—"

"No." O'Carroll shook his head. "I don't want you going anywhere. Do not leave the building. Am I clear?"

Boyle swallowed.

He said, "Of course."

"Five minutes, Kevin."

Boyle waited until O'Carroll was out of sight.

Then he sprinted to the car park.

CHAPTER 89

Joe arrived at Ken Wall's property filled with dread. He'd driven as fast as he could, with the lights in the grille flashing and his siren blazing, until he got close.

He found the property down a narrow road that wound through hills and forest. It was certainly isolated.

The gate was open. Not what Joe had expected, but he wasn't sure what to expect anymore. Some junk lay just inside the gate. A rolled-up rug, tied with rope, and a worn-looking barrel.

He eased the car forward, wondering if he was being watched. There was a two-storey house ahead. To the right was a ramshackle stone building, maybe old stables. He pulled in at the right, behind the building, so his car wouldn't be obvious to someone in the house.

Joe hoped Dunne had rounded up the whole power of the force, but even if she had, they were maybe ten or fifteen minutes behind. And when they arrived, they wouldn't be as quick as Joe was to go in. They'd be thinking strategy, collateral damage, the veracity of the information, whether a warrant was required, if they hadn't had time to get one. In other words, all kinds of shit that would make them sit on their thumbs.

Joe's strategy was simpler.

He got out of the car and pulled out his Sig. His first order of business was to put a bullet in Barry Wall's head. He figured if Wall and Ken were there, they'd be holed up in the big house, but he could be wrong about that. The stables were closer, so he decided to clear them first.

He jogged to the door, which was locked. He went around the side, but found nothing there except weeds. Moss grew on the side of the building. It must have been a long time since any horses were kept there. He continued on to the end of the building. There was another door there.

Joe tried the handle and it opened. At first the building appeared to be empty. It was pitch dark. After a moment, a voice pierced the silence.

"Help us."

There were figures in the darkness. The voice belonged to his son.

"Christopher?"

"Dad?"

Joe's heart skipped a beat. He stepped in, cursing himself for not bringing a torch. He reached out his right arm and felt around for a light switch.

"Other side," a voice hissed in his ear.

Joe spun around, but he was too slow. A fist connected with his nose. He saw stars as he hit the ground.

He forced himself to get back to his feet fast, shaking off the blow.

The light came on.

Wall stood in the doorway, his bulk practically blocking out the sun. He looked like a mountain, bigger than Joe remembered. Somehow his shaved head made him look larger still.

"Give it up, Wall."

Joe tried to raise his gun, but suddenly Ken was at his side. Ken grabbed Joe's wrists and wrenched them behind his back, tying them together with rough rope. The Sig dropped from Joe's hand.

Wall stepped closer, his biceps gleaming.

Joe said, "What do you want with my son? He's innocent."

Wall's voice was a growl. "What would you know about innocence?"

From behind, Ken pushed Joe towards his brother. Wall unleashed an almighty volley of blows, lightning fast but with a power that took the wind out of Joe. It was like a pair of huge steel pistons pounding his chest. He was expecting them to tear through his chest and exit through his back.

It felt like Wall was breaking every bone in Joe's body. And he just kept going. After five, Joe lost track of the blows. He was in too much pain to count. Christopher was crying out, somewhere behind, in the dark.

"Dad!"

Not Joe, but Dad.

Then the thought was obliterated.

Joe couldn't reply. Couldn't say anything. If Ken hadn't been holding him up, he would have fallen to his knees. That was for sure.

Wall paused.

As far as Joe could tell, he hadn't broken a sweat.

"My wife is dead," Wall said. "What of her innocence? Where's her justice?"

Joe gasped for breath, struggled to reply. "It's – it's not my fault. And it's not my son's."

Wall took Joe's chin in his hand, lifted it up.

"Of course, it is. You punish the innocent and let the guilty walk free. Your sham justice system failed. You failed. You could do nothing for my wife. You didn't protect her, and you couldn't find justice for her. Now you're going to learn how that feels."

With that, Wall gave Joe a punch that just about took his head clean off his shoulders. He didn't know how he held onto consciousness, even for a moment.

Joe felt Ken let go of him.

He wobbled on his feet for a moment.

Then a plastic bag was slipped over Joe's head. Ken squeezed it tight around Joe's throat.

And he started to kill him.

CHAPTER 90

Christopher watched helplessly as Ken choked his Dad until his body went limp and fell to the floor. Christopher screamed and strained against the chains holding him to the wall. He pulled them with all his might, willing them to snap, trying to lift his backside off the cool concrete floor and get to his feet, but he only succeeded in hurting himself. He fell back on the floor, defeated.

He squinted through the dark, trying to detect the slightest twitch on his Dad's face, through the plastic bag over his head. Anything to let Christopher know that he was alive. But there was nothing.

Dad couldn't be dead. No way. Not now, when he'd finally come into Christopher's life.

Barry Wall leaned back his foot and pushed Joe over onto his back. He looked down at Joe for a moment in silence.

"I'll put him with the others," Ken said.

With a terse nod, Wall turned and disappeared out the door.

Ken dragged Joe a short distance to the wall, where another set of metal rings were set into the stone. He lifted Joe up, only to throw him hard against the wall. Then he took a pair of hand cuffs, attached to a chain, and closed them over Joe's wrists.

He must be alive, Christopher thought. Otherwise Ken wouldn't be binding him. He felt a glimmer of relief at the realisation. But Dad looked awful. There wasn't a trace of life visible on his face or in his body. He looked exactly like a corpse.

Ken crouched down in front of Dad and slapped him across the face with an open hand, like he was trying to wake him up.

No reaction.

"Ha," Ken said, and stood up again. He looked at Christopher. "What a disappointment, eh? A couple of slaps and it was over."

"Please let him go," Christopher said. "Please."

Ken paused, then came and stood in front of him.

"Should I tell you a secret?" Ken said. "We have a surprise in this building. In fact, there are surprises all over my land… ones with timers… volatile surprises… So talk quietly. You wouldn't want to set something off. Better breathe gently too… Or else, *kaboom*."

Smiling, Ken pointed to the corner of the room. Christopher saw an innocuous-looking barrel that he hadn't even noticed before. His heartbeat began to race. Was there really a bomb inside it? And there was nothing any of them could do about it.

Ken switched off the light and followed his brother out the door. Christopher was plunged into semi-darkness. He heard Ken stop outside the door and make a phone call.

"How's my favourite officer? Tell me, what's new? I didn't put fifteen k in your bank account for nothing. Tell me something I don't know. Really? Okay... FYI, there's a dead boy here. Someone you know. And there'll be another one soon."

Christopher heard Ken's voice fade as he walked away. After a moment, all he heard was the sound of his own blood pumping. He started to cry.

"Whoa," Aidan said. "That's not going to help."

"I'm going to die," Christopher said, through his sobs. "We're all going to die. Do you think there's really a bomb? Why do they have bombs here?"

"I don't know. Maybe to get rid of evidence. So no one will know we were here. Look, don't lose hope. You never know how things will turn out." Aidan picked at his upper lip. "I thought I was going to die before."

"When?" Christopher looked up.

"Six months ago. After I was in court, Barry Wall tried to blow me up. Only your dad stopped him."

"Another bomb?" Christopher shuddered. He remembered hearing about it at the time, but Joe had done his best to downplay it. "My dad saved your life?"

Aidan nodded. "Yeah, he did."

"But he thought you were a killer."

"I thought he would have been glad to let me die. But he saved my life."

Christopher looked around. "Now we're both going to die here," he said.

"That's no way to talk. Don't say that. You hear me? You're going to be alright."

Christopher nodded. But he couldn't see how.

*

Dunne hadn't wanted to take Lisa O'Malley with her. After Joe drove away, Dunne had gone back up the driveway to the house. Lisa was standing in the doorway, looking all mournful and willowy. Hard to imagine what Joe ever saw in her.

Dunne said, "Stay here. We're going to take care of this." She turned to go.

"Wait," Lisa called. "You can't leave me like this."

"It's better for everyone if you stay at home. We'll be in touch as soon as we have more information."

"No, I can't stand it."

Dunne didn't have time for a lot of talking. She needed to go.

"Fine," she said. "But you have to stay in the car. I don't want you getting hurt. Or compromising the response."

"I will," Lisa said.

"Whatever happens, you stay in the car. Got it?"

"I promise."

"Okay then."

They hurried out to the Lexus. Lisa's hands had shaken as she struggled to fasten her seatbelt.

Dunne checked the address again, and then hit the accelerator.

CHAPTER 91

Joe came awake slowly, feeling like he'd been hit by a freight train. The room was dark, dimly lit by a tiny window near the ceiling. Everything was blurry. Ken hadn't killed him, but he'd left the plastic bag loose over Joe's head. Maybe it was to taunt him.

You're dead anytime we like.

At least it was clear plastic, so Joe could still see.

"Dad? Are you okay?"

Joe turned his head, sending a jolt of pain down his neck. Christopher was straining forward.

"Yeah."

But he didn't feel okay at all. He'd never been in so much pain in all his life.

"Are you okay, Christopher?" His voice was muffled by the layer of plastic.

"Yeah. They didn't hurt me."

Joe squeezed his eyes shut and said a silent thank you. Someone coughed. Farther down the room, past Christopher. Another dim shape loomed in the darkness.

"Who's there?" Joe said.

"Me."

A familiar voice. Joe squinted at the man.

Christopher said, "It's Aidan Donnelly. He's lost a lot of blood. Th-they cut off his fingers."

Joe didn't want that murdering little creep talking to his son.

Christopher said, "They think he killed that woman."

"He did."

"I don't think he did."

Joe's head hurt, and he didn't want to talk. The only thing he wanted to do was get Christopher out of there. And he had no idea how he could do that.

CHAPTER 92

Boyle reached the property as quickly as he could, which wasn't as quick as he would have liked. The drive there had been infuriatingly slow. In any case, the important thing was that he arrived before the uniforms. He needed Joe dead and the cash retrieved, both in next few minutes, or he'd be paying with his own life.

From the road, Boyle could see a Honda that looked like Joe's, parked right next to some badly crumbling stables. A big house stood in the distance, down a dirt road.

Boyle didn't enter the gate. Instead, he circled around the side of the property. It was a long detour, which led him uphill, around a patch of forest.

Big place, Boyle thought.

Eventually, he made his way to the back gate. After parking, he climbed over the wooden fence and struggled through a thorny shrub that cut the backs of his hands, and his cheeks and nearly took his eyes out.

The things I have to do, he thought. *Me, a sick man.*

On the other side of the fence stood a big metal shed. The door was unlocked. Boyle opened the door. Two motorbikes were parked inside.

Bingo.

The Wall brothers were here.

Boyle walked over to the beginning of a steep path, from where he could survey the property. He was looking at the back of everything he had been looking at a few minutes ago, but from a higher vantage point, because of the hill. He could see the back and roof of the house below, and, in the distance, the stables. He also saw a white van parked around the side of the house. This was definitely the place.

Boyle shunned the dirt path. Instead, he trudged into the pine trees and made his way laboriously through the forest, so he could stay out of sight.

He caught a glimpse of Barry Wall in the house as he passed it.

Bingo again.

He'd get Wall later. He had priorities, and nailing Joe was far more important than nailing Wall.

As he approached the stables, he crouched down and jogged over to Joe's car, nervous now that he was out in the open. He approached cautiously in case Joe was sitting in it, but there was no one in the car.

The backpack of money was sitting on the back seat.

Bingo bingo bingo.

Boyle was beginning to feel a lot better. He tried the door handle. It was unlocked, and no alarm sounded as he opened it. Finally, things were going his way.

Leaning into the car, he unzipped the backpack and looked inside. The cash was still there. Or most of it was. The bag seemed a little less packed than it had been earlier. Boyle wondered if that was just his imagination or if Joe had already spent some. Fucking asshole. In any case, most of it was there, and that was what mattered. He could always supplement it if he had to. He'd find a way. He'd do whatever he had to do to stay alive.

Boyle wrinkled his nose. A faint but unpleasant smell suffused the car, as if an animal had died under the seat. Boyle looked around, but he could see nothing that would cause the smell.

He leaned back out of the car, and swung the backpack over his shoulder. Closing the back door, he opened the driver's door and looked inside. He could see nothing there that might explain the smell.

Maybe it was coming from the boot?

He walked around the back and popped the boot. The smell was stronger now. Something bulky was wrapped up in a sheet of plastic. Boyle reached out and pulled at the edge of the sheet, taking a peek at what was wrapped inside. His eyes widened when he saw a body.

"Bloody hell, Joe."

He pulled back the plastic far enough so he could see that the corpse belonged to a young man in a school uniform. Could that be John Kavanagh, the missing kid? Whoever he was, his body was starting to go bad.

What the hell had Joe been up to lately?

He let out an amazed laugh, then closed the lid of the boot and walked around the stables. A heavy bolt held the door shut. Boyle slipped it open and went inside.

"Jesus," Boyle whispered.

A teenage boy and a bloody mess that looked like Aidan Donnelly were chained to the walls of the building. And a short distance away, Joe Byrne was chained up too. A clear plastic bag covered his bloody face.

He looked up when Boyle stepped into the room.

"What the fuck?" Boyle said.

Joe's eyes widened. "Get us out of here. Christopher has just told me there's a bomb," Joe said.

"Here?"

"Yeah. I think it's going to blow soon."

If Byrne lived, Ger Barrett would come after Boyle. That was clear. And if Boyle didn't get Barrett his money, he was dead. Boyle wasn't a killer. He'd never ever wanted to murder anyone. Even though he hated Joe, he didn't want to shoot him. But here, a solution had been provided. If he did nothing, and let events take their course, his problem would be solved.

Boyle took a step back.

"What are you doing?" Joe said.

"I'll be back."

"Help us now."

"I'll call the bomb squad. Just hang tight, okay?"

"No, it's not okay. Get us out of these chains." Joe looked furious. "Is that the money?" Joe said, eyeing the backpack slung over Boyle's shoulder.

Boyle didn't answer. Instead, he said, "I saw what you've got in your car, Joe."

Joe flinched. "Get us out of here. Then we can talk about that."

Boyle said nothing as he turned and walked outside. He ignored Joe's shouts as he slid the lock shut.

Boyle allowed himself a smile. He had the money and Joe was going nowhere. Things were working out well. The sooner the bomb went off, the better.

CHAPTER 93

Wall stepped out the door of the big house. He was frantic. He clawed at his cheeks, running the fingernails from his cheekbones down to his jawline. A bad habit that he'd had as a teenager. He hadn't done it once for over a decade, but now he just couldn't help himself. His chest felt constricted. Ken followed him outside, and tried to calm him down, but Wall wasn't listening. He was wrapped up on his own thoughts.

"Donnelly couldn't have held out all this time. Why would he? I… I was wrong."

Ken shook his head. "He did it. I'm sure he did. He'll crack once he sees our surprise."

Wall squeezed his eyes shut. "I cut off his fucking fingers, one at a time, and he stuck to his story."

"That doesn't mean anything. You're right. I'm right. Even the cops are right. Everyone knows the little shit did it. We'll make him tell us."

Suddenly Wall burst forward and grabbed Ken by the shoulders.

"Don't you understand? He didn't kill Valentina. If he did, he would have told us by now."

Ken shook himself free. He pushed his brother back.

"Get a grip, Barry. He's tougher than he looks. You said it yourself. That's all."

"No." Wall clawed his face again. "Someone else did."

"Impossible. You know the evidence all points to him."

"I nearly killed him, and he admitted nothing."

Ken cocked his head. "Do you hear that?"

Wall listened. A helicopter.

"They're coming," Ken said. "They'll be cautious about coming in. We still have some time. Not a lot, though."

Ken started to walk towards the stables, but Wall turned and went back to the house. He opened the door with a kick of his boot.

"Hey," Ken shouted, halting in his tracks. "What are you doing?"

Ignoring him, Wall entered the house. In the kitchen, he put his fist through the microwave's door. He opened the door of the fridge, and then slammed it shut.

He made his way to the hall.

Stupid.

The rage was overtaking his rational mind, and he didn't care. If he was wrong about Donnelly, everything he'd done since Valentina went missing was a mistake. Heaping pressure on Byrne to make Donnelly talk, trying to kill Donnelly, torturing him now, taking Byrne's kid… even killing the barrister and that stupid, pompous judge.

That stupid pompous judge had been *right*. And Wall had been the idiot. He unleashed an animalistic howl of pain and frustration.

Ken was behind him, his hand on Wall's shoulder.

"Barry, please, calm down."

"Fuck that."

"You're destroying my house!"

Wall reached the hall, where the dart board was hung on the wall. Joe Byrne, Aidan Donnelly and Judge Roberts all stared back at him.

What if they were all good people – and he, Barry Wall, was the monster?

He drew back his arm and launched his fist at the board with all his strength.

Wall's knuckles connected with the dart board, passed through the back, and punched through the wall behind. Wall stared at the hole. He pulled the dart board away and dropped it on the floor. He realised that a plywood door was blended into the wall. The dart board had hidden the handle.

"What is this?"

"It's the basement," Ken said. "Come on, let's check on Byrne."

Wall had known there was a basement. On the other side of the kitchen, there was a doorway down to it. He hadn't known there was another entrance. One that was concealed.

Wall opened the door.

Wooden stairs disappeared downwards into the darkness.

Ken said, "Come on, Barry, we have more important things to do."

"I didn't know the door was here."

Ken shrugged. "You weren't in the mood for a tour of the house, remember? Your exact words were, 'Don't give me the estate-agent bullshit'."

Wall descended the steps one at a time, moving slowly. He stood at the bottom, waiting for his eyes to adjust to the darkness. He saw that there was a small window near the ceiling. The basement wasn't completely submerged, but it was dim. Suddenly the room blazed into light. Ken had flicked on the light switch. A workbench stood on one side of the room, with a small steel box on top.

"What's that?" Wall said.

He walked over to the box.

Ken said, "It's nothing. Let's go back upstairs."

Wall glanced at his brother, then lifted the lid.

*

Maureen squirmed and wriggled. She was exhausted. After struggling for twenty minutes, she'd only managed to worm her way a few inches towards freedom, at the end of the rug which was wrapped tight around her. She still had a long way to go.

Claustrophobia had never troubled Maureen during her sixty years on Earth, but she could feel the condition sizing her up now.

She rested for a moment.

She knew she had to hurry, that no one was going to release her. No one was going to look for her here, wherever *here* was.

If she was going to get away, she needed to make it happen herself.

Was Aidan here too? Maureen hoped not.

She resumed her efforts, ignoring the discomfort and the stifling heat, forcing herself to move towards the end of the rug, inch by painful inch.

Faster, she told herself.

Before that man came back.

CHAPTER 94

When Boyle walked outside and shut the door behind him, Joe knew he wasn't going to come back. Joe had to get Christopher out of there himself. Joe had known Boyle was corrupt, that he'd taken bribes, but he had no idea he was happy to see him and Christopher die.

Joe turned to Donnelly.

"Any tips for getting out of handcuffs?" Joe said. His voice was muffled by the clear plastic bag over his head.

"What?"

"People slip out of handcuffs all the time, right?"

"Why would I know anything about that?" Donnelly made a disgusted sound.

Joe knew that when you were putting cuffs on a suspect, the optimal position was right on the bone that juts out at the wrist. Not above it, not below it. Firmly on it. But that was not what Ken had done to him.

"You've got small hands," Donnelly said, squinting at him from across the room. "Maybe you can slip out if you keep trying."

"They're not small hands."

Joe swallowed. He could make out, in the dim light, the bandaged stumps on Donnelly's hands.

Joe struggled to use his left hand to pull down the cuff on his right. It was awkward and he wasn't getting very far, so he brought up his leg and pushed against the cuff with his foot. The cuffs still weren't passing over his hands. Metal ground against bone, the sensation setting his teeth on edge.

"Up there," Donnelly said, nodding to the shelving unit beside him. "There's a tin of oil on the shelf."

Donnelly kicked out at it. It took a few kicks to shake the shelf, and make the bottle of motor oil fall to the floor. Once it was there, he kicked it towards Joe, who drew it closer with his foot, until he could take it in his hands. The tin was light.

"It's empty."

But he unscrewed the top anyway and tipped the bottle upside down. A single drop fell out. It missed the cuffs and fell on the floor.

"Damn it."

He kicked the air and pulled madly on the chains.

Christopher said, "Keep going, Dad! Maybe you can pull the chain off the wall."

Joe lost his temper and roared at him, punctuating each word with a kick of his feet and a savage pull against the chains.

"I. CANNOT. BREAK. METAL. CHRISTOPHER."

With an explosion of pain, his right hand slipped out of the handcuff as he gave an especially angry pull. He sat looking at his free hand in astonishment.

"Well done," Christopher said.

Donnelly looked impressed too. "Fair play, Joe."

Joe got to his feet. With one hand loose, he was able to reach the shelf beside him with his foot. He spied a pair of bolt-cutters. Hooking them with the toe of his shoe, he pulled them towards him. They fell on the floor within reach.

"Yes," Christopher squealed.

Joe grabbed them, managed to cut the chains holding him. He tore the bag off his head, relieved to finally be able to breathe unconstrained.

He freed Christopher and then Donnelly. He had to help Donnelly to his feet. Joe could hardly stand to look at his bloody bandages.

"Take my son, and go out onto the road and look for help. Don't look back."

Christopher's mouth fell open.

"Dad, come with us."

"Go ahead," Joe said. "I need to finish this."

"But, Dad, I hear a helicopter. That might be help coming."

"Even if it is, they might be too late. I have to stop that psycho." Joe turned to Donnelly. During the last few minutes, Joe had been thinking about the torture the young man appeared to have suffered at the hands of the Walls. If he had known where Valentina was, surely he would have told them already. "Aidan… maybe… maybe I was wrong about you."

"Now you believe me?"

Joe shook his head. "I don't know. Maybe. I was just trying to save a woman's life. But I went about it the wrong way. Really, I apologise."

"Apology accepted," Aidan Donnelly said after a moment.

It pained Joe to think that Donnelly was a bigger man than he was. But whatever. He'd faced a lot of hard truths lately.

"Go," he urged them.

Donnelly had lost a lot of blood. He needed to get to a hospital fast. Once out the door, Donnelly set off for the gate. In the doorway, Christopher stopped. He lowered his voice so Donnelly wouldn't hear.

"That other detective? What did he mean? He said he found something in your car."

Joe decided to be completely honest.

"John Kavanagh's body… It's in the boot of my car."

"What? Why?"

"Your mother told me what happened. That she was protecting you. Well, I came along after it happened. I found the body."

"Didn't you tell anyone?"

"No, you would have got into very bad trouble if I had."

"You hid his body to protect me and mum?"

Joe shrugged. "If anyone asks, you know nothing about what happened to Kavanagh or where his body is. I just want to get you to safety, ok? Don't worry about me."

Christopher ran to Joe and gave him a hug.

"I'm sorry for being a crappy father," Joe said.

That just made Christopher hug him tighter.

"I'm sorry for being a crappy son," Christopher mumbled into Joe's shirt.

"You're not. I'm proud of you." He meant it.

Christopher looked up at him. "I heard Ken on the phone. He said something about a dead kid. And something about money. A bribe."

"Later," Joe said. "We can talk about that when we get out of here. Now go. I'll be there as soon as I can."

Christopher set off running after Donnelly. Joe turned the other direction. He headed to the house, to end this.

CHAPTER 95

Ken watched his brother open the trophy box, his most prized possession. It was something he'd never planned to share with anyone, but now that Barry was here, looking at it, Ken was riveted, absolutely fascinated to see how he'd react. Barry didn't say anything when he looked inside first. Then slowly the skin on his cheeks seemed to sag and a choked breath came from his throat. His voice was very small when he spoke at last.

"What is this?"

He lifted up a necklace with fake opals and a metallic chain. That one had belonged to Susan Keogh, the second woman Ken murdered. He was still a beginner at that stage, and had made some mistakes, but he'd got away with it all the same.

Ken walked over to the other wall where his tools hung from hooks. He selected a claw hammer.

"What's this?" Barry said again. He still sounded confused but there was a certain dawning realisation in his tone. He picked up a necklace with a bright yellow sunflower pendant. "Did – did you take this from Valentina before she died?"

"Who said she's dead?"

"What?"

When Barry spun around, Ken smashed him across the side of the head with the hammer. The blow knocked Barry to the floor and left him looking even more dazed. A trickle of blood ran down the side of his head. He groaned, then rolled on his side and looked up with an idiotic expression on his face.

"What are you doing?" Barry said.

The detonator for the remaining portion of the explosives sat on the worktop. Ken hadn't expected to have to use it so soon, but it seemed that the time to go was rapidly drawing near.

"Just what I have to do."

"I – I don't understand."

"I think you'll find it's pretty simple."

Barry shook his head. "It was you?"

"Don't take it personally."

"*You* took Valentina?"

"In fairness, you're better off without her. She was only a prick tease. And you know how it is with girls like Valentina – they look so firm and juicy until they turn thirty and then they inflate like a fucking airbag. You're left with a ball of lard that just gets rounder every year. I'd say Valentina was in her prime when we had her. It would have been all downhill after that. She wouldn't have been any fun."

Ken had thought she would have been easier, even if she was a raging Catholic. Ken had wanted to fuck her ever since Barry married her. He bided his time. Valentina wasn't the only woman in the world, after all. Then there was that June weekend last year, when Barry and Valentina were getting the house painted. Ken had been after Valentina all week and she still hadn't put out. He was the one who had put them in touch with Aidan Donnelly, recommending the painter to Barry.

A year or two earlier, Barry would have done the painting himself, but now he was too full of himself, what with his gym and his Z-list Hollywood clients and his whole big man schtick.

Ken knew Aidan was a dope, twenty-four years old, with about twenty-four brain cells, and an unshakeable conviction that the world was run by lizards, that aliens were behind 9/11, that the government drugged the population with chemicals in the water supply. A cocktail of conspiracy theory bullshit.

Ken had an idea he could use him.

Boy, was he right.

The day he killed her, Ken sent Valentina a few texts to get her excited. Then he'd gone to the house.

Donnelly had finished the painting and was loading gear into his van. Ken chloroformed him and tossed him in the back.

Then he waited.

Valentina was a curious bitch and Ken and knew she'd be annoyed if Aidan seemed to be hanging around in her driveway.

Sure enough, after just a couple of minutes she came out to check. She'd already called Barry, of course, but he hadn't answered. Ken knew his brother had a packed schedule that morning.

Ken had pushed her back into the house.

She put a good fight. Tried to claw at his face up good, but Ken wore a balaclava so she couldn't leave any visible marks on him, and so any neighbours, if they saw anything at all, would not be able to describe him.

He dragged her to her own bed. To her credit, she never gave up. Never stopped trying to get away, even when Ken threatened to kill Barry unless she was quiet.

He remembered her screaming, "Get your dirty hands off me."

Ken had to gag her in the end. Once he'd fucked her, he took her downstairs.

"My dirty hands? Let's take care of your dirty hands," Ken said.

He was glad she was already gagged because she tried to scream the house down when he got the garden shears.

It wasn't easy to take her fingers. He had to beat her around a little to stop her squirming. He arranged the fingers in the garden as a joke. Barry always had hated mushrooms, the sight of them poking up through the soil like strange little creatures.

Ken left the garden shears in the bedroom. He figured Barry would find them there.

He took Valentina and Donnelly in Donnelly's van. He'd driven them to a quiet place, then transferred Valentina to his car. It was a piece of crap he'd bought cheap for occasions like this.

Before driving her back to his place, he transferred a few tantalising clues to Donnelly's van. Her underwear. A few other pieces of evidence for the forensics team to find. Then he left Aidan there, after splashing him with a bit of gin. Ken had no doubt that he'd soon be found.

After dropping Valentina to his place, he left her, with some reluctance, in order to go back to Barry's house, and collect the car he'd driven there in. All the driving and changing cars had been a bit convoluted, but he'd had to do it.

Then he'd gone back to his house, and enjoyed a little more time with Valentina. She was still alive, and he fucked her again. He didn't have to gag her this time, and it was funny the way she tried to fight him off with her stumpy hands. But all good things must come to an end, and Ken had to get back to the city centre, so he had finished her off with a pickaxe.

He'd showered, headed back to his office, and waited for Barry to call. It had been an exhausting day.

"What did you do with her body?" Barry said.

Tears were streaming down his face.

"She didn't go very far."

"How far?"

Ken had never seen his brother look so pathetic.

"Not far at all."

"Where did you bury her?"

"I didn't bury her."

"Tell me what you did," Barry said miserably.

"It's the cycle of life. Every creature is prey for another. We're all eaten up and shitted out the other side. But you can take comfort. Not everyone will be so delicious."

Barry's voice went as high as a little girl's. "You don't mean… you couldn't mean… you ate her?"

Ken laughed. "Of course not. Why would I want to eat her? *You* ate her."

*

Maureen staggered down the country road. Although she felt like hell, she was finally free. Her cardigan, and one of her shoes, had been lost when she wriggled out of the rug, but she didn't care. Putting some distance between herself and that house was all she wanted to do. Maybe that man would chase her. A terrifying thought. She urged herself on.

CHAPTER 96

Joe sprinted towards the house, shaking off the stiffness he felt from being chained up. He reached the house without being seen, as far as he could tell. Once inside the kitchen, he stopped. A creepy stillness suffused the building.

Joe's Sig lay on the worktop. As quietly as he could, he picked the gun up and checked that it was loaded.

Muffled voices carried from somewhere else in the house. Then the crashing sounds of a struggle. From above or below?

Moving carefully, he followed the sound to the open door to the hall, then to an open doorway. He poked his head through. Steps led downwards. Joe could see nothing of what was in the basement. But he could hear voices.

He stood there and listened, feeling a chill of horror as Ken spoke.

Wall said, "You don't mean… you couldn't mean… you ate her?"

"Of course not. Why would I want to eat her? *You* ate her."

"What?"

"After she disappeared, I served her up to you, one meal at a time. Remember all those chilli dinners I brought you?" Ken laughed. "A good food processor can handle just about anything."

Joe began to creep down the steps. They were old and wooden, and he didn't trust them not to creak, so he kept the gun raised, ready to shoot. And though he'd never shot anyone in the line of duty, he would have no problem with making Ken Wall the first.

"That can't be true," Wall said.

"I can assure you that it is. And you wouldn't believe the amount of seasoning I needed to make her palatable. So much basil. So many peppers. I tasted her, but only to make sure she was edible. I have to say, it was funny watching you look for her everywhere, while you literally had her right in front of you, day after day. For weeks, you ate her."

Ken broke out laughing.

As Joe reached the bottom of the staircase, he caught sight of the brothers. Ken was standing with his back to Joe, a hammer in his hand.

Barry Wall lay on the floor at Ken's feet, a trickle of blood coming down the side of his head. Wall was dry heaving, his eyes half-closed, and he looked to be losing whatever will to live that had carried him along over the last year. Perhaps he was in shock. No surprise given what Ken had just said.

Joe continued down. The next stair, the third from the bottom, creaked when Joe stepped on it. Ken looked around.

Joe brought up the Sig. Before he could squeeze off a shot, Ken hurled the hammer through the air. The bastard had good aim. The hammer caught Joe in the stomach and the blow winded him. He doubled over in pain.

When he'd recovered, Ken was disappearing from view. Joe ran after him and saw him jump up on a workbench and squeeze himself through a narrow window near the ceiling.

Joe swore, then went to check on Barry Wall.

He hunkered down next to him and checked his pulse. It was weak. His eyes were unfocused and he looked disoriented.

After all the work Joe had done to capture this man, it was sad to see him like this.

"I heard what Ken said."

"I was wrong," Wall said in a small voice.

"I was too. I'm sorry."

"Promise me…"

"What?"

Wall held out his closed fist. He opened his fingers to reveal a necklace. "Give this to Valentina's parents."

"I will," Joe said. "Hold on, Barry. Help is on its way."

Wall shook his head. "There's a bomb."

"In the stables? I know."

Wall whispered. "There are more."

"Where?"

Joe leaned closer, but Wall's eyes closed. His chest stopped rising and falling. He had already joined Valentina.

CHAPTER 97

With the detonator in one hand, Ken jogged uphill to the shed at the back of the property. That was where the motorbikes were, and a motorbike would be better than the van for getting away.

Things hadn't gone as he'd planned. But he never had been very good at sticking to plans. Usually impatience set in quickly and, when that happened, plans went to hell.

The whole point of breaking Barry out of jail was to set him up for the murders – not just Valentina, but all the ones Ken had done over the years. That wasn't going to be easy now.

Oh, well.

He'd just have to leave a mess behind.

Ken could assume a new identity. It wasn't hard. He'd start a new cycle of murders somewhere else. Spain maybe. There'd be some irony in that. Or America. Or Australia. Anywhere but here. He was bored of Ireland anyway.

As he approached the shed, a helicopter *thud thud thudded* past, low overhead. Ken threw himself on the ground. He crawled to the treeline next to the path, waited for the chopper to pass, then got to his feet and hurried to the shed.

Everything was as he'd left it. Motorbikes weren't the only things there. Ken had other fun stuff, like a mini fridge stocked with beer, and a case containing a sniper rifle.

Joe Byrne would be coming after him. It would be a pretty thing to take that asshole's head off before Ken made his escape.

First he slipped the detonator into his jacket pocket, then opened the fridge and pulled out a bottle of beer. He realised he hadn't had anything to drink for hours. Beating the living shit out of Donnelly and Byrne had been thirsty work.

He tore off the cap and took a long drag on the bottle.

Then he loaded the sniper rifle, fitted the scope, and walked outside with the beer bottle tucked into his jacket pocket.

He walked down the path to a place where he could look over the property from an elevation of about forty-five feet.

It was a shame to waste such a good slope. Ken could almost hear his father's voice.

I'm gonna roll you down the hill, you little bastards.

Yeah, Dad would have loved rolling Barry and Ken down this fucking hill. Never a man likely to win Father of the Year. But Ken had learned lessons from him. Like the power you held over people when they feared you, and how much fun it was to blow shit up.

Aidan Donnelly and Christopher O'Malley were walking towards the gate.

Patrol cars with sirens blazing were coming up the road now, and the helicopter was circling back. Ken thought Barry was probably dead. Ken couldn't see Joe. He was probably still in the basement.

He'd better kill them all. There was always a chance that this could blow over, if he destroyed enough evidence, though that was pretty unlikely. Anyway, he'd see how the cards fell.

Ken drank the rest of the beer, then threw the bottle into the bushes.

He raised the detonator and squeezed the button.

CHAPTER 98

Joe didn't follow Ken through the basement window. Ken already had a head start, and if he wanted to, he could be waiting out there, with a hammer in his hand and a smile on his face. His confession had chilled Joe. Joe had encountered some violent men over the years, but none of them made his skin crawl the way Ken Wall did.

Joe climbed the stairs, gun in hand.

The idea of a number of bombs on the property made him feel sick. He hoped Christopher and Donnelly were far away by now.

As he got to the top of the stairs and ran to the door of the house, he thought of Kevin Boyle. Was he still lurking here too? Or had he taken the money and run back to Ger Barrett, in the hopes of saving his own life?

Joe stepped out into the air. The land rose to his right. He turned left, in the direction of the stables and the path to the road. Christopher and Donnelly hadn't gone far at all. In fact, they were standing at the gate like a couple of idiots.

And not only that, they were now walking back in, towards Joe. Forgetting everything else, he set off at a sprint towards them.

"Get back," he shouted. "Go onto the road."

But they didn't seem to hear. Ken didn't strike Joe as someone to hang around. He was going to want to get moving. And Joe doubt he wanted to leave anyone behind to tell the tale.

Donnelly had a horrified look on his face, and he was hurrying to the place at the inside of the gate, where a rolled-up rug lay next to a barrel. Joe couldn't figure out what Donnelly was up to. Joe kept running. As he got closer, he saw a yellow cardigan next to the rug. A shoe too.

Donnelly continued running in that direction and Christopher hurried after him.

Joe increased his pace. He shouted, "Get away from there!"

Christopher stopped, but Donnelly ignored him.

"Auntie?" Donnelly cried. "Auntie?"

"Get away from the barrel," Joe shouted. "For god's sake, Christopher, run!"

Joe kept running towards them. Christopher suddenly seemed to wake up. He turned away from Donnelly, the rug and the barrel. Joe reached Christopher and dragged him away from there. He shouted Donnelly's name over his shoulder, but at that moment the barrel exploded, and Donnelly was consumed by a ball of flame.

A moment later, the other bombs detonated too.

CHAPTER 99

Ken watched the explosions with a smile. The stables blast was huge, tearing the walls off the building and engulfing Byrne's car. A huge pine tree was also toppled by the blast.

The barrel near the entrance also blew nicely. Donnelly went up in it, but Ken wasn't sure if it took out Byrne's son. At the last moment, Ken caught sight of a man's figure near the boy. Maybe it was Byrne, or else it was the first of the emergency services, who were now streaming up to the gate. Ken couldn't see much through the swirling smoke and the tongues of flame arcing into the sky.

Another blast occurred in the basement of the house. From the hill where Ken stood, he saw the basement window blow out.

If Joe was still there, he wouldn't have survived.

Still, Ken watched the basement window through the sniper scope, in case there was any sign of movement.

After a minute, there had still been nothing, so he decided to go. Patrol cars were streaming onto the property and things were going to get hot. Ken retraced his steps to the shed. With the rifle swung over his shoulder, he wheeled his motorbike out of the shed. He looked towards the back gate.

Funny.

An old Ford Escort was parked just outside.

Out of the corner of his eye, Ken saw movement, in the trees next to the trail. Coming towards him. A man running fast.

Joe Byrne?

In one fluid motion, Ken swung around, brought the rifle up, and shot the man square in the chest.

CHAPTER 100

As bombs went off all around them, Joe pushed Christopher to the ground, and flung himself on top of him. The nearest blast swallowed Donnelly. He didn't stand a chance. A little earlier, Joe might have been glad to see him dead. Now he felt ashamed. He was only glad he'd had time to apologise.

Smoke and heat roared over them like a river. It felt like the flames were licking Joe's ears. Debris shot through the air – lethal shards of super-heated metal and stone.

He kept his head down and waited for the dust to settle. When it did, he helped Christopher to his feet. He looked back at where Donnelly had been standing. Nothing that could be obviously identified as a person remained.

Christopher said, "Look, an ambulance."

Joe turned and looked where he was pointing. Sure enough, an ambulance had pulled up on the road outside, waiting its turn to come in after a fire engine and a stream of patrol cars. Uniformed officers were jumping out of cars and vans, and swarming in.

Joe saw Dunne arrive in her Lexus. Lisa sat next to her in the front passenger seat. Joe would never forget the look of relief on Lisa's face when she caught sight of Christopher.

"Run over to your mother," Joe said.

"What about you?"

"I have to find Ken Wall."

Joe shoved Christopher towards the Lexus. Then he set off running, around the side of the stables, to where the treeline began, and into the undergrowth.

Joe took the long way around the property, moving as fast as he could through the thick forest. It was rough work, but he figured he'd be dead if he walked up the path by the house. He didn't want to become another trophy in Ken's box.

By the time he'd climbed the incline and skirted the property, he was out of breath. He found himself standing behind a shed. The back gate was within view, and Kevin Boyle's car was parked there. The sneaky bastard. Joe took a moment to catch his breath, so that when he came out into the open, he'd be ready.

He pulled out his Sig and was about to step out when he saw movement in the trees on the other side of the path.

He hunkered down and waited for a good shot.

After a moment, he realised that the running figure was Boyle, not Ken. He must have been trying to get to his car, and escape with Barrett's money before he got caught up in this.

Joe was about to call out, to tell him to stop, when a terrifyingly loud gunshot rang out.

Boyle dropped to the ground like a felled deer.

Joe's pulse was working overtime, a crazy, overclocked beat that would land him in hospital if he kept it up. He forced himself to stay motionless as Ken walked down the trail and came into view. Carrying a rifle with a scope, Ken ambled over to where Boyle lay.

Joe took the opportunity to sneak over to the back of the shed. Pressing himself against it, he peered around the side.

Boyle was still alive, but only just. Joe saw a spray of blood droplets shoot into the air when he coughed. His chest was a mess of gore. At point blank range, Ken pointed the rifle at him. Joe had never liked Boyle, but the man didn't deserve this.

Joe stepped out onto the path.

Ken heard him coming and turned. He brought the rifle up, but not fast enough.

Joe squeezed the trigger of his Sig.

The first shot hit Ken in the shoulder. The second got him between the eyes.

Ken dropped to the ground.

He was dead. No doubt about it. His trophy box fell out of his pocket. It opened, spilling necklaces onto the ground. Joe stared in horror. How many women had this monster killed? A chill went up his spine.

He went to check on Boyle. He was twitching.

"Hold on," Joe said. "Just hold on."

But even as he spoke, the light faded from Boyle's eyes. There was a look of confusion on his face –

pain too – but then acceptance washed over his features, and, finally, peace.

Joe stood there for half a minute, looking at the body at his feet. Then he put the Sig away, turned and walked down the path.

The uniforms were swarming all over the place.

Joe caught sight of Dunne, standing with David O'Carroll, surrounded by a retinue of uniforms. He walked over to them.

"Jesus," O'Carroll said, catching sight of Joe. "You're alive. You look dreadful."

The fire brigade was spraying the wreck of Joe's car. As soon as the blaze was out, they'd find the body inside. John Kavanagh. Or whatever was left of him.

It was all over.

The important thing was that Lisa and Christopher were okay. If Joe had to go to jail to make that happen, he would.

He closed his eyes and waited to be arrested.

CHAPTER 101

"What the bloody hell has been going on here?" David O'Carroll asked, looking around. The vein in the middle of his forehead looked like it was about to rupture. "Where's Barry Wall?"

Joe could understand his boss's confusion.

He said, "Wall is dead. So is Donnelly. We were wrong about him. *I* was wrong about him. Aidan Donnelly never touched Valentina López Vázquez."

"What?" O'Carroll gaped.

"Ken Wall killed her. And she wasn't his first."

"Is Kevin Boyle here?" Dunne asked.

Joe pointed up the trail towards the back of the property.

"He's dead. Ken shot him. You'll find his body up there."

O'Carroll said, "Where's Ken?"

"He's dead too. I shot him." Joe took out his Sig and handed it to a uniformed officer wearing gloves. She slipped the gun into an evidence bag. Joe said,

"You'll find Ken's body beside Boyle's. I wasn't able to save Boyle."

O'Carroll scowled. "I've never seen so much bloodshed in all my life. My head is spinning."

Joe was too numb to tell O'Carroll that his head was about to spin even faster, once he realised he'd have to arrest Joe in connection with John Kavanagh's death.

Lisa and Christopher had been speaking to a uniformed officer. But when Joe looked their way, it broke the spell. Christopher came running over. Lisa followed and they both hugged him. He was sore from the beating he had taken, but he hugged them both fiercely.

An unmarked car pulled up next to them. Detective Superintendent Michael Kavanagh stepped out. Joe couldn't recall a superintendent ever coming out to a crime scene. Only something tremendous would get one out of his office.

"Where's my son?" Kavanagh shouted. "Has he been found?"

Time to take the blame.

Joe opened his mouth – and then a thought struck him.

He said, "What makes you think your son is here?"

"I got a tip-off."

Dunne came up beside the superintendent. Now Joe's head was really about to explode. Maybe he wasn't thinking straight but he had trouble understanding what was happening. John Kavanagh's body was here, but there was no way the superintendent could have been aware of that. Who could have told him?

Joe's brain hurt. He was too tired to try and figure it out.

He pointed at his car, knowing that he was about sixty seconds away from being handcuffed and taken away in the back of a patrol car.

The fire which had engulfed Joe's car was now out, though a little smoke rose from the shredded, twisted heap of metal.

Joe had to let the boy's parents know he had passed away. He didn't them to suffer with false hope any longer than they had to.

"He's dead, sir," Joe said.

Superintendent Kavanagh looked at Joe's car. Then he got up in Joe's face and grabbed him by the lapels.

"Dead? What do you mean, dead? What did you do to him?"

Of all the people present, Christopher was the one who came between the two men.

"I can tell you," he said. "When I was tied up, Ken Wall told me I was lucky to be alive. He said he tried to kill me on Thursday afternoon, but he killed another boy by mistake."

"Is that right?" David O'Carroll said, his shrewd eyes narrowing.

"No," Superintendent Kavanagh said. "No, it's not."

Christopher continued. Joe didn't know where his son found the resolve, but his voice was firm and he spoke clearly and simply. Everyone was hanging on his words. "Ken wanted to kill me and put my body in my dad's car to find. But he got the wrong kid. He killed John Kavanagh."

Superintendent Kavanagh released Joe. Every feature on his face seemed to have slumped.

"Impossible… It can't be true…"

Dunne said, "I don't think I showed you my full credentials, Joe." She produced her ID from her jacket pocket. Joe read it. She wasn't a regular detective. She was with the Special Crimes Operations division, which meant she had joined the Barry Wall investigation under false pretences.

Dunne wasn't here to catch Wall.

She was investigating other officers.

"You're with the SCO?" Joe said.

Dunne nodded.

So this was it, she'd been investigating him all this time. She knew everything and Joe was done for.

Dunne said, "I'm here to make an arrest."

Joe was even more screwed than he had thought. O'Carroll looked unsurprised so he must have known about Dunne's investigation already. Superintendent Kavanagh looked shocked, though.

Christopher said, "I also heard Ken Wall talking to someone on the phone. It sounded like it might be a detective. They were talking about money. Fifteen thousand. And Ken said something like, 'there's a dead kid here, and there'll be another one soon'. He was talking about John, and me."

Superintendent Kavanagh's face went white, like a switch had been flicked.

"Rubbish. You're a lying little shit!"

"Hey," Joe said. "Don't talk to my son like that or I'll knock your block off."

Dunne's smile broadened. She took out a pair of cuffs – and slapped them on Superintendent Kavanagh's wrists.

"What the hell is this?" he roared, lunging at Dunne.

Two uniformed officers grabbed him from behind.

Joe stared, not understanding. They were meant to be arresting *him*, not the superintendent. What was going on?

Dunne said, "As I said, I'm with SCO. I came to Donnybrook to investigate corruption. Joe set the ball rolling months ago when he complained about various investigations and raids coming to nothing."

"I thought no one listened to me," Joe said.

David O'Carroll made a derisive snorting noise.

"I told you to butt out," he said. "I told you I was taking care of it."

Dunne said, "So SCO began looking into it, together with the Garda National Bureau of Criminal Investigation and the Garda National Drugs and Organised Crime Bureau. We knew Ger Barrett's organisation was learning things it shouldn't have known."

"I never gave him any information," the superintendent snarled.

"Correct. Kevin Boyle did, to pay his medical bills. But *you* were giving information to the Wall brothers. For pure greed. But it didn't stop them killing your son to get revenge on Joe."

Tears were streaming down Kavanagh's face now. The sight of it was a shock. He tried one more time to escape responsibility.

"You've no evidence for any of this."

"Actually, we do. Of many kinds. And Christopher here has just proved himself to be a credible witness."

"How so?"

"We bugged your phones. All of them. And we heard the call this afternoon which Christopher described. Including the bit about 15 K. That's a precise number. It matches an amount deposited into your bank account last week from an account in the Cayman Islands."

Kavanagh finally crumpled, falling to his knees, taking a last look at the wreckage of Joe's car, where his son lay dead, before burying his head in his hands. Despite the heinous acts he apparently committed, providing the Wall brothers with inside information, it was pathetic to see him on his knees in the dirt. He had nothing but a dead son and a ruined career. And a wife whose hate he had probably earned.

"Can I take my son home?" Lisa said.

David O'Carroll nodded. "Soon. We'll take a preliminary statement now and follow up later."

"Can Joe come too?"

O'Carroll hesitated.

"Well, we need to talk to him for a few minutes. But I suppose he can make his full statement later too. Does SCO have any problem with that?"

Joe held his breath.

He waited for Dunne to speak.

To decide his fate.

"Yes," she said. "I'm sorry, but Joe's not going home with you."

So this was it. He had been stupid enough to get his hopes up. He'd thought Christopher's words might have put him in the clear. But Dunne sounded unconvinced. She wasn't letting him go home. It could mean only one thing: arrest and detention.

O'Carroll raised an eyebrow but that was nothing compared to the anxiety Joe felt.

Suddenly Dunne's expression changed to one of concern. "I want Joe to spend the night in hospital. He looks like he's been through a lot."

O'Carroll looked at him. "She's right, Joe. You look bloody awful."

Joe took a long, deep breath. He tried to conceal his relief that he was going to hospital, not a holding cell. He had no idea what would happen later. Would his story, and Christopher's, stand up to scrutiny? Between Christopher covering for him and the destruction of evidence in the bomb blasts, Joe figured it just might be possible.

At that moment, Superintendent Kavanagh was loaded into the back of a patrol car and driven away at speed.

Lisa and Christopher were put in a separate car, and driven away at a more leisurely pace, headed home. Joe grinned as he watched them go.

Over the following half hour, Joe gave Dunne and O'Carroll an outline of events. Meanwhile, officers swarmed all over Ken Wall's property, soon joined by people from the Technical Bureau. By the time Joe had finished a bare-bones version of his story, exhaustion had caught up with him.

"That's enough for now," O'Carroll said finally. "Get checked out. Rest up. And report to the station tomorrow to write up a full statement."

The medics helped Joe into an ambulance and drove him to hospital, where he would spend the night.

As he was wheeled to an examination room, he tried not to think about what would happen the next day. It was hard not to worry that he might have missed something. Some shred of evidence that would sink his story.

But after he'd been examined by a doctor, and his wounds had been dressed, Joe fell into the deepest sleep of his life, and he worried no more.

CHAPTER 102

Joe drove to the station the next afternoon. O'Carroll had let him borrow an unmarked car, a nondescript Toyota, until Joe could arrange a replacement set of wheels for himself. He would be interested to see what his insurance company said about the Honda.

It was a lovely Saturday with a gentle breeze and a clear, blue sky. The cemetery next to the station would be peaceful, but Joe didn't feel the need to go there today. His body ached, but he was refreshed after sleeping for eleven hours. This morning, after the doctors had discharged him, he'd gone home to his apartment and phoned Lisa.

She and Christopher were doing well. Lisa said she had heard nothing from Graham and she didn't seem to care. Christopher's mood had improved ever since a girl from school texted him asking if he was okay. Apparently, everyone at the Highfield Academy was talking about his ordeal and John Kavanagh's death, and Christopher was now some kind of celebrity.

Joe still couldn't believe that Christopher had managed to save him, to re-contextualise the events in a way that fitted the facts, and which Joe thought no one would be able to contradict. Smart kid. He must have got that from Lisa.

The station was quiet, which suited Joe, but he ran into Anne-Marie Cunningham. He'd just made himself a coffee and was returning to the District Detective Unit office when he met her in the corridor. She had a golden retriever on a leash.

"Beautiful dog," Joe said.

"This is Babe," Cunningham said. "She was Kevin's. I guess now she's mine."

Joe hunkered down and patted the dog's head. She lay down, inviting Joe to rub her belly.

Cunningham cleared her throat. "With what's emerging about Kevin, I wanted to come in and apologise in person. I mean, I can't believe he helped Ger Barrett's gang, but it seems he did. I was wrong. I'm sorry."

"Forget it," Joe said. "You wouldn't believe how many times I've been wrong recently."

Cunningham gave a weak smile. She seemed genuinely surprised to find out Boyle was corrupt, and Joe appreciated the apology.

"I better go," Cunningham said. "Babe needs a walk. I guess I'll see you after your week's leave."

O'Carroll had insisted that Joe take some time off.

Joe brought his coffee to his desk and set to work writing his statement. He'd been working on it for an hour when heavy footsteps, and shouting, interrupted him.

He stepped into the corridor in time to see Alice Dunne walking at the head of half a dozen uniformed officers, who were marching two men to the holding cells. Dunne wore a navy jacket with SPECIAL CRIMES OPERATIONS written across the chest in gold.

The first man, a blond-haired fellow with a scar, was familiar to Joe. Ger Barrett's right-hand-man. He was struggling and shouting, but the uniforms held him tight. They threw him in the first holding cell.

The second man looked calmer. He was easily recognisable, with his grey curls. Barrett himself. He didn't look Joe's way, instead keeping his head down as he was locked in the second holding cell.

Dunne had been busier than Joe had known. He caught her eye, gave her a nod. Dunne nodded back.

All of a sudden, Joe remembered a dream from the previous night, in which Dunne had visited him in hospital. She had emerged from the darkness beside his bed. She'd sat next to him, leaned over and slowly kissed him on the lips, while her cool hand stroked his chest. It had been almost unbearably erotic.

Where did *that* come from?

The reality of his hospital stay had been more sobering. Aidan Donnelly's aunt, Maureen, had been in the ward just down the hall from Joe's. He'd visited her this morning. Physically, she was fine, the doctors said. It was a miracle that she'd escaped the Wall brothers. An ambulance had picked her up just down the road. However, since getting away, she hadn't said a word to anyone. Her gaze had passed right through Joe when he stood in front of her and admitted he had been wrong about her nephew.

Thinking about it now, Joe shook his head. There would be plenty of time later to reflect on his mistakes.

He returned to his office to continue writing his statement. Once it was complete, he e-mailed it to David O'Carroll, who was upstairs, working overtime because of all that had happened. Joe was sure that he and O'Carroll would have many conversations about the events of the previous days. But for now, for a little while, Joe wanted to forget about the whole thing.

He took out his phone and brought up a photo of Lisa and Christopher. The events of the last few days had just hammered home to him how much he cared about them. Joe didn't know what he would have done if anything happened to either one of them. He looked at the picture for a full minute, thinking how lucky he was.

Then he walked out to the car park. Before getting into the Toyota, he paused and looked up at the sky, stretching into infinity. There was so much to be grateful for. Joe was alive, he was free, and he had people who cared about him.

He even had plans for the day.

Lisa had invited him over for dinner. He would get there early, and just enjoy spending time with his family. Lisa was going to make Joe's favourite meal: burgers, chips and milkshakes. That happened to be Christopher's favourite too.

CHAPTER 103

Alice Dunne pushed through the steel door at the back of Donnybrook Garda Station. She stepped into the car park, shielding her eyes from the afternoon sun, as she watched Joe walk to his car. He was probably going off to play happy family with his ex and their son, and that was fine. Joe deserved a little time to catch his breath. But he wasn't the kind of man to be content with such a mediocre life.

It had been a fun case, and Dunne was glad Joe got out of it alive. She liked so many things about him, from the way he looked in his leather jacket, to the dry sound of his voice, to the gleam in his cool, blue eyes. She liked his will to win, to get the job done, whatever it takes. She liked his intelligence and his impatience with rules. In a way, he reminded Dunne of herself.

As Joe drove away, Dunne's phone rang. It was David O'Carroll. She turned and looked up at his office window where he was standing. She listened while he told her that a body had been found at a nearby house. An irate landlord had broken into his own property in order to forcibly evict his tenant. He was only admitting this behaviour because, once inside, he had found the tenant dead.

This kind of thing really wasn't Dunne's job, but the station was under pressure at the moment, what with the loss of Boyle and Kavanagh, with Joe being on leave, and with everyone else scrambling to sort out the previous day's mess. O'Carroll wanted a plainclothes officer on the scene. Would Dunne mind taking a look?

"Happy to help, David. I'll go right there," she said.

O'Carroll gave her Graham Lee's address, but, of course, she already knew it.

She was surprised his body had been found so quickly. She'd only killed him twelve hours earlier.

The previous day, Dunne had followed Joe to The Melford Hotel. She'd lost Joe inside and had wandered about the corridors for ten or fifteen minutes, getting more and more annoyed. But finally, she saw him leaving a room with a backpack slung over his shoulder. Dunne had been curious about what he'd been up to in that room, so, when he had gone, Dunne had knocked on the door. Graham Lee had let her in. She recognised him at once, having seen him at Lisa's house when she was doing surveillance on Joe.

Dunne could be persuasive when she wanted to be. She immediately grasped that Graham was furious at Joe, so she presented herself as a colleague with a grudge against him. With a little coaxing, Graham had told her everything – how Lisa had killed John Kavanagh, how Joe had covered it up, and how Graham had tried to blackmail him.

Joe had been naïve to think that Graham would leave Dublin, and even more naïve to believe that he'd keep Joe's secret. Graham was the kind of man who would use a juicy piece of information like that for the rest of his life. He'd be like a bad penny that never stopped coming up.

Dunne decided to help Joe out. An act of kindness. The neuroscientists said that people like her couldn't be kind, that such a thing wasn't in their nature. Consumed by egotism, they lacked all empathy, all remorse.

Untrue, Dunne thought. She could be kind when she liked. She wanted to be with Joe. Helping him was helping herself, and if that wasn't a win-win situation, she didn't know what was.

After leaving the crime scene in Wicklow late the previous night, Dunne had headed to Graham's house. She had picked his lock and moved through the house as silently as a cat. Of course, Graham had broken his promise. He hadn't left Dublin, just as Dunne had expected.

She found him asleep in bed, snoring loudly.

Graham didn't wake, even when she slipped the needle into his arm.

She'd arrested a drug dealer the previous year, before she joined Special Crimes Operations. The man ended up going down for manslaughter. He'd been cutting his heroin with strychnine. In fact, it was more like he'd been cutting his strychnine with a hint of heroin. Two users had died. Dunne figured he was trying to get rid of addicts who couldn't pay. She had kept a little of his mixture for herself. You never knew when rat poison would come in handy.

Dunne gave Graham a generous dose of the heroin/strychnine mixture and watched him until he stopped breathing. It didn't take long.

She made sure to get his fingerprints on the syringe and on the small plastic bag which contained a little more of the drugs, plus some related drug paraphernalia, which she placed strategically around the house.

Then she left, her good deed for the day done.

Before going home, she'd visited Joe in hospital, sneaking into his private room. She missed him and wanted to see his face. When he stirred in his sleep, perhaps sensing her presence, she kissed him. Then she slipped out.

Now, Dunne walked to her Lexus and sat behind the wheel. It would be interesting to see what colour Graham's skin had turned. How did he look now? She could also make sure that the uniforms and forensics people came to the correct conclusions about his death.

Dunne smiled. She loved being a cop.

She remembered the way David O'Carroll had brought her into the corruption investigation. Dunne had asked if Joe could be one of the officers taking bribes. O'Carroll had broken out in an extended laughing fit.

When he'd recovered, he said, "Not a chance. Joe's a good guy. He can be a little wild, but he'd never take a bribe. Not in a million years."

Yes, Joe was a good guy. And a little wild.

Her watch was still at his apartment, on top of his bookshelf. One day soon, she'd go back and get it.

Maybe Dunne would request a permanent transfer to Donnybrook. She'd have to leave Special Crimes Operations and go into the regular detective unit, but she was sure she could make that happen. Dunne was extremely persuasive when she wanted to be.

Joe would be so happy. He liked her. She'd seen the way he looked at her. He just didn't want to admit it to himself, because he had a kid. But that was no reason to ruin the rest of his life. He needed to let go of the past and embrace the future.

She'd work her way into his heart, inch by inch, and settle there for good. Eventually, he'd admit his feelings. Then they could be together. One day, when he was ready, he'd find out what she'd done for him, what she'd done for both of them, and then he'd finally understand the kindness of psychopaths.

Acknowledgements

I was lucky to receive a lot of help while I worked on this novel between May 2019 and November 2020. I owe a debt of gratitude to everyone mentioned below.

Thanks to Detective Inspector Joseph Mc Laughlin for his assistance in my research of Garda practice and procedure, specifically detective work, and for welcoming me to Donnybrook Garda Station in late 2019. He was very generous with his time and help.

Thanks also to the other members of An Garda Síochána I met at the station. They are better people than their fictional counterparts!

I would also like to thank the numerous Gardaí involved in obtaining permission for my visit.

Thanks to retired Detective Joe McCabe who generously spoke to me about his career on the force. My mother, Margo Gorevan, made this possible.

The well-connected Alison Boydell was a great help in beginning my research on several aspects of this book.

Thanks to Officer McNeill of the Irish Prison Service for taking the time to speak to me about his line of work.

Needless to say, any errors, omissions or deliberate distortions of Garda or prison procedure are entirely my responsibility. If at any point, I had to choose between putting the story or strict research accuracy first, I always chose the story. (This is fiction.)

KC critiqued early versions of a number of chapters and discussed ideas with me as they developed, making the book much better than it would otherwise have been.

John Gorevan acted as first reader for the complete manuscript. His feedback improved the book considerably.

Long overdue thanks to Niall McMonagle for encouraging my literary endeavours over the years.

I would like to reiterate that the characters and plot in this book are entirely fictional. And my hero was named Joe long before I met any of the "Joes" who helped me with this book!

By the same author

Better Confess

Better Confess: an online forum where you can anonymously reveal your darkest thoughts and actions.

But be careful what you write.

When Florence Lynch finds out her boyfriend is cheating on her, she feels like her whole world has collapsed.

In a drunken rage, she confesses that she wishes he was dead.

And someone offers to help…

Out of Nowhere

Zookeeper Nathan Green lives a lonely life. He's more comfortable with gorillas and wolves than with people. But one night, a stranger shatters his solitary existence.

A woman with no name.

With no past.

Helping her might cost Nathan everything.

Hit and Run

Jake Whelan ought to be happy. He has a devoted girlfriend and a job at a prestigious law firm, where he expects to make partner. Yet he's crippled by terrifying panic attacks and a suspicion that his life isn't as it should be.

When Jake is passed over for promotion, he thinks his day can't get any worse.

He's wrong.

A terrible accident is about to change his life forever.

The Hostage

Lindsey O'Reilly is at home, cleaning up after dinner, when she sees armed police swarming over her garden wall.

There's a noise downstairs.

A knock on the door.

She opens up, but it's not the police.

It's the man they're chasing.

A stone-cold killer.

Now he's inside...

The Forbidden Room

You and your partner are looking forward to a romantic break in the rugged landscape of West Cork, on the south west coast of Ireland. Cliff walks, seafood dinners and spectacular views of the Atlantic Ocean.

But a storm is brewing.

Your car breaks down in the middle of nowhere. There's no phone signal. So you start walking.

You search for help.

And you find it. At an isolated house, a family gives you shelter… but something is wrong.

The husband has a head wound. The son is too terrified to speak. And the wife forbids you from going near her other son's bedroom.

Printed in Great Britain
by Amazon